LYING IN WAIT

I'd been watching Kimberly splash through the water, but now I looked past her. It took a few seconds to spot the dinghy. And there was Andrew, closing in on it.

I got my eyes back to Kimberly in time to watch her dive. She vanished under the waves for a few moments, then surfaced and began to swim with quick, sharp strokes.

Man, she was fast!

Not fast enough, though.

She was only about halfway there when Andrew arrived at the dinghy.

"He made it," Billie said.

Way off in the distance, he reached up out of the water with both hands. He grabbed a gunnel near the bow. Then someone stood up in the dinghy.

I thought I'd have a heart attack.

Connie made a gasp.

Billie cried out, "My God!"

We couldn't see who it was. We couldn't even see whether it was a man or woman. Just that it was a person, and that it came up suddenly out of the bottom of the boat and raised an object overhead with both hands.

The object looked like an ax.

RICHARD LAYMON

ISLAND

LEISURE BOOKS NEW YORK CITY

*This book is dedicated to Frank Coghe,
a legend in his own time. When they made you,
Cog, they broke the mold.*

A LEISURE BOOK®

March 2002

Published by

Dorchester Publishing Co., Inc.
276 Fifth Avenue
New York, NY 10001

ISBN 0-8439-4978-3

Visit us on the web at www.dorchesterpub.com.

ISLAND

INTRODUCTION:
THE FOX IN THE CHICKEN SUIT
BY DEAN KOONTZ

On February 14, 2001, at far too young an age, Richard Laymon left this world for another. Within a large community of suspense, horror, mystery, and fantasy writers, news of his death was received with shock and grief. His writing was edgy, often disturbing, and definitely not for everyone, but even those colleagues who didn't read Richard Laymon's work nevertheless acutely felt the loss of him because he was such a reliably cheerful, forthcoming, likable man. Years before we lost Dick, I wrote this tribute to him for a special occasion. It made him laugh then, and in rereading it recently, I smiled because it reminded me of how amiable Dick was. Therefore:

At the moment that Richard Laymon was born, a mysterious rain of one million frogs fell on Cleveland, Ohio, and over seven hundred citizens were severely injured by large plummeting amphibians. In Tibet, at that same hour, a holy man suddenly levitated twelve feet off his monastery floor and, seized by some strange entity, began barking like a dog and shouting the word "gravy" in seventy-nine languages. While the holy man was aloft and shrieking, two archaeologists, at work outside Jerusalem, unearthed the altar of a third-century devil-worshipping cult on which was carved an image of Satan that bore an uncanny resemblance to the Warner Brothers' cartoon character Yosemite Sam. Even as the doctor slapped Richard Laymon's butt and the author's first cry echoed through the hospital delivery room, a group of nuns in Boston inexplicably fell into a ferocious hysteria and, racing through the streets of that city, set fire to anyone they encountered who was named "Herman." In London, the queen's favorite feathered hat exploded for no good reason, causing no harm to her august personage but putting her in such a foul mood that, forgetting what century she was in, she ordered the royal hatmaker beheaded.

In zoos all around the planet, elephants broke out of their enclosures and squashed anything cute and furry that they could find; for a few minutes, bears addressed startled onlookers in clear, grammatical English, speaking with better diction and projection than the greatest stage actor who ever lived—although according to all reports, none had anything interesting to say; and gorillas performed entrechats with a grace that made thousands of ballerinas weep. Perhaps the greatest mystery of that fateful day was the bewildering presence of so many ballerinas in so many zoos.

Then the world settled into its usual routines. Frogs stopped falling from the sky and were to be seen only in French restaurants where they belonged. The Tibetan holy man floated back to earth, stopped shrieking about gravy, and returned to his usual pursuits: prayer, meditation, and betting on the ponies. Wiping the bloodied remains of squashed bunny rabbits off their thunderously huge feet, the elephants ambled back into their enclosures. Their passion for ballet forgotten, the gorillas just ate bananas and stood around scratching their asses. Calm ensued. Peace reigned on God's good earth.

But all the while, Richard Laymon was quietly

growing up.

With his sunny face, disarming manner, unfailing cheerfulness, and singularly good humor, he passed through high school and college as smoothly as a fox in an exceedingly convincing chicken suit could pass through a flock of Prozac-numbed hens—that is, of course, if foxes were sufficiently talented tailors to make chicken suits and if hens were able to obtain Prozac prescriptions. If you met Richard Laymon (who, for some reason I don't fully grasp, is known as "Dick" to his friends) he would strike you as one of the most amiable men you have ever met. He is one of those guys who—were he a movie actor—would most often play the best buddy of the male star: in comedies, he would be lovable and bumbling; in romances, he would be lovable and adroit at bringing the estranged lovers back together after they had quarreled over one stupid misunderstanding or another; in police action pictures, he would be the lovable partner who would be shot stone-cold dead by the villain at the end of act two, sending the star on a flinty-eyed, tight-lipped race for justice and vengeance; in a horror movie, he would be eaten alive. Thus, he was able to appear sufficiently mild-mannered to obtain a job after college as a ninth-grade English teacher in a Catholic girls' school. The nuns adored him—and they weren't those crazy nuns in Boston who set fire to anyone named "Herman"; these were *nice* nuns. The students thought Dick was just swell, and their parents thought he was a particularly wholesome young gentleman.

But all the while, Richard Laymon was quietly writing.

Later he worked in the library at Marymount College, where he probably wore a bow tie, a jacket with leather patches on the elbows, and a look of bookish bemusement. There, I imagine, he kept the card catalog in impeccable order, dusted the shelves, staffed the lending desk, regretfully sent out overdue notices, murmured of Socrates and Plato to his patrons, and gently reminded boisterous students to whisper at all times. If he were a fox, he would have sewn for himself a chicken suit so thoroughly convincing that any farmer would have reached under him in search of eggs.

He married Ann in 1977, as sweet-tempered and gracious a lady as you would ever hope to meet. In 1979, Ann gave birth to Kelly, a blond little girl who appeared to have been modeled after the cutest cherubim in certain paintings in the Vatican. No one could look upon this young family without smiling approvingly and feeling that all was right with the world.

In 1980, however, Richard Laymon published his first novel, *The Cellar*. No doubt every nun who had ever known him began to pray for his soul, and every library patron who had ever been alone with him among the stacks at Marymount felt a chill along his or her spine, and all the Catholic school girls to whom he'd taught English said, "Hey, *cool!*" *The Cellar* was the scariest, fastest-paced, darkest, just-plain-nastiest thriller in years. In that debut, he established a style that has often been imitated but never equaled: plunging, pull-out-all-the-stops, no-limits, in-your-face, shock-packed, take-off-the-top-of-your-head, gonzo suspense and horror that will appall some people and exhilarate others.

Over the years, in thirty novels and numerous short stories, Dick has never compromised his unique vision in order to please the market-place, yet he has found an audience of devoted readers. Curiously, as I write this, he is better known and more widely admired in England than here in his native country. This situation arose, I believe, because many American editors favored the light diet of "quiet horror" rather than the meaty stew that Dick cooked up, and along with the *good* novels of quiet horror, they shoveled into bookstores uncountable self-conscious pseudo-literary exercises in obscurantism by writers who had yet to learn correct grammar and syntax, books that gave quiet horror—*all* horror—a bad name. Those unreadable tomes, combined with the usual yearly total of 3,568 vampire novels, virtually destroyed the genre on these shores even while Dick was trying to build a career doing something different from the work of others.

He has survived, however, and prospered, because a significant number of readers like a bowl of stew in their literary diet from time to time. By being politically incorrect in his fiction and singularly clear-eyed and cold in his portrayal of evil, he writes stories that read like the work of no one else—which is essential if a writer is to stay afloat in the sea of sameness that is modern publishing. Now that he has written so many books, however, he has revealed himself and can never again quite squeeze all the way back into that chicken suit.

Indeed, when Gerda and I go to the Laymon

house for dinner, we sometimes wonder if *Ann* is really the gentle lady she seems to be or if she is engaged in a masquerade as clever as her husband's. When she's cooking, I pop into the kitchen unannounced—just to be sure that she's adding only herbs and spices to each dish and not anything lethal. When she picks up a carving knife, I ease to the edge of my chair, prepared to leap away from the table and throw myself out of the nearest dining-room window if she should move in my direction instead of toward the turkey or roast. Several times, I've been a bit too edgy, misjudged her intention, and hurled myself through a pane of glass, only to look back into the house from the lawn and see her standing over the roast, looking astonished and bewildered. Too embarrassed to admit my suspicions, I always claim to have been catapulted out of the room by a catastrophic muscle spasm, and I think she buys that story because she keeps giving me the names of medical specialists who might be able to help me—though lately they have all been psychiatrists.

I keep a sly watch on Kelly, too. When she was a tiny little girl, she was so cute that you could have dangled her from one of the branches of a Christmas tree, and everyone would have been so dazzled by her that they wouldn't have noticed any of the other decorations—yet she always had an unexpected wit that was more sophisticated and astringent than the average child's sense of humor. One night, when six of us adults sat around the Laymon dinner table, having a grand good time, Gerda realized that Kelly was standing in the doorway, in her pajamas, quietly commenting on our conversation; Gerda nudged me, and when I tuned out the adults and tuned in Kelly, she was funnier than any of us—even though we thought ourselves reasonably amusing. Not long thereafter, during a visit to an amusement park with the Laymons, as we were suddenly swept up in a surging crowd, little Kelly—then no bigger than an elf—reached for my hand, gripping it tightly, and I was touched by her genuine vulnerability and more deeply touched by the fact that she trusted me to keep her safe; yet this *same* little girl eschewed the usual dollhouse and played, instead, with a miniature haunted castle full of monster figures and beheaded victims. That is a fact, not a comic exaggeration. Now, many years later, Kelly is a young lady, quieter than the sprightly imp of yore, even demure. Nevertheless, she is her father's daughter, with those same strange genes, and if at dinner some evening she were to say, "Let *me* carve the roast, Mom," I'm certain I'd have another catastrophic muscle spasm and wind up on the lawn amidst shattered window glass.

If *Island* is your kind of book, I'm pleased you've found the work of Richard Laymon. I only wish all of you could have had the additional pleasure of knowing Dick Laymon as well as I did. In truth, the strangest thing about him is that he tolerated me as a friend.

The Journal Of
Rupert Conway, Castaway

Today, the yacht exploded.

Fortunately, all of us had gone ashore to have a picnic on this island, so we didn't get blown to smithereens. All of us, that is, except Prince Wesley.

Prince Wesley wasn't actually a prince. He was actually an asshole. Sorry about that; you're not supposed to speak ill of the dead. But he was a royal pain in the butt and I wouldn't be at all surprised if the explosion was his fault. He probably picked the wrong time and place to light up a cigarette.

Kaboom!

Now he's fish nibbles.

I'm sorry he's dead, but he *was* a ridiculous, arrogant jerk. He was a grown man; all of thirty, I suppose, but he went around all the time wearing one of those stupid white yachting hats. And you never saw him that he wasn't strutting around the deck with his ivory cigarette-holder hoisting up a Marlboro in front of one eye or the other. Oh yeah, he wore aviator sunglasses, too. And an ascot, more often than not.

Anyway, that was Prince Wesley. He's dead, so I won't spend any more time running him down. His actual name, for the record, was Wesley Duncan Beaverton III. He died today, April 1, 1994, which is not only April Fool's Day, but also happens to be Good Friday. What a day to go.

He is survived by his wife, Thelma. Who ought to consider herself lucky to be rid of him, but instead seems to be terribly upset.

Wesley and Thelma didn't have any children, but they'd only been married for about a year.

Personally, I think he married her for her money.

He sure didn't marry Thelma for her good looks. Her sister got all of them. The sister, Kimberly, is about twenty-five and a knockout. To think I'm marooned on a tropical isle with a babe like Kimberly . . . ! Whoooey!

Not that anything much is likely to come of it. Aside from the fact that I'm a few years her junior and here as the guest of her half-sister, Connie, she's married. Her husband, Keith, is one of those incredibly handsome, bright, sincere and capable guys who makes ordinary jerks (like me) look like we got stalled somewhere low down on the evolutionary ladder. I'd hate him, but he's too nice to hate.

The other male with us here on the island is the sire of all three gals, Andrew (never Andy) Collins. His first wife, mother of Thelma and Kimberly, bit the big one in a snow skiing accident at Lake Tahoe. He subsequently married Billie, and together they had Connie.

This little yacht excursion in the Bahamas was a gift from the children to celebrate the twentieth wedding anniversary of Andrew and Billie. (Wesley came down to Nassau a week ahead of everyone else to set it up – scout the situation, check up on the hotel reservations, rent the boat, and so forth.) Andrew is probably in his mid-fifties. He's retired Navy, rich because he invested in some sort of oil scheme that paid off huge, and a pretty decent guy. If you're going to get marooned, he's probably a good fellow to have along. A straight arrow, smart, and tough. He treats me okay, sort of, even though I'm sure he suspects I've been 'putting it' to Connie.

Connie's mother, Billie, is only a couple of years older than Thelma. In other words, she's young enough that you'd logically take her as one of Andrew's daughters, not his wife. She's a lot better looking than Thelma, though not quite as hot as Kimberly.

She and Connie look more like sisters than like a mother and daughter. They both have dark tans and golden hair, and wear their hair in the same short, pixie style. Connie is slightly taller. Her mother is a lot fuller in the chest and hips, and of course looks older in the face. Actually, Billie is quite a bit more attractive in many ways than her daughter.

(I'd better make sure none of these folks gets a chance to read what I'm writing here. I've only just now started working on this journal, and I've already thrown in some stuff that could get me in trouble.)

My plan, by the way, is to keep a detailed account of things, and use it as the basis for a 'true adventure' sort of book. Which won't pan out if we get rescued too soon. I'm hoping we'll have to spend a while here, long enough for there to be a few more dramatic events. For the record, the reason I brought my writing pad when we came to the island is that I've been working on some short stories. I plan to win the Belmore fiction writing contest . . . Man, what an optimist! Maybe none of us will ever get off this island, in which case I might as well forget the writing contest. And a few other things.

Never mind.

Gonna depress myself, if I don't watch out.

Anyway, back to the introductions.

Connie, daughter of Billie and Andrew, is my 'girlfriend.' We're both freshmen at Belmore University. That's how I got to know her. We kept being forced together by the alphabet: she being a Collins, I a Conway. At a university, you can't remain strangers for long with the person who immediately precedes you in the ABCs. Soon, we began talking to each other. After a while, we started going out. Before I knew it, she was inviting me to spend spring break with her family on a yacht in the Bahamas.

You don't turn down an offer like that.

I don't, anyhow.

I decided to postpone the inevitable – breaking up with her – until after the excursion.

Now, there might not *be* an 'after.' Yee gads, stuck with her for life. No no no. Won't happen. We'll probably be rescued shortly. There's just no way this can turn into some sort of Robinson Crusoe deal. At most, we might spend a few days here. More likely, we'll be picked up before dark; that's if somebody heard or saw our boat explode.

It was one hell of an explosion.

For a while, crap kept falling out of the sky and plopping into the water. Pieces of the boat – and undoubtedly Wesley. (I expected to see a foot or a head or a big looping coil of entrails coming down, but nope.) Many of the pieces were on fire. They got snuffed out when they landed in the water. Nothing came down on the beach, luckily.

Then there wasn't much left but a bunch of junk floating on the water, and a smudge of drifting smoke.

At the time it went up, we couldn't spot any aircraft or boats. We sure did look. Some of us did, anyhow. Not Thelma, of course. That's when Thelma clutched the sides of her head and started shrieking, 'No! No! Oh my

God, no! Wesley! My poor Wesley! No!' And like that.

After a few seconds, Kimberly put her arms around her. They stood there hugging each other, Kimberly patting her sister's back and murmuring to her. Kimberly was wet. She'd gone in the water for a little swim after our picnic lunch on the beach, and had just waded ashore a minute or two before the explosion. Her black hair was matted against her skull and hung in a sheath down the nape of her neck. Her back was golden and smooth and dripping. She wore a white bikini. The pants of her bikini hung a little crooked, lower on one hip than on the other, showing more of the top of her right buttock than her left. And the middle of the seat had a crease in it . . .

Enough of that.

She looked damn fine, that's all. I couldn't help staring. But I also spent my share of time looking out across the water. The cloud of smoke had moved on and thinned out. I could see a couple of islands, way off in the distance. But not much else except water and sky.

Kimberly led her sister away from the rest of us. They sat shoulder to shoulder on the blanket where we'd had our picnic.

'Poor thing,' Billie said, watching them.

'Splendid move on Wesley's part, blowing up our boat.'

'Andrew!'

'Fumes in the engine compartment,' he went on. 'The idiot *knew* they could blow us to hell and gone. My mistake. Shouldn't have let him stay on board, nobody there to keep an eye on him. Should've known he'd fuck up the works. The bastard. He was too dumb to live.'

'Andrew!'

'At least he blew *himself* up with the boat. That's the silver lining.'

'Don't let your daughter hear you say such things. She loved him.'

'He sure as shit didn't love her. Anyhow, good riddance. Rest in pieces, Wesley.' And he hocked a wad of spit onto the sand at his feet.

After that, Andrew and Keith went out on the dinghy to see what they could find at the scene of the explosion. I offered to go along, but they said it wouldn't be necessary. Typical. Maybe it's because they think of me as a useless kid or because I'm not part of the family. Maybe there's a reason I don't know about. Even though they're generally nice to me, they treat me like an outsider. I get excluded a lot. I'm sort of used to it by now, having spent several days with this bunch.

Anyway, they left me behind with the women while they puttered out and started picking up nearly everything that was still afloat.

Connie stood on one side of me, her mother on the other.

'They won't bring back Wesley, will they?' Connie asked, making a face like the one she'd given me once when we talked about eating beets.

'We should give him a proper burial,' Billie said.

'He's probably in chunks,' I added.

'They'd better not bring back *chunks* of him. God! That's just what we'd need.'

'If we're stuck here very long,' I said, 'we might want to eat him.'

'Rupert!' Billie gasped.

'God!' Connie snapped. 'I can't *believe* you sometimes. That's disgusting!'

'We'd have to jerk him right away,' I said, 'so he doesn't go bad on us.'

Billie shook her head at me. She was smiling slightly. 'You're demented,' she said. 'Just don't say anything like that around Thelma.'

'I wouldn't,' I assured her.

She swayed sideways and bumped me a little with her shoulder. 'I know,' she said. 'You're demented, but sensitive.'

'That's me.'

'Cut it out, huh?' Connie said. I think she meant both of us. I'd noticed before how it seemed to annoy her when Billie and I talked or goofed around. Come to think of it, just about everything about Billie seems to annoy her. Maybe it's one of those competition things, and she knows she doesn't measure up. I mean, her mother has her whipped in every department: looks, brains, sense of humor, compassion, you name it.

Must be hard on Connie. I'll have to be more understanding.

After she told us to cut it out, we just stood there silent as the 'men' gathered floating treasures.

The sand of the beach was almost white. The water lapped in gently – no big combers, I guess, because of the reef. (There'd been some pretty good waves right after the explosion, but they didn't last long.) The water, pale blue, was a little murky. It had been incredibly clear until the boat blew, and would probably be that way again in a while. There was a soft, warm breeze taking away the worst of the heat. And there were the gals.

Man oh man.

It's a shame that Prince Wesley had to go (I'm sure), and it's too bad that Thelma is taking it so hard, but I couldn't help thinking how lucky we were to be stranded in a place like this.

At least for a while.

The longer the better, as far as I'm concerned.

Not really. But I wouldn't mind a couple of weeks, as long as we don't starve (no need to worry about fresh water, because of the stream).

After a while, Andrew and Keith returned with a boat full of odds and ends – including some packets of food, but no bits or pieces of Wesley. I'm sure Connie was relieved.

'Is his body out there?' I asked.

'Bet on it,' Keith said.

'We're going back out,' Andrew said. 'We've gotta salvage what we can.'

'I could go with you, this time, if you need an extra set of hands.'

'That's all right, chief,' Andrew said. 'Somebody's gotta stay here and watch out for the ladies.'

Chief. He calls me chief quite a lot. It's like a thing with him. I'm almost nineteen years old, and he calls me chief like I'm a kid.

Oh, well, maybe it's quaint.

'Whatever you say, skipper,' I told him.

He hoisted an eyebrow.

Anyway, Thelma and Kimberly came over. Thelma had stopped crying, and seemed groggy. They pitched in, and everyone helped to unload the boat. Then Andrew and Keith cranked up the dinghy's motor and took off to scour the inlet for more loot.

The gals got to work on the goodies we'd just unloaded, so I went over to our picnic area to get my notebook and a pen. They were in my book bag along with a couple of paperback books. Instead of taking them out, I just swung the bag onto my back and took the whole thing with me.

I called out, 'I'll be back in a while.' Before anyone

could ask questions or offer to accompany me, I hurried off.

I walked alongside the stream, figuring to follow it into the jungle. Keith and Kimberly had gone exploring before lunch while the rest of us dinked around on the beach, and they said the stream led to a great little lagoon, complete with a waterfall – if you hiked inland far enough.

My impression was that they took the hike to get away from the rest of us. They probably skinny-dipped in the lagoon, and I'd bet a million bucks they screwed.

I sort of wanted to see it and maybe take a little dip, myself – but I was more interested in sitting beside the lagoon and getting to work on my journal.

When I started into the jungle, it looked pretty dense and creepy. No telling what sort of creatures might be lurking there. The open beach seemed a lot safer. So I gave up on following the stream, and went along the sand toward a big tower of rocks on the point.

The inlet is shaped like a large U, with the stream running down its center to join up with the salt water, and rocky points at each tip. The one ahead of me was higher than the other. It would give me a good view and all the privacy I needed.

The climb to the top winded me, but was worth it. The summit was probably forty or fifty feet above the water. When I got there, I took a while to look around. I could see the gals down on the beach. Also, I saw 'the men' on the dinghy, hauling crap out of the water.

In places, the water was clear enough that I could see to the bottom. Mostly, though, it was still cloudy because of the explosion. I turned away pretty quick – afraid that I might spot some leftover Wesley.

On the other side of the point, there's a lot more beach

and jungle. No docks, no houses, no roads, no telephone poles, nothing to indicate the island has inhabitants.

I studied the sky and ocean. No aircraft, no boats.

After a check of our beach to make sure nobody was coming my way, I found myself a nice, sheltered nook in the rocks, sat down and started to write.

It's been very nice. No one can see me here. An overhang keeps the sun off me, and there's a wonderful breeze. All I can see is a bit of ocean and the sky.

Now, I'm caught up to the present.

I feel like I've been at it for at least an hour, maybe a lot longer. I didn't keep track of the time. My butt's a little sore. I'm about ready to head back down and see what's going on.

Maybe I should leave my journal up here. Hide it in the rocks.

No, I'd better take it with me. If I leave it here, might be tough to retrieve it in case we suddenly get rescued. Also, something could happen. Some sort of wildlife might attack it – I don't want my precious pages getting munched by an iguana or ending up as insulation for a bird nest. I'll keep it in my book bag, and take it with me everywhere so nobody will have a chance to lay eyes on what's written in here.

That's all for now.

The First Supper

I'm back.

It's early evening, and we're still here. Looks like we probably won't be going anyplace tonight.

Andrew and Keith spent most of the afternoon making trips to the scene of the explosion to salvage things. Keith even did some diving and brought up stuff that had sunk. They managed to retrieve quite a lot of items that should make our stay on the island more endurable: food and clothes and utensils, not to mention a few bottles of booze that had somehow survived the blast and some fresh fish that hadn't. But they came back without anything *really* major – such as a flare gun or transmitter – that we could use to alert rescuers of our position.

Andrew, a great hand at everything, cleaned the fish. He is not only retired Navy, but an Eagle Scout. He is nothing if not prepared. Just as I never go anywhere without my writing implements and reading material, he is forever equipped with a slew of useful items, including a Swiss Army knife and a butane lighter for his pipe.

While Andrew gutted the catch of the day, the rest of us trooped over the beach and gathered driftwood for our fire. It is plentiful. In about ten minutes, we had a pile six feet high.

Done with the bloody work, Andrew built a tidy little fire about twenty feet from our huge stack of driftwood. He used his butane lighter to ignite it.

Keith had recovered a skillet during one of his dives.

Billie did the cooking. We didn't have any grease for the skillet, so she opened one of the liquor bottles and cooked up the fish in bourbon. It wasn't bad.

This is sort of like being on a camping trip. A trip where you messed up and left most of your supplies behind – a trip where you don't necessarily have a way to get home. Those are the negatives. On the other side of the coin, this is better than any camping trip I ever went on because this one includes the gals.

I've had a hard time keeping my eyes off Kimberly in her white bikini. And Billie isn't any slouch, either. Her black bikini is a lot bigger than Kimberly's, but seems smaller because there's so much of her that it doesn't cover. She was really something to see, crouched beside the fire and shaking the skillet. The skillet wasn't the only thing that shook. She seems to like showing off what she's got. I try not to let Connie catch me looking at her.

I'd be looking at Connie, but there's not much to see. She's spent most of the day wearing an extra large T-shirt over her swimming suit. Also, even though she has a decent build, she looks scrawny compared to her mother. And unlike her mom, she doesn't seem to have any tendencies toward exhibitionism.

As for Thelma, she's sort of cute in a thick, blocky way, but nothing much to look at. I don't mean to be unkind. She's a pretty nice woman and I actually like her quite a lot most of the time. The whole trip, I haven't once seen her in a bathing suit. She always wears a big floppy straw hat, a loose blouse that she doesn't tuck in, baggy shorts, white socks and Reeboks.

I probably shouldn't be writing this stuff about the women. It'll be embarrassing if someone happens to read it. Also, it sort of makes me look shallow and creepy. As if all I care about is how a gal looks in her bikini.

That isn't *all* I care about.

The thing is, it's probably easy to be nonchalant about gorgeous, semi-nude babes if you're a handsome, confident guy who has nailed about fifty of them. But I'm eighteen, short and skinny and zitty. My name is RUPERT, for Godsake. (I was named after Rupert Brooke, the poet. He was a great poet, and I love his stuff, but if my parents had to pick a poet's name for me, why not Robert Frost, Carl Sandburg, or Walt Whitman? Rupert? Please! I guess I should count my blessings; at least they didn't name me Wilfred, Ezra or Sylvia.)

Anyway, I'm basically a shrimp with a dumb name and an attitude. Connie goes for me – to the extent that she does – because I'm nonthreatening, she thinks she generally controls me, and she often finds me amusing. There might be other reasons, but those are the most obvious.

I think there are always *other reasons* for everything. Invisible reasons. Sometimes, they're so well hidden that nobody knows about them at all.

There might be some deep, dark reason why I've been going out with Connie. I hope so. Otherwise, it's just because she's the only gal at school who has ever shown the slightest interest in me. It certainly isn't her glamorous looks or her winning personality.

Among other things, she's a real prude.

I mean, I've gotten nowhere with her in the romance department.

Which is about as far as I've gotten with most girls,

which might explain why I'm so interested in *looking* at people like Kimberly and Billie.

Or maybe there are hidden reasons.

It's almost too dark out here to see what I'm writing. I'll quit now and go over to the campfire, where everyone else is.

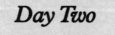

Day Two

A Mysterious Disappearance

Keith is missing.

It must've happened while he was standing watch.

Right after I joined the bunch sitting around the campfire last night, we had a discussion about whether we ought to take turns on guard duty. Most of us were against it. Why bother, since we'd been on the beach since late morning and hadn't found any reason to consider ourselves threatened? But then Andrew said that, even if we didn't seem to be in any danger, it's better to be safe than sorry. Also, he thought we shouldn't let the fire go out.

'We ought to keep it going day and night till we're picked up,' he said. He was packing tobacco into his briar pipe as he spoke. 'Don't need to get caught with a dead fire when a search plane comes along. Besides, we let it go out and we'll wind up lighting new ones all the time. That'll get a bit more difficult after my Bic runs out of juice. I've stopped using it to light my pipe, of course.' As he said that, he pulled a stick out of the fire and sucked its flame down onto the tobacco in his pipe. He puffed to get things stoked up. Then he explained that the men should take turns staying up to keep watch and feed the fire.

There were three of us, and he figured about nine hours till morning. That meant that we would each have to stand a three-hour shift. (Finally, I get to participate as one of the guys! Thanks a heap, skipper.)

Then Kimberly asked why the women weren't being included in the guard duty. 'Do ovaries disqualify us?' she asked.

Which made me laugh. Which won me some points with Kimberly and Billie, but didn't seem to be appreciated by the others.

There was a general discussion. It stayed friendly, and the decision was made that the women could be responsible for watch duty on the second night, if we're still here by then. That ended the complaints.

Andrew was supposed to take first watch, then wake up Keith, who would do his three hours and then wake me up at about four in the morning to keep an eye on things for the rest of the night.

With that settled, we all turned in except Andrew, who remained by the fire.

The night was warm and nice. We each made up our beds with assorted blankets, clothing, and whatnot that we'd either brought with us when we came for the picnic, or that Keith and the skipper had retrieved from the water. (Everything was dry by then.)

All of us stayed in the general area of the fire. Couples made their beds together. Not Connie and I, though. We helped each other build separate sleeping places – side by side, but with a space between us. Which was fine with me.

She gave me a goodnight peck on the mouth, then we retired to our rag piles.

There was method in her arrangement.

Billie's bed was only about ten feet away. Once we were lying down, however, I couldn't see her; Connie blocked my view.

I might've been able to see Kimberly in the other direction, but she and Keith had insisted that Thelma share their quarters. It was nice of them. Otherwise, Thelma would've had to spend the first night of her widowhood alone.

Kimberly, unfortunately, stretched herself out between Thelma and Keith. Which ruined any chance I had of watching her.

Thwarted on both sides, I shut my eyes and let my imagination take over.

The next thing I knew, someone was shaking me by the shoulder. I opened my eyes. It wasn't Keith waking me up. And the sky wasn't dark anymore.

At first, I didn't recognize the guy squatting over me. It was Andrew, of course. The skipper. But he was wearing nothing except his khaki shorts. I'd hardly ever seen him when he didn't have on a T-shirt, sunglasses and ballcap. He had a gray fur all over his chest, his eyes looked sort of pale and bare, and he was bald and shiny on the top of his head. He seemed older than usual, and not as tough.

'What's going on?' I asked.

'You tell me.' He didn't sound angry. Concerned, though. 'Why aren't you up and standing watch?' he asked.

I had to think about that for a minute. Then I said, 'Nobody woke me. Keith was supposed to, wasn't he?'

'And he didn't?'

'No. He was supposed to, though. Yeah. When he was ready for me to relieve him at four.'

'That was the plan.'

'If he didn't wake me up, it's not my fault. I mean, I haven't got an alarm clock.'

I sat up to see what was going on with Keith. Thelma

and Kimberly were sleeping side by side, but Keith wasn't there.

I gave the whole area a quick scan, and didn't see him anywhere.

'Where is he?' I asked.

'I don't know.'

'Uh-oh,' I said.

'*You* don't know?'

'Huh-uh. I fell asleep right away. You were over by the fire, and Keith was with Kimberly. That's the last I saw of anybody till now.'

'I never took Keith as the sort to desert his post,' Andrew said.

'If he had a good reason.'

'Such as?'

'I don't know, a bad case of the trots?'

'He should've gotten you up three hours ago,' Andrew said, making a point of the *three hours* part.

A mighty long time to spend squatting in the jungle.

'Maybe he decided to let me sleep . . .' I looked over at where the fire used to be. Only a smokeless pile of ashes remained. Obviously, nobody had fed the thing for hours.

I suddenly got sort of a sickish feeling in the pit of my stomach.

'What's the matter?' Connie asked, sounding groggy. With a yawn, she pushed herself up on one elbow. Her hair was a messy tangle, in spite of being almost as short as mine, and her T-shirt hung off her shoulder. She actually looked sort of cute that way. This was the first time I'd ever seen her wake up in the morning.

Andrew explained to her about Keith. 'Did you notice anything last night?' he asked.

She yawned again and shook her head. Then she added,

'I bet he went jogging or something. He's such a fitness freak. Probably on the other side of the island by now.'

'Maybe,' Andrew said, but I knew he didn't buy it. I'd noticed before how he sometimes agreed with his daughters and wife even when they were obviously wrong. It was just his way of keeping the peace.

Anyway, our discussions were getting nowhere fast.

So Andrew went over to Billie, bent down and shook her. She seemed to be quite a heavy sleeper. She moaned and rolled onto her side. She'd gone to sleep in her bikini, and wasn't covered by anything else. Looking between Andrew's legs, I saw that her upper breast had gotten dislodged a little. About half the nipple showed. I kept watching, hoping her entire breast would fall out. But then Andrew turned around, so I had to look the other way quick.

'Honey, go on over and wake up your sisters, would you?'

Connie groaned like it was a chore, but she followed orders. While she was on her way to where Thelma and Kimberly were sleeping, I got to my feet. I checked on Billie. She was sitting up and rubbing her eyes. One of her elbows was in the way, so I couldn't see much of her bikini top.

I turned my attention to the others. Connie nudged Thelma with her foot and said, 'Guys, wake up.'

Thelma, flat on her back, blinked up at her and scowled.

Kimberly was covered to the shoulders by a blue blanket. (It wasn't the good one that we'd brought with us to spread on the beach for our picnic. Andrew and Billie claimed that one.) Kimberly's blanket had been retrieved from the inlet. A survivor of the boat explosion, it was missing a corner, had a rip down one side and a bunch of burn holes with dark, charred edges. I could see her skin through some of the holes.

She didn't move when Connie said, 'Guys, wake up.' Then came, 'Keith's disappeared.'

Kimberly threw the blanket aside and sat up fast. Frowning, she swung her head from side to side as she got to her feet. She was still in her white bikini. She looked terrific. She also looked worried.

Andrew and Billie were already striding toward her. (Billie had straightened her bikini top so nothing showed that wasn't supposed to.)

Kimberly said, 'Dad, what's going on? Where's Keith?'

'We don't know, honey. He was supposed to wake up Rupert at four, but he didn't. From the look of things, he's been gone a long time.'

Kimberly suddenly shouted 'Keith!' toward the jungle. She got no answer, so she cupped her hands to the sides of her mouth and belted out, 'KEITH!'

Then we all started yelling his name.

We even tried calling out in unison. That was Billie's idea. She counted to three, and we all yelled 'KEITH!' at once.

Then we waited, but no reply came.

'Do you have any idea where he might've gone?' Andrew asked Kimberly.

'No. Are you kidding? He wouldn't go anywhere, not when he's supposed to be keeping watch. Not Keith. Except maybe for five minutes, if he had to go to the john. He wouldn't take off for *hours*. No way!'

I'd never seen her this upset. She wasn't hysterical, though. She didn't cry, but her voice sounded tight and she had a frantic look in her eyes like she wanted to scream for help.

'Something's happened to him,' she said. 'He's had an accident, or . . .' She shook her head. 'We've gotta go and find him.'

We might've started a general discussion about the various possibilities, but Kimberly didn't hang around. She picked up her shoes and started running toward the jungle.

'Kim!' Andrew yelled. 'Wait for us.'

Still running, she glanced back over her shoulder.

'Stop!' he ordered.

She quit running, turned around, and walked backward toward the jungle.

'Somebody should stay here,' I suggested. 'You know, in case Keith shows up. If he comes back and everyone's gone . . .'

'Good idea,' Andrew said. 'You wanta stay?'

'No, but . . .'

'I'll stay,' Connie volunteered.

'I don't want you here by yourself,' her dad said.

'Rupert'll stay with me.'

'I want to help search for Keith,' I said.

The skipper pointed at me. 'Stay with her.' He dug into his pocket, came up with the lighter, and tossed it to me. 'Get the fire going, Rupe.'

'Aye-aye, sir.'

Andrew, Billie and Thelma spent a couple of minutes picking up odds and ends such as shoes, hats, and sunglasses. Then they hurried to catch up with Kimberly.

Before long, they vanished into the jungle. Connie and I stood by ourselves on the sand.

'He'll turn up,' Connie said.

'I hope so.'

She frowned the way she does when she wants you to

know she's concentrating hard. 'What do you think happened to him?'

'He went out in the jungle to take a dump last night, and the local headhunters nailed his ass.'

'Ha ha ha. Very funny. You're sick if you think that's funny.'

'Maybe not headhunters,' I said.

'I should think not.'

'Maybe a snake got him. I bet something did. Might've been one of those giant spiders I heard about – they're indigenous to these islands. They have this special venom that turns your blood to acid so you burn up from the inside out.'

'Yeah, right.'

'Really.'

'Get fucked,' she told me, then spun around and walked off toward the water.

'By you?' I asked.

'In your dreams,' she said, not even glancing back.

Not in *my* dreams, I thought. I didn't say it, though. I'd already said enough, pretty much.

She went in for a swim, so I built a new fire in the ashes of the old one. When the fire was going good, I fetched my pen and journal and got to work.

The search party still hasn't returned.

Connie's been leaving me alone.

After swimming around for a while, she went climbing on the rocks at the point. (Good thing I didn't leave my journal hidden up there. She probably would've found it and read it, and then I'd be in some real trouble.) Later, she climbed down and swam some more. Then she sprawled out on the sand. She's acting like I'm somewhere else.

We didn't exactly have a model relationship *before* this trip, but it started to really deteriorate as soon as the others entered the picture. I think she considers it a big mistake that she asked me to come along.

Oh, well.

I'm having a good time, mostly, in spite of her.

On the negative side of things, it's not a good sign that the search party has been gone so long. I'm afraid something bad might've happened to Keith.

I sure hope *they're* all right.

Shit! What if *they* don't come back?

I don't want to think about that. Besides, it isn't very likely.

So long for now. I've got a few personal matters to take care of while I've got the place pretty much to myself.

Keith Turns Up

Oh, man. Oh, shit.

The search party hasn't come back yet. No wonder. They're still out there looking for Keith, probably.

I found him.

I didn't have to look far, either. Just *up*.

Here's what happened. Since there was nobody around, and I'd been holding things in for a while, I decided to take advantage of the privacy to answer nature's call. I took a paperback book with me. Not for reading purposes. I figured I could start ripping out pages from the first half, which I'd already read. (It's not that great a book anyway.)

I went wandering over to the area that our group has been using since our arrival yesterday – in the jungle and a pretty good distance south of the stream. It wasn't very far to walk, and the foliage in there was thick enough so that you could disappear after just a few steps.

Most everyone had gone in, at one time or another.

It was the first place that Kimberly and the others had searched, too.

But they'd missed him.

I didn't stop at the first likely trees, but went in a little deeper. After all, no telling when the searchers might return.

I found a good place, and did my business.

I had taken off my swimming trunks to make the job easier, so then I had to put them back on. The problem was, I *hadn't* taken off my shoes. When I stood on one foot and tried to slip the other into the leg hole of my trunks, the heel of my Nike got caught and I lost my balance. I hopped and tried to work my foot loose. All of a sudden, though, I was out of control. My shoulder slammed into the trunk of a tree in front of me. The blow turned me, and I landed flat on my back.

Which is when I found Keith.

I'd crashed into *his* tree.

It wasn't a palm tree, by the way. The jungle here was full of regular, non-palm trees of maybe a zillion different varieties. This one looked like a normal tree – the sort that has a thick trunk, branches starting about ten feet up, and normal-sized leaves instead of fronds.

Keith was a little higher than the first set of branches.

All I saw, at first, was the bottom half of a naked man dangling almost directly above my face.

I pulled my trunks on, fast as I could, then got out from under him.

He was up there so high that I couldn't see enough of his face to recognize him. There was no doubt in my mind, though. This was Keith. He'd lost his flip-flop sandals. He'd also lost his trunks. What he still wore was his bright green, blue and yellow Hawaiian-type shirt. It was fluttering in the breeze up there. And he was swaying just a bit from side to side.

I was pretty sure he'd been hanged, even though I couldn't make out the rope.

Suicide didn't seem real likely.

Which meant someone had *done* this to him.

I got the hell out of there.

Connie was down near the shore, stretched out on the sand. Sunbathing, maybe asleep.

I went back to my journal, and here I still am.

I'm still pretty shaky. This stuff is barely legible. It isn't every day you run into a murder victim. He was a nice guy, too – unlike Prince Wesley.

Now we've got two dead husbands. And two widows.

Poor Kimberly. It's sure going to be tough on her.

I could keep it to myself about finding the body, but that won't really solve much. I mean, it's not like Keith got lost in the jungle and if we wait around long enough, eventually he's going to turn up. All he's likely to do is rot.

Besides, everybody needs to know we have a killer out there.

One or more killers.

Savage natives?

Who knows?

Maybe one of us did it. Possible, but not likely. Andrew's probably the only one strong enough to hoist Keith up a tree like that. Unless a couple of the women teamed up to do it. No motive for anything like that, though, as far as I can see.

Oh, shit. The search party is coming back.

Gotta go.

We Deal With It

They came out of the jungle with Andrew and Billie supporting Thelma. She was hobbling along between them, putting almost no weight on her left leg. Her left ankle was wrapped with Andrew's black leather belt.

Kimberly brought up the rear. She kept turning around and looking back into the jungle.

All of them were flushed and sweaty.

As they walked closer to me, Andrew shook his head.

'No luck?' I asked.

'He could be anywhere out there. No sign of him at all. I take it he hasn't put in an appearance around here?'

'Nope,' I said. Then I asked Thelma, 'What happened to you?'

'I'm such a klutz,' she said. 'I slipped and twisted my ankle.'

'Could've happened to anyone,' Billie told her.

'We'll go out looking again,' Andrew said. 'Needed to bring Thelma back, and we ought to get some food in us.'

They lowered Thelma onto the collection of rags and towels that she'd shared last night with Kimberly and Keith.

Kimberly kept walking. 'I'm going in to cool off,' she said as she passed us. She was scratched, shiny with sweat,

31

dirty, and had bits of green sticking to her skin.

'Did something happen to her?' I asked, when she was a fair distance off.

'There wasn't any stopping her,' Andrew said. He shook his head as he watched her stride toward the shore. 'She crawled into tight places, went through bushes, scampered up rocks. Wore me out just watching her. What a kid – all I could do to make her come back with us. Keith better have himself one damn good excuse if he turns up okay.'

'He won't,' I said.

Andrew, Billie and Thelma all suddenly looked at me.

'He won't what?' Andrew asked.

'Turn up okay. I found him. Just a few minutes ago. He's been killed. Hanged, I think.'

Thelma's mouth fell open and she started to blink at me very rapidly.

Billie murmured, 'Oh, my God.'

Andrew mashed his lips together and shook his head. Then he said in a low voice, 'Better show me. You two stay here,' he told the gals.

'What about Kim?' Billie asked.

I turned my head just in time to see Kimberly, up to her thighs in the clear blue water of the inlet, raise her arms and dive under.

'No point in telling her anything until we're sure,' Andrew said. 'Jesus wept. What is there, some damn conspiracy to turn all my daughters into widows?'

When he said that, Thelma started to cry.

Kimberly surfaced and began to swim, her back flashing sunlight.

'Let's go, chief.'

We hurried. As we went, he asked how I'd discovered

the body and was I sure it was Keith. I left out the part about falling down, but told him the rest. As for being sure of the identity, I pointed out that Keith was the only guy who had disappeared and the body in the tree was wearing a shirt exactly like Keith's, so I figured it was a pretty good bet.

'Don't be smart about shit like this,' he told me.

I apologized.

'That's my girl's husband you're talking about, and he was a good, decent man. Unlike that fuckhead who blew himself out of the water yesterday.'

When we got into the jungle, we had to wander around for a while, but finally I found the right place. The crumpled pages of a paperback book marked the spot, so to speak. That wasn't Keith's tree, but it worked as a landmark. I took a few strides away from it, looked up, saw Keith and pointed.

'I reckon that's him, all right,' Andrew said.

'I think he probably came out here during his watch,' I said. 'You know, figuring it'd be a good time to take care of business, everybody else being asleep. Only someone was out here waiting for him.'

'Or followed him when he left the beach,' Andrew added, and gave me a look. I couldn't see his eyes too well, his sunglasses being in the way, but I knew what sort of look he was giving me.

'If you think I did it, you're nuts. Why would *I* do it?'

'You've got the hots for Kimberly, so you take Keith out of the picture . . .'

'You're nuts!'

'You can't take your eyes off her.'

'Bull. And anyway, I'm not dumb enough to think she'd fall into my arms just because Keith isn't around. What kind of a moron do you think I am? And how in hell do you think I could possibly hoist a guy Keith's size that high into a tree?'

'It could be done,' Andrew said.

'With a winch, maybe.'

'A block and tackle.'

'Have you seen me running around the beach with a *block and tackle* hanging outa my trunks?'

'Steady there, chief. Don't blow a gasket, I'm just speculating.'

'Well you can quit speculating about me. How do I know *you* didn't kill him? I bet you could hoist a guy up there *without* a block and tackle.'

'What's my motive, Sherlock?'

'You tell me.'

'Shit. He was the salt of the earth, that boy. Shit!' Andrew suddenly jabbed a finger toward the body. 'Get up there and cut him down. Kimberly sees we're gone, she might get suspicious and come looking.'

'You want *me* to climb up there . . . ?'

'You betcha, chief. I'm a sixty-year-old man, for Godsake.'

'Sixty?'

'Bet yer ass.'

'You're in better shape than me, anyway.'

'I know that, and you oughta be ashamed to admit it.' He dug the Swiss Army knife out of a front pocket of his shorts, and tossed it underhand to me.

I fumbled it and had to bend down to pick it up.

'Get up there. Haul yer ass. Kimberly comes along and sees him swinging up there with his dick in the wind, she'll have nightmares the rest of her life.'

I figured that Andrew was probably right about that.

My swimming trunks didn't have a pocket and I wasn't

wearing any shirt, so I kept the knife shut and slid it down the top of my right sock. Then I started climbing the tree.

It wasn't my idea of a good time.

For one thing, I was worried about falling. For another, I was on my way up to a dead guy. I'd had about as much experience with dead bodies as I'd had with live gals. Basically, none. And I would've liked to keep it that way. (Not about the gals, about the corpses.)

If being dead wasn't bad enough, he was as good as naked. There's just about nothing I'd rather see less than some guy without any pants on. Especially the front of him, which is the section that was turned toward the tree trunk – and me.

I made sure not to look at him, and kept my eyes on the tree while I climbed. After a while, his bare feet showed up in my peripheral vision.

I turned my head and saw where the rope was tied off. I didn't look up to see where it came from. Obviously, though, it went upward from around his neck, was looped over a limb above his head, then came down – sort of behind him. It was wrapped and knotted around a limb just a little distance below his feet.

Which meant I could cut him down without climbing any higher, if I was willing to squirm out on the limb. The idea didn't appeal to me. To get within reach of the rope, I would need to go under Keith – and nudge his feet out of my way. If that wasn't bad enough, what was going to happen when I cut the rope? He would fall on me, that's what.

I wanted to be out of harm's way when I cut him loose.

So I turned my face to the tree again, and kept on climbing.

Even trying not to look, I couldn't help but see a lot

more of Keith than I liked. You just can't *avoid* taking glances, now and then, when you've got something like that hanging next to you.

For instance, you want to make sure you aren't about to bump into him, or something.

And you want to know if he's got something on him that might, say, leap across the gap. I mean like a snake or other beast.

Anyway, it made me feel pretty sick, the way he looked. The whole business disgusted me, especially that he didn't have any pants on. But then I got up high enough to see his face, and things got a hundred times worse.

I won't even get into what he looked like.

'It's him for sure?' Andrew called.

'I think so.'

'Do you think so, or know so?'

'He's all wrecked up. His face. But I guess I'm sure.'

'Hung?'

He meant 'hanged.' Hung meant something very different, also applicable to the situation. I was in no mood to make any cracks, though. I said, 'Yeah. But he's got blood all over his hair and face. It looks like maybe someone whacked him on the head, *then* strung him up.'

'Go ahead and cut him down.'

'Just a second.'

I checked out the rope. It didn't look very new, and was a little thicker than an ordinary clothesline. It had an actual 'hangman's knot.' I counted thirteen coils. They were tight against Keith's right cheek, and the thickness of the knot had shoved his head sideways. From the top of the knot, the rope went straight up to a limb several feet above his head. It looped over the limb, then stretched down behind his back, straight as a rod to where it was tied off on the limb below his feet.

He'd probably been hauled up by someone standing on that lower limb.

Maybe he'd been killed first, or at least knocked out.

'What're you doing up there?' Andrew called. 'Cut him down!'

I wondered if there might be a way to lower him.

If he could be hauled up, why not lowered?

Because, looking down, I could see that there was no extra rope at the lower limb. After tying it off, the killer must've cut off any excess.

I hated to just cut him loose and let him drop.

'Damn it, Rupert!'

'He'll fall,' I called back.

'So what? He's dead. He won't feel a thing.'

'Okay, okay.'

I climbed a little higher. Hugging the tree with my left arm, I brought up my right leg and pulled the knife out of my sock. I used my teeth to open the blade. Then I reached out over the top of Keith's head and pressed the edge of the blade against the rope.

Andrew's knife must've been awfully sharp.

One slice, and the rope popped.

Keith dropped.

It was worse than I expected.

He hit the limb underneath him, all right. But it went in between his legs and slammed him in the crotch. The whole limb shook. He sat there for a few seconds, head hanging. In his bright shirt, he looked like a flamboyant cowboy who'd fallen asleep in the saddle. Then he slumped over sideways. He fell the rest of the way head first.

Andrew let out a grunty noise and pranced backward to get out of the way.

Keith hit the ground with the back of his head. His spine seemed to bend in half. His legs shot down and his knees struck the ground on both sides of his face. For a second, he gazed up at me from down there like some sort of mutant that was half-face, half-ass. Then he tumbled over sideways.

I pushed my face against the tree trunk and sort of trembled for a while.

Pretty soon, Andrew started telling me to quit stalling and climb down – and bring the rope with me.

I did it. I had to climb out on that lower limb to get the rope. My hands shook too badly for me to untie the knots, so I used Andrew's knife to cut it loose. Then I just let it fall.

On the ground, I gave back Andrew's knife. He'd already picked up the rope and coiled it.

'What're we going to do with him?' I asked.

'Kimberly can't see him this way.' He handed the rope to me, then crouched by the body and took off Keith's noose. 'She'll want a look at him, though. We can't get around that. If she doesn't see his face, she'll never believe he's really dead.'

At that point, Andrew pulled and tugged at the body until it was stretched out flat on its back.

'Where's his damn trunks?'

'The killer must've taken them.'

'Look around.'

I did, but couldn't find Keith's swimming trunks, sandals, or anything else.

'Wanta give him yours?' Andrew asked.

'No way. Are you kidding? Not mine. You want to go around volunteering pants, volunteer your own.'

He gave me a smirk. 'Run on back to camp, then, and

grab a beach towel . . . a blanket . . .'

'Maybe we should cover him with leaves or something.'

'Do what I told you.'

So I did, even though it seemed like a mistake.

When I came out of the jungle, Kimberly saw me. She must've just waded out of the water. She was striding up the beach toward Billie and Thelma, but then she spotted me and broke into a run.

Maybe I should've run off. I thought about it, but just couldn't. She's too nice for me to run away from.

'You found him,' she said. She must've figured it out from the look on my face. 'Oh, God. Where is he?'

'Your dad's with him. He doesn't . . .'

'He's dead, isn't he?'

'Your dad's fine.'

'Keith.'

Before I could think of a good way to answer, she dodged past me and raced for the jungle. She must've seen where I came out, because she was headed straight toward it.

'Wait!' I yelled. 'Kimberly, don't! Just wait!'

She didn't stop. She had too big a headstart on me, so I didn't try to chase her down. Besides, what was I supposed to do, tackle her?

Andrew shouldn't have sent me back to the beach. I'd warned him not to. But he'd insisted.

Anyway, I still had a job to do. I took my time, though. Walked slowly to our camping area, picked up a blanket, answered a few questions from the women, then made my way back to the jungle.

When I got there, Kimberly was sobbing in her father's arms.

He was just in his white briefs.

He must've heard her coming, and had enough time to make Keith less indecent. He'd covered the lower parts with his own khaki shorts, and he'd draped a white handkerchief over the poor guy's face.

While he was busy consoling Kimberly, I went ahead and covered the body with the blanket. Then I reached under and plucked out Andrew's shorts and hanky. I stood off to the side, holding his stuff, and waited for them to get done.

The Funeral

After Kimberly stopped crying in her father's arms, she insisted on giving Keith a close inspection. (All our worries about covering him up seemed a little absurd.) Andrew tried to stop her, but she ignored him and pulled the blanket off and crouched beside the body.

She was awfully grim. She didn't say a thing, but she didn't cry, either. She actually lifted Keith's head, turned it from side to side, and searched through his hair with her fingers. (I think she was trying to figure out what killed him.)

After a while, she unbuttoned the front of his shirt. She asked us for some help, so we lifted him into a sitting position and Kimberly pulled his shirt off. She put it on right away, over her bikini top, but didn't fasten the buttons.

Then the three of us, working together, wrapped Keith in the blanket. Andrew wound the rope around it, so that the blanket would stay put. The result was a tidy, man-shaped bundle. Tidy except for the fact that Keith's feet stuck out the end.

Andrew slung Keith over his shoulder. With him in the lead, we made our way back to the beach.

Billie, Connie and Thelma were waiting for us at the

campsite. They were all pretty much in tears. When we showed up, they gathered around Kimberly, shaking their heads and sobbing, hugging her and muttering. Kimberly seemed to be taking things pretty well. She was grim, but didn't fall apart. Something about the way she stood there, being really brave and wearing Keith's festive shirt, got to me so that I choked up, myself.

We had a discussion about what to do with Keith's body. Since we don't expect to be castaways for any great length of time, we didn't want to dispose of it in any sort of permanent way. We wanted it handy and easy to recover.

We let Kimberly make the final decision. She chose to bury Keith (*store* him, more like it), over where the rocks jutted out to the south side of the beach. The place was close enough so we could keep an eye on it and get to the body easily in case of rescue. It was also far enough away so that the thing wouldn't exactly be living with us. I'm hoping we won't be able to smell it.

Bad enough that we can see it.

Not the body. It's out of sight. But every time I turn my head in that direction, I can't help but look at the pile of rocks covering it. Not to mention the cross. Kimberly made the cross out of driftwood, this afternoon. She stood it up at the head of Keith's 'grave.' It's gnarled and twisted and as white as bleached bones.

That's getting ahead of things, though.

First came the decision about where to put Keith. Then we all trooped over there, Andrew marching in the lead with the body slung over his shoulder. (Thelma came with us. Her ankle injury had been pretty minor, and she was able to hobble along okay without help by the time we had our funeral procession.)

Kimberly picked exactly the spot where she wanted the

grave to be. Then Andrew and Billie and I helped her to clear some rocks out of the way.

Thelma stood by and cried like a maniac.

Connie didn't help, either, but acted strange; she stood rigid and watched, had this far-off look in her eyes, and rubbed her upper arms as if she was cold. Personally, I don't think she was grieving over Keith. I think she was scared witless.

After we'd cleared a depression in the rocks, Andrew and Kimberly loaded Keith inside it.

Then Billie said, 'Someone should say something.'

'Let's bow our heads,' Andrew said. We did. In a low and steady voice, he said The Lord's Prayer. Knew it by heart, which came as a surprise to me. I wouldn't have taken him for the religious sort.

While everybody still had their heads down, I broke into 'Danny Boy.' God only knows what possessed me. I've got a pretty good tenor voice, but I'm not a guy who goes around singing in public. It was a sappy thing to do. The guy's name wasn't even Danny.

But I'd liked him, and I felt so sorry for Kimberly . . .

When I got into 'Danny Boy,' the waterworks were a sight to see. *Every*body cried.

Even Kimberly teared up. After the song was done, she came over to me, wet-eyed and sniffing. She put her arms around me and hugged me.

I'm hoping she'll do that again sometime, under more favorable conditions.

Fat chance.

She was too overcome with emotion to know what she was doing.

Anyway, I'm glad I went nuts and sang 'Danny Boy.' She wouldn't have hugged me, except for that.

When it was time to finish the burial, she asked everyone to leave. 'I'll take care of it,' she said. So we all left her there.

Away from the rocks where Kimberly was working, Andrew called the rest of us together.

'I don't want anyone to go straying off alone,' he said. 'Keith didn't have an accident. He was murdered.'

Thelma let out a high-pitched, squealy sound. She seemed embarrassed by it, and plastered a hand across her mouth.

Connie started to shake.

Billie, frowning with concern, put an arm across Connie's shoulders. 'It's all right, honey,' she said.

'We think it happened out in the jungle where we found him,' Andrew went on. 'Someone knocked him on the head, and then hung him. That's how we figure it.' He glanced at me.

'It was probably just one person who did it,' I added. 'I mean, the sneaky way it was done.'

'Somebody strong enough to hoist Keith's body fairly high up in a tree,' Andrew said.

'What'll we do?' Billie asked.

'I'm not sure yet. Need some time to think things through. Let's figure on a pow-wow later on. For now, we'll probably be all right as long as nobody goes off alone. I don't think the killer'll come after any of us out here on the beach in plain sight.'

'What about . . . when we need to relieve ourselves?' Billie asked. 'Do you want us to do it right here on the beach?'

Connie joined the party. 'Not me. Huh-uh.'

'We'll work something out,' Andrew said. 'For the time being, we can keep on using the same area as before. But not without an escort. Let me know, and I'll go with you.'

'Oh, charming,' Connie said.

'I changed your diapers, babe. But don't worry, I won't peek.'

'This really sucks,' Connie said.

Andrew suddenly looked steamed. 'You've got two sisters whose lives have been blown all to hell in a matter of less than twenty-four hours. There's an asshole out there who'll probably try and kill more of us the first time he gets a chance. What we do not need at this particular juncture is any kind of adolescent shit from you. We *know* you're deeply inconvenienced by all this, but . . .'

'Go to hell!' she blurted. Bursting into tears, she whirled around and ran toward the water.

Thelma, by the way, was already on her knees, sobbing into her hands. This had happened at about the time Andrew made the remark about the two sisters whose lives had been 'blown all to hell.'

Billie scowled at Andrew and shook her head. 'That was really uncalled for, do you know that?' She didn't wait for an answer, but went hustling after Connie.

I was the only member of the group still standing in Andrew's presence. He seemed to be glaring at me from behind his sunglasses.

'*I* didn't say anything,' I told him.

'Don't be a smartass,' Andrew said. And stalked off himself.

I was left on my own, so I got my bag and came up to my tower. (Violating the new rules about straying off, I suppose, but nobody called me on it.) There was a lot of journal to catch up with. Instead of going to the place I'd found yesterday, I picked a spot in the rocks where I had a view of our beach.

When I arrived, Kimberly was still busy on the other side of the inlet, picking up rocks and gently arranging them on top of her husband. After she finished with that, she took care of making the cross. (I've been keeping an eye on her while I write. The others are down there, too, but they haven't been doing anything worth mentioning.)

For a while now, Kimberly has been sitting on the beach. She is still wearing Keith's bright, Hawaiian shirt. Her legs are out in front of her, her knees drawn up, her arms around her shins. She seems to be gazing out at the water. A breeze is stirring her hair, and fluttering the shirt a little behind her back.

She looks so beautiful and alone.

I wish there was some way to make things better for her.

The important thing, now, is to make sure that the killer doesn't get any more of us.

Pow-Wow

We ate supper early. Billie did the cooking again. It was a mixture of noodles and beef from some foil packets that Andrew and Keith had gathered out on the inlet, yesterday. We also had some canned peaches, and bread from a loaf that had gotten through the explosion with its cellophane bag intact. We drank stream water, pouring it into our plastic cups from a pot that we passed around.

None of us had eaten anything all day, as far as I knew.

I, for one, was pretty hungry.

We sat in the sand around the fire, eating, passing the water pot around, and not saying much. Everyone seemed pretty upset.

Afterwards, Billie asked me to help her with the dishes, and I agreed. Glad to get away from the group, for one thing.

The 'dishes' were a mix of things: a couple of metal pots rescued from the bottom of the inlet by Keith, plus plastic plates, cups, knives, forks and spoons that we'd brought ashore for our picnic.

We didn't want to mess up our beach with food scraps, so we carried everything out to the north point – leaving the beach behind and stepping carefully from rock to rock until we reached the very end (forty or fifty feet below the place where I like to work on my journal). We went around the tip, just a bit.

There was nothing to see on the other side. Just more water, beach and jungle.

Billie sat on a rock and dangled her legs in the water. She washed her dishes by bending forward and dipping them into the water between her knees. When I knelt near her and tried to scoop up some water in a pot, she shook her head. 'Just put it down. I'll take care of washing these things. I just wanted you along for the company.'

'I'll help.'

'Don't be ridiculous. There isn't enough here to worry about.' She had brought a rag with her. Also, back on the beach, she'd scooped up some sand in one of the pots. While I watched, she rubbed the dishes with sand, wiped them with the rag, and leaned forward to rinse them with a dip in the water.

She didn't seem to be in any hurry.

I sure wasn't.

I liked being out there with her. For starters, Billie is great to look at. She had some major cleavage showing, and her breasts wobbled and shook because of the vigorous way she was washing the dishes. And then there was the way she kept bending forward to rinse things . . .

It wasn't just her looks, though. Also, she's a cool lady. She has always been very nice to me (too nice, if you ask Connie), she treats everyone decently, she has a sense of humor, she isn't prudish (she's almost immodest), she doesn't fly off the handle every two seconds, and she seems to have loads of common sense.

Unfortunately, she didn't pass on many of these traits to her daughter. Connie has some of Billie's looks, but apparently didn't inherit much of her temperament.

Anyway, it was very nice to be out there on the point with her. I tried not to stare at her *all* the time.

Each time she finished cleaning an item, she twisted sideways and reached up and handed it to me. I made a neat pile on a slightly higher rock.

We were almost done when she gave me a plastic fork, looked me in the eyes and said, 'I have a feeling it might be Wesley.'

Her words took me completely by surprise, but I knew right away what she meant.

'It's occurred to me, too,' I said. 'He blew the boat on purpose?'

'Some kind of timing device, so he'd have a few minutes to swim clear before she went up.'

'I've seen that sort of thing done in some movies,' I said.

'And so, I'm sure, has Wesley.'

'Do you think he'd have the guts?'

'Never underestimate the guts of a weasel,' she told me. She patted the rock beside her, so I sat down. 'I haven't mentioned this to Andrew, yet. Not to anyone else, either. Wanted to see what you thought of the idea. You're not an actual member of the family, for one thing. And you're a good, sensible guy.'

'Well, thanks.'

'Look at the whole deal as an elaborate set-up,' she said. 'Whose idea was it to give Andrew and I this boat trip for our anniversary? Wesley's. Who made all the arrangements? Wesley. Who came down in advance to look things over? Wesley. Who picked this island for our little picnic yesterday? Who stayed on board while the rest of us came ashore? Who got blown up – supposedly?'

'He might've actually *chosen* this island as the place to stage the accident,' I suggested. 'Maybe he toured around last week till he found a nice, uninhabited one.'

'Exactly,' she said. 'He would've needed not only a deserted island, but one that's out of the way – where we're not likely to get found immediately.'

'Or at all.'

'And while we're on *that* subject,' Billie said, 'he could've left a trail of false information to make sure nobody misses us – or knows where to come looking.'

I nodded. I'd been nodding fairly regularly since the start of our talk.

'I bet he even came ashore,' I said.

'Here?'

'Yeah. He must've brought in a bunch of supplies and hidden them somewhere. For his own use, you know? Whatever he's got in mind for us, I'll bet his plan doesn't include screwing himself out of stuff to eat and drink.'

'And what,' Billie asked, 'do you suppose his plan might be?'

'What do *you* think?' I asked her.

'I asked you first.'

'Okay.' I took a deep breath. 'For starters, Wesley wouldn't do any of this if he really loved Thelma.'

'I agree. And he didn't. I think he could barely tolerate her.'

'So why did he marry her?'

'She's very rich. As are we all, thanks to Andrew.'

'Yeah. Okay. Is there a way that this business of marooning us might make Wesley rich?'

'Sure. If he's the only survivor.'

We looked at each other, and we both grimaced.

'What would he inherit?' I asked.

'What wouldn't he?'

'Jeez.'

'So that's his plan. Kill us all.'

'Maybe,' I said. 'He's gotten off to a great start – killed the toughest male in the group.'

'I don't know about that.' She smiled. 'Andrew's a pretty tough *hombre*.'

'He's probably next on the list.'

She shook her head. 'Won't let that happen.'

'We'll have to talk to the others about this.'

'That'll certainly endear us to Thelma. We'd better leave her out of it.'

'Talk to them one at a time,' I suggested.

'Yeah.'

'We might be completely wrong, you know. I mean, this is all guesswork – sort of farfetched, too.'

'But it all fits,' Billie said.

'Yeah. The only thing is, sometimes things *are* the way they seem. Maybe Wesley *did* get blown up with the boat.'

'And Keith was killed by . . . ?'

'A restless native?'

A corner of Billie's mouth turned up. 'Maybe Gilligan did it.'

'Or the Howells.'

Billie smiled and shook her head.

I suddenly felt a little guilty for kidding around about Keith's death. Getting serious, I said, 'In a way, it doesn't matter *who* did it. What matters is that it happened and the killer's probably still out there. Whether he's Wesley or someone else, it's pretty much the same deal.'

'Except I'd sure like to know who we're dealing with.'

'Yeah,' I said. 'Me, too.'

'It isn't quite as scary when I think of Wesley out there trying to knock us off. At least he's not a complete stranger.

If it's *not* him, it might be someone ten times more dangerous.'

'Better him than some sort of deranged jungle-man.'

'I'll say.'

'So, what are we going to do about our theory?' I asked.

'You don't see any major holes in it?'

'No. I think there's every reason to believe it is Wesley – except that maybe he was blown to bits yesterday.'

'Or maybe he wasn't.'

'Nobody found any bits,' I admitted. 'Which doesn't mean he *wasn't* blown up . . .'

'I've picked up one lesson from many long years of watching crappy TV mysteries,' Billie said. 'Here it is: if the body isn't found and identified beyond a shadow of a doubt – then the person ain't dead. It's almost always a ruse, and the "dead" guy is up to no good.'

'I've noticed that, too,' I said. 'But that's TV. TV ripping off Agatha Christie. Or maybe . . . is there a Holmes story where a "dead" guy is a perpetrator?'

Billie frowned at me. 'I wouldn't know, Rupert. Do you think it *is* or *isn't* Wesley?'

'Might be.'

She slapped the side of my arm, but in a sort of playful way. 'Don't be difficult.'

'Sorry.'

'What I'm getting at . . . should we tell the others about our suspicions?'

'We'd better.'

'Good. That's what I think, too.'

'But maybe we'd better bring it up in front of everyone,' I said. 'Including Thelma. Otherwise, what'll happen if he *is* the killer, and she runs into him?'

'You're right,' Billie said. 'We'd better let everyone in on it.'

With that settled, we gathered the dishes and returned to the beach. I was all set to work on my journal. Before I could get started, though, Andrew called everyone together for a group discussion.

We all sat around the fire.

Everyone seemed solemn except for Connie, who gave me dirty looks from the other side of the fire. Odds are, she's put out with me for disappearing around the point with her mother. She probably thinks we were making out.

'There are things that need to be said about our situation here,' Andrew began. 'And we need to make some decisions about how to proceed. This time yesterday, our only real concern was how long we might have to wait before being picked up by a rescue party. Now, Keith has been murdered. That changes . . .'

Thelma raised her hand like a schoolgirl.

Andrew gave her a nod.

'I've been thinking,' she said. 'About Keith's murder and . . . about Wesley.' Her chin trembled. She pressed her lips together. After a couple of seconds, she went on. 'Doesn't anybody find it funny that Keith got killed so soon . . . It was just yesterday the boat exploded and . . . you know. Wesley. What I'm trying to say . . . you all think the boat was an accident. But maybe it *wasn't*, though. I've been thinking about all this, you know? Maybe somebody blew up the boat on purpose. What I mean is, maybe *Wesley* was murdered, too. Not just Keith. Maybe they blew up the boat to kill Wesley and strand us here. Maybe the idea is, they want to pick us off one by one. Or maybe they only just want to kill off all the men.'

'If that's the plan,' Kimberly said, 'they're halfway home.'

I didn't much like the sound of that, me being part of the remaining half.

'What "they" are we discussing here?' Andrew asked. He seemed a little annoyed. 'I'm not aware of any "they."'

'Whoever's behind all this,' Thelma told him.

'You think we're the victims of a conspiracy?'

She stuck out her lip. 'You're just *so* sure Wesley got careless . . .'

'If he didn't blow up the boat by accident,' Andrew said, 'then why *did* it explode?'

'I don't know,' Thelma said. 'Anything's possible. Maybe it got hit by one of those rocket things. Or somebody might've swum up to it underwater and attached a bomb to it. You know?'

'Who would do such things?' Andrew asked.

'Drug dealers? Maybe we've stumbled onto a nest of drug dealers, and they need to eliminate us. Or maybe there's a secret military base on the island.'

'Maybe it's Dr No,' I suggested.

Nobody seemed amused. Not even Billie, who sort of cringed when I said it.

'We'll have no more of that,' Andrew told me.

'Yes, sir.'

'All I'm trying to get at,' Thelma went on, 'is that in my opinion I think Wesley didn't get killed because he did something stupid on the boat and blew everything up. I think he got murdered, the same as Keith.'

Staring toward the fire, her voice very calm, Kimberly said, 'Has it occurred to anyone that maybe Wesley isn't dead, at all?'

Billie's eyes latched on mine.

'Suppose he arranged for the boat to explode – after he got off it?'

'What do you mean?' Thelma asked.

Kimberly grimaced at her. 'I'm sorry. It has to be said, though. I think there's a chance that Wesley's alive, and that he might be the one who murdered Keith.'

Then she spelled it out. The whole scenario, just as if she'd been listening to Billie and I out on the point. She used nearly all the same reasoning, but presented her argument in a more logical, concise way than we'd done. About the only thing she left out was my theory that Wesley visited the island in advance and hid a cache of supplies for his own use.

Through the whole thing, Thelma sat there looking stunned, betrayed, aghast.

When Kimberly finished, Thelma said to her, 'You're out of your fucking mind.'

'If she is,' Billie said, 'so am I.'

'Me, too,' I said.

Thelma turned her gaze to Connie, looking for an ally.

'Don't ask me,' Connie said, then went right on and added, 'All I know is that I've always thought Wesley was a pig . . .'

'Constance!' Andrew snapped.

She flinched, but went right on. 'So it wouldn't exactly come as any big shock if he pulled something like this. I mean, I don't wanta hurt your feelings, but I thought you were nuts to get involved with him in the first place, much less marry him.'

Andrew glared at her.

'Well,' Connie said in a whiny voice, 'she asked.'

Thelma looked as if she'd been slapped silly. She turned to Andrew. In a sad, pathetic voice, she said, 'Dad?'

'You know good and well how I felt about Wesley. But I'm on your side in this.'

'There aren't sides,' Billie put in.

'Whatever. Thing is, it makes a cute theory – Wesley set us all up and faked his own death. But I'd say it's too cute. He didn't have the smarts or ambition or guts to pull off a stunt like that.' Andrew stuffed some tobacco into the bowl of his pipe.

'Maybe we never knew him,' Kimberly said.

'You didn't,' Thelma blurted. 'None of you knew him. He wouldn't . . . *do* something like this. You don't know how sensitive he could be.'

Andrew took a burning stick from the fire. As he sucked the flame down into his pipe, Billie said, 'I think most of what we saw from Wesley – including you, honey – was false. I don't know that we ever saw an honest emotion from the guy.'

'Slick Wesley,' I said.

'*You* shut up,' Thelma snapped at me.

After a few puffs on his pipe, Andrew said, 'There's the matter of the rope. It didn't come from our boat; I would've seen it. Which leads me to the conclusion that the rope was on this island before we got here. More than likely in the possession of the fellow who used it on Keith.'

'And that lets Wesley off the hook?' Kimberly asked.

'In my opinion.'

'Suppose he had the rope in his luggage?'

'He didn't.'

'How do you know?'

Andrew blew out a pale plume of smoke, then said, 'I inspected his luggage.'

Thelma's eyes bulged. 'You *what?*'

'Settle down, honey. It was as much for your protection

as ours. Just wanted to see that he hadn't packed anything worrisome. Drugs, a firearm . . .'

'Dad!'

'Who else's stuff did you search?' Connie asked. She looked ready to blow her lid.

'Nobody's. Just Wesley's.'

'Yeah, I'm sure.'

'It isn't any wonder that he felt like everybody was always against him,' Thelma said. 'I just thought he was being overly sensitive, but . . .'

'We're not against him,' Andrew said.

'Like fun.'

'*I'm* not, anyway,' he told her. 'I'm saying the rope didn't come from the boat. If it didn't come from the boat, where could Wesley have gotten his hands on it? He's innocent. Keith was murdered by a stranger. A stranger who had access to that rope.'

'Wesley might've brought in a load of supplies last week,' Billie pointed out.

'That's right,' Kimberly said, nodding eagerly. 'If he set things up to maroon us, he almost *had* to lay in supplies for himself.'

That was my idea, of course. But I was happy to let them take credit for it. Seemed as if I'd already opened my mouth once too often.

I had to open it again, though. With a look at Thelma, I said, 'Whether it's Wesley or some stranger, there probably is a bunch of supplies hidden somewhere on the island. I mean, the rope came from *somewhere*, right? Tomorrow, we oughta go and try to find where the stuff is being kept.'

'What we oughta do tomorrow,' Connie said, 'is climb into that dinghy and haul our asses out of here before we *all* get killed. I mean, isn't that the smart thing to do? Just leave? Whoever this guy is, he won't be on the dinghy with us. We just trot ourselves over to a *different* island, where there isn't some lunatic trying to wipe us out. I mean, you look out there and you can *see* those islands.'

'They're farther away than they look,' Andrew pointed out.

'So?'

'We'd run out of gas before we got anywhere close to them. Then we'd be stuck on a dinghy with limited amounts of food and water . . .'

'But nobody trying to kill us,' Connie pointed out.

'We're a lot better off here, believe me. We've got everything we need to sustain life. We could spend our entire lives here in relative comfort, if it came to that.'

'Swiss Family Collins,' I said. Couldn't help it.

'God save us from *that*,' Billie said.

'Wesley'll murder us all first,' Connie said.

'It's not my Wesley!' Thelma cried out.

'Well, whoever!'

'Stop it,' Andrew said.

I'll have to stop pretty soon, myself. Gotta hurry things along; it's almost too dark to see what I'm writing.

The upshot of the pow-wow was that either Wesley or a stranger killed Keith and might be after more of us or all of us. We won't try to get away in the dinghy tomorrow, but we might keep it in mind in case things get worse. We'll probably spend tomorrow exploring the island. We are posting double guards tonight: first Andrew and Thelma; then Kimberly and Billie; and finally me and Connie. Obviously, nobody is supposed to go off alone.

After the pow-wow, we all ran around and gathered a whole bunch of firewood. We also picked up rocks to use as weapons. Then I had a chance to sit by myself and start writing. I've been at it for a long time. Almost done, though. If I don't hurry, I'll have to finish tonight's entry in Braille.

While I've been working on the journal here, Thelma has been pouting. Connie has been sitting by herself, over near the dinghy, gazing off into space. Andrew, Billie and Kimberly have been putting together a nice little arsenal: aside from a pile of throwing rocks, we've now got spears, clubs, and makeshift tomahawks. We'll be in great shape if we end up in a pitched battle with Fred, Wilma and Barney.

I shouldn't joke about it. I like the idea of having weapons.

What'd I'd *really* like, though, is maybe an M-16.

Oh, well. Castaways can't be choosers.

Day Three

What Happened With The Dinghy

Here's what happened.

Some time during the night – we don't know whose watch it was – he got the dinghy.

No big trick. Though we'd kept it beached above the high-tide line, it wasn't close enough to keep an eye on. For one thing, the beach had a slight downward slope from where we camped. For another, the area where we left it was beyond the reach of the firelight.

Nobody was really paying attention to it, anyway. We were worried about each other, not the boat.

What he must've done was sneak in from a side, staying close to the shore, and drag the dinghy into the water. Then he probably swam away, towing it by the bow line.

Connie and I started our watch at four in the morning. We sat so we faced each other across the fire. That way, between the two of us, we had a 360-degree view and nobody could approach without one or the other of us spotting him.

It was Connie who suggested our positions. Not only were we beyond touching distance, but we couldn't carry on a conversation without raising our voices. So we stayed silent, for the most part. Fine with me.

Even though we just sat there, looking around and not

talking, neither of us noticed anything wrong. Maybe the dinghy was already gone by then.

An hour or so into our watch, I got up from the fire and went over to the rocks and took a leak. I must've walked within twenty feet of where the dinghy was supposed to be. I don't recall seeing it, but I don't recall *not* seeing it. More than likely, it had already been taken. But I can't swear to that.

A little later, Connie headed toward the same area – for the same reason I'd gone there. I started to get up and go with her, but she said, 'I don't need an audience, thanks all the same. Anyway, I can take care of myself.' She was holding one of the spears, and gave it a shake. 'You just stay here and mind your own business.'

So I stood with my back to the fire and watched her. After she left the firelight behind, she was just a dim shape. All I could see was her T-shirt, because it was white. It seemed to float above the beach as she walked. Then it started to rise, which meant she was climbing the rocks. When she got up into them, the T-shirt sank out of sight.

At the time, I thought how it would've served her right if she'd gotten nailed right then and there.

She didn't, though.

Pretty soon, she came back.

'Real nice,' I congratulated her.

'Sorry. I'm sure you would've loved to watch.'

'Guess who would've gotten the blame if our resident Thuggee had taken the opportunity to kill your ass while you were over there? Me, that's who. Your dad thinks I'm worthless, as it is. There'd be no living with him if I let you get killed.'

'Ha ha ha. I'm sure you wouldn't mind, otherwise.'

'You think I want you to get killed?'

She let out a huff. 'You wouldn't exactly consider it a great loss. All you care about is my mom – and Kimberly. I don't exactly stack up, do I?'

'Well, no.'

'See?'

'That doesn't mean I'd like you to get killed. What I'd really like is if, by some miracle, you stopped being such a bitch all the time.'

She gave me a sneer and said, 'Oh, isn't that cute.' Then she strutted over to her side of the fire. She sat down, crossed her legs, and lay the spear across her thighs. 'Don't even look at me,' she said.

So I didn't look at her.

Not for about half an hour, anyway.

But she drew attention to herself by raising the spear overhead. Just as I turned my eyes to her, she threw it.

At me.

It flew over the top of the fire, its whittled point coming straight for my face. I whipped an arm up just in time, and knocked the spear aside.

'Real nice!' I told her. 'Shit! You could've *hurt* me with that thing!'

'That was the general idea.'

'Try it again some time, and maybe I'll forget to be a gentleman and shove it . . .'

'Fuck you.'

'Just shut up before we wake everybody up,' I said. Then I muttered, mostly to myself, something about her being a 'crazy fucking bitch.'

'What did you say?'

'Nothing. Shut up, okay? We're supposed to be keeping watch.'

Oddly enough, our quarrel didn't wake anybody up. At

any rate, nobody yelled at us to knock it off.

Connie and I didn't say anything to each other for the rest of the night. I tried not to look at her again, but couldn't help it. I had to make sure she wasn't about to hurl a weapon at me. Whenever our eyes met, she never failed to give me a dirty look.

Dawn finally came.

Andrew woke up and came over to the fire. He was shirtless, barefoot, and wearing his khaki shorts. He said, 'Lovely morning, eh, kids?' Then he did a couple of quick knee-bends, arms forward for balance. Then he rubbed his hands together. 'How was the watch? No trouble, I take it?'

'What're *you* so peppy for?' Connie said.

'Ah, the child's in a snit, and it's barely sun-up. Lover's quarrel?' he asked.

'Give me a break.'

'Tell you what, a good brisk swim oughta set things right. I'll race the both of you.' Grinning and rubbing his hands together, he looked toward the inlet. 'We'll make it a race to the . . .' His face changed. Something was wrong. As I stood up to see what it was, he said, 'What's *that* doing out there?'

A boat was floating on the water, maybe four hundred yards out. For a second, I thought that rescuers might be on the way. But then I checked the beach and saw that our dinghy wasn't where it ought to be.

Connie stood up, too. She studied the situation, then made a face.

Andrew turned on me. 'What do you know about this?'

'Nothing,' I said.

'Connie?'

'Don't ask me.'

'You two were supposed to be keeping watch.'

'We didn't notice anything unusual,' I said.

'Well something unusual sure as hell *happened*. That dinghy didn't just get up and *walk* off the beach.'

'No, sir.'

As if the three of us all wondered the same thing at once, we turned suddenly toward the sleeping areas. Billie, Kimberly and Thelma were where they ought to be: none of them had snuck past us and taken the boat out for an early-morning excursion.

'And you are sure you two don't know anything about it?' Andrew asked Connie and me.

We both shook our heads.

'We obviously had a visitor last night,' Andrew said. 'He slipped right past you and set our boat adrift. Did you fall asleep?'

'No, sir,' I said.

'You?' he snapped at Connie.

'No.'

'Mess around?'

'With *him*?' She wrinkled her nose. 'Get real.'

'We didn't do anything,' I said.

'Apparently, that includes keeping watch. Good thing our friend didn't decide to slit a few throats while he was in the neighborhood.'

Connie cringed and looked a little sick.

'A couple of terrific sentries you two are,' he said.

I considered pointing out that the visit might've occurred during someone else's watch – even his – but decided not to bother. After all, we should've at least noticed that the dinghy was missing.

Connie didn't try to give the skipper any excuses, either. The way she looked, I bet she was thinking about how she'd gone over to the rocks, all by herself, to take her leak last night. I bet she was wondering where the killer might've been while she was there.

'What's all the fussing about?' The question came from Billie. We looked over at her. She lay on her side, propped up on one elbow. Her upper breast seemed about ready to fall out of her bikini, but so far it was staying put.

'Our friend,' Andrew explained, 'snuck in here last night right under the noses of our two sharp-eyed sentries and set the dinghy adrift.'

Frowning, Billie thrust herself up to a sitting position. She was wonderful to watch – all that shifting flesh barely contained by her black bikini. Nothing came loose, though. Once she was on her feet, she took a few moments to adjust her top and bottom. While she fiddled with the bikini, she frowned out at the dinghy.

'Maybe a wave just came in and took it off,' she suggested.

'Not a chance,' Andrew said. 'This was done on purpose. By a person. By the man who murdered Keith, more than likely.'

'What'll we do?' Billie asked. 'We aren't going to just let it go, are we? What if we decide we want it? Even if you don't think we should try for another island . . .'

'It isn't going anywhere,' Andrew said.

'It's almost gone *now*.'

'I'm going out to get it.'

She looked at him. She gazed at the boat. 'No, you're not.'

'Yes, I am.'

'You can't swim that far.'

'Of course I can.'

'I don't mean you *can't*. I mean you're not *going* to. You're sixty years old, for Godsake.'

'Don't give me that age crap. I can outswim anyone here.'

I raised my hand a little – like a schoolkid who thinks he might know the answer but isn't quite sure. 'I'll swim out and bring it back,' I offered.

'Don't make me laugh,' Andrew said. 'I've *seen* you swim – if one can call it that.'

'Maybe we should just let it go,' Billie said. 'It's not worth . . .'

'No!' Connie blurted. 'It's our only way out of here! We've got to get it back!'

'She's right,' Andrew said. He unbuckled his belt.

Billie put a hand on his shoulder. 'No. Come on, now. Kimberly's the swimmer of the family. She should be the one to go, if anyone.'

Kimberly appeared to be asleep. She was face down in her nest of rags, sprawled limp, one leg out to the side and bent at the knee. One arm was under her face. The other stretched away from her as if she were reaching for something.

Maybe reaching for Keith.

She still had his Hawaiian shirt on. The gaudy fabric rippled in the breeze. The shirt had gotten mussed in her sleep, so it let some of her back show above her bikini pants.

Man, she looked great.

'I'm not going to wake her up for this,' Andrew said. 'No, sir. Not me.' He took off his khaki shorts, handed them to Billie, and stood in front of us wearing nothing except his white briefs. They were sagging a bit, so he tugged them up. (Like Thelma, Andrew had come to the picnic with no intention of swimming. They both left their suits on the boat.)

69

Billie was frowning. 'Andrew,' she said. 'Don't . . .'

'For Godsake, woman.'

'Don't make *me* a widow,' she told him.

He narrowed an eye at her. 'The day I can't swim out as far as that dinghy, I might as *well* be dead.' He winked, then grabbed her upper arms, pulled her against him and planted a big kiss on her mouth. 'That'll have to last you till I get back.'

'I wish you wouldn't go.'

'Christ, now, you're gonna jinx me!' He smacked her on the rump.

Hard enough to make her flinch and wince.

'Back in a flash,' he said.

Then he whirled around and marched with a jaunty swagger toward the water.

'The idiot,' Billie muttered. Even though she was annoyed, she seemed proud of him.

'He'll be all right,' Connie said. 'He can swim that far without even getting winded.'

'He *is* in great shape,' Billie admitted.

The way he was wading through the knee-deep water, I thought he looked rather like an old, bow-legged monkey. But I kept the observation to myself.

'Should I go with him?' I asked Billie.

'Get real,' Connie said.

'I wasn't asking you.'

'He wouldn't like it,' Billie told me, not taking her eyes off Andrew. 'He thinks he's perfectly capable of doing everything.'

'Made me climb the tree and cut down Keith yesterday,' I said.

Billie shook her head. 'Did he? He isn't fond of heights.'

'Dad'll be fine in the water,' Connie said.

The water of the inlet was very shallow. Andrew waded out nearly as far as the point before he began to swim. Because of the reef, there was no real surf. Just small, calm waves that shouldn't give a swimmer any trouble at all. He moved along smoothly, taking his time. The dinghy kept drifting farther away, but he was slowly gaining on it.

The next thing I knew, Kimberly stood beside me.

'Hi,' I said.

'Hi,' she said. 'What's happening?'

'Your father's swimming out to get the dinghy.'

'That's our dinghy out there?'

'Yeah.'

'How'd it get away?'

'We don't know,' I said.

Billie joined in, saying, 'Andrew thinks the killer snuck in and set it adrift last night.'

'Jesus,' Kimberly muttered. She put a hand against her brow to shade her eyes. 'It sure is far out there.'

'We were going to have you go for it,' Billie said, 'but your father insisted on doing it himself.'

'He didn't want to wake you up,' I added.

'Figures,' Kimberly said. Then, without asking for advice or permission, she flung off Keith's shirt and bolted for the water. She didn't jog, she sprinted. It was great to watch. She dashed over the beach, shiny black hair flowing behind her, arms swinging, long legs striding out, feet kicking up sand, then water. The water flew as she splashed forward. It sparkled in the sunlight. It gleamed on her dark shoulders and back and legs.

'He doesn't *need* her,' Connie whined. 'God! She always has to butt in and take over.'

'It's fine,' Billie said.

'Yeah, sure. What's the point, anyhow? She isn't even

gonna catch up to him in time.'

I'd been watching Kimberly splash through the water, but now I looked past her. It took a few seconds to spot the dinghy. And there was Andrew, closing in on it.

I got my eyes back to Kimberly in time to watch her dive. She vanished under the waves for a few moments, then surfaced and began to swim with quick, sharp strokes.

Man, she was fast!

Not fast enough, though.

She was only about halfway there when Andrew arrived at the dinghy.

'He made it,' Billie said.

Way off in the distance, he reached up out of the water with both hands. He grabbed a gunnel near the bow. Then someone stood up in the dinghy.

I thought I'd have a heart attack.

Connie made a gasp.

Billie cried out, 'My God!'

We couldn't see who it was. We couldn't even see whether it was a man or woman. Just that it was a person, and that it came up suddenly out of the bottom of the boat and raised an object overhead with both hands.

The object looked like an ax.

It swung down and appeared to strike Andrew on top of his head. He let go of the gunnel.

He vanished under the water.

I felt like I'd been kicked in the stomach.

Connie went nuts. She started shrieking, 'Dad! Dad!'

But Billie kept her head. Like me, she must've known it was a waste of time to cry out for Andrew. If we'd seen things right, he was past help.

Kimberly was the one in danger, now.

She was still swimming toward the dinghy. Hadn't she

seen? Maybe she *had* seen, and planned to do something about it.

Billie shouted, 'Kim! Kim! Watch out! Get back here!'

'What's happening?' Thelma called. I glanced around and saw her staggering toward us.

Billie ignored her and kept yelling at Kimberly.

Connie was on her hands and knees, head up, staring out toward the scene of the murder, shrieking, 'Dad!'

I flung my shoes away and hit the water at a run.

God only knows what I hoped to accomplish.

Save Kimberly, I guess.

As I splashed my way forward, I heard the sound of a motor. So I stopped running. In water up to my thighs, I saw the dinghy start moving away to the right. The killer sat hunched over low at the stern, steering.

Maybe it was Wesley.

Could've been almost anyone.

The boat picked up speed.

Kimberly kept swimming, but the boat was long gone by the time she reached the place where it had been.

Three Down, One To Go

I'm the only guy left. On the surface, that might be an enviable position. Here I am, the lone male marooned on a tropical island with four women.

There's one big drawback, though.

The other three males have been killed in quick succession. (That's if you include Wesley, who is dead unless he's the killer.)

The women are still here, intact.

Makes me think it isn't safe to be a man on this island.

In other words, guess who's next?

I'm not sure what to do about it. I can't exactly *leave* – the killer made off with our dinghy. No telling where it might be, by now. The last I saw, it was heading toward the north end of the island. Kimberly and I had just dragged Andrew's body onto the rocks around the end of the point. (About where Billie and I did the dishes last night.)

Now that I've seen the wound, there's no doubt that the weapon was an ax. It chopped Andrew's head pretty much in half all the way down to his jaw. The back of his head was still intact, sort of. But the front was split open wide – including his face. Bloody yuck was slopping out when we pulled him onto the rocks. I've never seen such an awful mess in my life. You wouldn't even know who he was, if all you had to go by was his face.

It was terrible for Kimberly to see her father that way. Ironic, too. He'd tried like mad, yesterday, to protect her from the shock of seeing Keith's body. Now here *he* was, ruined a lot worse than Keith – and he couldn't do anything about it.

I threw up.

Not Kimberly, though. After we hauled him out of the water, she sat on the rocks with her back to both of us. She was facing out to sea, her legs bent, her arms around her shins. It was the same way she'd sat for a long time yesterday on the beach after she'd finished with Keith's body.

The dinghy, by then, was almost out of sight.

I thought about sitting down with Kimberly and maybe putting an arm around her. I sure *wanted* to do that. Comfort her. But it might look as if I was trying to put moves on her, so I gave up the notion.

After a while, I said, 'What should we do?'

She shook her head.

'We don't want the others to see him like this,' I said, figuring that's what Andrew would've said if he'd been able to talk.

She just sat there, staring out to sea.

'Maybe I should go and get a blanket or something,' I suggested.

'Yeah,' she said.

'Will you be all right out here?'

She nodded.

But when I turned to go, she said, 'No, wait.' Then she got to her feet and turned around. She was crying softly. She wiped her eyes and sniffed. 'Just a second, okay?'

'Sure.'

'I'll be all right . . . just a second.'

I tried not to stare at her. It made me feel guilty, because a guy shouldn't be paying attention to how great someone looks in her bikini – not when her father is sprawled on the rocks three feet away with his head hacked open.

She wiped her eyes again. Then she said, 'Thanks for helping, Rupert.'

I shrugged.

'You're right, what you said. About how he shouldn't be seen this way. God knows, I wish I hadn't . . . He'd want to be remembered the way he was. You know?'

'That's why I thought I'd go back and get something. To cover him with.'

'I'm going to tow him out beyond the reef.'

'What?'

'Bury him at sea. That's what he always wanted.'

'Don't you think we should, maybe, put him over with Keith? So we can take him back with us when we're rescued?'

Kimberly shook her head. 'It's different with Keith. Dad would want it this way.'

'Shouldn't Billie have a say?'

'Bring her out here. Connie and Thelma, too. Have them all come out. I'll wait with Dad in the water.'

'Do you want a hand?'

'No, go on back.'

I had a choice of swimming, or walking along the rocks. Since I was shoeless, I swam. Billie and Connie were still sitting on the beach, Billie with an arm around her daughter. Thelma stood nearby, watching me and shaking her head and sobbing.

Nobody objected to Kimberly's plan. Apparently, Andrew had made it quite clear to Billie and his daughters that he desired to be buried at sea.

I put on my shoes, and the four of us made our way out along the rocks to the point.

Kimberly hadn't gone far. She was treading water, thirty or forty feet away. Andrew's body floated beside her. In spite of the water being crystal-clear, you couldn't see what a mess he was in. There was the distance. Also, Kimberly had him face down. The main thing, though, was probably the way the sunlight glittered on the water's surface – it was almost blinding. All you could see really well was Andrew's gray, furry back. And his right arm.

The arm was stretched across the water because Kimberly had it by the hand.

'I'm going to tow Dad out,' she said. 'Is that all right with everyone?'

Connie and Thelma were both sobbing like crazy.

Billie wiped her eyes, then said, 'I want to come, too.' Then she stepped down off the rocks into the water and swam out to Kimberly and Andrew. She went to the other side of Andrew, and came up with his left arm.

They both started swimming away, towing him between them.

It was a hell of a thing to watch. I ended up crying, myself – and I never even liked the guy very much.

That was a couple of hours ago. We all returned to the beach after the 'burial at sea.'

It's mighty gloomy around here.

Billie, Kimberly and Thelma have all lost their husbands (one way or another) since we came to this island a couple of days ago. If that isn't bad enough, Kimberly, Thelma and Connie lost their father today.

I'm the only one who hasn't lost one or two loved ones,

and I'm worried about the killer coming for me next.

I've been writing in the journal, here on the beach. It doesn't exactly take my mind off our plight, but at least it gives me a chance to think about something other than how much danger *I'm* in.

There's no doubt that I'm next on the hit list, is there?

He kills me, then there won't be any more men to stand in the way.

In the way of what?

The women.

He wants the women.

We'd better figure out something before it's too late.

We Hatch A Plan

It was only mid-morning, but I was feeling hungry by the time I finished catching up with my journal. Nobody else had eaten any sort of breakfast. The way things looked, it might be a while before they got around to thoughts of food.

It seemed like bad castaway etiquette to eat by myself – which might be looked upon as trying to sneak more than my share. I didn't want to bother any of the women, though. They were busy mourning.

I felt like more of an outsider than ever, since I was the only person who hadn't lost a husband or father (or both). I hadn't lost anyone I really cared much about. They were going through these huge, awful changes, while I was unscathed.

I actually resented it, to some extent. Maybe because I was keenly aware that I might be the next person to get killed. Also, because I was hungry and they seemed too wrapped up in moping around to care.

As far as they were concerned, I didn't even exist. That's how I saw it, anyway.

I figured nobody would miss me anyway, so why not take a hike? I'd been wanting to see the lagoon – and swim in it – ever since hearing about it from Keith and Kimberly.

Now seemed like a good time to visit the place. So I put the book bag on my back, picked up one of the spears, and started striding toward the jungle.

I was fearless.

If any jungle creatures came after me, they'd better watch out.

As for the killer – I counted on him being too far away to nail me. Even though I had no idea how large the island might be, and he'd had about three hours to make his comeback, I was convinced that he must still be miles away.

Anyway, he was bound to kill me sooner or later.

And nobody would likely give a damn, anyhow.

I was still on my way through the sand, striding with bitterness and determination toward the place where the stream entered the jungle, when Kimberly called out from behind me, 'Rupert! What are you doing?'

I glanced back. 'Just thought I'd check out the lagoon.'

'Are you nuts? Get back here.'

'I won't be long.' I started walking backward. All four of the gals were looking at me.

'Rupert!' Billie yelled.

'You can't go off by yourself,' Kimberly called to me. 'If you *have* to go to the lagoon, we'll all go.'

'I don't *have* to.' I suddenly felt a little bit like a jerk. Pleased that somebody cared, after all – but a jerk for being so self-centered and making myself a nuisance.

'I think we all oughta have something to eat,' Thelma said. 'What do the rest of you think? Cause, I mean, I'm kind of starving here.'

'Good idea,' I said.

As soon as I started back, all the gals quit paying attention except for Kimberly. She didn't take her eyes off me. I pretty much kept my eyes on her, too.

She stood in the sand with her feet apart, her Hawaiian shirt blowing behind her in the breeze, her hair blowing, too. Her left hand was planted on her hip, which was bare except for the thin band of her bikini pants. Her right hand held a spear. With its end in the sand by her foot, the spear was higher than her head.

I wish I could've taken a picture of her.

Andrew did bring a camera with him. (Which I'd forgotten about until seeing Kimberly in such an awesome pose.) It should be in the picnic basket. As far as I know, nobody has taken it out since the boat exploded. I guess I'll leave it there. For one thing, the camera doesn't belong to me. For another, I'd look pretty creepy trotting around shooting snapshots on a day like this.

We should've taken photos of the bodies.

Nobody thought of it. Everyone else must've forgotten about the camera, the same as me.

Photographs would've been a really good way to show the authorities how Keith and Andrew were killed. (Andrew is out to sea, but we could still unearth Keith and get some shots. I'm not about to suggest it, though.)

Anyway, my mood underwent a major change because of Kimberly calling me back – not to mention the way she looked.

We gathered at the supply pile (preferring to avoid the campfire with its heat), and sat on the sand around it. As usual, Billie took charge of the food. We ate crackers and cheese left over from the picnic. There was sharp, Swiss cheese, and smoked Edam. She sliced the cheeses with Andrew's Swiss Army knife. She also popped open a bottle of wine that Keith had brought up from the bottom of the inlet. It was a Glen Ellen Cabernet Sauvignon. Though warm, it tasted awfully good. We passed it around, and took sips while we ate our cheese and crackers – and talked.

There was 'small talk' at first. About the food and wine and weather. Like everyone wanted to avoid mentioning the nasty stuff. After about ten minutes of that, Kimberly said, 'I saw who did it.'

Wham.

Silence.

Everybody stopped chewing and stared at her.

We knew she meant the killer.

She'd been swimming out toward the dinghy with her head down, most of the time, so I think the rest of us assumed she hadn't gotten a look at him.

We waited for her to say the killer's name.

But her face told us who she'd seen.

Thelma said, 'No.'

'I'm sorry,' Kimberly said. She looked terribly solemn.

'Wesley's dead!'

'He isn't. I saw him plain as day.'

'No, you didn't!'

'I'm sorry, Thelma. It was him. He's the one I saw. He's the one who murdered Dad.'

'You're lying!'

Kimberly shook her head. 'I thought long and hard about whether I should tell. I almost decided to pretend I hadn't seen who did it. Pretending wouldn't do us any good, though. I know it's tough, but you've got to face it. Wesley's alive, and he's killing us.'

'No!' Thelma blurted. 'It's a lie!' She started to blubber. She still held a half-eaten cracker with a slab of half-eaten cheese on top. I expected her to throw it. Instead, she shoved it into her mouth. Then she flopped over and scurried away from us on her hands and knees. When she was clear of the group, she staggered to her feet and trotted away.

Kimberly started to get up.

Billie raised a hand and shook her head slightly. 'We've gotta make some plans. She'll be all right.'

Kimberly stayed.

Thelma stopped just short of the water's edge, then sat down on the sand, her back to us.

With Thelma out of earshot, a change came over Kimberly. She let her anger out. 'The dirty bastard. I *knew* it had to be him. He's gotta be the one who killed Keith, too.'

'He probably plans to kill us all,' Billie said.

'Guys first,' I added.

'What're we gonna do?' Connie asked. She seemed more frightened than her mother or Kimberly.

'We can't just sit around and wait for him to make the next move,' Billie said.

'That'd be me,' I said.

Though Billie nodded in agreement, she said, 'It might just be the next person he happens to catch off guard. I realize he started with Keith, then got Andrew, but . . . he couldn't possibly have known who'd be going after the dinghy this morning.' She hesitated. 'When I think how close we came to letting it go . . .'

'If I'd kept my big mouth shut,' Connie said.

'It wasn't that,' I told her. 'Andrew wasn't about to let it go.'

'I could've stopped him,' Billie said.

'Nobody's to blame,' Kimberly said. 'Nobody but Wesley.'

'He's awfully damn sneaky,' I said. 'We'll really have to watch ourselves.'

'We'll have to do more than that,' Billie said.

Kimberly nodded. 'We need a plan of action.'

'I still think we oughta get off the island.' That was Connie, of course.

'No,' Billie said. 'Your dad was absolutely right about that: we've got food and water here. We can survive indefinitely.'

'Yeah, right. Look what happened to him.'

'Wesley did that,' Kimberly said. 'What we've gotta do is eliminate Wesley.'

'Or eliminate ourselves,' I suggested.

Billie asked, 'What do you mean?'

'He can't kill us if he can't find us.'

'You mean we should try to hide?'

'It's just a thought. The thing is, we'd have to *find* him before we could do anything to put him out of action. That might be a pretty good trick. But he knows exactly where we are. We're almost always in plain sight, here on the beach. All he has to do is hang back in the jungle and spy on us till he spots an opportunity to strike. But what if he comes looking for us and we aren't here?'

'He'd find us,' Connie said. Always the optimist.

'Not necessarily.'

Frowning, Kimberly said, 'I'm not too crazy about playing hide and seek with the bastard. I want to take him out. Hunt him down and kill him.'

'Why not *draw him in* and kill him?' Billie suggested.

'How would we do that?' Kimberly asked.

'Pull a disappearing act,' Billie explained, giving me a nod. 'Lure him in and ambush him.'

I liked the sound of that.

From the look on Kimberly's face, so did she. 'How would we pull it off?' she asked.

Billie shrugged. 'We'll have to figure something out.'

So we sat there talking about it, tossing schemes back and forth as we passed around the bottle of wine. We were in agreement on the general principle of the thing, but kept running into the same snag; we had to figure that Wesley might already be watching us. How could we possibly pull off a vanishing act (especially one that would allow us to hide nearby and attack him), right in front of his eyes?

Even in the middle of the night, with the fire out, the beach wouldn't be dark enough to completely hide our activities. The sand was too pale, and too much light came from the moon and stars.

'We need to keep the fire going,' Billie said. 'It'll screw up his night vision.'

'But if we don't put it out,' Kimberly said, 'he'll be able to see us in the firelight.'

'Maybe we can figure a way to make that work *for* us,' I suggested. 'You know? Make him see what we want him to see. And while he's watching that, the rest of us might be sneaking to our positions.'

Billie nodded. 'Distract him.'

'Right,' I said. 'If, say, one of us creates a diversion he can't take his eyes off of, the rest of us could do just about anything.'

'What sort of diversion do you have in mind?' Connie asked. From the look on her face, she must've already suspected what I had in mind.

I shrugged and said, 'I don't know. We could stage a fight, maybe.'

Not what I really had in mind, but I would not be the one to suggest a striptease.

'A fight would take at least two people,' Billie pointed

out. 'That only leaves three to maneuver around and jump him.'

'It's just the first thing that came into my head,' I explained.

Right.

'Three could be enough,' Kimberly pointed out. 'I want to be one of them, that's all.'

'Connie and Rupert,' Billie said. She glanced at each of us, then met Kimberly's eyes. 'They can have a quarrel during their watch tonight.'

Typecasting.

Billie didn't stop there. 'A real knock-down drag-out fight.'

'A quiet one,' Kimberly added. 'They don't want to wake us up.'

'Right. And while they're at it, we'll slip out of our beds and hide.'

'Hide where?' Connie asked.

'You'll be out in the open, fighting with Rupert.'

'I don't mean me. Where'll *you* go, where Wesley won't be able to see you? The rocks are too far away.'

'We'll do some digging this afternoon,' Kimberly said. 'Make ourselves a hidey-hole or . . .'

'He'll think we're digging a latrine,' Billie said.

'So,' I said, 'Connie and I get his attention by having a big fight. You guys sneak over to your ambush positions. But how do we get Wesley to come out of the jungle?'

'You and Connie split up,' Billie suggested.

'She runs off,' Kimberly elaborated.

These two women made quite a team.

'She runs to the water to get away from you,' Kimberly continued.

'Leaving you alone and upset by the fire,' Billie added.

'We should have him walk toward the jungle,' Kimberly said to Billie.

'Right. After all, he's the one Wesley probably *really* wants to kill next.'

'Let's not make it too easy for him,' I suggested.

'Don't worry,' Kimberly told me. 'We'll be right there, just out of sight. When he comes for you, we attack.'

'What if he's got that ax?'

'He won't get a chance to use it,' Kimberly said.

'We'll kill him before he gets close enough,' Billie said.

Connie raised her hand. She had a bit of a smirk on her face.

Our plotting sure had pulled these gals out of the doldrums. They were acting as if they'd forgotten all about Keith and Andrew being dead. Apparently, scheming vengeance is a great cure for the blues.

Anyway, Connie had a little problem with our plan. 'What makes you so sure Wesley's gonna be in the jungle while all this is going on? I mean, I'm supposed to go running down to the water, right? Just suppose that's where *he* is? And there I am, all by myself, while you guys are waiting for him all hell and gone over here.'

Billie grimaced. 'You're right.'

'Why does she have to leave the fire?' I asked.

'So you'll be alone,' Kimberly said.

'I'll be alone, anyway, when I walk to the jungle.'

'Connie can't be watching,' Kimberly explained, 'or Wesley won't make a try for you. He'll be afraid she might see what's going on and raise the alarm.'

'He'll be thinking the rest of us are asleep in our usual places,' Billie said. 'If Connie yells and wakes us up, we might come running to help you. He doesn't want that.'

'He *has* to think he's got you alone,' Kimberly added.

Connie started up again. 'If you think I'm gonna go running off by myself . . .'

'Wesley'll probably be in the jungle,' Kimberly said.

'Like last night when he took off with the dinghy?'

'I know how we can do it,' I said, meeting Connie's frown. 'We're having our big fight by the fire, okay? Now, suppose I really land one, and knock you out?'

'Oh, terrific,' she said.

'It's pretend,' I told her. 'I wouldn't actually hit you, but you'd go down and stay down. Like you're unconscious. That way, you'll be safe and sound by the fire, in plenty of light and not very far from help. But you'll be out of the picture, as far as Wesley knows.'

'Sounds good to me,' Billie said.

'Yeah,' said Kimberly. 'I don't see any problem with that.'

Connie wrinkled her nose. 'I don't know,' she muttered.

'What's the matter?' I asked.

'It seems . . . kind of corny.'

'Corny?' I asked. 'This guy killed your father.'

Wrong thing to say.

'You think I don't know that? Fuck you!' She flung a handful of sand at me.

At least it wasn't a spear, this time.

I turned my head away, shutting my eyes and mouth. The grains of sand stung my cheek. They got in my ear, too.

'That's enough, Connie,' Billie told her.

'He's such a creep!'

'Just calm down, honey. The thing is, we've got to do whatever we can – whether it's corny or not. It isn't just that he killed your dad and Keith; he'll kill us all if we don't stop him.'

'Maybe, maybe not.'

I said, 'Maybe everything'll turn out wonderful, and he'll stop after he nails *my* butt.'

Connie glared at me. 'Yeah, maybe so.'

A smile actually lifted the corners of Kimberly's mouth. 'You guys oughta be able to pull off a very convincing fight.'

'Only why don't you save it for tonight?' Billie suggested.

Connie was sort of snarling. 'Yeah, yeah,' she muttered. Then she turned her head and looked over at Thelma. 'What about her?'

We had a brief discussion about that. The upshot was, we decided to keep the plot to ourselves. For one thing, Thelma wasn't in good enough physical shape to be much help in eliminating Wesley. For another, she's his wife. She apparently loves him, even if he did chop her father's head in half.

After deciding to leave her in the dark, we figured out where to construct our ambush site.

The 'latrine' would go about two-thirds of the distance from our campfire to the edge of the jungle, then off quite a way to the south of the stream that cuts down through the middle of the beach. (The route to be taken by Kimberly and Billie shouldn't cross the fire. Diversion or no diversion, we don't want them backlit as they sneak to their position.)

For the next couple of hours, we dug in the sand with our hands, with our spears, and with cups and pots. Thelma wondered what we were doing. We explained that we were making a latrine so that we wouldn't have to risk our lives by going into the jungle. She seemed to think that was a good idea, and she even helped.

While digging, we came up with the idea of adding an enclosure. So we made a couple of frameworks out of branches, then went to the edge of the jungle and gathered foliage. When we were done, we had a double-sided stall with two walls about four feet high. They ran parallel to the edge of the jungle, so Wesley wouldn't be able to see in – not if he was watching from the general area where we expected him to be.

The make-believe latrine should provide a great hiding place for Kimberly and Billie, if they could just get to it without being spotted.

A problem came up, though, a while after we finished. Thelma wanted to use it.

I had already started to write, but I was sitting within earshot. Kimberly intercepted her. 'What are you going to do?' she asked.

'Well, what do you think?' Thelma said.

'That wouldn't be a good idea.'

'What do you mean?'

'You can't use it.'

'I helped build it.' She was indignant. 'What're you talking about?'

'Nobody can use it till tomorrow.'

'Why on earth not?'

'It has to set,' Kimberly explained.

Thelma frowned and looked confused. 'What?'

'The sand needs time to set. Otherwise, it'll all fall in and fill up the hole.'

'Are you crazy?'

'No, it's true.'

She shook her head. 'I've never heard of such a thing.'

'It's true,' I chimed in. 'You never use a sand latrine the first day. I thought everyone knew that.'

Thelma wrinkled her face. She looked quite perplexed, and vaguely suspicious.

'Where am I supposed to go, then?' she asked her sister.

'The same place as always.' She nodded toward the jungle. 'I'll get Billie and Connie. We'll all go together, from now on.'

'What about me?' I asked.

Thelma narrowed her eyes at me. Kimberly, though, is always a sport. She knew I was mostly kidding. 'I think you'll be fine right here. We won't go far.'

'Don't you think you might need a guy along for protection?' I asked.

'We'll be fine, Rupert.'

'Have it your way.'

So all the gals went trooping off into the bush without me. I stayed where I was, but quit working on the journal for a while. I didn't want any distractions, in case Wesley might pop up out of nowhere and make a try for me.

Even though I felt vulnerable, I was fairly safe. I was surrounded by stretches of sand, for one thing. For another, I was fairly well armed – a spear, a club and a selection of rocks within easy reach.

Also, the gals never went very far. They only pushed into the jungle far enough so I wouldn't be able to see them. I could hear their voices, though, so I knew they'd be able to hear me if I had to yell for help.

Nothing happened.

It's been pretty uneventful, since then. I've just kept working on the journal here, taking my time, keeping an eye on the gals. Kimberly and Billie went in swimming for a while. Connie went for a climb on the rocks, but never wandered out of sight. Thelma has mostly just sat around and napped.

I'll probably try to take a nap, myself.

It may turn out to be a long night.

Day Four

The Diversion

Thelma turned in, last night, shortly after dark. That seemed to be a good thing, since we needed her out of the picture. She'd worried me, the way she had spent so much of the day sleeping. I was afraid she might be wide awake, ready to stay up all night, and manage to wreck the ambush we had planned.

I said as much to the others, after she'd gone off.

'It's not uncommon at all,' Billie said, 'for people to sleep a lot more than usual when they're going through tough times emotionally. It's a way of escaping from the pain of the situation.'

Billie had been a high-school teacher before marrying Andrew. She'd taught English, but you have to learn a lot of psychology to become a teacher – at least in California. That's probably how she picked up the stuff about escaping with sleep. Or maybe she picked it up watching Oprah.

Kimberly said, 'Sleeping's about the *last* thing I feel like doing.'

'You're a lot stronger than Thelma,' Billie said.

'A lean, mean, killing machine,' said I.

Which earned a friendly smirk from Kimberly, a roll-upward of the eyeballs from Billie, and a snarl from Connie. (You can't please all the people all the time . . .)

Anyway, we kept sitting around the fire and talking about this and that for another hour or so. We mostly avoided the topic of the ambush, but I bet it was the main thing on all our minds. We were talking about trivial stuff to keep ourselves from dwelling on it.

I felt awfully shaky, and even got goosebumps from time to time. Not because there was a chilly breeze, either. There was a breeze, but it was warm and felt good. It felt so good that I'd taken my shirt off, just after sundown.

I'd started wearing a shirt, now and then, especially during the hottest times of the day – to keep from getting a sunburn. It wasn't so much a shirt as a blouse, actually. A bright pink silk blouse that belonged to Billie. It had been retrieved from the inlet, along with so many other things, by Andrew and Keith. The lower back of the blouse had gotten burnt off, but otherwise it was fine.

Billie is the one who picked it out for me to wear. That was way back on the day after the yacht blew up. (Seems like about ten years ago.) It was the best of the lot. I said she might want to keep it for herself. She told me, 'If I need it, I'll know right where to find it.'

So far, she hasn't asked for it. She's been happy just going around all the time in her bikini. (As I might've written way back at the start of all this, she is sort of a borderline exhibitionist. We'd be seeing a lot more of her, I bet, if her daughter wasn't around.)

Billie uses some pretty heavy-duty sunblock. When she runs out of that, maybe she'll start wearing more clothes. I'm not looking forward to it. I like her attire just the way it is.

The way things are going, however, we'll probably all be dead long before we need to worry about running out of sunblock.

Never mind. I don't want to think about what the future might hold for us.

Back to a subject I can write about with a certain amount of pleasure – the wardrobe.

Kimberly has continued to wear Keith's bright and flowery Hawaiian shirt most of the time. She never buttons it. The shirt is always open, often blowing behind her in the breeze, giving me a wonderful view, whenever I look, of her bare brown skin and her skimpy white bikini.

Connie wears her own skimpy bikini. Hers is orange. But she keeps her T-shirt on nearly all the time. The T-shirt is white, large and loose. Sometimes, it hangs off one shoulder or the other. It covers her all the way down to about mid-thigh, like a short dress. The material is so thin that you can see through it.

Thelma has continued to wear the same . . .

Thelma.

I guess I'd better stop wasting time, and get to what went wrong.

I'm not real eager to do that.

Procrastination, thy name is Rupert.

'We'd better get on with it,' as Billie said last night by the fire.

We had been doing some procrastinating, ourselves.

'Is everyone about ready?' she asked.

Kimberly didn't say a thing, just made a single nod with her head.

'Are we really gonna go ahead with this?' Connie asked.

'Unless you have a better idea,' Billie told her.

Connie wrinkled her nose.

'He hasn't left us any choice,' Kimberly said. 'It's him or us.'

'Are you two really gonna kill him?'

'If we can,' Billie said.

'You've got the knife,' Kimberly said to her.

Billie had Andrew's Swiss Army knife on her hip. The thick plastic handle was tucked down the waistband of her bikini pants, all the blades and tools folded in.

'Do you want to be the one to use it?' Kimberly asked.

The two women stared at each other, the firelight flickering in their eyes.

'You want to, don't you?' Billie said.

'Yes.'

They were not exactly beating around the bush.

'Okay,' Billie said. She pulled the knife out, leaned sideways and passed it to Kimberly.

Kimberly shut her hand around it, and pressed her fist against her belly.

Billie glanced from me to Connie. 'Do either of you have any questions?'

'Guess not,' Connie said.

'I'm ready,' I said. 'Just don't let him kill me, okay?'

Kimberly got to her feet.

So did Billie. 'Good luck, you two,' she told us. 'Make it look good.'

'We will,' I promised. 'You be careful out there.'

Side by side, carrying their spears, they walked away from the fire. I was facing the fire (and Connie on its other side) so I had to look over my shoulder to watch them. They went to the stream – the usual routine – drank from it and brushed their teeth (using fingers). Then they wandered over to the rocky area at the north side of our beach. As they started to climb, Connie snapped, 'Quit watching. Jerk.'

'I can't see anything,' I said.

'Not that you aren't trying.'

I faced front – to be on the lookout in case Connie chose to throw her spear at me. 'I'm *not* into watching ladies take a leak,' I explained. 'Maybe *you* are, but . . .'

'Fuck you.'

'Give it a rest, okay? Why don't you just sit quietly and try to work on your vocabulary?'

'What a wit.'

I looked back over my shoulder, but couldn't spot Billie or Kimberly.

'This is such a treat for you,' Connie said.

'Really.'

'A dream come true.'

'Right.'

'Trapped on an island with a band of women.'

'And a maniac who wants to kill me. It's a blast. Why don't we save all this for our big fight scene, okay?'

She didn't come back with a crack, so maybe she liked the idea.

After a while, Billie and Kimberly reappeared. They climbed down from the rocks and came across the beach. After crossing the stream, Billie waved and said to us, 'Night, now.'

'See you in the morning, people,' Kimberly said.

They split up and went to their own sleeping nests – beds, as Billie calls them. Billie lay down alone. Kimberly, a few yards away, eased down into her place beside Thelma.

From where I sat, not much could be seen of them. They weren't completely beyond the glow from the fire, but the light that reached them was pretty dim and murky. Just the way we wanted things.

'Let's wait a little while,' I said to Connie.

'Your wish is my command.'

I sighed.

'What?' she asked.

'Nothing.'

'Yeah, sure.'

'Okay. First off, we're in a real mess. You know? People have died . . .'

'Tell me about it,' she muttered.

'I just think that, under the circumstances, it'd be nice if we didn't have to fight among ourselves. I mean, my God, it's pretty weird to be bickering with each other about a load of insignificant crap when there's a guy out there killing us off. I know you're upset and scared, but that doesn't give you any excuse to go around making everyone miserable.'

She showed me her teeth. 'Do I make you miserable?'

'You make me want to smack you silly.'

'Well, two can play that game.'

'Why the hell did you even ask me to come on this damn trip? All you've done the whole time is dump on me.'

'Maybe I *like* to dump on you,' she said.

'Sure.'

'You're such a fucking loser.'

'Why did you ask me to come? I don't get it. Did you just want to show your family what a loser you've got for a boyfriend? That doesn't exactly make sense. Not that I ever exactly *expect* you to make a whole lot of sense, but . . .'

'Up yours.'

'Why am I here? Why did you invite me? You needed someone your own age to pick on?'

She sneered at me. 'What was I supposed to do, come by myself? I figured, better you than no one.'

'Oh, thanks a heap.'

'Well, you asked. Besides, I used to think I liked you.'

That one actually sort of hurt.

'I thought I *loved* you,' she said.

That one stunned me so much I wondered if it was a lie.

'If you loved me,' I said, 'you had a funny way of showing it.'

'What, because I wouldn't jump into bed with you?'

'No!'

'I happen to be very particular about who I jump into bed with, buddy. It's a very select few, as a matter of fact. I have to be one hundred per cent sure of a guy . . . and I had my doubts about you from the start. Thank God I didn't give in. But maybe you'll have more luck with my mom . . . or Kimberly. It's so disgustingly obvious that you'd rather fuck one of them . . .'

'Knock it off,' I said. 'Man! Your father got his head chopped in half this morning; how in hell can you be talking like this?'

'Maybe it's time for a little honesty, that's how. Why go around lying and being a phoney about everything if we're all gonna get killed anyway? You know? Screw it. From now on, I say what I think.'

'You mean, you haven't been? Could've fooled me. But you know what? I don't see more honesty here; all I see is that you're getting more energetic in your nastiness.'

'Fuck you.'

'That's original.'

That was apparently the final straw.

Or she just figured it was time to start the show.

She started it by twisting her face so she looked like a maniac. Then she hissed through her teeth and she leaped at me. Didn't bother to go around the fire – sprang over it, instead. I didn't even have time to stand up before she crashed down on top of me and slammed me backward into the sand.

She seemed to be all knees and elbows and fists.

Next thing I knew, she was sitting on my stomach. The knees and elbows no longer jabbed into me, but her fists kept smacking me in the face.

I put up my arms to block them.

And gasped things like, 'Stop it! Shit! That hurts! Hey!'

I knew better than to think she was simply trying to make our fight look good for Wesley; she was trying to inflict damage on me.

And succeeding.

I've got a thing about hitting girls.

The thing is, I don't do it.

If you aren't some kind of a pervert or shit, you've got a deep-down revulsion when it comes to hurting a female.

So even though Connie was pounding me pretty well, I couldn't bring myself to slug her. I tried to defend myself by blocking her blows. Then I managed to catch hold of her arms. She lurched and twisted.

'Stop it!' I gasped.

She kept trying to jerk her arms free, so I bucked and threw her off me. We rolled, and I got on top of her. I sat across her hips and leaned forward and pinned her arms down. She wouldn't stop squirming, though. Afraid she might throw me off, I stretched her arms up past her head and put as much weight on her as I could. We were belly to belly, chest to chest, face to face.

Pretty soon, she quit struggling. She lay under me, gasping for air.

We were so tight together that I could feel the pounding of her heart. I also felt the push of her breasts against my chest. And her breath on my lips.

'Get off,' she said.

I stayed.

She was between my legs, and our groins were pressed together. She had sort of a mound down there that pushed against me.

'Get off, damn it!'

I'd never been this close to her before, never had so much actual contact. It started having an effect on me.

'Oh, terrific,' she muttered.

She'd noticed.

'Get off me, for Godsake. We're supposed to be *fighting*. Leave it to you . . .'

'Sorry.' I let go of her wrists and shoved against the sand and started to push myself up.

'Get it over with,' she said.

'What?'

'What do you mean, what? Slug me, knock me out.'

'Shouldn't we get on our feet first?'

'What, so I get a chance to fall down? I'm already down. Go ahead and do it.'

'This isn't the right way. It won't look right.'

'Okay,' she said. And her right arm shot up. She punched the side of my face so hard that I toppled over sideways. I flopped onto my back. She stood up.

'This how you want it?' she asked.

'Yeah,' I said.

She wasn't playing the game I expected, but at least she was on her feet, up where Wesley could get a good view of her. When I tried to stand, she rushed in and kicked me over. On my second try, I blocked her kick and staggered up.

More like it.

We started circling each other, hunched over, hands out like a couple of disarmed knife-fighters. She made a lunge as if to grab me. I leaped out of reach.

Suddenly, she pulled her T-shirt off. She tossed it to the sand. 'This better?' she asked.

I couldn't believe she'd done it. Miss Prude. Up till then, she hadn't even taken off the shirt to go swimming. She had a tan, though. She must've gone without it sometime, just not in front of me.

She didn't look bad.

'Think I've got his attention now?' she asked.

'Probably.'

'Yeah? Just probably?'

Her right hand darted out.

Slapped my face.

Not a hard slap. It didn't hurt as much as her punches, but it stung my ego. It was a humiliating taunt, just as she'd meant it to be.

I pressed a hand to my face.

She slapped the back of my hand, then pranced backward.

'They're on the move,' she said.

'Huh?'

'Your girlfriends. Remember? The plan?'

I started to turn my head.

Connie stopped me. Stopped me dead by crossing her arms and grabbing the front of her bikini top with both hands and tugging it up. Her breasts seemed to spring out from under it. And there they were, right in front of me. Loose all of a sudden, they jiggled. They lifted and nearly went away, turning into small slopes, as she raised her arms and shucked the bikini top off over her head. When she put her arms down, her breasts came back out.

They looked so *naked*. They weren't tanned at all, but had a pinkish hue from the firelight. The nipples looked big and dark.

'Think he's distracted now?' she asked.

I didn't even try to answer.

Letting out a huff of laughter, she tossed her orange top aside with one hand and slapped my face with the other. Before I could do anything about the slap, she leaped out of range.

We went back to circling each other.

She was wonderful to watch – the way she was bent over with her arms out, naked except for the waistband and meager orange front panel of her bikini pants, her skin ruddy and shimmering in the firelight, her hair golden – and how her prancing, lurching movements made her breasts bounce and bob.

For me, it was like something in a wild dream.

For Wesley, it must've been pretty exciting, too.

The absolute perfect diversion, just so long as the guy you're trying to distract isn't dead, blind or gay.

If our campfire was in view of Wesley's hiding place, his eyes were glued to Connie. Not a shadow of a doubt about that.

Connie darted in and slapped me again.

I didn't mind.

It was a good, sharp smack, but the view was stunning.

'Do it now,' Connie said, circling again.

'What?'

'Knock me out.'

I shook my head. 'Too soon.'

'Isn't. They're there.'

'Are you sure?'

'Damn it, Rupert! Quit stalling.'

'I can't hit you.'

'It's pretend, remember? My Christ, this was *your* plan in the first place. Let's do it! I'll come in at you.'

'I don't . . .'

'Now!'

'Okay, okay.'

She charged straight toward me, arms out as if she wanted to give me a bear hug.

I threw a roundhouse in the general direction of her chin.

She ran right into it.

Honest. I never intended my fist to connect with her. It was an accident. Really and truly.

But what a punch! The blow snapped her head sideways. Her cheeks flopped, her lips almost jumped off her face, and a glittering banner of spit flew toward the fire. Her legs kept coming, but the rest of her body stopped fast and started on its way down. Her back struck the sand, *whup!* Her breasts flattened as if mashed against her chest by invisible hands. An instant later, they were springing up. Then her legs landed.

She lay sprawled on the beach, motionless.

Scared, I hurried over to her and dropped to my knees. Her eyes were shut. Her mouth drooped open. My punch had taken her out, no question about that. She was breathing, though. I could see the rise and fall of her chest, so I hadn't killed her.

I looked around.

Thelma appeared to be asleep. Kimberly and Billie were nowhere to be seen, but they might be watching me. Wesley was probably watching, too. So I didn't allow myself to spend much time enjoying the view of Connie. Also, I kept my hands to myself.

On my feet, I went over to my place by the fire and picked up my 'tomahawk.' The weapon, made by Kimberly, consisted of a sturdy, Y-shaped limb with a rock at the forked end. The rock was wedged in and strapped secure with strips of denim cut from some jeans that had been salvaged after the explosion.

I looked back at Connie. She was still sprawled on her back. I grimaced. I'd *really* nailed her. Which made me feel guilty, but secretly pleased. Also, I felt sort of pleased about my self-control; I'd wanted to feel her up so badly it hurt, but hadn't done it. What restraint! I deserved a medal.

Actually, restraint didn't have much to do with it. I was just afraid her mom might see me. I sure wouldn't want Billie to know what a horny degenerate I really am.

Anyway, I gave Connie one last, long look. Then I turned away and headed for the darkness beyond the firelight.

The Ambush

Thelma lay on her bed of rags where she belonged. Curled on her side, she slept with an arm under her head for a pillow.

Kimberly and Billie had left human-shaped mounds of sand covered with scraps of cloth at the places where they usually slept. A pretty lame trick, really. The sort of thing a kid might do before he sneaks out his window at night.

In fact, our entire ambush plan seemed to be made of lame, childish tricks.

Tricks that didn't stand much chance of fooling a reasonably intelligent adult.

(In spite of the opinions of Andrew and some others in our group, Wesley isn't stupid.)

As I walked away from the firelight, I got a terrible feeling that we hadn't even come close to outsmarting him. He hadn't been distracted by Connie. He'd watched Billie and Kimberly sneak to the fake latrine. Maybe he'd already silently killed them both.

About halfway between the fire and the latrine, I stopped walking. The area ahead looked so damn dark. I needed time for my eyes to adjust.

That's what I told myself, anyway.

Actually, I stopped because I was suddenly scared to

keep going. I wanted to be back at the fire, safe in its light, with Connie. (Even out cold, she'd be better company than nobody.)

I couldn't turn back, though. I'd look like a chicken.

So I forced myself to start moving again. It seemed to take forever, but finally I reached the latrine.

From the side, I saw the dim shape of someone low down in the darkness between its walls. There seemed to be only one person. I couldn't tell who it was. Or whether it was a woman.

I stood there, staring.

The person hiding in the latrine didn't make a sound.

I told myself: This has to be Billie or Kimberly.

Unless it's Wesley.

The way the body kept so still, I thought it might be one of the gals, but dead.

I started to feel like running away.

Which, of course, would've blown everything.

Finally, I choked out, 'Who is it?'

'Rupert?' A hoarse whisper. But it seemed to be Billie's voice.

'Yeah.'

'Thought it must be, but . . .'

'Where's Kimberly?' I whispered.

'Get in here,' Billie said, rising up slightly higher in the darkness.

We hadn't exactly rehearsed this part. I stepped in between the bushy walls. They were about as high as my waist. Billie seemed to be standing below me in the hole, her face level with my knees.

'What am I supposed to do?' I asked.

'Pretend you're taking a whizz.'

Great, I thought.

But I saw the point. After all, the whole charade was for Wesley's benefit. If I was going to visit the latrine, I should appear to be using it.

So I clamped the tomahawk under my arm, then started going through the motions – as if I'd just stepped up to a urinal.

Of course, I didn't haul anything out.

'What happened to Kimberly?' I whispered.

'She went off. Thought we ought to split up.'

I looked around, but couldn't spot Kimberly. The beach between me and the jungle looked gray and desolate. Beyond the line of trees, the jungle was black. Turning my head the other way, I checked on our campsite. The sleeping area looked like a field of dark lumps. Connie was still sprawled on her back near the fire.

'Do you know where she went?' I asked.

'The jungle.'

'She out of her mind?'

'She wants you to go there. If Wesley doesn't attack you here.'

'Oh.'

'If the attack happens here, she's gonna come in and take him from behind.'

'I don't think it'll happen here,' I said.

'Let's give it some time.'

'It doesn't take all that long to . . . you know, take a leak.'

'Stop looking around.'

'Okay. Sorry.'

'Wesley hasn't got a stopwatch on you. I'm sure he isn't keeping track of the time.'

'I don't know. I'd be done by now.'

Her arms came up, barely visible in the darkness, and I

felt her hands curl softly against my calves. 'Just stay for a while,' she whispered. 'Give him a chance.'

'Okay.'

Her hands glided up and down a little, caressing me. 'How are you holding up?'

'So far, so good.'

'I don't know what we'd do without you.'

'Thanks,' I said. 'I hope you don't get a chance to find out.'

She patted one of my legs. 'Wise guy.'

'How are *you* doing?' I asked.

'Getting along. I'll fall apart later. After we've dealt with Wesley.'

'Must be awfully hard on you.'

She was silent, and her hands went motionless on my legs. Then she said, 'I've still got Connie.'

'Yeah.'

'I saw some of what happened with her over there.'

'You did?' Apparently, the low wall of bushes at the front of the latrine wasn't as thick as I'd thought. I felt my face go hot. 'What did you see?' I asked.

'Oh, her little strip show.'

'Ah.'

'She's a beautiful girl, isn't she?'

'Takes after you,' I said, which was more flattering to Connie than to Billie, and untrue.

'Bet she surprised you with that.'

'I'll say.'

'She's got spunk.'

'Yeah.'

'She sure knew how to get Wesley's attention.'

And mine, I thought.

'She shouldn't have slapped you, though.'

Billie had seen that, too. My face flamed up again. 'Like you say, she's got spunk.'

'She can be a real bitch, sometimes. But she's a good kid. Under it all. You probably know that already.'

'Yeah,' I said.

Yeah, my ass.

'You just have to stand up for yourself. Don't take any crap from her, you know?'

'Didn't you see me punch her lights out?' I asked.

'You what?'

'It was an accident.'

'You mean you *hit* her?' Billie sounded concerned, but not angry.

'Weren't you watching?' I asked.

'I must've been looking away when that happened. All of a sudden, I looked back again and Connie was on her back. I thought . . .'

'No, it wasn't any act. I mean, it was supposed to be, but she walked right into my fist. She's okay, though.' I looked. Connie was still spread out on the sand. 'I bet she's conscious by now. She knows better than to get up.'

'Well . . .'

'I'm sorry. It really *was* an accident. I would never hit her on purpose.'

'I hope not.'

'Honestly.'

'Okay.'

'I'd better get going,' I said. 'I've been here way too long. Wesley'll know something's up.'

'Yeah.' She squeezed the backs of my legs, then took her hands away. 'Kimberly'll be at the regular place. Go slowly and keep your eyes open.'

'Okay. See you later.'

I stepped backward away from the latrine, hitched up my trunks a bit, then took the tomahawk out from under my arm and started walking toward the jungle.

I got more and more scared. It helped, though, to tell myself that Wesley might not even be there. For all we really knew, he could be miles away. Or maybe the dinghy had gone down with all hands aboard. Maybe he'd fallen off a cliff. Maybe he'd been dropped by an aneurism or a coronary. Maybe he'd run afoul of a man-eating critter, a poisonous snake, a headhunter, or Dr Moreau.

Endless ways he could've met a demise.

But I figured that he was probably lurking among the trees, watching my approach and fully intending to lay me to waste.

The only thing that kept me going was Kimberly.

Wishful thinking aside, *she* was probably in there lurking among the trees, watching my approach and fully intending to jump the bastard when he made the try for me.

Unless she'd already been jumped by him.

My legs were shaking pretty good, but I kept going.

I was half a dozen strides from the edge of the jungle when the whole deal went to hell.

A shout came from Thelma. 'HELP!' she yelled. Then, 'WHAT'S GOING ON?'

I turned around fast.

She was on her knees beside Connie's sprawled body, her arms raised and spread out wide as if to show us all the size of her confusion and fear.

'RUPERT!'

She'd spotted me.

I flapped an arm, signaling her to stay put.

But she scurried to her feet and started running straight toward me.

I muttered a curse.

She was ruining everything.

I kept waving her back, but she kept coming, chugging closer, her bosom leading the way, her head thrown back. If her bra had broken during the charge, her leaping breasts would've torn open her blouse, whammed her in the face and probably knocked her over backward.

When she came to a halt in front of me, I considered whamming her in the face.

I'd like to have done it with my tomahawk.

But I don't hit women.

Anyway, she didn't *know* she was ruining everything. All she knew was that she'd woken up to find herself alone – and to find Connie unconscious and topless.

Wasn't Thelma's fault she went nuts.

Wasn't her fault she'd wrecked our whole scheme.

Wasn't her fault I suddenly hated her guts.

She staggered to a halt in front of me and stood there, huffing for breath, her mouth hanging open.

'What's . . . going on?' she gasped out.

'I've gotta take a dump,' I said.

'*What?*'

'You know.'

'I don't know. You're . . . way over here. Connie's *out cold*. What's the matter with her?'

'I slugged her.'

'You what?'

'We had a fight.'

'A fight? What kind of a fight? How come she's half-naked? Did you do that to her?'

'No!'

'Where's Kimberly? Where's Billie?'

'I don't know.' Not exactly a lie. I wasn't entirely sure

where they were – mainly, I wondered why Billie hadn't hopped out of the latrine to intercept Thelma.

Suddenly, I was worried about her.

'Billie!' I called. 'Are you okay?'

'Yes.' Her voice came from the direction of the latrine. It didn't sound joyful.

'You might as well come on out.'

A few moments later, Billie crawled out from between the dark, leafy walls. She stood up and walked slowly toward us, shaking her head.

Thelma said to her, 'What *is* all this? What were you doing in there?'

'I was using the facility,' Billie explained. 'Is that all right with you?'

Thelma's mouth fell open. 'It isn't supposed to be used till tomorrow!'

'What?'

'It has to set. The *sand* needs time to set.' She turned to me for support.

'That's right,' I told Billie.

'None of us were supposed to use it till tomorrow,' Thelma protested.

'Oh.'

'Now you've probably ruined it.'

'We forgot to tell you,' I said to Billie. Then I faced Thelma and said, 'See? *I* knew better than to use it. That's why I was heading for the jungle.'

'By yourself?' Thelma asked.

'Who am I supposed to take with me?'

She opened her mouth as if to give me a suggestion, but then she grabbed Billie's shoulder and shook it. 'Did you see what he did to your daughter?'

Billie nodded.

We all looked toward Connie. She was still stretched out in the sand near the fire, but not on her back. While nobody was watching, she must've rolled over.

'Guess she's okay,' I said.

'Rupert attacked her,' Thelma explained.

'I did not.'

'Bull!' she snapped at me. 'You tried to tear off her clothes.'

'Settle down,' Billie told her. 'Connie took off her own top.'

'No, she didn't. Why would she do that?' Thelma glared at me. 'And what did you do with Kimberly?'

'Nothing.'

'Then where is she?'

Billie and I shared a glance. She shook her head; I shrugged.

'If we don't tell her the truth,' Billie said, 'we'll be making up stories till Hell freezes over.'

'Yeah. I know. But look, the thing is, I've got a little, uh, chore to take care of. Why don't you two go on back to the fire. See how Connie's doing, and you can tell Thelma all about our plan. I'll be back in a few minutes.'

'Where's my sister?' Thelma demanded.

'I'll see if I can find her,' I said. Without waiting for any more trouble, I turned around and headed for the jungle. When I was just about there, I looked back. Billie and Thelma were walking slowly away, side by side. They seemed to be talking, but I couldn't make out the words.

I was so annoyed and frustrated, thanks to Thelma, that I forgot to be afraid.

A short distance into the trees, I looked back and couldn't see much of the beach anymore – just a little flicker from our fire.

The bit I'd told Thelma about 'taking a dump' had been a fib. I truly did need to pee, though. Right where I stood seemed like as good a place as any.

Nobody seemed to be nearby.

Of course, Wesley or Kimberly might've been standing three feet away without being seen. Awfully dark in there.

I told myself, *If I can't see them, they can't see me.*

I half believed it, too.

My trunks don't have a fly. I got clear of them by tugging the crotch up and sideways, which gave me a window of opportunity through the left leg hole. I kept the trunks out of the way with my right hand, and kept the tomahawk in my left.

One more glance around, then I started to go.

It promised to be a long one.

Which didn't thrill me. I wanted to get it done with and *amscray* back to the beach.

Also, I wasn't thrilled by the noise I was making. A loud, papery, splattery sound. Obviously, I was hitting leaves or some other variety of foliage. It's damn near impossible to take a silent leak in a jungle. I tried swiveling from side to side. The noise changed directions, but not volume.

It was just starting to taper off when I heard someone take a step. At first, I didn't *know* it was a footstep. I didn't know for sure until I heard the second one.

Then came the third, closer to me than the others.

By that time, I had shut down my irrigation project and stowed the equipment.

I switched the tomahawk to my right hand.

Then I stood still and held my breath.

And wished to God I had stayed on the beach where I belonged.

The footsteps stopped.

Maybe two yards away?

I strained my eyes to see who was there, but all I could make out were different shades of dark gray – and a lot of black.

It's probably Kimberly, I told myself.

But what if it isn't?

I knew, really, that it had to be her. She'd heard me and started to come toward me, then stopped, afraid I might be Wesley.

We were both standing there, trying to convince ourselves that the other person *wasn't* Wesley.

Suddenly, I had a bad thought.

What if she decides I'm Wesley, and attacks me?

She wouldn't do that. After all, I was supposed to come out here and act as bait. She was *expecting* me.

But she also expected Wesley to show up.

It was actually possible that she might goof and kill me by mistake.

Anyway, we couldn't just stand here all night.

In a quiet voice, I said, 'Kimberly? It's me. Rupert.'

The voice came back, 'Rupert? It's me. Wesley.'

Close Shaves And Rescues

Wesley, being the asshole that he is, apparently couldn't resist the chance to scare the hell out of me. If he'd just kept his mouth shut and snuck in closer and used his ax, I'd be a dead boy right now.

But he had to answer me back.

My reactions surprised me.

I didn't scream and whirl around and make a mad dash for the beach. Which is what I would've *guessed* I'd do, if anyone had asked.

Maybe everyone isn't like this, but I seem to have at least two different people inside of me: one is timid and plays by the rules; the other is a little nuts – and the nut pops up at odd, unexpected times.

I was standing there, scared half to death even before Wesley answered – my knees shaking, my heart slugging. Then he said, 'Rupert? It's me. Wesley.'

Instead of having a panic attack, I heard myself greet the guy. 'Hey, Wesley, how's it going?'

'Having a ball.'

'Glad to hear it.'

'What was this supposed to be, tonight? Some sort of trap?'

'Yep.'

'Guess who got caught in it?'

'You tell me.'

I hoped to God he wasn't about to say, 'Kimberly.'

Wesley said, 'You.'

'Sure thing,' I said.

He laughed.

I threw my tomahawk at the sound. Threw it hard. It went smashing through bushes. I didn't wait for the outcome, but made a one-eighty and ran.

Behind me, Wesley let out a yell. He sounded more angry than hurt.

Then I heard him come charging after me.

I dodged between a couple of tree trunks, rammed my way through a bush, and raced onto the beach.

I almost collided with Kimberly.

What a sight! I'll never forget it as long as I live. She stood only a few strides in front of me, bare and dark except for the white of her bikini. (Not wearing Keith's Hawaiian shirt, for a change.) Her feet were planted in the sand, legs apart and slightly bent, one foot forward. Her left arm was stretched out toward me, her right arm cocked back near her ear – the spear all set to throw.

'Hit the deck!' she commanded me in a quick, loud whisper.

I dived for the sand, pounded against it chest first and slid toward Kimberly's bare legs. About to plow into them, I threw myself sideways. Did a half-roll and looked up just as she hurled her spear.

It shot straight forward.

Snapping my head around, I kept track of it.

The spear raced toward Wesley as he came charging out of the jungle.

This was the first I'd seen of him since the explosion.

He appeared to be stark naked. His skin gleamed black in the moonlight – some sort of camouflage, I guess, for sneaking around at night. (He hadn't put the stuff on his backside, I discovered pretty soon.) He held his ax in both hands, raised high over his left shoulder, ready to split me like a log.

His grin was big and white.

The grin went away when he saw Kimberly – and the spear speeding at him.

His mouth opened wide.

He yelled, 'YAAAH!' and tried to dodge the spear, giving himself an awkward half-twist to the left in the moments before it struck.

The whittled point of Kimberly's spear caught him in the chest area. He was a husky guy, and he had pretty good boobs on him. The spear hit him in the left one. He was partly turned away, though, so all it did was poke through one side of his tit and come out the other side, just behind his nipple and maybe half an inch under his skin.

He squealed. Dropping the ax behind him, he grabbed the shaft of the spear with both hands and stumbled and fell to his knees. Though he clutched the spear, he didn't try to pull it out.

I think he was afraid to pull it out.

Afraid of the pain.

He held on to it the way he did, I think, to keep the weight of the spear from dragging open his wound. If he'd just let go, it probably would have split the front of his boob wide open from one side to the other.

Anyway, I scurried over to where the ax had fallen.

While I did that, Kimberly rushed Wesley and reached for her spear.

'No!' he cried out. 'Don't touch it!'

Kimberly touched it, all right.

She grabbed its end and tugged. On its way out, it must've hurt him pretty good. He screamed so hard I thought my ears might bleed.

He fell onto his side and curled up and squirmed and whimpered.

I picked up the ax.

When I looked at Wesley again, he was on his hands and knees. Trying to crawl away.

Kimberly rammed the spear into his bare ass.

It missed his anus (the likely target), but jabbed into his right buttock. He squealed again, and flopped down flat.

Kimberly pulled out her spear and planted it in the sand by her feet. Then she pulled her father's Swiss Army knife out of her bikini pants. She flung a leg over Wesley and sat down in the middle of his back. With both hands, she worked on prying open one of the knife blades.

'Look out!' Billie yelled from a distance. 'Watch it! Thelma!'

We both turned our heads and saw Thelma coming at us. Billie was chasing her. (Connie stood by the fire, watching. She'd put her T-shirt back on. She hugged her chest and rubbed her upper arms as if she had a chill.)

Billie was faster than Thelma, but Thelma must've had a good headstart. Too good a headstart. Billie wasn't likely to catch her in time.

'Don't let her interfere,' Kimberly told me. 'I've gotta finish him off.'

Thelma must've heard that. She cried out, 'No! Don't you dare! Leave him be! Kimberly, leave him be, damn it!'

Kimberly muttered, 'Yeah, right.'

I put myself in Thelma's way, the ax at port-arms. I had

no intention of hurting her, of course. I planned to block her, that's all, and give Kimberly the time she needed.

Coming at me, growling, stocky as a bulldog, she gave me a bad case of the creeps. This woman, normally so plain and innocuous and rather dumpy, had somehow changed into a raving lunatic.

At the last second, she veered to avoid me.

A quick sidestep put me into her path again.

'Stop!' I yelled.

The rock in her hand came as a surprise. She hurled it, point blank, at my face.

It almost missed.

Nicked my cheekbone and cut a hot path all the way back to my ear. I stayed on my feet, but staggered a little – enough to let her slip by.

Billie made a flying leap for Thelma's feet.

She came up short and plowed a furrow through the sand.

'Shit!' Kimberly shouted.

Stumbling, I saw her still sitting on Wesley's back. She had the knife open in her right hand. Her left hand clutched Wesley by the hair. The way he was thrashing and whimpering, though, I knew she hadn't gotten a chance to use the knife. Her torso was twisted sideways as she watched her sister.

'Stay back!' she shouted.

Thelma snatched the spear out of the sand. With a bellow that gave me goosebumps, she swung the spear at Kimberly. It whistled as it cut the air. Kimberly flung up her right arm to block it. The spear lashed in underneath her arm and whacked against her side.

'Leave him be!' Thelma shrieked, and raised the spear overhead to strike again.

Kimberly was already tumbling off Wesley's back.

With a leap, I put myself in front of Thelma. I blocked her spear's downward stroke with my ax. When it crashed against the haft of the ax, it broke in half.

Half of it flew off into the darkness.

Thelma still held the other half. She rammed it in low, shoving its sharp, broken end into my belly. It didn't go in. Not very far, anyway. But it felt red-hot and rammed my wind out. I staggered backward, tripped over Wesley's feet, and fell.

Fast as I could, I raised my head.

Wesley was starting to crawl away.

Billie was on her knees, trying to get up. Thanks to her skid through the sand, her breasts had come out of her bikini. (Normally, I would've been thrilled by such a development. Not then, though. I noticed, but didn't much care.)

Thelma smacked Billie across the face with what remained of the spear. Down went Billie.

'Get up!' she yelled at Wesley, who was still crawling. 'Get up and run!'

She kept shouting as she rushed over to where Kimberly was struggling to stand up. She kicked her sister in the side and knocked her over, then kicked her again – this time in the stomach. I heard Kimberly grunt.

Wesley, whimpering and sobbing, scrambled to his feet. I still had his ax.

He didn't come for it, though. He started to run, in a lurching jog, toward the jungle.

Thelma yelled, 'Run! Run! Go!'

She followed him like some sort of rear guard, twisting and turning to keep her eyes on us.

I used the ax handle to push against the sand and keep

myself steady as I got to my feet. When I was up, I glanced at the others. Billie lay on her back, holding her face and moaning. Kimberly, curled on her side, made wheezy sounds as she tried to breathe.

Connie was now dashing toward us, a spear in one hand. She must've decided to join the fray when she saw Thelma slam her mother in the face.

She was still too far away to do a lot of good.

None of the three gals on my team was in any position to stop Wesley's escape.

It'd be me or nobody.

I'm not exactly a hero-type, but I sure as hell didn't like the idea of letting him get away. So I hefted the ax with both hands and went after him.

I would've caught him, too.

And hacked him to death, probably.

But Thelma, guarding his rear, turned on me and blocked my way. I should've gone through her. That's just what I would've tried, if she'd been a guy. But instead, I cut to the right and tried to dodge past her side. She leaped and got in the way again. Head up, arms out, hunched over at the waist, she looked like some kind of butch sports-fiend determined to stop me from scoring.

'Get out of the way!' I yelled in her face.

I dodged to the left, but she sprang in front of me again. 'No no no no no,' she said. 'You think you're getting him? No no no. Think again, shithead.'

Meanwhile, Wesley had almost made it to the jungle.

I'd wanted to nail him while he was still on the beach, but the chance for that was gone.

'Get out of the way or I'll chop you down!' I shouted.

'Like fun.' Suddenly, she dropped her arms and stood up straight, her eyes wide with alarm at something going on behind me. 'NO!' she yelled.

I whirled around.

Connie, in mid-stride, launched her spear. Its long, pale shaft soared through the night high above our heads.

I think they call such a throw, in football, a 'hail Mary.'

It flew over us and kept on going like a Tomahawk missile homing in on the naked, pale back of Wesley as he lurched closer and closer to the darkness.

Thelma yelled, 'Wesley! Look out!' She bolted after him.

Wesley twisted sideways and looked back. He stumbled. He fell sprawling. A moment later, the spear zipped down and planted itself in the sand – probably ten feet to his right.

Behind me, Connie yelled, 'Fuck!'

I glanced back at her. She had quit running – must've thought the spear would take care of business. She looked disgusted and punched at the air with her fist.

I spotted Wesley again, just in time to see him vanish into the jungle.

Thelma was chasing him.

'Wait up!' she called out, and waved a thick arm. 'Wait! Wesley! I'm coming with you!'

A couple of seconds later, she was gone, too.

Battered Angels

Nobody went in after Thelma and Wesley.

Would've been too dangerous, for one thing.

For another, our ambush had turned into a disaster. We were stunned, disappointed, angry, confused – and injured.

Mostly thanks to Thelma.

After the end of the mess, we stood around together on the moonlit beach where it had happened. I had the ax resting on my shoulder. Billie, hands on hips (and breasts back inside her bikini), frowned toward the jungle. Connie was bent over, hands on knees, still trying to catch her breath after racing almost to the edge of the jungle to retrieve the spear she'd thrown at Wesley. Kimberly shook her head and shut the blade of her Swiss Army knife.

We must've all been thinking about Thelma.

'How could she do it?' Kimberly said.

Billie made a snorty sound. 'She loves the guy.'

'But he killed *Dad*. My God! Her own father! I can see how she might not turn on him for a little thing like killing *my husband*, but he murdered *Dad*.'

'Oh, her dear Wesley wouldn't do *that*,' Connie said. 'The dumb bitch.'

'She knows he did it,' Billie said. 'She might not be a genius, but she's not *that* stupid.'

'I think she just went nuts,' I said. 'All this stuff the past few days – and then seeing her father get whacked this morning – it unhinged her.'

'You might be right,' Billie said. 'This sure wasn't the behavior of a rational person, tonight.'

'We knew she might cause trouble,' I reminded everyone. 'That's why we didn't let her in on the plan.'

'Never thought she'd do something like *this*,' Kimberly muttered. 'Jesus H. Christ.' She tucked the knife down inside her bikini pants. 'We should've tied her up.'

'Thought she was asleep,' I said.

'Well. Nothing we can do about it now.'

'Let's go on back to the fire,' Billie suggested.

So we turned our backs to the jungle. We walked side by side, me with the ax on my shoulder, all of us battered (me the only one bloody). We must've been a sight to see – if anyone was watching.

Charlie's Angels and the Tin Woodsman.

All messed up and nowhere to go.

Or whatever.

I'm starting to lose it. I've been writing for hours, trying to get down all of last night's events in this journal. My hand is turning into a claw – my mind into mush. Anyway, I've got to finish about last night.

Before something else happens.

If I let the journal fall behind, I might have real trouble catching up.

On second thoughts, I'm going to take a break.

Hello, I'm back. Took a nice swim, then sat around with the gals for a while.

Maybe it was a mistake, but I finally admitted that I'm keeping a journal. I'd been telling everyone, before, that I was working on a series of short stories. But it was finally time to trust them with the truth. I mean, there's only three of them, now.

I wanted them to know about it. To know I'm not just fooling around while I'm sitting by myself for hours. To know there's a record of our ordeal being kept. (Maybe it'll be important for them to know that, at some point. Especially if something happens to me. Yuck. Made me feel squeamish, writing that little line.)

We had quite a long talk about the journal. They wanted to know what I've written about them (which made me sweat big-time), but I explained that I wouldn't be able to write truthfully if I had to worry about pleasing an audience. Finally, they promised to respect my privacy and make no attempts to sneak a peek.

They'd better stick to their promises, or there will be some mighty embarrassed and angry people on this beach. (I couldn't stand to face any of these gals, knowing they're aware of certain things I've written about them.)

Shit. They gave their word. If they read this stuff, they deserve what they get.

Maybe I shouldn't have told them.

Seemed like the right thing to do at the time.

Anyway, now that I've rested and shot off my mouth to the ladies, I'm ready to knock out the conclusion of last night's events.

I left off when we were on our way back to the camping area.

Okay.

We got into the firelight, and the gals suddenly noticed my wounds. They seemed pretty concerned – even Connie. In fact, she's the one who insisted on tending to me. She told her mother and Kimberly that they should try to get some sleep. She would fix me up, then she and I would stand watch for the next few hours.

I urged them to go along with it. I mean, they both seemed worn out and hurting.

While Billie and Kimberly settled into their sleeping places, Connie grabbed a couple of rags. She went to the stream, dipped them in, and came over to where I was sitting by the fire. She made me turn so the firelight would shine on the wounded side of my face – the right. Then she knelt in front of me.

The firelight lit up the swollen left side of her jaw.

Where I'd punched her.

'I'm sorry about that,' I told her. 'It wasn't supposed to connect.'

'Wasn't, huh?'

'I swear.'

She started dabbing at the raw trench that Thelma's rock had torn in my face and ear. She was gentle about it, but every touch ignited pain. 'I had it coming,' she said. 'I got in my shots, you got in yours.'

'It was an accident.'

'Sure.'

'I never would've hit you on purpose.'

She smirked. 'If you say so.'

'It's the truth.'

'What'd Thelma get you with, anyway? It sure fucked up your face.'

'A rock.'

'Look at this.' She pulled back the rag and showed it to me. It was red with my blood. The other cloth was still clean. She used it to mop off the blood that had run down my face and neck and right shoulder and arm. Then she wrung out both the rags, squeezing and twisting them. Bloody water spilled onto the sand between us.

She scowled at my lower wound.

Thelma's broken spear had gouged me just above my belly button. The hole wasn't deep, but it had bled a lot. The front of my swimming trunks was soaked, and trickles had even made their way down my thighs.

Connie shook her head. 'We'd better just go over to the stream.'

She took the rags with her. I carried the ax.

Gaining possession of the ax was the best thing to come out of our disastrous ambush. Next to a gun, you couldn't ask for a better weapon. Now it was ours, not Wesley's. I planned to keep it close by.

Connie led the way to the stream. We stepped down its shallow, sandy bank and waded in. The water felt great — slightly cooler than the night air.

The stream is basically so narrow that, during most of its course from the jungle to the inlet, you can jump across it without much trouble. It is also fairly shallow. Ankle-deep in many places, knee-deep in a few.

Connie and I entered one of the deeper areas. She faced me. We were out of range of the firelight. 'You can put down the ax,' she said.

I swung it underhand, and let go. The heavy, steel head thumped onto dry sand near the shore. The haft dropped toward me, and splashed into the stream where it would be easy to grab in case of an emergency.

Crouching in front of me, Connie rinsed the bloody rags. She stayed down. After draping one of the cloths over her knee, she reached up with the other and began to wash my wound. To hold herself steady, she clutched the waist of my trunks with her left hand, over near my hip.

I couldn't help but feel the backs of her fingers in there.

Couldn't help noticing how she'd tugged my trunks down a good inch – just by virtue of hanging onto them.

Not to mention, her face was straight in front of my groin.

I tried not to let these things affect me.

They affected me quickly and obviously.

'Not again,' she said when my trunks started sticking out.

'Sorry,' I told her.

She stopped patting the wet cloth against my wound. She lowered that hand, but the other stayed. 'Don't apologize, make it go away.'

'Huh?'

'You heard me. I'm trying to help you, and here you've got your *thing* in my face.'

'I don't have a lot of control over it. You know? It just . . . responds. To things like you.'

'Things like me.'

'Yeah, you. The way you look. Your hand there. The water. It all . . . adds up.'

'So then, it's *my* fault?'

I smiled. 'Pretty much.'

'I'm supposed to be flattered, or something?'

'Maybe,' I said.

She looked up at me and didn't speak for a few seconds. Then she said, 'You had one when we were fighting, too.'

'Yeah. When I was on top of you.'

She dipped the rag in the stream, then lifted it and began mopping the blood off the area between my wound and the top of my trunks. 'And when I took my top off,' she said.

'You noticed that?'

'Of course.'

'Thought maybe you were too busy slapping me,' I said.

'Ha ha, very funny.'

She dipped the rag again. As it came up soaked, her left hand plucked the waist of my trunks away from my belly. She mashed the sopping cloth against my skin, and a flood washed down. It drenched my works, then spilled out through the leg holes of my trunks and streamed down my legs.

Keeping my trunks pulled out, she dunked the rag into the stream again. She swished it around. 'Would you like me to take my top off again?' she asked. 'I could do it, you know. Right here, right now. You want me to?'

'Sure.'

'Or would you rather have me pull your trunks down?'

All I could think of to say was, 'You're kidding.'

'Take your pick.'

'How about both?'

'One or the other.'

It wasn't a very difficult decision. 'My trunks,' I said.

'Why?'

'Sort of tight in there.'

'I'll bet. Why else?'

I thought about that for a second, then said, 'It'll make it easier for washing the blood off me.'

'Lousy reason. Give me another.'

I shrugged. 'Well, I've already seen . . . you know, seen you topless.'

'And once was enough, huh?'

Woops.

'No,' I protested. 'But it's too dark here. I wouldn't be able to see.'

'You could touch.'

'Really? You didn't say that before. Okay, I pick that.'

'What?'

'Taking off your top.'

'Too late. You already made your choice.'

'Can't I change my mind?'

'No.'

'Okay.'

'You sure give up easy.'

'I just don't want to argue.'

'You just really don't want to see me topless again. Don't worry, pal – you won't.'

With that, she pulled at the waist of my trunks as if she wanted to see how far the elastic would stretch. She drew it out about half a foot, then let go. It shot in and snapped me.

And it hurt.

I staggered backward to get out of her reach – not knowing what to expect next.

She stood up. 'Fuck you,' she snarled. 'You're such a pathetic fucking loser. You really thought I'd pull your trunks down? Or take off my top? No way. Not a prayer. Last thing I want is your stupid cock in my face. And the only reason I let you see my tits back at the fire was to let you take a good look at what you're never gonna see again.'

I doubted the truth of that. Fact is, I doubt that she *ever* says what's really going on in her head – maybe doesn't even *know* what's going on in there.

But she was looking for trouble, so I gave her some. Not a smart move, but what I said was, 'I figured you took off your top 'cause you wanted to show off your boobies – such as they are – to Wesley.'

Her mouth fell open.

A moment later, she blurted, 'That's the thanks I get for trying to be nice to you.'

Whatever that meant.

I was afraid she might go for the ax. She didn't, though. She stomped through the water and ran up the bank and didn't stop till she reached the sleeping area. There, she flopped down on her usual assortment of rags.

I was left standing in the stream, a bit confused about what had gone wrong.

She'd been getting pretty friendly there for a while.

Unless it had been an act.

When it comes to Connie, it's just mighty damn awful hard to tell what's real from what isn't.

All I can be sure of is that she is never likely to react the way I'd expect a person to react. Not like Billie or Kimberly, for instance. You can make sense out of them. Unlike Connie.

Could it have to do with the fact that she's still a teenager? At eighteen, though, you'd think she might be past the usual adolescent crap.

Doesn't seem to be.

She reminds me of a cat I used to know. One time, I was petting its head. The cat was really into it, eyes half shut, its purr rumbling away. But all of a sudden, God knows why, it went nuts and shredded my arm.

I was thinking about that sort of stuff while I finished at the stream. What I did there was kneel in the water, wash the blood off my body as well as I could, then work at getting my trunks clean. Finally, I waded out, picked up the ax and returned to camp.

Connie was probably not asleep. I considered going over to her and trying to make amends, but that didn't seem like such a hot idea. I might just end up setting her off again.

So I went to the fire and sat down, figuring I might as well keep watch – even though sentry duty didn't seem very necessary.

Our ambush hadn't been a complete failure – Kimberly had delivered a couple of nasty wounds to Wesley. They were probably not fatal (barring infection), but they were pretty sure to keep him in major pain for a while.

And out of our hair.

Though I didn't expect an attack, I stayed awake and kept watch. There was plenty to occupy my mind. My plan was to stay up all night, so that the gals could get plenty of sleep. A while before dawn, though, Billie woke up and came over to the fire.

She sat down next to me. The side of her face was swollen and discolored by the blow from Thelma's spear. 'How's it going?' she asked.

'I don't think there's much chance of them bothering us tonight.'

'There isn't . . . How about you? How are your wounds doing?'

'Connie washed them off for me.'

'Let's see.'

I leaned back and turned toward her. Looking at my injuries, Billie grimaced. 'Must hurt.'

'How about you?'

'I'll live.' She put a hand on my leg. 'Why don't you go on to bed, now?'

'I'm not that tired.'

'Sure you are. Go on.'

'Why don't I stay and keep you company?'

'Thanks. But you know what? I'd rather be alone for a while. You know?'

I wanted awfully badly to stay with her – not to keep *her*

company, but because I felt sort of lonely, myself. When it comes right down to it, I'd rather spend time with Billie than with anyone else I can think of.

But she probably wanted time to sit by herself and think about Andrew. I said, 'Sure. See you later.'

Then I went over to my sleeping place.

Before you know it, I was out like a light.

Odds And Ends

So much for last night. This is still day four, and I've spent the better part of it working on my journal here.

I'm just back from another break.

It's late afternoon, now. This has been a fairly uneventful day. Thank God.

I already went into how I took the earlier break from my writing and told the gals about the journal.

There are a few other matters worth mentioning.

For instance, we've started using the latrine as a toilet. Laid some branches across the hole, to stand on.

Also, Billie and Kimberly, with some help from me, constructed a couple of shelters. We made them like the walls of the latrine, by lashing bushes and fronds to frameworks of sticks. Instead of being walls, though, these are roofs. We set them up on poles, near our sleeping area. The purpose is to have places where we can escape from the sun. I'm using one, now. Though the sun hasn't been terrible (the heat is fairly moderate, and there's usually a pleasant breeze), I really enjoy being able to sit in the shade while I write.

Billie and Kimberly also made new weapons to replace the ones that were lost or broken last night.

Connie has spent most of the day by herself. She's

hardly spoken to me since our squabble at the stream. The few times she's been near me, she has thrown narrow-eyed glares my way.

The good part is, she spent hours fishing. This morning, she borrowed the knife from Kimberly and used it to whittle a special point on the end of her spear. The point is very long and thin, with three barbs carved into its side. They look like small, sharp limbs, and sweep back at an angle away from the tip. The one nearest the tip is the smallest. They get bigger as they go. The obvious purpose for the barbs is to stop fish from falling off, once they've been speared.

It's a wicked-looking piece of work, though. Sure hope she doesn't get into a tiff and decide to use it on me.

Anyway, she stood in the inlet for hours, way out where it's waist-deep. Must've taken a long time to get the hang of using the spear. Every once in a while, I heard her yell 'Fuck!' Finally, she yelled, 'Yes! Gotcha, you bastard!' I looked up and saw her hoisting a big, silvery fish toward the sky on the tip of her spear. Everyone cheered, including me. She brought the fish ashore. Kimberly went running to her with our biggest pot, scooped it full of salt water, and Connie tossed in the fish.

She ended up with four of them.

We'll be having a real feast, tonight.

That's about it for today's events. So far, so good.

We've done pretty well when you take all the circumstances into account. Yesterday, we'd had to deal with the killings of Keith and Andrew. Today, on top of that, there was the failure of our ambush to think about and the defection of Thelma – plus all the injuries from last night.

In the injury department, I'm the worst off, if you don't count Wesley.

Kimberly is probably the most beat up, after me. Her skin didn't get broken, but she has a horrible bruise on her ribcage, just below her right armpit. She also has bruises on her stomach and right hip from Thelma kicking her.

Billie and Connie have bruises on their faces. The swelling went away, leaving behind dark smudges that almost look like dirt. Billie's is on the left cheek, Connie's on the left side of the jaw. Billie got dealt a much meaner blow from Thelma's spear than Connie got from my fist.

I'm going to knock off now, and help prepare the fish for supper.

The fish was great. Billie fried it up on the skillet with bourbon – her special method. We also passed the bottle around, and had a few nips to help our finny friends go down smooth.

One thing really struck me during the meal.

The size of our group.

Or the lack thereof.

Four of us.

Jesus.

There used to be eight of us. Eight is a fair number of people, a pretty good crowd.

Four is measly.

And I've got to say, four looked a lot like three, from where I sat. I'm sort of like a movie camera, you know? I don't see myself, most of the time. I see Billie, Kimberly and Connie. One, two, three. That's all.

We've been whittled down considerably.

We didn't talk much while we ate. About the time we finished, though, Billie said, 'We'd better do something, tomorrow.'

Connie looked offended. 'Hey, *I* did something today. You just ate it.'

'We should've gone hunting,' Kimberly said, 'not fishing. Hunting for Thelma and Wesley.' She met Billie's eyes. Pressing her lips together in a tight line, she shook her head. Then she said, 'I just didn't want to deal with it today.'

'Yeah,' Billie said. 'I know. Neither did I.'

'Not after last night,' I added.

Connie gave me a quick, sour glare.

'But we'd better go looking for them tomorrow,' Billie said. 'We can't give Wesley time to recover. He's gotta be in bad shape after last night. If we find him while he's still laid up, he'll be a lot easier to finish off.'

'What'll we do about Thelma?' I asked.

'Save her,' Billie said.

Connie let out a snort.

Ignoring it, Kimberly said, 'Yeah. He'll probably kill her, sooner or later.'

'Maybe not right away,' Billie said. 'He'll want her around to take care of him, at least till he gets better.'

'You're both nuts,' Connie said. 'He isn't gonna kill Thelma.'

I decided to stay out of it.

'Why not?' Kimberly asked her.

'For one thing, she saved his bacon last night.'

'You think he'll spare her out of gratitude?' Kimberly asked.

'He's got no *reason* to kill her. She's on *his* side, you know?'

'He might not see it that way,' Billie said. 'Maybe he just sees her as an obstacle.'

'In the way of what?'

'Why is he doing any of this?' Billie asked. 'That's the real question. In my opinion, he set up this whole operation in order to make himself rich. Most of the family wealth is in Andrew's name. And mine. With both of us dead, you two girls and Thelma inherit everything. With the three of you dead, your spouses would get it. Connie hasn't got a spouse . . .'

' And he killed mine,' Kimberly muttered.

'Right. So that leaves Wesley. He stands to make a pile if he's the only survivor.'

'I'd bet he's also got a life insurance policy on Thelma,' Kimberly said. 'So you can add that to his take.'

Connie had a sick look on her face. 'I think you've all been watching too much *Murder, She Wrote.*'

'Why do *you* think he's doing all this?' Billie asked her.

She wrinkled her nose and shrugged. 'Because he's nuts?'

'He's nuts, all right,' Kimberly said. 'Nuts if he thinks he's gonna survive. First thing in the morning, I'm going after him.'

'We'll *all* go after him,' Billie said.

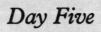

Day Five

War Dance

I didn't have to stand watch last night. The women took turns, and let me sleep.

I woke up on my own. The sun had risen over the tops of the jungle trees, and threw warm gold across our beach. It sure felt good. I wanted to just keep lying there, enjoying it.

Billie and Connie were asleep nearby, but I couldn't see Kimberly. After a while, I raised my head to look for her.

She was about midway between the campfire and the shoreline, swinging the ax. Exercising with it. Or practicing. She was as graceful as a dancer, twirling and smiting the air, springing forward to cut down an invisible enemy, taking swings to one side, then the other. She was a little spooky to watch. So smooth and graceful, yet wielding such a vicious weapon. The head of the ax glinted like silver in the sunlight. Her thick dark hair flowed and shook like the mane of a stallion.

She wore her dead husband's Hawaiian shirt. Unbuttoned, as usual, its gaudy fabric flew out behind her like a cape when she lunged or twirled. Her white bikini flashed. Her bronze skin gleamed with sweat.

She was spooky, elegant, primitive, beautiful. It made me ache, watching her. I couldn't force my eyes away.

Being stuck on this island *is* the best thing that's ever happened to me. By that logic, of course, I ought to be thanking Wesley, not trying to kill him. Except that I hate him for bringing grief to Kimberly and Billie. And I hate him for what he might do to them, if he gets the chance. (I'm not tickled by the fact that he wants to kill me, either.)

Anyway, Kimberly was spectacular to watch.

Until she noticed me watching. I felt like a peeping Tom who'd been caught in the act, but I smiled and waved. She waved back. I sat up, gave myself a couple of minutes to calm down, then got to my feet and wandered over to join her.

'Preparing for the big battle?' I asked.

She rested the ax on her shoulder, and smiled. She has a spectacular smile. 'Just fooling around,' she said. 'Getting a little workout.'

'You must be part Viking,' I said.

'That's me, Nordic through and through.'

She was making sport of me, but I liked it. 'I wasn't referring to your complexion,' I explained. 'It's the way you swing that ax. Like you've got battle-axes in your blood.'

'Ah. That might be my Indian blood.'

'You're Indian?'

'Injun. Part Sioux . . . Lakota.'

'You kidding me?'

'I swear.' With her free hand, she drew a quick X in the middle of her chest. 'On my mother's side. Her grandfather fought at Little Big Horn.'

'You're kidding.'

'I have it on good authority that he *personally* scalped Custer.'

'Really?'

She grinned. '*That* was kidding.'

'Glad to hear it, because I don't think Custer *got* scalped.'

'I don't really know if my ancestor scalped anyone at all. He was there, though. That's a fact.'

'My God.'

'So I guess maybe things like tomahawks, spears and knives might run in my blood. I'm also part Sicilian.'

'Sioux and Sicilian. Man! Red blood *and* hot blood. That's a dangerous combination. Remind me not to make you mad at me!'

'Yep. Watch it. I'm hell on wheels.' Her smile died and her eyes went dark. For a while there, she must've forgotten about the murders of her husband and her father. But she had just remembered. I could see the pain in her face. And the anger.

Wesley had made a very big mistake, killing people Kimberly loved.

He's already paid for the mistake, but I've got a feeling that his torments have hardly even started.

Wanting to take her mind off her grief, I said, 'Boy, I didn't think we'd be stuck on this island more than a day or two, did you?'

'An *hour* or two,' she said. 'I thought for sure somebody must've seen the explosion. And even if nobody *did* . . . My God, it's like a century too late to be getting marooned on an island.'

'Just goes to show, anything can happen.'

'Especially when there's a devious bastard scheming to *make* it happen.'

'He *must've* filed a false itinerary,' I said. 'Or, what do they call it, a float plan?' It was something I'd thought about and mentioned before, but now I felt certain of it. 'That's about the only way I can figure why we haven't gotten rescued yet. Nobody's looking for us. Either that, or they've been tricked into searching in the wrong places.'

'At this point,' Kimberly said, 'I don't even *want* to be rescued.'

Her words stunned me.

They echoed my own feelings on the subject.

This was the start of our fifth day on the island. In some ways, it seems like we'd been here for years. Mostly, though, it seems like much too short a time. Thanks to all our troubles with Wesley, we haven't even explored the island, yet. There's no telling what we might find, or what adventures we might have over the coming days – or weeks. Or even months.

Rescue would put an abrupt end to all the fabulous possibilities.

I figured that Kimberly must feel the same way, but then she said, 'I'm not leaving this island till I've taken care of Wesley.'

'You already got him pretty good.'

'I'm going to kill him.'

The way she said it, and the way she *looked* when she said it, gave me a shiver up my back.

Preparations

I did some quick catch-up on the journal while the gals got ready for our jungle excursion.

Our hunt.

Our mission to rescue Thelma and finish off Wesley.

Before leaving, we had a small meal and discussed what to do about the fire. So far, we'd followed Andrew's advice about never letting it go out. But we figured we might be gone all day. If we wanted to keep it burning, we would almost have to leave someone behind to tend it.

We were not about to leave anyone alone.

But if we let two stay behind to guard each other and watch the fire, that would leave only two for the hunt.

Which, we all agreed, would be ridiculous.

We decided to let the fire burn out.

Anyway, we still had Andrew's lighter.

Billie went over to her sleeping area and looked for it. She found Andrew's khaki shorts, picked them up, and searched the pockets. She emptied them as she went along, pulling out such things as his pipe, tobacco pouch, billfold, keys, and the white handkerchief that he had placed over Keith's dead face. Soon, she came hurrying back with the shorts in one hand, the lighter in the other.

She tested the lighter. A flick, and the flame leaped up.

She had brought the khaki shorts over to us because she thought someone ought to wear them. 'They've got such great, deep pockets,' she explained.

Obviously, we could use something for carrying odds and ends.

Aside from Andrew's shorts, the only pocket in sight was the one on the chest of Kimberly's Hawaiian shirt – a pocket so loose and flimsy that she didn't even trust her Swiss Army knife to it.

There was my bag, of course. I'd hidden it under some rags over at my sleeping place, for safe keeping. I planned to leave it there, because I sure didn't want to spend the day hiking through the jungle with *that* on my back. (It's the home of my journal, which is a big thick spiral notebook – probably weighs at least two pounds.)

'Who wants to wear them?' Billie asked, holding up Andrew's shorts.

Nobody volunteered.

Probably because the shorts would be too bulky and heavy and hot, especially for gals who were used to going around in scanty bikinis.

'You wear 'em,' Connie told me. 'They're men's shorts, and you're the only guy around here.'

'I don't want to wear them,' I said. I remembered how Andrew had taken them off and spread them over the lower parts of Keith – who'd been naked down there and dead at the time.

'Just put 'em on over your trunks,' Connie said.

'That'd be too hot.'

'I'll wear them,' Kimberly offered.

She didn't sound eager, and I didn't like the idea. In fact, I didn't want to see *anybody* wearing them – but especially not any of the gals. 'That's all right,' I said. 'I'll put 'em on.'

I took them from Billie, bent over, and raised a foot to step into them.

'No,' Billie said. 'Get your trunks off, first. You'd smother in all that. Besides, your trunks are a mess.'

They aren't a *mess*. I'd gotten most of the blood off them, so they were only a little bit gory.

I looked around for a place to change.

'Just do it here,' Kimberly said. She was pretty matter-of-fact about it.

I shook my head. 'I can go over to the rocks . . .'

'Don't be silly,' Billie said. 'Just do it here. We won't peek.'

Connie smirked. 'Who'd *want* to?'

I sighed. Then I said, 'Well, okay.'

After their backs were turned, I pulled my trunks down and got them off. It felt weird. I was naked on a beach in broad daylight, and the three gals were almost near enough to touch. They weren't wearing much, themselves – but more than me.

I got enormous, all of a sudden. I stepped into Andrew's shorts and pulled them up as fast as I could.

'You decent?' Billie asked.

'Almost.'

I shoved myself inside the fly and got the zipper shut. The shorts were big and loose, drooping well below my waist. But I hitched them higher and got the belt cinched.

'All set?' Billie asked.

'Uh, yeah.'

She turned around. They all did.

I bent down fast and picked up my trunks. When I straightened up, I held them in front of me.

Connie said, 'Good God, Rupert.'

I shook my head. I felt as if my face might burst into flame. 'What's the matter?' I asked.

Big mistake.

'Your *hard-on*'s the matter, you fucking degenerate.'

'Connie!' Billie blurted.

'Well, look at him!'

'He doesn't need you pointing it out to everyone,' Billie scolded her.

'It's *already* pointing out to everyone,' Kimberly said, smiling.

I think I moaned. I think I muttered something like, 'Oh, man.'

In the meantime, Kimberly's comment had cracked Billie up. Even Connie was laughing about it.

The object of their amusement, meanwhile, was shrinking like an icicle in Hell.

I stopped trying to hide behind my trunks. 'Yeah, well,' I said. 'These things happen, you know?'

'Happen to *you* all the time,' Connie said.

'It's nothing to be ashamed of,' Billie told me, being sort of solemn now that she'd finished laughing. 'Don't worry about it, honey.'

Honey?

Kimberly said, 'Looks like the big fella's out of commission, anyway.'

'Do we have to talk about it?' I asked, feeling awfully squirmy inside.

'You're the one who brought it up,' Kimberly said. She gave me that smile again. That spectacular smile.

I actually laughed, myself.

'Okay, okay,' I said. 'Now, can we get on with things?'

'Here.' Billie tossed me Andrew's lighter. 'You've got the pockets.'

I dropped it into a front pocket of my shorts, and felt it way down against my thigh. 'How about the knife?' I asked Kimberly.

Normally, I avoided looking at it.

This gave me an excuse, though.

It was tucked into the front of her bikini pants. The thickness of the plastic handle made the flimsy white triangle purse out. I could see bare skin down there.

Kimberly's open right hand suddenly covered it all.

Patted it.

'I'll hang on to the knife. It has an appointment to keep with Wesley.'

Over at the supply pile, we gathered a few items so that we'd have something to snack on. The food went into the pockets of Andrew's shorts. (My shorts, now.) Then we gathered our weapons.

I volunteered to carry the ax.

'It's awfully heavy,' Kimberly said.

'I can handle it.'

'Let's take turns.'

'Okay,' I said.

'You start out with it, if you want. Just let me know when you get tired.'

'Okay.'

The ax required two hands. I wanted to have a back-up weapon, though, so I loosened my belt enough to slip a tomahawk under it, by my right hip.

Billie watched me do that, then pushed her tomahawk down the side of her pants. The waistband couldn't take the weight. 'Woops!' The pants were at about a forty-five-degree angle by the time she grabbed the weapon.

'Mom!' Connie blurted. 'For Godsake!'

'Oh, calm down.' She pulled out the weapon, hooked a

finger under her waistband, and corrected the slant.

'You did that on purpose.'

'Don't be an idiot.'

At that, Connie glared at me as if I were somehow to blame.

I just gave her a goony look and shrugged. 'I wasn't even looking,' I said. Which was a lie, and she knew it.

Billie, still determined not to carry the tomahawk in her hand, came up with the section of rope that had been around Keith's neck. Someone had untied the hangman's noose, so she had four or five feet of rope to work with. As all of us watched, she knotted the ends together and made a sling for her tomahawk. She slipped the loop over her head and put her right arm through it, then adjusted the rig so that the rope crossed her chest like a bandolier, the weapon hanging at her hip.

'I oughta do that,' Kimberly said.

As it turned out, Kimberly and Connie both did it. They used sections cut from the main length of the hanging rope, which we'd kept coiled with the rest of our supplies.

It took a few minutes. Worth the wait, though. They each had a spear. Would've taken both hands just to carry their weapons if they didn't have the tomahawks suspended by the rope slings.

We didn't burden ourselves with water bottles. For one thing, we wanted to travel fast and light. For another, we figured that we would never stray very far from the stream.

At last, we were ready.

Kimberly led the way. I went second. Connie followed me, and Billie took the rear.

We left the beach behind at the place where Wesley and Thelma had escaped into the jungle.

The Hunt

At first, we tried to follow the trail of Wesley's blood. Kimberly moved slowly through the bushes, often stopping, sometimes crouching for a closer inspection.

Even though Wesley must've bled plenty from his chest and buttock wounds, it wasn't easy to find the places where he'd left dabs of it behind. The jungle was so dense, in most places, that you couldn't see for more than a few feet in any direction. Also, not a lot of sunlight made it down to our level. We spent most of our time trudging through deep, murky shadows.

We probably would've had no luck at all finding traces of Wesley's blood, if Kimberly hadn't been so persistent. Or talented. Or psychic. She often seemed to know, by instinct, where to look.

Maybe it's the Sioux in her genes.

In spite of her uncanny abilities in the tracking department, we eventually lost all trace of the blood. By then, however, Kimberly had determined the general direction of his travels.

'He's going for the stream,' she whispered to us.

'That makes sense,' I said. 'He's gotta have fresh water.'

'Why didn't we go there in the first place?' Connie said. 'We could've skipped all *this*. This place blows.' With that, she smacked a mosquito that had landed on the side of her neck. She said, 'Yuh!'

Today was the worst mosquito trouble we'd had so far. They'd mostly left us alone, on the beach. They hadn't even been a major nuisance during the few times I'd ventured into the jungle.

But today they were awful.

We had no *6-12*, no *Cutter's*, no *Off!*, no nothing. The insect repellents had come on the sea voyage with us, but had been left aboard the yacht when we set out on our picnic. An oversight that we paid for today.

We'd been slapping mosquitoes ever since leaving the beach.

Some of us had been, that is.

Kimberly didn't let them bother her. Basically, she ignored them.

I tried to follow her example, but couldn't stand the way the little monsters hummed around my ears and the way they tickled wherever they landed. They seemed especially fond of the injured area on the side of my face and on my ear. (Apparently, they dig scabs.) I was very glad that I'd worn my shirt – the pink blouse on loan from Billie. Also, Andrew's big old shorts probably gave me more protection than I would've gotten from my swimming trunks.

Connie was wearing her usual T-shirt, but it was so thin and clingy that the mosquitoes nailed her right through the cloth. Her only safe areas were those protected by her bikini. If I haven't mentioned it before, hers is the skimpiest of the three. (Why Connie, who likes to act the prude, would wear such a revealing swimsuit is beyond me. But then, when it comes to Connie, what isn't? Maybe the T-shirt is her way of maintaining an appearance of decency.) Anyway, the top of her bikini consists of twin orange triangles and a few thin cords. Its bottom is what they call a 'thong' – with a slightly wider strip in front than the one that goes up her rear. In other words, only a few very private inches of her body were safe from the attacking mosquitoes.

Billie, as usual, wore only her bikini. No shirt, and the swimsuit didn't cover much. Even though hers had at least three times the fabric of Connie's, there's a lot more flesh to Billie. She seemed to have acres of bare skin, all of it shiny and dripping with sweat. She looked like a wonderful hot meal for the little bastards. But they left her alone.

I noticed this when we stopped in a sunny clearing to rest on our way to the stream.

'Aren't they eating you alive?' I asked her.

'Nope. They never do.'

'What's your secret?'

'When I was about five, I saved a mosquito's life. Word got around. They haven't touched me ever since.'

'She told *me* that story when *I* was five,' Connie said. 'It's such bullshit.'

Billie gave her daughter a big understanding smile. 'Think what you like, dear.'

'I think they leave you alone 'cause they don't like your smell.'

'You're such a sweetheart.'

'You smell fine,' I told her.

Hell, I thought she smelled great.

'Thank you, Rupert,' she said.

'Whatever your secret is, I wish I had it. These things are driving me nuts.'

'All they want,' Kimberly said, 'is a little of your blood. They aren't asking much.'

'I'd just as soon keep my blood,' I told her. 'You're just *letting* them have at you?'

'Trying to fight them off is a losing battle. I accept what I can't change.'

Connie smirked. 'The bullshit's thicker than the mosquitoes around here.'

I smacked a mosquito on my forehead.

After a while, we got moving again and came to the stream. We gathered along its shore, and looked both ways as if we'd come to a highway and were worried about getting struck down by a speeding truck.

No sign of Wesley or Thelma or anyone.

The stream flowed along at a pretty good clip, splashing over rocks, coming down from the high ground to our right. Looking to my left, I saw it running downhill toward our beach. I couldn't see our beach, though. Or the ocean. Just trees and bushes and hanging vines – and birds swooping here and there. Not much of the stream was visible, either. About thirty feet away, it curved out of sight.

'Hold this for me,' Connie said. She thrust her spear into her mother's free hand, then climbed down into the stream. She knelt, bent over, and cupped some water into her mouth. Then she started splashing and rubbing herself, apparently to soothe the itch of her mosquito bites.

The way she acted, it must've felt really good.

The rest of us still stood on the bank.

'How are you doing with that ax?' Kimberly asked me.

'Fine.'

'Want me to take it for a while?'

'No, really.'

'I'm pretty sure we're just below the lagoon.' She stepped down into the water. Billie and I did the same.

'It'll be an easy hike from here,' Kimberly said, 'but we'd better keep our eyes open.'

We crouched and took drinks, then just stood in the stream to wait for Connie to finish. I sort of felt like rolling in the water and rubbing my itches, too. But it was only a few inches deep here. I preferred to wait for the lagoon.

Connie took her time, as if she enjoyed making us wait. I didn't mind much. It was just fine with me, watching her flop around all shiny and wet in her transparent T-shirt and her feeble excuse for a bikini.

Finally, she stood up. Billie returned her spear, and we got moving again.

We made our way single file up the stream bed. Sometimes we walked in the water, sometimes on dry rocks alongside it. It was much easier than trekking through the jungle. As we went along, though, the terrain got steeper. The stream tumbled down, loud and frothy. We had to climb, and sometimes leap from rock to rock. Luckily, things never got so steep that we needed our hands.

Kimberly had said it would be 'an easy hike' to the lagoon.

For her, I suppose it was.

The rest of us had to stop a few times along the way.

Our last halt was called by Kimberly, which surprised me. Had she finally gotten worn out enough to need a rest?

Nope.

She sat on a rock. As she waited for the rest of us, she set her spear aside, took off the tomahawk hanging by her hip, and slipped out of Keith's gaudy shirt. When we arrived, she said, 'We're just about there. I'll go on up. You guys wait here, okay? I want to take a look around.'

'You shouldn't go alone,' I said.

'I'll be in plain sight. Just up there.' She turned her head and nodded toward the higher rocks. 'I want to make sure the coast is clear.'

We agreed to stay behind.

Kimberly climbed the rocks to the right of the stream. Just below the top, she scurried part way up the face of a large slab that was at about a forty-five-degree angle. Then she sank to her belly and squirmed the rest of the way.

She lay flat, her head up. For a long time, she didn't seem to move at all. Then her head made small, slow turns from one side to the other.

The three of us watched her from below, and said nothing for a long time.

After maybe ten minutes, though, Connie muttered, 'What the hell's taking her so long?'

'Maybe she sees something,' Billie said.

'Maybe she just wants to make sure nobody's there,' I suggested.

'This is stupid, waiting around.'

'A few more minutes won't hurt anything,' Billie told her. All patience and calm. 'Just relax.'

A few more minutes passed. Connie spent them sighing and shaking her head and rolling her eyes upward.

It annoyed me. 'You late for an appointment?' I finally asked.

'Fuck you.'

Billie said softly, 'Cut it out, Connie.'

'He doesn't have to be such a fucking wise-ass all the time.'

'Would you please watch your language?'

'Oh, yeah. Take his side, why don't you?'

'I'm not taking any sides. I just think you should settle down, all right? You're not improving the situation. And it seems like all I've been hearing out of you lately is "fuck" this and "fuck" that. You wouldn't be talking that way if your father was around.'

'Well, he isn't.' She said that in a very snotty fashion.

'No, he isn't.' Billie said that in a sad way that made me get tight in my throat.

And Connie suddenly started to cry.

Her mother tried to put an arm around her, but Connie shoved it away and blurted, 'Don't touch me. Leave me alone.' She turned her back on both of us, and buried her face in her hands. She didn't make much noise with her crying – just a gasp or sniffle now and then. But she was crying pretty good. I could tell by the way her back and shoulders kept jumping.

As much as I sometimes can't stand Connie, it hurt to watch her crying. It sort of made *me* want to cry. It also made me want to comfort her. I knew better than to try a thing like that, though. So I kept my distance and silence.

She'd finished crying, but still had her back to us, by the time Kimberly climbed down.

Kimberly frowned at her. 'You okay?' she asked.

'Fuck off,' Connie muttered.

Which didn't seem to faze Kimberly. 'Sure. Whatever.' She turned to Billie and me. Crouching in front of us, she said, 'Doesn't look like anyone's up there. We shouldn't count on it, though. We'll have to be really careful, and watch our backs.'

'Wesley might be too weak to attack anyone,' Billie said.

'Good chance of it,' Kimberly agreed. 'But there's no telling what Thelma might pull. I think she'll do *anything* to save him.'

'Stands by her man,' I said.

Kimberly came very close to snarling. 'What a gal,' she muttered.

'We shouldn't blame her too much,' Billie said. 'She never could see straight, as far as Wesley was concerned. She probably *still* refuses to believe he killed Andrew and Keith. If she's even . . . still in the picture.'

Kimberly slipped the rope sling over her head and adjusted the tomahawk so it dangled by her right hip. 'I'd say it's ten to one she's still alive. And on his side. If she attacks, though . . .' Shaking her head, Kimberly squeezed her lower lip between her teeth. Then she said, 'We have to defend ourselves. I don't want her hurt, though. Not if we can help it. She's still my sister.

'You're my sister, too,' she said, turning her head to look at Connie. 'I'm not going to leave you sitting there, no matter how much you might prefer to spend the rest of the day sulking.' She took her spear and stood up. 'So get on your feet, all right? It's time to go.'

'Sure,' Connie muttered. 'Your wish is my command.'

'You better believe it,' Kimberly said, and smiled.

I'll have to quit writing, pretty soon. I went to work as soon as we got back to the beach, this afternoon. They let me stick with it while they prepared dinner. Then I took a break to eat, and came back to the journal. I'm going to run out of daylight before I run out of things to write about yesterday.

I'll be backed up pretty good.

What I really need to do is stop trying to write about every damn thing that goes on. Well, actually, I'm not writing about *every*thing. I've been leaving plenty out. There are a million little details that I haven't mentioned, and some might even be important.

You don't know what's important until later, sometimes.

For want of a nail, the shoe was lost. For want of the shoe, the horse was lost. For want of the horse, the battle was lost. I don't know what's coming, so I might not even mention the lost nail. Does that make any sense?

Maybe that's why I try not to leave out any details that I think might turn out to be important. Since I don't know how things will turn out . . .

Maybe if I stopped wasting time and paper with stuff like this, I'd get further.

I'd *better* cut down somewhere. At this point, about half of my notebook is filled up. I've been writing on both sides of each page, but it looks like I might run out of notebook before I run out of story – at least if things keep going on for very many more days.

I'll try being more careful about what I include. And from now on, I'll write *really small*.

What if I end up running out of paper because I spent too much space writing about running out of paper?

Life and its ironies.

Back tomorrow. I hope.

Day Six

The Hunt (Part Two)

Here we are, at the start of our sixth day as castaways.

It's dawn.

We agreed for me to take the final watch of the night, so that I would have daylight for working on my journal. A few minutes ago, Kimberly woke me up to relieve her. She has just gone over to her sleeping place. Billie and Connie appear to be sound asleep.

It is very pleasant and peaceful, sitting here alone by the fire at sunrise. I hear the gentle swishing sounds of the waves. The fire crackles and snaps. Off in the jungle, a few birds are squawking.

I'd better get down to business.

Yesterday, and our hunt for Wesley and Thelma.

When I left off, we were just about to reach the lagoon.

We climbed the rest of the way, and found ourselves standing within a few feet of its shore.

The lagoon turned out to be larger than I'd expected – maybe fifty yards across and twice that size in length. I'd also expected its entire shoreline to be in sight, but there were so many curves and points and coves that fairly large portions of the lagoon and its banks couldn't be seen from where we stood.

It was a lovely sight, though. The surface was so still

that it had hardly a ripple except where the waterfall splashed down directly across from us.

The water of the falls looked like a curl of silver where it slid over the rock edge about ten or fifteen feet above the lagoon. It hung down the face of the rock, shiny and transparent. At the bottom of its drop, it splashed softly.

The rest of the lagoon was like a dark mirror. It cast a perfect, upside-down image of the rocky shores, the bushes and towering trees.

We stood for a while on the shore, looking around.

As expected, there was no sign of Wesley or Thelma. It was hard to believe that any human had ever been here before – even though I knew that Kimberly and Keith had visited the lagoon on our first morning at the island, before the boat blew up. The place seemed so remote and primitive that I wouldn't have been surprised to see a dinosaur wading through its water. Like in *The Lost World* or *King Kong*. Or *Jurassic Park*.

The only wildlife I could see, however, was of the winged variety. Bugs and birds. And not a pterodactyl in sight.

'I'm going in,' Connie said. She set down her spear and tomahawk, and started to take off her shoes.

'We'd better not all go in at the same time,' Kimberly said. 'Someone should stay on the bank with . . .'

Connie dived in.

'. . . with the weapons.'

'I'll stay,' I volunteered.

'We'll take turns,' Billie told me. 'I'll come out in a few minutes and take over for you.'

'Fine,' I said.

'Let's give ourselves about half an hour,' Kimberly suggested. 'Then we'll scout the shores, see if we can find any traces of my sister and Wesley. Maybe we'll be able to pick up their trail.'

'If they were even here,' Billie said.

'This is where *I'd* come, if I were Wesley. I'd have a hiding place somewhere near the lagoon, here. A base camp.' To me, she said, 'So keep a sharp eye out.'

'Don't let anyone sneak up on you,' Billie said.

'And watch us, too,' Kimberly added. 'We'll be sort of vulnerable out there.'

That was like our cue to look for Connie.

She had made it to the other side, and was standing under the waterfall. As we watched, she took off her T-shirt, wadded it into a ball, and started to rub her face with it.

'I sure wish she'd shape up,' Billie muttered.

'She's having a tough time,' Kimberly said.

'We all are. That's no excuse.'

'Come on, let's go in.'

They piled their spears and tomahawks on the shore, along with the rope slings, the Hawaiian shirt, the Swiss Army knife and their shoes. Then they entered the water.

Kimberly dived in. Did a much cleaner job of it than Connie had done – darting into the water with hardly a splash. I watched her slide along under the surface. She was long and sleek, black hair flowing down her back, the white seat of her bikini pants slipping through the gloom like a bright, winged fish. With the reflection on the water above her, she seemed to be gliding beneath a translucent landscape painting.

Billie, less athletic and more cautious than Kimberly, climbed down to the water and waded in. She made her way slowly, as if worried about what she might step on. When the water reached her thighs, she leaned forward, turning her body, and eased into a side-stroke.

Connie, still at the falls, was rubbing the wadded T-shirt up and down an arm.

At the moment, she was the most vulnerable of the three gals. Nobody appeared to be sneaking up on her, though. I looked around to make sure no one was sneaking up on *me*. Then I added my tomahawk, shirt, shoes and socks to the pile. I also emptied the pockets of my big old khaki shorts, since I planned to wear the shorts when I went in for my swim.

Then I climbed onto a good-sized boulder that stuck out into the lagoon, sat down on it and lay the ax across my lap.

It was sort of like being the lifeguard at a public swimming pool. All I needed was a whistle and some white goop on my nose.

I could've focused completely on any one of the gals. They were all worth watching, all exciting for one reason or another.

Connie, in spite of her attitude problems, had a slim, fine body and such a skimpy swimsuit that she almost seemed to be naked.

Billie, more appealing than her daughter from the get-go because she's so nice, also had the most fabulous body: wide shoulders, large breasts, a flat belly and full, firm buttocks.

Kimberly, gorgeous enough to be on the cover of a fashion magazine, was dark and slender and hard, an athlete and a warrior. Her body looked as if it had been carved from wood and polished to a high gloss.

Each was sort of a masterpiece, in her own way.

I could've spent all my time watching just one of them. All three were my responsibility, though. I had to force myself to turn my eyes from Kimberly to Billie, then force myself to abandon Billie for Connie. I could've lingered on Connie for an hour, but made myself look away to make sure Kimberly was all right. And on it went.

With me as the observer and guardian, each followed her own whims in the lagoon.

Kimberly swam the crawl. Back and forth, back and forth across the middle of the lagoon. Low and quick in the water, she swam for speed, not pleasure.

Billie luxuriated. She moved slowly, doing a languid sidestroke for a while, then rolling face down and breast-stroking, later flipping over and paddling along on her back. She never stayed long in any one position. She seemed to relish rolling over, sloshing. And I relished watching her. Which is putting it mildly.

Connie hardly did any swimming at all. She stayed in the waist-deep water below the falls, rubbing herself with the wadded ball of her T-shirt. Apparently, this was to relieve the itching of her mosquito bites. That's what I thought at first, anyway. Until, after a while, she took off her bikini. She put her back to me, *then* took it off and sidestepped away from the falls and tossed it onto a big, flat-topped block of stone. Keeping her back to me the whole time. And never letting the water level drop below her waist.

After ridding herself of the bikini, she returned to her place beneath the falls and resumed rubbing herself with the T-shirt. Always with her back toward me.

What a bitch.

I knew I should be keeping an eye on Billie and Kimberly, but Connie had me hooked. I couldn't look away from her.

She must've thought she would taunt me by keeping her back turned, so she would've been disappointed to find out how much the view of her bare back thrilled me: her delicate shoulders, the moving curves of her shoulder blades, the way she tapered to her slender waist, then flared out at the hips. Not to mention that I could see her buttocks, the crease of her ass, and the backs of her legs – all of which were perfectly visible below the surface of the water.

She also had me hooked because she kept rubbing her breasts with the wadded shirt. And rubbing her belly. And rubbing between her legs. It was very obvious *where* she was rubbing herself – she made sure of that.

What a charmer.

While she was at it, though, my time on guard duty ran out.

I hadn't been keeping track of time, hadn't even given much thought to going into the lagoon. But Billie had apparently noticed Connie's antics.

She rose to her feet in the waist-deep water just in front of me. At the sight of her, I almost immediately forgot about Connie.

Billie's short hair, clinging wet, looked golden. She was dripping and shiny and breathing hard. Her breasts, as brown as bread loaves, moved up and down, barely contained by her black bikini. From my position above her, I could see a strip of light at the bottom of her cleavage.

She said in a quiet voice, 'I'll take over. Jump on in and pay her a visit.'

'Who?'

'Who do you think? Connie.'

'You're kidding.'

'She needs a little visit.'

'Not from me.' A drop of water fell off the tip of Billie's

nose. It vanished into the crevice between her breasts.

'Go on,' she said.

'I'll go in the water,' I said, 'but I'm gonna stay away from her.'

Billie shrugged. 'Well, it's up to you.'

'It's up to me?'

'Sure.'

'In that case,' I said, 'why don't I stay here and keep *you* company? You're not as likely to dump on me. And you're better to look at.'

She smiled. 'Is that so?'

'Yeah. And you know it.'

'*She's* the naked one.'

'Big deal,' I said.

Which brought a quick, soft laugh from Billie. 'A big deal, all right. You'd better get over there, or she'll *really* hate you.'

'Oh, she really hates me *now*.'

'Only it'll be more so if you stick around with me while she's doing everything in her power to drive you nuts.'

'Think so?' I set the ax aside, and stood up. 'Hey, Connie!' I called.

She looked over her shoulder at me. She did not turn around. She scowled. 'What?' she snapped.

'Is that waterfall big enough to share with a friend?' I asked.

'Fuck you!' she yelled.

I smiled down at Billie, who still stood in the waist-deep water in front of my rock. She shook her head. 'You *like* to piss her off,' she said.

At the other side of the lagoon, Connie was now sidestepping toward the place where she'd left her bikini.

She didn't plan to take any chances.

173

'I'm *coming* for you!' I called.

'Just try it, and see what happens!'

Billie grinned. 'Clearly an invitation.'

'Should I take off my shorts?' I asked Billie.

'That might be pushing your luck.'

'I wouldn't, anyway.'

'I know. Now quit wasting time and jump in.'

Across the lagoon, Connie was bending over. On the nearby rock, her bikini had been replaced by the sodden wad of her T-shirt.

She straightened, pulling up her bikini pants. (To tell the truth, the addition of the thong didn't make much of a change to her rearview appearance.)

'What are you waiting for?' Billie asked.

'Nothing,' I said.

A few moments later, Connie finished putting on her top. Only then did she turn around. She gave me a smug little smile, and a wave.

Not wanting to look like a jerk in front of Billie, I refrained from giving Connie the finger. I just shook my head. Then I waited for Kimberly to swim by. When she was out of the way, I dived in.

The water felt great – cool enough to be refreshing, but not chilly. It slid against my skin like satin. No wonder Billie had rolled and wallowed in the luxury of it.

When I came up for air, I couldn't find the bottom with my feet. So I trod water, blinked my eyes clear and spotted Connie straight ahead. She was on her way back to the falls.

'Do you mind if I come over?' I asked.

'It's a free country,' she said, sounding like a six-year-old.

'You sure of that?' I asked. I started to paddle toward

her with a modified breast-stroke that kept my face above the water. 'I mean, what country *is* this?'

'Don't be such a wise-ass.' She turned her back to me and stepped into the gleaming curtain of water. Her body seemed to cut its own likeness into the falls. She spread out her arms and tipped back her head.

'I bet that feels good,' I said.

She didn't answer.

About six feet away from her, I was able to stand up. The water reached the middle of my chest.

'That was a nice show you put on,' I said.

She lowered her head and arms, then turned around. The turning around, I'm sure, was to give me a good look at her snotty smirk. 'Glad you liked it,' she said.

'Your mother was *very* impressed.' I hoped that Billie couldn't hear us. We were probably safe – at least if we kept our voices down.

'Good for Mom.'

'She's the one who sent me over here.'

'No kidding. Why did she do that?'

'She thinks you *want* me.'

Connie blew out a big puff of air. 'That's how much Mom knows. I want you like I want a hole in the head.'

'The feeling is mutual.'

'Yeah, right,' she said. 'Like you weren't *aching* for me to turn around.'

'Yeah, right,' I said. Two can play that game.

'Fuck off,' she said, and shut her eyes.

Instead, I stood there. If she'd really wanted me to fuck off, she wouldn't have shut her eyes.

Anyway, I couldn't just leave. Not with Billie watching. Besides, the view was too good.

The waterfall was splashing Connie behind her

shoulders, but missing her head completely. After a few seconds, she leaned backward. Her head made a hole in the liquid sheet. Water spilled down over her ears and face, splattered the tops of her shoulders, ran down her chest.

Maybe she really did want me to leave, and now she was trying to shut me out. Or maybe this was part of the game: her way of letting me look her over, unobserved – possibly to gain a full appreciation of what I would never be allowed to see naked, or touch.

Unless, as Billie might see it, this was Connie's bizarre method of trying to seduce me. Fat chance of that, in my opinion.

Since Connie had her eyes shut, I moved closer to her.

I watched how the water slid down her chest and the tops of her breasts. Her breasts were about half the size of Billie's. Each was partly covered by a clinging orange triangle, pulled taut by thin strips of elastic.

Her nipples were sticking out big and hard against the flimsy triangles.

Maybe Billie was right about her motives.

After all, Connie knew I hadn't gone away, knew I was standing close enough to touch her, knew I must be giving her a close-up inspection, knew what I was seeing and the effect it would have on me.

I suddenly wondered if she wanted me to touch her.

Maybe pull her against me and kiss her.

Prove to her that *she's* the one I care about – not Billie or Kimberly.

We *used* to kiss, back before we embarked on this excursion that somehow turned her into a monster. Kissing was *all* we used to do in the sex department. Hug and kiss, but no feelies below the waist, front or back, and her chest area was totally off limits. It got to be enormously frustrating and annoying.

I'd been all set to dump her, but then she'd invited me on the trip.

Now, she seemed to be waiting for me to *do* something.

Frankly, I didn't much want to kiss her.

You have to like somebody for that to be any good.

What I *wanted* to do was hook my fingertips under each of her breasts and give the elastic strip a big tug toward the sky so they'd leap out like they did by the campfire the night of the ambush.

With or without Billie watching, I couldn't pull a stunt like that.

Connie opened one eye slightly, to see what I was doing.

I said, 'See ya,' and started to back away.

Both eyes open, she took a small step forward and muttered, 'Yeah, go on and run away like a . . .'

'I'm just fucking off. Isn't that . . . ?'

'LOOK OUT!' Billie shouted.

The Hunt (Part Three)

As Billie shouted her warning, a rock the size of a coconut came straight down as if carried over the falls by the stream's current. I saw it an instant before it hit Connie. It struck the side of her head, then crashed onto her left shoulder.

The way her head jerked when the rock hit it, you'd think she'd been swatted by a baseball bat. Her hair flew. Her face shook. When the rock pounded her shoulder, she was knocked to the left. Half a second later, she dropped under water.

Billie and Kimberly were both yelling, but I'm not sure what they said.

I ducked and grabbed Connie under the armpits and hauled her up. She felt limp. Her head lolled sideways and water slopped out of her mouth. Her eyes were open, but rolled upward so that only the whites showed, mostly. Blood mixed in with the water running down the left side of her head.

I dragged her through the water, over to the place where she'd put her T-shirt. Then I thrust her up and backward, trying to sit her on the slab of rock. I couldn't get her high enough for that. But she started to slump backward, so I let go of her sides and hugged her around the thighs and hoisted her again. This time, I got her rump up there.

Kimberly arrived. 'Stay with her,' she gasped, then hurled herself out of the water and went scurrying up the rocks. She rushed for the top of the falls.

She didn't have a weapon.

I stood in the water, holding Connie by the legs so she wouldn't slide back into the lagoon. Before I had a chance to think about what to do next, Billie showed up. She brushed past me and climbed onto the slab. Kneeling by Connie's side, she leaned over and pinned her down by the shoulders. 'Got her,' she gasped.

Kimberly, near the top of the falls, raced out of sight.

I boosted myself onto the rock.

Kneeling on both sides of Connie, her mother and I lifted and dragged her until she was flat on her back. 'That's fine, that's fine,' Billie said. She sounded almost calm. 'You're gonna be fine, honey. Everything's fine.'

I wasn't so sure about that.

Connie was out cold, and bleeding from the side of her head. She was alive, though. Breathing. With so much bare skin showing, you couldn't miss all the parts of her that rose and fell. Here and there – at the side of her neck, just under her sternum – I could even see her skin throb with her heartbeat.

'What'll we do about her head?' I asked.

'There's her shirt.'

I was almost kneeling on it. I snatched up the sopping T-shirt, folded it into a big, thick pad, and pressed it against the bloody side of Connie's head.

She moaned and started to turn her head away.

Billie put a hand against the other side to hold it steady. 'That's all right, honey,' she said. She began crying softly. With relief, I guess, because Connie had moaned – a good sign. 'You'll be fine, honey.' She sniffed a couple of times. 'You had an accident, but you'll be fine.' With the hand that wasn't holding Connie's head, she wiped her eyes. She said to me, 'Do you think her shoulder's broken?'

The top of Connie's shoulder had a nasty abrasion. She looked as if she'd skidded across a sidewalk on it, rubbing it raw. The shoulder didn't appear to be swollen much, though, or knocked out of shape.

'I don't *think* it's broken,' I said. 'Not that I've had that much experience with broken bones.'

Connie squeezed her eyes tight and bared her teeth and moaned again.

Billie clutched the girl's good shoulder. 'You're gonna be fine, honey.' To me, she said, 'Thank God you were with her. She might've drowned.'

I shook my head. 'That rock was just there, all of a sudden,' I said. 'I didn't have time to *do* anything about it. If I could've pushed her out of the way, or something . . . I just stood there like a jerk.'

'You were great,' Billie said. 'It happened too fast, that's all.'

'Did it just *fall*, or what?' I asked her. 'Did you see?'

'It rolled off the edge of the falls.'

'By itself?' I asked.

'Not hardly. I don't think so, anyway. I think somebody threw it – or rolled it. Somebody up at the top of the falls, but far enough back to stay out of sight.'

'Wesley or Thelma.'

'I should think so.'

'How is she?' At the sound of Kimberly's voice, I raised my head and saw her trotting down the slope.

'She's banged up pretty good,' I said. 'She's coming around, though.'

'She'll be fine,' Billie said.

'What'd you find up there?' I asked.

'Nothing.' Kimberly squatted down for a better look at Connie, and her bare arm rubbed against mine. 'How are you doing, Con?'

The answer she got was a groan of pain.

'She's so thick-headed,' Kimberly said, 'the rock probably didn't even dent her.'

Connie murmured, 'Fuck you.'

With that, I'm sure we all figured Connie was well on her way to recovery.

'You didn't find *anything* up there?' Billie asked.

Kimberly shook her head. 'I didn't do much searching, though. Just took a quick look around, then tried to see if I could find any footprints. Nothing. I wanted to get back and see how Connie was doing. And I didn't want to get myself jumped. There must be about a million hiding places up there. I didn't have anyone to watch my back, so it didn't seem smart to hang around.'

'I could go up with you,' I offered. 'The two of us could do a search.'

'Not gonna leave Billie and Con. Anyway, all our weapons are over there.' She nodded toward the other side of the lagoon. 'We've taken enough casualties for one day. What we've gotta do now is get ourselves back to the beach.'

Which is what we did.

We waited a few minutes for Connie to recover some more. Then we helped her sit up. We needed a way to keep the bandage (her folded T-shirt) in place against the side of her head, so Billie volunteered my belt. While I held the bandage against the wound, Kimberly wrapped the belt around Connie's head – making passes over the top and under the chin, then fastening the buckle.

Then we lowered Connie into the water. We floated her across the lagoon on her back, and helped her out on the other side.

I was only half a help; my belt being otherwise occupied, I needed one hand to keep my shorts from falling off.

We found our stuff where we'd left it. I removed one of the tomahawks from its sling, and used the rope as a belt for my shorts. Then I refilled my pockets. (We hadn't touched the food yet, but nobody wanted any.)

It was agreed that Billie and I would work together on helping Connie back to camp, and Kimberly would take care of whatever weapons we couldn't manage. I put on my pink shirt, and stuck a tomahawk down the side of my rope belt.

Kimberly ended up in her Hawaiian shirt, with her chest crossed by rope slings, a tomahawk at each hip, her Swiss Army knife tucked down the front of her bikini pants, four spears hugged against her side with her left arm, and the ax in her right hand.

I took one side of Connie; Billie took the other. We held her by the arms.

With Kimberly in the lead, we started downstream.

Connie whimpered and groaned and sometimes cried. With Billie and I holding her steady, though, she was able to stay on her feet and support her own weight, most of the time. Every now and then, she sagged and we had to struggle to keep her from going down.

We stuck to the stream; it was easier going than the jungle, and seemed like the most direct route back to the beach.

Sometimes, the stream was too narrow for the three of us to walk side by side. We always managed to keep Connie up, through places like that.

We only had real trouble once. That happened when we were making our way down a fairly easy slope. We would've been fine, but some damn bird suddenly flapped up out of nowhere and crossed right in front of us. It startled the hell out of us. Billie yelped. All three of us, I think, flinched and jumped. But then Billie had a foot slip out from under her. We tried to hold each other up, but we all fell down, splashing in the shallow water and landing on the rocks of the stream bed.

Only Kimberly, a few strides ahead of us, got away unscathed.

The rest of us weren't scathed in any major way – not from that. It just added several new sore places to each of us.

Soon after that stupid fall, we hobbled out of the jungle and onto the clear, bright sand of our beach.

The big hunt was over.

We hadn't found our prey, but we'd been preyed upon.

Connie is mighty damn lucky to be alive.

All that was yesterday.

Andrew's lighter, in my pocket at the time of our fall into the stream, got soaked and stopped working. This had us very worried. A couple of hours in the sunlight yesterday afternoon dried it out, though, so we were able to get our campfire going again.

Connie is doing fairly well. The gash on the side of her head isn't large. It bled a lot for a while, then clotted and hasn't reopened. She's got quite a lump there, under her hair. She complains of fierce headaches and shoulder pains, but nothing serious has happened so far. I mean, she hasn't fainted or had dizzy spells or blurred vision.

We think she'll probably make a full recovery.

Agony, by the way, has improved her personality; she's in too much pain most of the time to be a bitch.

Also, she seems to be busy feeling sorry for herself and wanting everyone's sympathy. At least when she's awake.

She didn't have to do any guard duty last night. Kimberly, Billie and I took turns, with me taking the morning shift so I could work on my journal here.

Been writing like a madman, ever since dawn.

A while ago, Kimberly woke up. She came over to the fire and we said 'Good morning' to each other. She asked how the journal's coming along. I said, 'Fine. I'm just about caught up.'

'I hope you're making it clear that Wesley's behind all this,' she said. 'Wesley Duncan Beaverton the third. So there won't be any doubt about who murdered Keith and Dad.'

'It's all here,' I said.

'And he's probably the one who dropped that rock on Connie yesterday.'

'Yeah.'

'You got that?'

'Sure do.'

'Good.' She shook her head. 'I'd sure hate for him to get away with this. If he ends up killing all of us, maybe that diary of yours'll be the only way anybody ever finds out the truth.'

'My God, I hope it doesn't come to that.'

'It probably won't,' Kimberly said. 'Anyway, I'm going in for a swim. Can you hold down the fort for another ten or fifteen minutes?'

'Sure.'

So then she jogged down to the shore and charged into the water.

She came out of it a few minutes ago. When she first came out, she did some push-ups on the beach. Then sit-ups, knee-bends, etc. She just now walked over for the ax. I guess she plans to swing it around, the way she did yesterday. I'm going to watch. So long for now.

Thelma's Story

And who should wander out of the jungle this afternoon but Thelma?

At the time she put in her appearance, nobody was actually keeping watch.

Billie and Kimberly were out in the water, trying to spear some fish for supper. Kimberly was going after them with Connie's special spear, while Billie stood by with the pot. They'd just finished nailing their second fish when Thelma came toward our campsite.

Connie was asleep under one of the shelters. We'd let her drink a few slugs of bourbon after lunch to ease her aches and pains. It must've helped considerably, because she zonked out. She'd been snoozing for a couple of hours by the time Thelma showed up.

I was stretched out on my back beneath the leafy roof of the other sun shelter, my head propped up by a mound of sand, my paperback held above my face with both hands. I'd been reading, watching Kimberly and Billie, reading a bit more . . .

Thelma's shout of 'Help!' startled me so much that I flinched and the book jumped out of my hands.

I flipped over onto my belly.

The paperback had landed in the sand about four feet away.

Thelma was about fifty feet away, walking slowly toward me. More of a stagger than a walk, actually. Small, stiff steps. She was bent over a little, as if cramped. Her arms hardly moved at all. She carried herself like someone who'd recently fallen down the cellar stairs, or something.

She had some pretty good damage to her face, including a shiner and a fat lip.

One sleeve was missing entirely from her blouse, leaving her right arm bare to the shoulder. The blouse was filthy, spotted with blood, and untucked so it hung down in front of her shorts.

Even though her blouse was buttoned up, I saw right away that she'd lost her bra. You couldn't miss it. She has *large* breasts. Un-leashed, they swayed and bounced, making the front of her blouse leap around as if she had a couple of wild animals trapped inside.

One bare knee had an abrasion similar to the one on Connie's shoulder.

Her hands were empty.

There was no sign of Wesley. I figured he might be nearby, though, using Thelma as a diversion while he snuck in.

Also, Thelma had given us a taste of how dangerous she could be *without* any help from Wesley.

I reached out and grabbed the ax. Hanging on to it, I crawled out from under the shelter and stood up.

She raised an open hand.

I twisted around. Kimberly and Billie were still busy fishing. Apparently, they hadn't heard the shout.

'Hey!' I yelled. 'Billie! Kimberly!'

Their heads turned. Because of the slope of the beach,

I doubted that they could see Thelma. They could see me, though. I gestured for them to come out, and added, 'Hurry! Thelma's here!'

I looked over at Connie. She was curled on her right side, the same as before, to keep the pressure off her wounds. The shouting must've woken her up. Her eyes were open, watching me.

'Thelma's here,' I told her, even though I was repeating myself.

She didn't say anything. She barely moved. But her upper lip twitched slightly.

Kimberly and Billie were sloshing toward shore.

For at least a while, it would be just Thelma and me. And Wesley, if he was trying to pull off a sneak attack.

Thelma was still coming.

'Stop,' I said. 'Don't take another step.'

She stopped.

'Put both your hands up. Put 'em on top of your head.'

She obeyed. Her breasts lifted. So did her entire blouse, a little bit.

I thought about frisking her.

Not just so I could feel her up, either: the way her blouse hung down, big and loose, there was plenty of room for hiding weapons.

The other two gals would be here soon, though, so I gave up the idea of checking her.

'Do you have any weapons?' I asked.

'No,' she muttered. She had a dull, sullen look in her eyes. 'I didn't come here to cause any . . .'

'Thelma!' Kimberly blurted. I looked back and saw her break into a run. Billie hurried after her. Over at her shelter, Connie didn't want to miss out. She was getting to her hands and knees.

Kimberly raced past me, then slowed, then stopped a few strides from her sister.

Thelma started to lower her hands.

'Don't.' Kimberly jabbed out with the spear, prodding her in the ribs.

'Ow!'

'Stay put.' She held the spear in both hands, its point an inch or so away from Thelma's chest.

Billie arrived. Both of us moved in and stood with Kimberly.

'Can I put my hands down, now?' Thelma asked.

'No. Don't move. Billie, you wanta search her?'

With a nod, Billie stepped forward. She went behind Thelma. Using both hands, she started at the armpits and worked her way down Thelma's sides.

'I haven't got anything.'

'We'll see,' Kimberly said.

Billie patted the pockets of Thelma's baggy shorts. After checking around the waist, her hands moved up Thelma's front. She stayed outside the blouse, but pushed in the fabric until she met flesh. She rubbed up and down, lifted and shoved Thelma's breasts this way and that as she checked underneath and between them.

Thelma grimaced while this went on. She also winced a lot, as if she were being hurt.

'Does *he* have to watch this?' Thelma wanted to know.

Meaning me.

'Make him look the other way.'

'Shut up,' Kimberly told her.

Squatting, Billie squeezed Thelma's rump, patted the legs of her shorts, and shoved a hand up between her legs. When the hand jammed against her crotch, Thelma gasped and went to her tiptoes.

'Nothing,' Billie announced.

'Okay, you can put your arms down.'

She lowered her arms.

Billie came around to the front, and stood beside me. A second later, Connie joined us. This was the first time since the attack yesterday that she'd been up and walking without any help. But she seemed to be on the verge of falling over. She leaned against her mother.

We all stared at Thelma.

Her chin was trembling. She sniffed. 'I . . . I know you're all mad at me. You have a right to be, I guess. I shouldn't have . . .'

'Cut the shit,' Kimberly said. 'Where's Wesley?'

She struggled to speak. When her voice came out, it sounded so high it was almost a squeak. 'Dead.'

'What?'

'Dead!' she blurted. 'He's dead!'

'Yeah, right,' Connie muttered.

'He is!'

'When did he die?' Kimberly asked.

'Yesterday.'

'When yesterday?'

'Morning.'

'Who did that to Connie at the falls?' Billie asked.

Thelma blinked and shook her head.

'Did you do it?'

'Do what?'

'Throw that damn rock over the falls?'

'No! We . . . We weren't at any falls.'

'Where were you?' I asked.

'His place. Wesley has this . . . secret place. It's past the falls. It's nowhere near the falls.'

Billie glared at her. 'If you didn't throw the rock, who did?'

'I don't know!'

'Did Wesley throw it?' I asked.

Before Thelma could answer, Kimberly said, 'He was dead by then, remember?'

'That's right,' I said.

'Which means *you* did it,' Kimberly said, and gave Thelma another quick poke with the spear.

'Ouch! Don't!' She grabbed the hurt place.

'*You* did it,' Kimberly said, and jabbed the back of her hand. The spear put a pale dent in it.

'Stop that!'

'Tell the truth.'

'Wesley made me!'

'What do you mean, he made you? He was already dead.'

'No. He wasn't. We were there. We were watching you all. We were up there above the falls, and spying on you, and he wanted to, you know, kill *him*.' She nodded at me.

'Me?' I asked.

'Yeah, you. I told him we shouldn't. I didn't want anybody else getting killed, but Wesley said he'd kill *me* if I didn't do it. What could I do? He would've *killed* me. So I went and snuck down to the stream and did it.' She glanced at Connie. 'It wasn't supposed to hit you. It was supposed to hit *him*.'

'Stupid bitch,' Connie muttered.

'I'm sorry. What can I say? I couldn't see what I was doing. Just a quick little peek or two. Somebody would've seen me up there watching, so I just had to throw it blind, and it got you by mistake.'

'Sure,' Connie said.

'It's the truth! If you think I hurt you on purpose . . . I *never* would've done it on purpose. Look what Wesley *did* to me!' She raised both hands, open fingers trembling toward her face. 'He beat me. Look how he beat me! All because I hit *you* instead of that *boy!*'

That boy.

Nice.

'He didn't want *you* getting hurt. And he wanted *him* getting killed – so when I hit you instead, he blamed me for screwing up everything. He . . . he beat me and . . .'

'Pretty damn active for a dead guy,' Kimberly said.

'He wasn't dead then.'

'Ah. So you were lying when you said he died yesterday morning.'

'It was after you all left the lagoon and everything.'

'He beat you up, and *then* he died.'

'Must've taken a lot out of him,' I said.

Glaring at me, she blurted, '*I* killed him!'

The rest of us went silent. I think we were stunned.

'What did you all think, he died from those old spear wounds? They were nothing. He was getting *over* them. *I'm* the one who killed him. You have *me* to thank for it, and nobody else.'

Kimberly looked her in the eyes and said, 'I don't believe you.'

Thelma's mouth dropped open.

'You wouldn't harm a hair on that asshole's head. He can do no wrong, as far as you're concerned. He's your god.'

'He hurt me!' she blurted. 'After I hit Connie with the rock, look what he did to me.' She gestured to her battered face again. 'And *this!*' She fumbled with the top button of her blouse, then stopped and said, 'He has to turn around.'

Kimberly gave me a nod.

I turned my back to Thelma.

A few seconds passed. Then she said, 'See? See what he did?'

Kimberly murmured, 'Jesus.'

I took a look over my shoulder.

Thelma's head was down. She had her blouse off.

Her huge breasts were striped with scratches, smeared with livid bruises. Some of the bruises were shaped like fingers; others were crescents. From the look of her breasts, she'd been lashed by a switch, slapped around with open hands, and bitten.

Sobbing, still not raising her head and noticing me, she turned around. 'And *this*!' Her back didn't look as if anyone had slapped or bit it – just whaled the crap out of it with a switch. Her skin was streaked with threads of dry blood. She must've taken fifty lashes back there.

'And that isn't *all*!' she blurted. Keeping her back to us, she started to put her blouse on. 'I'm not gonna show . . . not gonna pull my shorts down . . .'

I took that as my cue to turn away.

'But he . . . he made me strip . . . take off everything . . . and then he beat me and beat me . . . all because I dropped that rock on *Connie* by accident . . . He didn't want her damaged. But oh, God, he was sure the hell happy to damage *me*. And he got all turned on, beating me, so then he . . . he did other things to me.'

'He raped you?' Kimberly asked. She sounded upset.

'That was . . . yeah, and worse, too.'

I looked over my shoulder again. Thelma had her blouse on, and was trying to fasten its buttons. Her eyes were red and wet, her nose was runny and her hands trembled so much that she was having real trouble with the buttons. She saw me watching, but didn't complain about it, so I went on and turned around.

'What else did he do to you?' Kimberly asked her.

'No. I can't . . . I won't tell. It's too awful. But at least . . . It wore him out. That's the good part. When he was done, he was so tired he couldn't stay awake. He fell asleep and that's when I killed him. I bashed his head in. There was a rock nearby and I grabbed it and I *bashed* his head in.' One of her hands fluttered away from her blouse. It held an imaginary rock. She raised it and hammered it down. '*Bashed* him till there was nothing left of his head but a big bloody pile of *crap!*'

Kimberly shoved her spear into the sand. She opened her arms and Thelma staggered into them. They hugged each other and Thelma bawled her head off.

Thelma On The Hot Seat

After Thelma finished her story and finally got done crying her eyes out in Kimberly's arms, we went over to the shelter where I'd been reading, and sat down on the sand. We couldn't all be in the shade, but Billie and Kimberly prefer the sun, anyway. Thelma, Connie and I got to be under the roof.

Thelma crossed her legs the best she could, and wiped her eyes. She sniffled. Then she said, 'I've just gotta tell you all how sorry I am. I just went crazy the other night.' Meeting Kimberly's gaze, she said, 'I should've let you kill him, right then and there.'

'That's for sure,' Kimberly said.

'I'm sorry.'

'I'll just bet,' Connie muttered.

'I *am*.' She glanced at the rest of us. 'Maybe I deserve getting punished for what I did. I was wrong, and stupid, and I hurt *all* of you.'

'Fucking right you did,' Connie said.

'I know, I know. But . . . I paid for it, didn't I? Wesley saw to that. He hurt me a lot worse than all of you could ever come *close* to. And I . . . even though I rescued him, *I'm* the one who bashed his brains in. So I think . . . I think I paid for my mistakes.'

'You're very forgiving of yourself,' Billie told her, perfectly calm. 'You nearly killed my daughter. You *did* mess her up badly. God only knows how long she'll be in pain from that stunt you pulled.'

'I'm sorry,' Thelma muttered.

'Sorry,' Connie said. 'Big deal.'

'What am I *supposed* to do?'

'We'll figure out something,' Kimberly told her. 'We can't just forget what you did. My God, you not only attacked us and injured us, you *betrayed* us. You went over to the enemy. He's the guy who killed Dad and Keith, and you *helped* him. You're a traitor to your own family.'

Thelma started crying again.

'We can never trust you,' Kimberly went on. 'Never.'

'But . . . But I made things right. I killed him.'

'Did you?' Kimberly asked.

'Did I what?'

'Kill him.'

'Yes!' She sobbed a couple of times. 'What do you think, I'm *lying*? I made it all up?'

'It's crossed my mind.'

'You . . . you saw what he did to me!'

'That's no proof you killed him.'

'What kind of . . . proof do you need? Do you wanta see his body?'

'Until I *do* see his body,' Kimberly said, 'I'm assuming he's alive.'

'This is the same guy,' I pointed out, 'who tried to make us think he'd blown himself up with the yacht.'

'It smells like a trick to me,' Billie said. 'I don't think she killed him.'

'She didn't,' Connie said. 'No way.'

Thelma wiped her eyes and uncrossed her legs. 'Let's

go,' she said. 'I'm ready.' She sniffed. 'I'll take you there now, and you can see for yourselves. You'll . . . you'll see I'm not a liar.'

'Not a liar?' Kimberly curved a corner of her mouth. 'Give me a break. You lie like a rug. Do you think I've got amnesia? I grew up with you. My Christ, you lied every chance you got – even when you didn't have any *reason* to lie.'

'You're full of it,' Thelma said.

'The question isn't whether you're a liar, the question is whether you're lying about Wesley being dead. And the consensus is, yes.'

'Well, you'll just *see*.' She scooted backward to get out from under the shelter. 'Let's go. Come on. You'll see.'

'No hurry,' Kimberly told her.

'Well, maybe *I'm* in a hurry.' No longer crying, she now seemed to be in a huff. 'Nobody's gonna believe me, and you're all gonna keep on treating me like some kind of a leper till this is settled.'

'Nobody's treating you like a leper,' Kimberly said.

'You're not a leper,' Billie said.

'You're a traitor,' Connie said.

'That's exactly right,' Kimberly said. 'A traitor. But we're giving you the benefit of the doubt because you're my sister.'

'What benefit of the doubt?'

Kimberly paused a moment, then said, 'We probably *ought* to execute you.'

'What!'

'Kill you. The way I see it, you committed a capital offense when you helped him escape from our ambush. If you weren't my sister – and Dad's daughter – I would've probably killed you by now.'

Thelma suddenly looked as if she might throw up. 'You're kidding,' she murmured.

'Do you think so?'

Connie smirked and said, '*I* don't think she's kidding.'

'We're being easy on you,' Kimberly went on. 'We're giving you a second chance. But you'd better not be lying about Wesley.'

'He's dead and I killed him! I'm not lying about that! If you don't believe me, let's go right now!'

'Maybe tomorrow,' Kimberly said.

Which took us all by surprise.

'Or the day after tomorrow,' she added.

We all stared at her.

'Shouldn't we get it over with?' I asked. 'I mean, it'll be really nice to know for sure. If he *is* dead, we won't have to worry about him sneaking up on us . . .'

'*I'd* sure like to know,' Billie said.

Thelma brightened. She obviously had the impression we were on her side. 'See?' she said. 'They're for going now.'

'We haven't heard from Connie yet,' Kimberly said.

Connie grimaced. 'I'm not going anywhere. Are you kidding me?'

'Is it okay if we leave you here?'

'Alone? I can't stay here alone. This whole deal might be a trick. Maybe the minute you're gone, Wesley comes out and *gets* me.'

'Don't worry,' Billie told her. 'We won't leave you by yourself.'

'I'm *not* going with you looking for his body. I can't. I'm too . . . I feel like shit.' She fixed her eyes on Thelma. 'Thanks to you, you stupid fuck.'

'I'm sorry.'

'Sorry. Can't *tell* you how much "sorry" helps the throbbing *pains* in my head and neck and shoulder and arm and . . . I'm one big fucking pain from head to toe, thanks to you. So don't give me "sorry." Piss on you.'

Kimberly held up a hand. 'We won't make you come with us,' she said. 'Not in your condition. And it'd be stupid to leave your mom or Rupert behind to protect you. We don't want to be splitting up our forces like that. What I suggest is that we stay put. We wait a day or two before we go out and . . .'

'A day or two!' Thelma blurted. 'That's ridiculous!'

Kimberly raised her eyebrows. 'He isn't going to walk away, is he?'

'No! Of course not!'

'If you hadn't busted up Connie with that rock, we could go right now.'

Thelma scowled.

'So we'll wait until Connie can travel?' Billie asked.

'Yep.'

Billie smiled. 'That sounds like a pretty good idea.'

'Thanks.'

Connie, an oddly sly smile on her face, added, 'It'll give Wesley time to die.'

We all looked at her.

'We don't really believe she killed him,' Connie explained, 'but we *know* he's badly hurt. Maybe he's *not* getting better. Maybe he's getting weaker all the time, and has some infections setting in. I mean, that could happen to me, you know? Which is what made me think of it.'

'It won't happen to you,' Billie told her. 'You're going to be fine.'

'Yeah, I guess. I'm not too worried. But I have all you

guys sort of taking care of me. Wesley doesn't have anyone. We've got Thelma, so she isn't there to help him. Long as we've got her, he's on his own. If we give him enough time, maybe he'll just waste away and die without us ever having to touch him again.'

'That's right,' Kimberly said. 'But even if he isn't wasting away, it might screw him up if we don't come looking for him right away.'

'He'll think something went wrong,' I added.

Billie grinned. 'Something *did* go wrong.'

'You're all crazy,' Thelma said. 'He's dead.'

'He'd better be,' Kimberly said. 'That's another thing about our waiting period – it'll give you time to reconsider. Maybe you'll want to change your story.'

'There's nothing to change.'

'You'd better think about that. If you *didn't* kill him, you'd better let us know before we pay a visit to his body. If we get there and find out you've led us into a trap, there's gonna be hell to pay.'

'I'm not lying.'

'In the meantime, we can't exactly treat you like one of the gang. Go get some rope, Rupert, would you?'

'From the tomahawks?'

'No, we'll need to keep using those. Bring over what's left of the hanging rope.'

'What're you gonna do?' Thelma asked.

I'd started to scoot out from under the shelter, but I didn't want to miss anything, so I stopped.

'Tie you up,' Kimberly answered.

'Tie me *up*?' Thelma sounded shocked.

In a calm voice, Billie explained, 'You're his accomplice. What do you expect?'

'I *killed* him.'

'Yeah, right,' Connie said.

'Rupert,' Kimberly said. 'The rope?'

'Oh. Okay.' I went ahead and left them. I ran across the sand, found the remaining length of rope among the supplies, snatched it up and hurried back toward the shelter.

Approaching it, I heard Thelma complaining, '. . . stayed out in the jungle by myself, if I'd known you were going to treat me like a criminal.'

'Maybe so,' Kimberly said.

'You should've,' Connie said.

'You want to do the honors?' Kimberly asked me.

'Sure.' I ducked under the roof.

'Go ahead and tie her hands in front, for now. We'll see how it goes. If she gives us any trouble at all, we'll put 'em behind her. Do you hear that, Thelma? You don't want them behind your back, do you?'

'No.'

'Then you'd better cooperate.'

I knelt in front of Thelma. She glowered at me and held out her hands. I bound them together, wrapping the rope around her wrists, going in and out between them in a figure-eight pattern. I made it tight enough to keep her secure, but tried to avoid cutting off her circulation.

When I was done, a lot of rope was left over.

I picked up the hanging tail. 'What about this? Should we cut it off? I could tie it around her feet, or . . .'

'Maybe just let it hang,' Billie suggested. 'That way, we'll have something to grab hold of if she tries to run.'

'A leash for the bitch,' Connie said.

'You're all just horrible,' Thelma said. 'How can you do this to me? I know I made a little mistake, but . . . I'm all beat up. It isn't fair. You saw what he did to me. How

201

can you tie me up? I saved you. I saved you all from Wesley, and . . . you're treating me this way. You're horrible.'

'Why don't we put a gag on her?' Connie suggested.

'No!'

'Then do yourself a favor,' Kimberly said, 'and stop whining.'

Thelma shut her mouth and turned its corners down.

Soon after that, we broke up. Thelma wanted to lie down, so Kimberly, Billie and I led her over to her sleeping place. We helped lower her onto the bed of rags. She curled on her side. With her tied hands up close to her chin, she looked like she was about to start praying. But then she plucked up the end of a beach towel – one of the several towels we'd brought along on the picnic – and covered her face with it.

'Don't get up without asking,' Kimberly told her.

'Go away and leave me alone,' Thelma said through the towel.

Kimberly crouched beside her. 'Look,' she said, 'cut the attitude. We're being damn nice to you, under the circumstances.'

'Like fun you are. Am I supposed to be grateful . . . ?'

With the flat of her open hand, Kimberly smacked her on the side of the head.

Thelma let out a startled yelp.

In a slow, steady voice that wasn't like anything I'd ever heard from her before, Kimberly said, 'You brought Wesley into our lives, sister. We warned you about him. You wouldn't listen. You thought he was *so* damn wonderful. Now, my husband is dead. Dad is dead. It's all because of Wesley – and Wesley is because of you. Do you get it? *You* did this to us! *You!*'

She gave Thelma's head another slap.

Billie put a hand on Kimberly's shoulder.

Kimberly raised her head. Her eyes were brimming with tears. As she looked up at Billie, she blinked. Tears spilled out and trickled down her face.

It's amazing to see Kimberly cry. She is so tough, most of the time. But when she weeps, it's like watching a heartbroken kid trying to act brave.

I choked up, myself, at the sight of her tears.

It made me remember Keith's funeral, and how I'd sung 'Danny Boy' like some sort of idiot, and how she had hugged me afterward.

The best hug I've ever had. All sloppy and sentimental, but coming from the most beautiful woman I've ever known – not to mention that Keith's shirt was open so I could feel all that bare skin against me, and the soft push of her breasts through her bikini.

I wonder if I'll ever get another hug like that from her.

Who knows? There's always hope, I guess.

I'd really like a lot more than a hug. I'd like her to fall madly in love with me, and seduce me.

Fat chance of that happening. I'm not much of a prize. Gals who look like Kimberly don't give guys like me a second glance.

Though, who knows? As long as we're marooned on this island, anything is possible. I am, after all, the only living male. (If you don't count Wesley.) Maybe, eventually, all three of the gals will get after me.

Who am I kidding?

Anyway, it's nice to imagine. Except that the fun of imagining such things has sharp edges that hurt.

With me as the only guy on the island, these gals would probably turn to celibacy or lesbianism before they'd throw themselves at my feet. That's the kind of luck I have with babes.

What got me started off on this tangent, anyway?

Kimberly crying.

I would've liked to kiss the tears off her eyes.

Licked them off her cheeks.

Licked her *everywhere*.

I just stood there watching. She'd hardly begun to weep before she stood up, brushed the sand off her knees, and wiped her eyes. 'Keep an eye on her, Rupe,' she told me.

'I will.'

Billie still had the hand on her shoulder.

Together, they turned away and headed for the water. They went back to spear-fishing. Connie had already returned to her shelter, and was lying down. I went to mine, took out my journal, and got down to business.

I started to write about Thelma coming out of the jungle.

But I was facing the inlet, which put Thelma behind my back. So I changed positions, turning sideways. Now, I've got Thelma off to my left, Kimberly and Billie in the water to my right, and Connie straight in front of me.

Connie is lying on her side, like before.

Facing me.

She is probably suspicious of the fact that I turned myself in her direction. It would never occur to her that I did it in order to keep Thelma in sight. She is sure to think I'm ogling her.

Every so often, she has opened her eyes and sort of gazed across the sand at me.

She hasn't said anything, though.

No 'What're *you* looking at!' No 'Fuck off!'

Getting beaned by Thelma's rock really took the starch out of her.

I ought to give Thelma my thanks.

Anyway, I'm all caught up, now.

Day Seven
———————————

My Visitor

With Connie out of commission and Thelma as our prisoner, the watch duty last night was being divided among me, Billie and Kimberly. Last night, they gave me first watch.

I stayed by the fire. After everyone else went to bed, I had nothing to do except sit there, sometimes toss in some driftwood, and keep watch.

I sat with my back to the inlet. That way, nobody would be able to come out of the jungle and sneak up on the gals without me spotting him.

I kept wondering if Wesley was really dead.

He had sure done a number on Thelma, no question about that. An awfully good reason to kill a guy, even if you weren't especially bothered by the fact that he had murdered your own father.

I sure hoped she'd done it. If Wesley was dead, I could stop trying to spot him sneaking through the dark toward where the gals were asleep. I could stop glancing over my shoulder every few minutes to make sure he wasn't creeping toward my back.

I kept wishing we'd gone ahead and checked on the body, right after Thelma came in and told us about it.

Then we'd know by now, one way or the other.

On the other hand, some of us might be dead right now. Especially me.

I'd always figured I was next on the list. It stood to reason, considering that Wesley had killed off both the other males almost as soon as we got to the island. But now we'd had it confirmed by Thelma. Over at the falls, Wesley had given her orders to nail *me* with that rock.

Sitting there by the fire, though, I wasn't especially worried about myself. The danger to me didn't seem as important as my duty to watch over and protect the women. I felt very protective of them.

While they were asleep and I was on guard, they were my flock.

I occupied my mind, now and then, with some gallant fantasies about rushing to their rescue. With other fantasies about them, too. I won't get into that stuff.

Anyway, about an hour into my watch, Thelma came over.

When I first saw her getting up, I thought she might be making an escape attempt. Instead of running for the jungle, though, she stepped cautiously away from the sleeping area, and walked toward me. The leftover rope hung between her legs and dragged behind her.

None of the others stirred. Which convinced me that they were asleep. Kimberly would've raised holy hell if she'd seen Thelma up and around. The same goes for Billie and Connie.

Looking back on it, that's what *I* should've done — raised holy hell.

It's what I *almost* did.

My first inclination, when I realized none of the others would be putting a quick end to the situation, was to shout for Thelma to halt.

A shout would bring the whole gang running. (Except maybe Connie.)

But I kept quiet.

No need to wake everybody up. I can handle this on my own.

That's what I told myself.

It wasn't the whole reason I didn't shout, though. There was also the fact that I was curious. What did Thelma have in mind? Why was she coming to me? I wanted to find out.

As she walked closer, I grabbed the ax, stood up, and stepped around the fire so it wouldn't be in the way if I needed to get at her. I held the ax in both hands, at waist level, to let her see that I meant business but didn't have any immediate plan to chop her.

Neither of us said anything until she was just a few paces away. Then she stopped and said, 'I couldn't sleep. I mean, I *was* asleep, but I woke up a while ago and . . . I couldn't get comfortable.' She raised her bound hands. 'I don't guess you'll untie me?'

'No, I can't.'

She shrugged and winced a bit. 'I didn't think so. No harm in asking, though. *You* oughta try to sleep with your hands tied together like this.'

'Did you try sleeping on your back?' I asked.

'On *my* back? Have you seen my back? No, I guess you haven't.'

I didn't correct her.

'Wesley whipped me. My back is so sore and tender . . . *everything* is. He really hurt me, Rupert. He hurt me *everywhere*. There *is* no comfortable position to lie in. It's a wonder I was able to fall asleep at all.'

'I'm sorry about that,' I said.

'It's not your fault. I'm the one that was fool enough to marry him.'

I said, 'Well . . .'

'Anyway, that's all over and done with, now. The thing is, would you mind a whole lot if I just stayed here for a little while? I won't cause any trouble, I promise. I just *can't* go back there and lie down. All I do is toss and turn . . . it's just so miserable. Can I stay with you? Please?'

A. She *had* to be in a lot of physical discomfort. She wasn't lying about that.

B. What could she do to me? Her hands were tied and I had the ax.

C. I could always shout if she tried to pull a stunt.

D. I was *still* curious. Did she have some sort of secret reason for coming over? Did she have a trick up her sleeve? Just exactly what *would* happen if I let her stay? Maybe something interesting, or even exciting.

Not to mention that I really wanted to ask her about a few things.

'Okay,' I said. 'You can stay, but just for a while.'

'Thanks, Rupert.' She sounded sincere. 'You're sure a life-saver.'

'One condition, though,' I told her.

Some of her friendliness suddenly evaporated. 'What's that?'

'You have to answer me, no matter what I ask you.'

She blew out some air. 'Oh, forget it. I thought you were different from them. You're just like them, aren't you? For once, I thought somebody was being nice to me around here.'

'All I want to do is find out a few things. What's the big deal?'

She took a deep breath and used it to form a long, annoyed sigh. 'Everybody wants to give me the third degree.'

'Maybe you'd better just go back to bed,' I said.

'No, no, no. I'll talk. Whatever you want. Lord knows, why should you be any different from the bitches? What do you want to know?'

'Let's sit down,' I said.

I went back to my place at the other side of the fire, sat down, crossed my legs and rested the ax across my thighs. I told Thelma where to sit: in front of me but over to my left, facing the fire. That way, we didn't have the fire between us. Also, it would be easy to give her a nudge with the head of the ax, if she caused trouble.

'For starters,' I said, 'did Wesley tell you why he did all this?'

'Did what?'

'Blew up the boat, marooned us here, killed . . .'

'He *didn't* blow up the boat. I asked him all about that. What happened is, he smelled gas and jumped overboard just in the nick of time. He was almost killed. He no sooner got off the boat than it blew sky-high.'

'That's what he told you?'

'Yes.'

'And you believed him?'

'Why shouldn't I?'

I could only think of about a *million* reasons. 'If that's what happened,' I said, 'then how come he didn't swim in to the beach? We were all there. He knew we were there. He obviously wanted us to think he'd been blown up.'

'Well, that was the whole idea.'

'What? What are you talking about?'

'He *had* to disappear. He was afraid he'd get all the blame for the explosion. Which is *just* what happened. You heard my dad. It was all Wesley's fault.'

'And that's why Wesley pulled his vanishing act?'

'Sure. Lord only knows what you all would've done to him.'

'Yeah, Lord only knows — somebody might've called him an idiot.'

'You don't know anything.'

'Was he afraid Andrew might make him walk the plank? Or keel-haul him? Whip out the cat-o'-nine-tails?'

'There's no telling.'

'Nobody would've done anything to him, not for having an accident.'

'You haven't got a clue. You have no idea how *cruel* Dad could be. How vicious. If you knew half the things he's done . . . what he used to do to me . . . and to Kimberly, too.' She shook her head.

I suddenly found myself very interested.

'Like what sort of things?' I asked.

'Do you have any idea how *uncomfortable* it is, having your hands tied like this?' She held them toward me. 'Kimberly made the rope too tight.'

Before turning in for the night, Kimberly had freed Thelma's hands for a visit to the latrine — then had retied them.

'You knew the right way to do it,' Thelma told me. 'When you tied me, the rope didn't cut in this way. Kimberly did this to hurt me.'

'No, she didn't.'

'Look. Just look, why don't you?'

I leaned toward her and checked. The rope did appear to be awfully tight. It was making grooves in her wrists.

'Can you make it looser for me? Please?'

'I don't know. Maybe Kimberly had a reason . . .'

'She had one, okay. She just loves to hurt me. It turns her on.'

'Sure,' I muttered.

'If you make it looser,' she said, 'I'll tell you whatever you want to know.'

Naturally, I was suspicious of her motives. I couldn't get around the fact, though, that the rope was digging into her wrists.

'I'll redo it,' I told her. 'But you'd better not try anything.'

'I won't. I promise.'

I put the ax out of reach behind me, then moved in close to Thelma on my knees and picked open the knot. When the knot came apart, I began to unwrap the rope from around her wrists.

She suddenly pulled her hands free.

I was left holding empty loops of rope.

Before I could do anything, she swung both her arms around behind her back and started shaking her head. 'Please. I'm not doing anything. Don't tie me up again, okay? Please? Give me a break. I can't *stand* having them tied. Just give me a few minutes, okay? Please?'

'No. Come on, you promised.' I glanced over at the sleeping area. The gals were still down, thank God. I faced Thelma. 'You'll get me in all kinds of trouble.'

'They don't have to find out. I won't tell them if you don't.'

'Damn it.' Dropping the rope, I leaned forward on my knees and reached out and grabbed Thelma's upper arms. They were thick, but not flabby. They felt strong. Squeezing them, I tried to pull her arms out from behind her.

She struggled not to let me. After a few seconds, though, she said, 'Stop it or I'll scream.'

I let go fast.

It took a while to catch my breath. Then I said, 'Come on. If somebody wakes up and your hands aren't tied . . .'

'You'll get in more trouble than me.'

'We'll *both* be in trouble. Come on.'

'I'll make you a deal,' she said.

I picked up the rope. 'Like what?'

'Just let me stay untied for a while, okay? Just while we sit here and talk, and then – I'll let you tie them up again, I promise.'

'Somebody might wake up. And besides, you tricked me. You took advantage of me trying to do you a favor. So just give me your hands.'

She shook her head, and kept them behind her back.

'Come on,' I said. 'Please. I'll make it really loose.'

'I thought you wanted to ask me a lot of stuff about Wesley. And about Kimberly? Don't you wanta know about how Dad used to abuse her?'

'He *abused* her?'

'He used to do all sorts of things to her. To both of us.'

'Really?' I glanced over at the sleeping area. So far, so good.

'You're so worried, we'll just *pretend* I'm tied.' Thelma offered her hands. I wrapped the rope around them a few times to make it look good, but left it loose and unknotted. 'There,' Thelma said. 'Now you're covered if anyone comes snooping.'

'Just don't try anything,' I warned her. Then I went back to where I'd been sitting, sat down and put the ax across my thighs. 'What did he do to her?' I asked.

'To both of us,' Thelma said.

'Okay.'

Family Ties

'It's . . . awful nasty. Sick. Are you sure you want to hear about it?'

I nodded. Already, I was feeling a little shaky inside with a mixture of dread and excitement.

'Well, okay then. You asked for it. Don't blame me if you don't like what I have to tell you.'

'I won't. I promise. Come on.'

'One thing was, he used to make us strip naked and then wrestle on the floor. We'd *all* be naked. Me, Kimberly and Dad.' She spoke in a quick, hushed voice, as if she were sharing a very juicy bit of gossip. 'He'd start off by making just me and Kimberly go at it, while he watched from the side and . . . like cheered us on, gave us orders. He'd try to get us to hurt each other. And do perverted things. Then, after a while, he'd join in.'

'Jeez,' I muttered. 'How old were you?'

She shrugged, shook her head. 'I don't know. It went on from the time I was nine or ten, all the way through high school.'

'What about Billie? They were married for . . . twenty years? She let all this . . . ?'

'He never did anything in front of her. But she worked, you know. Dad found plenty of time to be alone with us.'

217

'Wasn't he away at sea a lot?'

'Not that much. Not *nearly* enough, if you ask me. And when he did come back from sea tours, he was worse than ever. He had all sorts of games. The wrestling was just one of them. But it was his favorite, I think. He wanted to do it whenever he had us alone. He used to get these holds on us, and make us scream. We'd be screaming and crying, squirming around with him on the floor and he'd – you know, stick his fingers in us. And his tongue. And he'd bite us.'

'Billie didn't know any of this was going on?'

'No, huh-uh. It was our dark little secret. Dad said he'd kill us if we ever told on him.'

'What about Connie?'

Thelma shrugged. 'I don't know. I stopped living at home when I went away to college. I mean, that's like twelve years ago. Connie would've only been like . . . how old?'

'She's eighteen now.'

'So that would've made her only six when I left. I know he kept it up with Kimberly after I was gone. We never talked about it, but I knew. I mean, they weren't *about* to stop. But I don't know if they got Connie doing it. It sure wouldn't surprise me, though.'

'"Weren't *about* to stop"?' You almost make it sound like Kimberly was . . . a willing participant.'

Thelma blew a huff of air out her nose and mouth. 'Kimberly *didn't* go away to college. What does that tell you? An honor student, class president, you name it, she could've gone to Princeton or Yale if she'd wanted to. But what did she do instead? Enrolled at the community college and lived at home.'

'You think she kept on *doing* things with him?'

'Hell, yes. She really got into it. The whole pain thing. Delicious pain. That's what Kimberly always called it, *delicious* pain.'

'Really?' I was a bit dumbfounded by all this. 'She hasn't got any scars. Not that I've seen, anyway.'

'No, no. Of course not. Scars are a dead giveaway. She's always been very careful not to let herself get hurt in any ways that show. You don't want people knowing about your nasty little secret life. They'll think you're a degenerate, a sicko. You know what I mean?'

'What about her and Keith?' I asked. 'I mean, she married the guy. If she was having this thing with Andrew . . . ?'

'Keith was the same way.'

'*He* liked to hurt her?'

'Sure, he did. I walked in on them, one time. This was just before I got married to Wesley. I had to go to Dad's house to pick up . . . a book. I needed Billie's etiquette book for my wedding plans. And I walked into the house without ringing the doorbell. I thought nobody was home. But I heard noises upstairs, so I snuck up to see what was going on. I was afraid there might be a burglar, or something. It wasn't any burglar, though – it was all three of them in Kimberly's bedroom.'

'All who?'

'Kimberly, Keith, and Dad.'

'Having *sex*? All three of them?'

'Yes, having sex. *And* torturing her.'

'Torturing Kimberly?'

'She was strapped down to her bed, spread-eagled, and . . .'

'Never mind,' I said.

'Dad was in her mouth.'

'Cut it out. I don't wanta hear . . .'

'Keith was kneeling between her legs. He was reaching up with pliers in each hand, working on her nipples, while his mouth . . .'

'Shut up! I don't believe you. You're making it all up. Kimberly wouldn't . . . She *said* you're a liar. This is all a load of bullshit.'

'Anyway, Wesley knew all about Dad and Keith. You see? He knew what a couple of sick degenerates they were. So when the boat blew up . . . he was afraid they'd blame him and he knew how they liked to torture people. He was terrified. Not just for himself, either. He was terrified for me and Billie . . . *all* of us. Can you imagine being stranded on an island with a couple of sadistic bastards like them? He *had* to kill them.'

'So why did he want to kill *me*? I never tortured anybody.'

A strange smile tilted up one side of Thelma's mouth. The other side, dark and swollen from the beating Wesley had given her, didn't move. 'You'd like to, though, wouldn't you?' she said.

Which wasn't exactly what I'd expected her to say.

'Like to what?' I asked.

'Torture somebody.'

'You're nuts!'

'Somebody like Kimberly,' she said.

'No!'

She smirked at me. 'Who are you trying to kid? It makes you hot, just thinking about it. You'd just love to take her nipples and pinch them till she wept and squirmed and begged for mercy.'

'You're nuts.'

'Or bite them.'

'It's time for you to go,' I said. I set the ax aside, picked up the rope again, and shuffled over to her on my knees. 'Put out your hands.'

'Look at you,' she said.

She was looking at the front of my shorts.

'So what. Hold out your hands.'

Instead of holding them out, she started to unbutton her blouse.

'Stop that,' I said.

'You can pretend I'm Kimberly,' she said, and pulled her blouse open. The firelight shimmered on her huge breasts. 'Here. Feel. I know you want to. You're *aching* to.'

'No. Stop it.'

She reached under her breasts and lifted them, raised them toward me. 'Here,' she said. 'They're all yours. You want to squeeze them, don't you? And slap them around? Make them swing and bounce? Wouldn't you love to take my nipples and twist them till I cry out for mercy?'

'No.'

She lowered her breasts, but only to free her hands. Then she started to finger her nipples. She pinched them, pulled at them, twisted them. While she did it, she clamped her lower lip between her teeth. She breathed through her nose, air hissing in and out her nostrils.

I watched.

'You do it,' she gasped. 'I know you want to. You'd *love* to.'

I had to admit, I was tempted. This was sort of like the kind of thing I'd been hoping for. But only sort of. Thelma was the only woman on the island who'd never figured in my fantasies.

I couldn't help being aroused, though. She'd been talking dirty, getting me all turned on with that stuff about Kimberly, and now she was showing me her breasts. They were huge, covered with bruises and welts and scabs. They excited me, anyway.

Frankly, I was pretty disgusted with myself. And with Thelma.

I felt like, if I took her up on the offer, I'd feel very guilty and very dirty. I'd want to wash my hands afterward.

'Come on,' she gasped. 'Come on.'

'Thanks, but no thanks.'

'I'm Kimberly. Just shut your eyes, and I'll be Kimberly for you. Come on. Take my tits, and I'll unzip you and . . .'

'Forget it,' I said. 'Now stop it. Button up and hold out your hands.'

'Okay, okay. Just a minute.'

She started to get up.

'Wait. What are you doing?'

'I just want to be on my knees, that's all. I don't wanta be sitting down. It's too hard to get up once your hands are tied.'

That made sense. I waited until she was kneeling in front of me, then said, 'Give me your hands, now.'

Instead of obeying, she smiled at me, rubbed her hands down her thick belly and started to unbuckle her belt.

'Don't.'

She didn't stop. 'I'll show you what *else* Wesley did to me.'

'I don't want to see.'

'Sure, you do.'

She was right, of course.

I knew I should stop her. In some ways, though, I didn't really want to. Also, I didn't know how. If I tried anything Thelma didn't like, she might yell. The *last* thing I wanted right then, was for one of the other women to wake up and find us like this.

The Best in Horror!
Get Two Books Totally FREE!

PLEASE RUSH MY TWO FREE BOOKS TO ME RIGHT AWAY!

Enclose this card with $2.00 in an envelope and send to:

Leisure Horror Book Club
20 Academy Street
Norwalk, CT 06850-4032

So I just knelt there, watching while she unbuckled her belt, un-fastened the waist button of her shorts, and pulled her zipper down.

The shorts dropped to her knees.

I expected to see panties, but didn't.

She had no pubic hair, to speak of. Just a bulging triangle with dark whiskers like a guy might get on his jaw if he goes a day or two without shaving.

Is *that* what she'd wanted to show me – where Wesley'd shaved her?

Maybe there were injuries to see, but I didn't keep looking. I turned away fast. Off beyond the fire, there was no sign of movement at the sleeping area. I thought, *Thank God.*

Somehow, I had to make Thelma stop all this.

I had to do it on my own.

Things had gone way too far. I never should've untied her hands. One thing had led to another, and now I couldn't see how to end it. Not without shouting for help.

What would they think, if they found us like this?

What I *ought* to do, I thought, is back off, get away from her, grab the ax and stand up and order her, point blank, to pull her shorts up and . . .

Something tipped me off.

I still had my head turned and was staring toward the sleeping area. I had no intention of looking in Thelma's direction again until I'd backed away. But something happened. I don't know what. Maybe I'd heard a quiet sound that didn't belong. Maybe I'd caught a movement in my peripheral vision. Sensed a change in the air. Something.

I turned my head.

Glimpsed Thelma's hand lurching up toward my belly with a straight razor.

No fooling, a *straight razor*. The kind with a blade that folds into its handle – the kind of thing that nobody in his right mind would even *own*, except a barber. Because they're so damn nasty, and it's too easy to cut yourself by accident if you try to shave with one, and you can't help but think about the sort of damage a crazy woman might do to you if she got her hands on it.

I don't know where the hell Thelma got it.

All I know is that all of a sudden I found her with the damn thing in her hand, and she was about to run it up my belly and split me open.

I let out a yelp and threw myself backward off my knees.

She missed.

I didn't feel anything, but saw her razor-wielding hand sweep up past my face as if she still had hopes of dividing my nose in half.

Then I flopped against the sand.

I shoved myself up with my elbows, not sure whether to kick at her or try scurrying away on my back.

For the moment, she wasn't coming at me. Her head was turned aside.

Was Kimberly getting up?

I didn't waste time trying to find out what Thelma was looking at. She was distracted, at least for a moment. That's what counted.

An extra second to put some distance between me and that blade.

I dug in my elbows and heels and started scooting myself across the sand on my back.

Right away, she noticed.

The instant her eyes shifted in my direction, I cried out, 'Help! Help!'

She came waddling toward me like someone whose

legs had been chopped off at the knees. Her shorts were still down. They had her trapped, so she couldn't move very fast. Not fast enough to catch me as I kept scooting away.

She was a real vision.

Lurching and flopping flesh, too well lit by a long shot, in spite of the shadows – her bruised, swollen face *grinning*. She waved both arms overhead as she kneed her way after me. The razor in her right hand flashed firelight.

'You stay put!' she gasped. 'Stay put, you little cocksucker!'

I kept shouting for help.

Then I spotted the ax in the sand, not far from my left elbow. I hauled it toward me by its haft.

'Thelma!'

Kimberly's voice, an angry shout.

Thelma glanced in the direction it had come from. Gasped. Then flung herself at me.

I swung the ax as hard and fast as I could.

The flat side of its steel head struck her in the forearm. The right forearm.

She cried out and the razor leaped from her hand.

She landed on me. Her head knocked me in the crotch. A second later, though, she rolled off. Making grunty noises, she rolled over a few times and got to her hands and knees. As she staggered to her feet, she snatched up her shorts. Holding them up with both hands, she ran for the inlet.

Kimberly went sprinting after her.

Lean and quick, dark except for the white of her bikini.

At the water's edge, she leaped and reached with both hands for Thelma's shoulders.

A great flying tackle.

Except that Thelma twisted around and smashed her elbow into the side of Kimberly's face. The blow deflected Kimberly. And dropped her. She smacked down on the water, and Thelma kept going.

I was on my knees by then, in spite of the bash to my nuts. I turned to look for the others.

Back at the sleeping area, Connie was sitting up and staring in my direction. Of course, she was too battered to come running to the rescue. And Billie didn't dare leave her behind. Billie, on her feet, a spear in her hands, was standing ready to fight in case Wesley should spring an attack on her and Connie.

I got to my feet and hurried toward the inlet.

Thelma was lunging through thigh-deep, black water. I couldn't see her very well. Suddenly, I thought she was coming *back*. Which scared the hell out of me. I stopped short. I fought with an urge to turn around and make a run for it.

If I ran, she would finish off Kimberly.

I had just decided to go back for the ax and fight to save Kimberly when I realized that Thelma was smaller than before. Nothing showed below her waist – because she was in deeper water. She wasn't returning. She'd been wading away, the whole time.

I hurried to help Kimberly.

She was on her hands and knees, head hanging, her face a few inches above the surface of the water. When I reached her, she didn't look up.

'Are you okay?' I asked.

She didn't answer.

'Kimberly?'

'Go and get her,' she muttered. 'Don't let her get away.'

I looked for Thelma. At first, I couldn't find her. Then

I spotted a dim shape way out near the point.

'She's awfully far away,' I said.

Kimberly muttered, 'Damn it, Rupert.'

'I wouldn't be able to catch her.'

She groaned.

'Can I help you up?' I asked.

'Don't touch me.'

She sounded disgusted.

'I'm sorry,' I said.

'You're sorry, all right. Jesus H. Christ.'

'I almost got killed.'

'That would've been a big loss.'

Man. I was beginning to wish Thelma *had* killed me.

'Okay,' I said. 'I'll go after her. If that's really what you want. What do you want me to do if I catch up to her? Am I supposed to try and bring her back? Or do you want me to try and kill her? Maybe I'd better take along a knife, or something. Can I have your knife?'

Head still hanging, Kimberly said, 'Forget it. Just forget it. Go to bed, or something. Shit.'

I'd never felt so low. I mean, you could tell she was completely disgusted with me and thought I was a waste and a loser.

Which is true. I am.

I decided to follow her advice, and go to bed. The problem with that, though, was Billie and Connie. They were there waiting for me, and I was crying pretty good by then. I just couldn't help it.

'What happened?' Billie asked. She didn't sound disgusted with me. She sounded like she cared.

'I'm sorry,' I said. 'Thelma got away. I let her get away.'

'Neat play,' Connie said.

'Hush up,' Billie said. Then she poked her spear into

the sand and came over to where I was standing and put her arms around me.

It was one of the nicest things anyone has ever done.

She was all soft and warm and gentle, stroking my hair with one hand and my back with the other while I cried against the side of her neck. She kept murmuring, 'It's all right, honey. It's okay. Everything's fine.'

She's the best woman I've ever known.

I calmed down pretty soon, thanks to Billie. Then Kimberly came along, so I got out of Billie's arms and turned around to face the music.

'Are you okay, Rupert?' she asked.

'No. I really screwed up.'

'You're not hurt, though?' I shook my head.

'How the hell did she get loose?' Connie asked.

'I . . . I untied her hands.'

'You outa your fucking mind?'

Billie put a hand on the back of my neck, and rubbed me.

'We'll talk about it in the morning,' Kimberly said. 'Everybody go back to sleep, now. I'll keep watch.'

'I'm sorry,' I told her.

'What's done is done,' she said. Then she turned away and walked back to the fire.

That's about it for last night.

More than enough, if you ask me. Aside from the fact that so much happened – good stuff and bad stuff and some very weird stuff – it's taken me most of the morning to write it down.

And I'm not even caught up yet.

The Inquisition

Anyway, I had all last night to worry about explaining the fiasco with Thelma. I wanted to make up a good story about it, so I wouldn't look totally stupid and gullible and perverted.

Also, there was a whole lot I didn't want to talk about.

But I couldn't concentrate very well. I was lying there on my 'bed,' trying to focus on coming up with a good lie, but all I could think about was what had *actually* happened. I kept reliving everything in my head. Not just remembering, but sort of *feeling* most of it – the confusion and fear and excitement and revulsion and arousal and terror – though in milder forms than when all of it was going on for real. And in jumbled order.

I couldn't even get away from Thelma by falling asleep. My nightmares were *worse* than what had really happened. I don't remember much about them, just that they had a lot to do with sex and razor blades, and that they were awful.

I was glad when morning came, so I wouldn't have to suffer through any more nightmares.

After everybody was up, we gathered around the fire and ate the last of the canned ham for breakfast.

Have I mentioned the canned ham before? It was one of

the things Keith and Andrew salvaged after the explosion. We got into it for the first time a few days ago when we didn't have any fish. Anyway, now it's gone – and we're starting to get low on things to eat.

We'd started off on the trip with a *lot* of stuff, a great deal more than eight people could hope to finish off during a week at sea. The explosion happened when we still had four days left, and I guess that Keith and Andrew recovered about half of the food that was left. Including some good stuff like the canned ham.

They didn't fare nearly so well with the drinks – we must've had enough soda, beer and hard stuff on the boat to keep an army happy. All that survived the explosion, though, were a few bottles of booze. (Nothing carbonated – soda, beer and champagne – survived the explosion. They all blew.)

Anyway, I'd say we were pretty lucky to end up with as much as we did.

For most of the time here, there have been only four or five of us to share it. We eat fish whenever possible. So we've stretched out our food supply pretty well. It should last a few more days, if we're careful. Then we'll have to concentrate on fishing, hunting, gathering edible fruit and vegetables from the jungle, etc.

That shouldn't be much of a problem, except that we have to contend with Wesley and Thelma. With them out there, getting enough food isn't exactly on the top of our priority list.

Man, this was a lengthy digression. I think I'm loopy from so much writing today.

After we finished the ham, it was time for the Inquisition.

'You want to tell us what happened last night?' Kimberly asked.

'Not especially,' I said.

Nobody appeared amused.

I sighed. 'Where do you want me to start?'

'Why did you untie her hands?'

Relief. An easy one. 'I had to. You know how you untied her before she went to the latrine last night? Well, when you tied her back up again, you made the rope too tight. It was digging into her wrists.'

Kimberly frowned at me. 'That's nonsense.'

'It isn't. I checked. The rope was way too tight.'

'Not when *I* tied her up. I was very careful . . .' She glanced from Billie to Connie. 'Did either of you retie her last night?'

Billie shook her head.

'If I was gonna do anything with her rope,' Connie said, 'I would've strangled her with it.'

'Maybe *she* tightened the rope,' Billie suggested. 'Did it herself, so she'd have a reason for asking Rupe to untie it.'

'How could she do that?' Connie asked.

'With her teeth?' Billie said.

'I guess it's possible,' Kimberly admitted. She frowned as if thinking for a few seconds, then said, 'Shit, it sounds *exactly* like something she might pull. She goes around acting like a lame-brain, half the time, but she can be . . . crafty. Very crafty. She used to be, anyway. Maybe she's changed, but I doubt it. Once a sneak, always a sneak.'

'What sort of things did she do?' I asked. I was somewhat interested in hearing about Thelma's sneaky ways, but mostly I hoped to delay the interrogation.

'She was always doing stuff. But . . . one time when she was pissed off at me, she chopped up her *own* Barbie doll – cut off its hands and feet and head – and hid them under

231

my mattress. Then she acted all innocent, went around and asked Dad if he'd seen her Barbie doll anywhere. When it finally turned up, I caught living hell.'

'From your mother?' Billie asked.

Kimberly shook her head. 'From Dad. This was after Mom had died, and before he met you.'

'Did he beat you?' I asked. I was suddenly breathing harder than a second ago, and my heart was thudding.

'Who?' Kimberly said. 'Dad?'

'Yeah. You said you caught living hell.'

'Right.' She looked a bit offended. 'He didn't *beat* me, though. Are you kidding? Dad? He gave me a *talking to*. Which made me feel lower than a snake, and I hadn't *touched* the damn doll. You should've seen Thelma. She was so proud of herself for pulling it off and getting me in hot water.'

'Did you get even with her?' I asked.

Kimberly gave me an odd look – as if she suspected that something was up. 'Yeah. What're you getting at?'

I could hardly force the words out, but I managed. 'She said you used to beat her up.'

'What?'

'That you'd . . . you were always forcing her to wrestle with you. You'd throw her down on the floor and put head-locks on her . . . make her cry out for mercy . . . stuff like that.'

Kimberly smirked and shook her head. 'She would've liked that.'

'You didn't wrestle with her?'

'She's five years older than me. She always outweighed me. And she had a cruel streak. There's no way I ever would've wrestled with Thelma. The one time we actually had a fight, I pulled her hair and she stabbed me in the arm with a pencil. It went *in*. I had to go to the doctor and get shots.'

'She said you used to wrestle with her all the time.'

'Really?'

'Yeah.'

'Maybe in some alternate universe.'

I was tempted to go on and explain that they'd been naked and their father had joined in – that the matches were supposed to be some sort of sadistic sexual romp.

Already, though, I figured Thelma must've made up the whole wrestling business.

'So you two were over here last night talking about make-believe wrestling matches between me and Thelma?'

'Yeah.'

'Why did she tell you that stuff?'

'I don't know. We were just talking.'

I felt sort of cornered, and wished I hadn't brought up the subject. It was a relief, though, to discover that Thelma'd been lying. If she'd lied about the wrestling, it stood to reason that the torture and incest stuff probably hadn't really happened, either.

I felt a little cheated, a little disappointed. Part of me had gotten sort of excited, picturing Kimberly mixed up in that sort of thing. Mostly, though, I was relieved.

'She must've had a motive,' Kimberly said.

'Not that I . . .'

'I know,' Connie said. She gave me one of her snotty looks. 'I bet Thelma was trying to get him to wrestle with her.'

I almost denied it. But the idea seemed to have some merit. I sure didn't want the truth coming out. 'Well . . . That's sort of . . . She *did* want me to have a wrestling match with her.'

'What on earth for?' Billie asked, half of her mouth rising in a crooked smile as if she were amused but baffled.

'She made it a challenge,' I explained. 'If she won, I'd have to let her get away. If I won, she'd let me tie her hands back up. See, she'd pulled them away when I tried to loosen the rope for her.'

'That's when you should've called for help,' Kimberly said.

'Sure, and have everyone think I was some kind of a worthless jerk for being dumb enough to untie her.'

Kimberly grimaced a bit. She lowered her eyes and looked ashamed. She didn't actually apologize, but she regretted being so sharp with me last night. You could tell.

'Boy,' Connie said, 'that Thelma read you like a book.'

I looked at her and didn't make the mistake of asking, 'What do you mean by that?' I kept my mouth shut, but it didn't help.

Billie asked, 'What do you mean?'

'She knew just which buttons to push. Amazing. Rupert's got sex on the brain. There's no way in the world he's gonna miss out on the chance to wrestle with a woman.'

I felt like my face might go up in flames. I said, 'That's bull. We're talking about *Thelma*. God almighty, she's the *last* woman I'd ever want to wrestle with.'

'Yeah, right.'

'She's disgusting.'

'As if you'd let a little thing like that get in your way.'

'Yeah,' I said, 'look at you.'

'Go fuck yourself.'

Kimberly raised a hand. 'Let's not get sidetracked here, kiddies.'

Connie sneered at her and gave her the finger.

Kimberly ignored it. To me, she said, 'So, did you

agree to have this wrestling match?'

I frowned and tried to decide on the best way to answer. After a while, I said, 'Well . . . she pushed me into it. She called me a chicken, and said I was too much of a wimp and a loser to beat her in a fair fight.'

'So you went for it?' Kimberly asked.

'I had to.'

Billie sighed. 'You didn't have to prove anything to Thelma. She was just manipulating you.'

'I guess . . . Well, not all the way. I mean, at first I agreed to wrestle her. But then she started to take off her clothes. She wanted us doing it naked.'

'You figured you'd died and gone to Heaven,' Connie said.

'I did not! I told her no. I said the deal was off, there wouldn't be any wrestling match, and I wanted her to hold out her hands so I could tie them. She wouldn't listen, though. She didn't pay any attention, and started taking off her clothes. It was like we were going to wrestle, no matter what I said. Before I knew what was happening, she had her blouse wide open and her shorts down. I didn't know what to do.'

'Probably had a boner on you the size of the Washington Monument.' Connie said that. Who else?

'I did not.'

'Yeah, right.'

'Leave him alone,' Billie told her.

'The thing is, that's when I knew it had all gone too far. I started backing away from her. I was planning to go for the ax, and *make* her quit messing around, but all of a sudden she attacked me with a straight razor. She almost killed me.' I met Connie's narrow eyes. 'If you don't believe me, we can probably find the razor. I knocked it out of her hand. It's probably in the sand around here someplace.'

Kimberly, who was wearing Keith's Hawaiian shirt this morning, slipped her hand into its left breast pocket and pulled out the razor. She flipped the blade open.

Billie pursed her lips and made a 'Whuuu' sound.

I grimaced, myself, getting a good look at it in daylight and realizing how close it had come to slicing me up the middle.

'Has anyone ever seen this before?' Kimberly asked. She held it between her thumb and forefinger so that we could see the handle – which looked like mother-of-pearl.

Connie shook her head.

Billie said, 'Wicked-looking thing.'

'Do you recognize it?'

'Me? No. I haven't seen a razor like that in years. My father had one that folded like that, but his had a green handle.'

'How about you, Rupert?'

'I saw it last night. When she came at me with it.'

'It's probably Wesley's,' Connie said.

Kimberly nodded. 'Maybe. It might even be Thelma's, for that matter.'

'She didn't have it when I frisked her,' Billie said. 'I couldn't have *missed* a thing like that.'

'Well,' Kimberly said, 'she sure got hold of it somewhere.'

'Why didn't she just *use* it?' Connie asked.

'She tried,' I pointed out.

'No, I mean to cut herself loose?'

'Maybe she couldn't get to it while her hands were tied,' I suggested.

'But she must've gotten her hands undone *before* she came over to you,' Billie said. 'If we're right that she'd retied the rope to make it too tight, she would've probably had to *un*tie it first.'

Connie scowled. 'This is getting too complicated.'

'Yeah,' I said. 'We've got her untying her hands so she can tie them more tightly so she can come over here and trick *me* into untying them for her. That doesn't make any sense at all.'

'Yeah. It does.' Kimberly nodded and nibbled her lower lip for a few seconds. Then she said, 'Yeah, it makes a lot of sense. We've been looking at it wrong. This wasn't about Thelma getting herself untied so she could escape. This was about killing Rupert.'

'Terrific,' I said.

She raised a finger. 'Here's what I think happened.' Looking at me, she said, 'Back at the lagoon, Thelma tried to kill you by throwing that rock over the falls. She missed you, and hit Connie by mistake.'

'That's according to *Thelma's* version of what happened,' Billie pointed out. 'Might not be the truth.'

'Whatever Wesley has in mind, he wants all the men dead first. That's how I see it,' Kimberly said. 'The thing is, he was too injured to try for Rupert, himself, so he ordered Thelma to do it. She screwed up and hit Connie. Then – her story – Wesley trashed her, so she killed him and came back to join up with us. I don't think so.'

'You don't think he *trashed* her?' Billie asked.

'Somebody sure did,' Connie said.

Kimberly nodded. 'Yeah, Wesley probably did it to her. Or some of it. I bet most of it was self-inflicted.'

'Would she *do* that?' Billie asked.

'Beat herself up? Maybe. I don't know. It wouldn't surprise me.'

'You think she's a masochist?' Billie asked.

Connie snorted. 'She's gotta be, she married Wesley.'

'She couldn't have *bitten* herself in all those places,' I pointed out.

'Not in all of them,' Kimberly said. 'I think it was probably a joint effort. The beating was supposed to be Thelma's excuse for killing Wesley, so it had to look good. She almost *had* to do some of it, herself. The beating was just too severe for Wesley to manage it by himself. In his condition? He might've given her some bites, but he couldn't have slapped her around and whipped her like that. She had to do that to herself. Most of it, anyway.'

'Sick,' Connie said.

'It was her ticket into our camp,' Kimberly pointed out. 'She could come in, show us those terrible wounds, and we'd be all set to believe she'd paid Wesley back by killing him.'

'But we didn't believe her,' I pointed out.

'No. Not entirely. I had my doubts all along that Wesley could've done that to her. But what *I* suspected – and I think the rest of us did, too – was that she'd been sent in here to set us up. If we believed her about killing Wesley, we'd let our guard down. That'd leave us open for a surprise attack. We also suspected that she might try to lead us into an ambush when we went looking for Wesley's body.'

'Right,' Connie said.

'But we were wrong. Completely wrong. She didn't come in to distract us or lead us into a trap so Wesley could nail us. You know what it was? From the very start? It was a one-woman mission to take out Rupert.'

'Kill me?'

'Right.'

'What does it mean?' Billie asked.

'Means, for one thing, Rupert's a very lucky fellow.'

'That's me, lucky.'

'Also means that Thelma's in this all the way with Wesley. She's perfectly willing to commit murder for him. She's a lot more dangerous than we thought.'

'And trickier,' I said.

'I always knew she was tricky,' Kimberly said. 'I just didn't know she was homicidal.'

Billie, frowning, shook her head. 'Do you think she was in on it with him?'

'In on what?'

'Setting us *all* up. Blowing up the boat. Trapping us here. Is it possible that Thelma helped Wesley plan it? I mean, I'm beginning to wonder. For that matter, maybe this whole thing was *her* idea.'

'I tend to doubt it,' Kimberly said. 'She might be a hell of an actress, but I think she really and truly believed that Wesley got killed in the explosion. She didn't know what was going on. She just got into this whole mess when she found us trying to ambush her husband. That's the way I see it, anyhow.'

'If Thelma *wasn't* in on the plan,' Billie said, 'then all this was Wesley's idea like we thought in the first place. So how does Thelma fit into it?'

I saw where she was heading. 'If we're right about Wesley's motives,' I said, 'she'll be killed like the rest of us.'

'He can't possibly let her live,' Billie added.

'That'll be her tough luck,' Kimberly said. 'But he won't kill her as long as he has uses for her. And maybe he doesn't intend to kill her at all. We *suspect* he's doing all this so he can be the sole survivor and inherit and so forth, but we don't really know *what* the hell his reasoning is. Or what to expect from him.'

'I expect he'll try to kill me again,' I put in.

'I suspect you're right,' Kimberly said, and smiled at me. 'We'll try not to let that happen.'

'Thanks,' I said.

'So, what do we do?' Connie asked.

'Nothing,' Kimberly said. 'Not today, anyway. You're in no condition to go on another hunt for those two. I'm sure Rupert has a lot of writing to do in that diary of his.'

'Big deal,' Connie muttered.

'It is a big deal,' Kimberly told her. 'I want him to keep current with it. I want there to be *something* – a record of what's happened here. In case we don't make it.'

'That's a laugh. I'm *sure* Wesley's gonna kill us all and then let Rupert's little *diary* incriminate him. Are you kidding me? He'll burn it.'

'Thanks, Connie,' I said.

'Oh, get real.'

'Anyway, I'm not planning to get killed. I'm gonna make it out of here – I hope we all do. And then I'll find a publisher. We'll be famous. I'll make a ton of money. And everybody who reads my true-life adventure book will see just what a bitch you are.'

'Maybe I'll burn it myself.'

'Just try, and see what . . .'

'Knock it off,' Kimberly said. 'Both of you.'

'And *you* leave Rupert's diary alone,' Billie told her daughter.

Her daughter said, 'Yeah, right, take *his* side, why don't you?'

That was pretty much the end of the conference. It hadn't turned out so badly, after all.

Being the intended target of Thelma's hit, I came out of

things looking a lot better than expected. I was now the survivor of an assassination attempt, not the dork who'd let Thelma escape.

I couldn't help feeling a little scared, though.

It's one thing to have somebody pull a razor on you because she's your prisoner bent on making a getaway. It's a whole different ballgame if she dropped in on us with a battered body and a load of lies just so she could get close to me, late at night, and rip me open.

I'm damn lucky to be alive.

Day ?
Anybody's Guess

Musings On My Return To The Journal

It's where I left it. So I've opened it. So now I'm writing again.

I don't know why I'm bothering.

Except, like Kimberly said, we've got to have a record of what's been happening here.

Maybe the cops'll get their hands on it, someday.

Yeah, right.

Do they have cops in this goddamn armpit of the universe? Do they have *anyone*?

I know one thing: I don't ever want to see this thing get published. Not anymore. Not after what happened.

'After *what* happened?' you ask.

I don't *know* what happened.

It has been a few days since my last entry in the journal. I think. I'm not sure how long it's been.

I just now turned back a couple of pages to read what's there and refresh my memory. It's almost like somebody else wrote them. Wrote them a long time ago. Years ago. So much has changed.

I'm embarrassed to see what I wrote.

Example: *I expect he'll try to kill me again.* The placement of *again* makes it sound like I've already been killed once.

But that isn't the real problem. (One can't be held accountable for the grammar of dialogue, right? And who gives a rat's ass, anyway?) The real problem is my cavalier, jaunty fucking attitude. Ah, yes, my good Wesley? He'll likely make another try for me. Tut, tut. Have to be on my guard, won't I? Have to remember to duck.

Well, here's news.

It wasn't me he got.

It was them.

Kimberly, Billie and Connie.

They're gone with the fucking wind, and I'm not. I'm here, back at the beach, writing in my journal, alive and well and alone.

I'm not planning to get killed.

Another gem from my previous entry.

Talk about arrogance.

Talk about being the prime asshole of the world.

Talk about prophetic.

Of course, I don't actually know if the women have been killed. I think it's likely, but I'm not sure. I know some of what happened, but not everything. They were still alive when I went down, but what happened to them afterwards?

I don't know.

I know they're gone, though.

I can't handle this. I'm going for a swim. Maybe I'll be lucky and a shark'll eat me for dinner.

War Party

This is the next day.

I was too messed up to do any more writing yesterday. I went for a swim, like I said. The sharks didn't get me, though. I didn't see hide nor hair of any sharks.

I did consider suicide, though.

One of those really cool, melodramatic suicides like you've seen in a billion crappy movies – where some idiot goes swimming off into the sunset. The deal is, I guess, you keep swimming away from shore until you get too pooped to make it back. So even if you eventually change your mind, you're history.

There are several reasons why I didn't do it.

A. Drowning sucks.

B. Being dead sucks.

C. Being the lone survivor is *not* a fate worse than death.

D. I'm not one hundred per cent sure that all the gals are dead.

E. If I kill myself, I won't be able to do any of the things that I want very badly to do to Wesley and Thelma.

F. Like it or not, I do feel a certain obligation to play Ishmael and tell thee, to be the Horatio of our noble, lost band and report our cause aright to the unsatisfied.

Other than *not* kill myself, what I did yesterday is of little consequence. I swam, I ate, I wept, I slept.

Today, I'll tell what happened to us on day eight.

As much as I know, anyway.

Day six was when Thelma returned, battered and claiming that she'd killed Wesley. That night, she went at me with her razor. Then she escaped by swimming away.

Day seven, we did a lot of talking about what had happened on night six. And I did a lot of writing about it. Other than that, nothing of consequence happened. Connie's injuries were the main reason why we didn't take any action. She seemed to be getting better, though.

Nothing happened that night.

Day eight, Connie was still sore but she was ready for action. We all were. We knew it was time to go after Wesley and Thelma.

We hoped that Wesley was already dead.

We were fairly sure that Thelma had lied about killing him, just as she'd lied about nearly everything else. We thought there was a good chance, however, that Wesley had died from the wounds he got on the night of our ambush. Kimberly had put her spear through his left tit, and she'd rammed a hole into his ass. As a result of those wounds, he could've died from blood loss or from infection.

If he wasn't dead, we figured he might at least be incapacitated.

On the other hand, maybe he'd recovered enough to be a real threat to us.

We'd discussed every possibility that we could think of.

We'd concluded that *anything* was possible, but that we were more likely to have trouble from Thelma than Wesley.

* * *

We set out at mid-morning.

Kimberly wore Keith's Hawaiian shirt over her white bikini. She carried her tomahawk on its rope sling. The Swiss Army knife puckered out the front of her pants. The spear was in her left hand.

Billie wore her same black bikini and no shirt, of course. Her chest was crossed by ropes. The single line of the tomahawk sling swept down from her shoulder to her right hip. The remains of the hanging rope (which we'd used for tying Thelma's hands) crossed her from the other shoulder. It was long enough to make three loops. We'd decided to bring it along in case we took a captive.

Though Kimberly was the one with Indian blood in her veins, Connie looked more the part. Because of her headband. She wore it to hold the bandage in place against her wound. The bandage was a pad of cloth made from her old T-shirt. The T-shirt had been ruined, anyway, so Billie had washed it in the stream and cut it up.

Connie also wore a vest. She'd made it herself, using my razor on day seven to cut it out of a beach towel. It had yellow and white horizontal stripes. Even though it didn't weigh much, it helped to hold a bandage down against her left shoulder. It also protected her shoulders and upper back from the sun, though it had no sleeves and was so short that it left her arms and lower back exposed. Not to mention her rump, which was as good as naked in that thong.

Before we set out, I offered to spread some of Billie's sunblock on her butt. She told me to fuck off. (Like I said, she was feeling better.)

The vest couldn't be shut in front, but the towel panels covered her breasts – her *real* reason for making and wearing the thing, more than likely. To keep them out of my sight. To taunt me and punish me.

Logically, she should've made herself a skirt, too. But she didn't. Did she think I had no interest in her lower regions? It didn't make any sense, really. But then, you could go crazy trying to make sense out of Connie.

She was sure good to look at, though. They all were.

To think that I might never see any of them again . . . It isn't fair. I know this is a terrible thing to write, but I feel cheated.

They're dead, and *I* feel cheated.

Sooner or later, maybe one of them would've . . . either fallen for me or gotten so desperate . . .

Maybe not. We'll never know.

What is for sure, though, is that they aren't here to *look* at, to daydream about, to talk with, to sometimes hold.

Which makes me realize that I've had hugs from all three of them, at one time or another.

I've seen Billie's breasts and Connie's, but never Kimberly's. Now, I never *will* see hers. Along with all the other things I'll never . . .

I had to stop writing for a while.

It depressed me too much – to put it mildly. I miss them so much. I can't stand the thought that they are dead.

I don't know for sure that they *are* dead.

A big mistake, around here, to assume that *anyone* is dead.

What I need to do is find them. I need to know whether they are dead or alive. If they're alive, they are almost certainly being held captive. Maybe I'll be able to rescue them. If they're dead, I'll . . . I don't know what. In either case, though, I have to kill Wesley and Thelma.

I should be out searching for them right now, not sitting here on the beach.

But I want to bring the journal up to date first. That way, in case I don't come back, there will be a record.

Back to the story.

I'd been telling about Connie's towel-vest. Because of the injury to her left shoulder, she wore the rope of her tomahawk sling on her right shoulder. The rope crossed her chest, and the tomahawk hung by her left hip. In her left hand, she carried her spear – the special, wicked one she'd made for fishing.

As for me, the day seemed too hot for Billie's pink blouse, so I went without it. I wore Andrew's khaki shorts. I haven't worn my swimming trunks since the day I started wearing Andrew's shorts. I like having the pockets, and the shorts are so big and roomy that they give me plenty of freedom. I wore shoes and socks, too, by the way.

I haven't written much about footwear. That's because it doesn't interest me much, and so far it hasn't been of any great importance. We all had shoes to wear. Sometimes we wore them; sometimes we went barefoot. Not much else to say on the subject.

For weapons, I had the ax in both hands, a tomahawk at my hip (stuck under my belt, which I'd gotten back after the loan to Connie), and Thelma's straight razor. Kimberly thought I should get to keep the razor. For one thing, it was the weapon I'd almost gotten murdered with. For another, even though Kimberly had actually found the razor where it had fallen in the sand, she pointed out that I'm the one who'd knocked it out of Thelma's hand.

Besides, Kimberly had her Swiss Army knife, Connie didn't even want to *touch* the razor, and Billie thought I should keep it because I was obviously the one in the most danger.

Wrong.

We were so damn wrong about that.

Anyway, I had the razor safely folded inside the right front pocket of my shorts, along with Andrew's lighter and Billie's plastic bottle of sunblock. (My other front pocket bulged with chucks of fish that we'd smoked overnight and wrapped in some leftover cellophane.)

So that's pretty much the way we were – how we were dressed and armed and so on – when we set out on the morning of day eight to hunt for Wesley and Thelma.

We'd agreed to try our luck at the lagoon. It seemed the most likely place to find them.

But Kimberly said, 'This way,' and started walking toward the inlet.

We went after her.

'Where are we going?' I asked.

'We shouldn't look like we're on our way to the lagoon,' she said.

'Are you kidding?' Connie asked. 'Who do you think is *watching*?'

'Probably no one. But maybe Wesley or Thelma.'

'Give me a break.'

'We'll just go up the shore for a while, make them think we're off to explore the island.'

'Then what?' Connie asked. 'Sneak around *behind* the lagoon?'

'Yep,' Kimberly said.

'Fabulous.'

'I think it's a good idea,' I said.

Connie gave me a sneer. 'You would.'

'Look what happened last time,' Billie told her. 'We

252

don't want to repeat the same mistake. If we come in from the back, maybe we'll take them by surprise.'

'I think it's stupid,' Connie said. 'We'll probably get lost.'

She was outnumbered.

With Kimberly in the lead, we climbed the ridge of rocks just to the north of our beach, made our way down to the other side, and hiked along the shoreline.

Connie glanced back, now and then. 'How far are we gonna go?' she asked.

'Let's make it around that point,' Kimberly said.

It was pretty far off.

Connie wrinkled her nose.

'If anyone's watching,' Kimberly explained, 'they'll think we're trying to circle the island.'

'Maybe we *should* circle the island,' I said.

'Some other time. First, we've gotta take care of Wesley and Thelma. They're too big a threat. After we've killed them, we'll be able to explore the island to our heart's content. What we'll do, as soon as we get to the other side of the point, is take cover in the jungle and make our way back till we're sure of our bearings . . .'

'Why don't I just wait for you here?' Connie offered.

'You're not helping matters,' Kimberly said. 'We know you're hurt, but . . .'

'But you're gonna make me walk a few extra miles, anyway.'

'What *about* trying to circle the island?' Billie asked Kimberly. 'It might not be a bad idea.'

'It's a *fine* idea,' Kimberly said. 'For some other day.'

'No, hold on. Except for a couple of short little trips into the jungle, we've been cooped up on that beach ever since we got here. We don't know *what* we might find.'

'Probably the dinghy,' I said.

Connie stopped glowering. 'Yeah! If we find the dinghy, we can get outa here.'

'This might not even *be* an island,' Billie said. 'How do we know we didn't land on . . . the end of a peninsula, or something?'

'It's an island,' Kimberly said. 'Dad was showing me the charts the night before we got here.' She nodded. 'We're nowhere near any mainland. Nothing for miles around but scads of little islands.'

'Well, that was just . . . I *know* we aren't on a continent or something. But we don't know *what* island this is, or how big it is. It might very well be inhabited. We might even find some sort of town.'

'And police,' Connie said. She was perking up. In spite of her injuries, she would apparently be delighted to walk for miles in search of the dinghy or a precinct house.

Billie nodded. 'It couldn't hurt to just keep going on the beach and *see* what . . .'

'Be my guest,' Kimberly said. 'I'm not interested. The rest of you wanta bail out on me, that's your problem. I don't care if there's a metropolis around the corner, I'm going into the jungle after Wesley and I'm not coming out till I've got his head.'

I couldn't help it. I gave her a buggy-eyed stare and said, 'His *head*? You mean, like, figuratively speaking?'

She just looked at me.

Which was all the answer I needed.

I muttered, 'Jesus.'

Billie had that look on her face – a mixture of amusement and disbelief. 'You're not *really* planning to cut off Wesley's head?'

'He killed my husband and my father. You know how

we towed Dad's body out? I'd like to swim out to exactly the same place with Wesley's head, and let it sink there in the same place so Dad'll see that I took care of business.'

I didn't like the sound of that.

I wanted Wesley dead, too, but it disturbed me to find out that Kimberly had come up with such a bizarre, grisly plan. She'd obviously given it a lot of thought.

It seems she had depths of creepiness I had never even guessed at.

Connie, too, seemed impressed. With a look on her face as if she'd just encountered a little green man, she did a brief rendition of *The Twilight Zone*'s music — 'Doo-*de*-do-do, doo-*de*-do-do.' I'd heard her do that before, but never an impression of Rod Serling (or anyone else, for that matter). 'One Kimberly Dickens, cheerleader, prom queen, loving daughter and faithful wife. She came to a tropical island in search of a picnic, and found instead that she had slipped into a netherworld of primitive . . .'

'Knock it off,' Kimberly said.

'Hey, you're talking about de*cap*itating someone.'

'You have a problem with that?'

'Not with that, with you. I mean, you're creeping me out. You start talking about taking a guy's head off – even *his* – and it starts making me wonder if you've lost a few screws.'

Kimberly frowned at her, then shrugged. 'You're probably right, I shouldn't go around saying stuff like that.' She glanced at each of us. 'I guess maybe I got carried away. I'm not missing any screws. A couple of them might be slightly *loose*, but . . . don't worry, I haven't gone crazy.'

'I've had some pretty horrible thoughts, myself,' Billie said. 'Things I'd like to do to Wesley. Some of them are a lot worse than chopping his head off.'

'Me, too,' I said.

'Well, so have I,' Connie admitted. Meeting Kimberly's gaze, she said, 'The difference is, *you* mean to do it.'

'I don't know,' Kimberly said. 'I guess we'll see, won't we?' With that, she turned away and continued walking.

Billie, Connie and I gave each other looks.

Kimberly had spooked all three of us.

None of us talked much, after that. Connie didn't even raise any more complaints.

Our silence must've bothered Kimberly. After a while, she frowned over her shoulder at us. 'What's the matter with you people?'

Billie just shook her head.

'Nothing,' I said.

'Nope,' said Connie, 'nothing wrong here.'

Kimberly turned around and walked backward. 'You people! For Godsake, I was *kidding*. Okay? Christ! You'd think I was foaming at the mouth! I'm not gonna cut off anybody's head, okay? I didn't *mean* it. I never should've said it. Now you all think I've flipped out. Anyway, as a matter of fact, *so what* if I wanta cut off his head? You think he hasn't got it coming? He chopped Dad's head *in half*. In my book, anything he gets is better than what he deserves. If we're lucky enough to catch him alive, what we *oughta* do is skin him. We oughta spend a few days killing him a little bit at a time, make him scream till he's hoarse, make him beg for death. If you think cutting his *head* off is extreme, just wait and see what I do to him *before* I take his head. He's gonna pay big-time for murdering Dad and Keith. If you think I'm mad now, just wait and see. You've got no *idea* what I'm capable of.'

The three of us gaped at her.

She suddenly swung out an arm as if trying to bat away

a trio of pesky flies. 'Get out of here. Leave me alone. *I'll*
take care of Wesley and Thelma. I don't need the three of
you hanging around . . . You're all useless, anyway. None
of you has got the stomach for what's coming, so get outa
my face. Go! Get outa here!' She swung her arm again,
then spun around and took off running.

'Don't!' Billie yelled. 'Hey! Wait up!'

'Ah, let her go,' Connie said.

'Kimberly!' I shouted.

She kept running.

Billie took off after her.

'Mom!'

Billie didn't stand a chance of catching up with Kimberly,
so I joined the chase. Even lugging the ax with me, I was
able to gain on Billie. But Kimberly, faster than both of us,
kept drawing away. And I could tell that she wasn't even
running full tilt.

Connie shouted at our backs, 'Damn it! Come back!
Are you *all* out of your fucking minds?'

Billie, still slightly ahead of me, glanced over her shoulder.
So did I.

Connie just stood where she'd been. We were leaving
her quite a distance behind us.

Billie stopped running.

I dodged to keep from crashing into her.

'Leave the ax,' she gasped at me. 'Get her. This is . . .
gotta stop her.'

I let the ax fall to the sand. Then I put on all the speed
I could muster. As I dashed after Kimberly, I yelled, 'Quit
it! Come on! We're with you! Slow down! You're not
crazy! Please! Stop running! Please! We wanta go with
you!'

A lot of good my shouting did.

It was a waste of breath, so I quit yelling.

Soon, I found myself gaining on her.

She must've been *allowing* me to gain on her.

Not to catch her, though.

She let me approach to within about three strides behind her, but no closer.

I watched the way her black hair streamed behind her. I watched how the seat of her bikini pants, visible under her flapping shirt tail, moved with the flexing mounds of her buttocks. And how her slender legs strode.

As she ran, she held the spear low by her left hip, its shaft parallel to the sand, while her right hand held the tomahawk against her side to stop it from flinging about and pounding her right hip.

Though she didn't pump at all with her arms, she raced along swiftly enough to stay ahead of me.

After a while, she said, 'Give it up, Rupert. Go on back to them.'

'I'm coming with you.'

'Forget it.'

'Just stop and wait,' I gasped. 'You're the one . . . always against us . . . splitting up. We . . . gotta stay . . . together.'

'You'll get in my way,' she said.

'No. Please.'

'I'm gonna do Wesley *my* way. Don't wanta hear you guys whining about it.'

'We . . . won't whine.'

'Forget it. You had your chance. *Adios, amigo.*'

She started to pour it on. I made a dive for her.

My fingertips brushed the flying tail of her shirt. Moments later, both my hands buried themselves in the sand. They shoved ditches into the beach as I flopped on my chest and skidded.

The landing knocked my wind out.

I lifted my head and watched Kimberly sprint up the beach. Spear raised high, she pumped it up and down as she dashed along like a Zulu on the attack.

Missing People

On my hands and knees, I watched Kimberly until she vanished around the point. Then I stood up, brushed the sand off my body, and started trudging back to Billie and Connie. Billie was a couple of hundred yards away from me, Connie another hundred yards or so behind her mother.

The way we were separated, any one of us could've gotten picked off. Keeping an eye on the edge of the jungle, I quickened my pace.

Connie made no attempt to join us. She just stood where she'd stopped, and watched.

When I got within speaking range of Billie, I started shaking my head.

'You almost had her,' Billie said.

'It only looked that way. She slowed down to let me get close.'

'I can't believe she just ran off and left us.'

'She wants to go on by herself.'

Billie handed the ax to me. 'We can't let her.'

'We can't stop her,' I pointed out.

'But we can join her.'

'I guess so. If we can find her.'

'She's on her way to the lagoon,' Billie said. 'We'll just go there.'

We started walking toward Connie.

'What route should we take?' I asked.

'What do you think?' She wasn't being sarcastic; she was asking my advice.

'Well, we could circle around through the jungle, but that's what Kimberly's probably doing. I don't think we'd have any luck intercepting her, either. It'd be too easy for her to sneak past us. So maybe we oughta just go ahead and make a direct approach to the lagoon.'

'Go straight up the stream?'

'Yeah. That'd be the quickest way to get there. We might even reach the lagoon ahead of her.'

Billie made a rueful smile. 'Ahead of her? Think we wanta do that?'

'If we're careful.'

'I'd hate for us to get attacked without Kimberly around to help.'

I shrugged. 'We can probably handle it. I mean, we're talking about Wesley and Thelma. Unless they take us completely by surprise . . .'

'What gives?' Connie called to us.

'Kimberly doesn't want us in her way,' I explained.

'Is she still going to the lagoon?'

'Guess so.'

'Good. We can go back to camp now, right?'

'Sort of,' I said.

'What do you mean, *sort* of?'

'We'll go back,' Billie said, 'but then we're heading straight up the stream.'

'Oh, really?'

'That's the idea,' Billie told her.

'I've got a better idea,' Connie said. 'Let's *not*, and say we did.'

We reached Connie. Then the three of us started walking back toward camp.

'I mean,' Connie said, 'Kimberly obviously doesn't want us with her. Shouldn't we do what she wants, and stay out of it?'

'She'd be outnumbered two to one,' I pointed out.

'That's just assuming Wesley hasn't already bought the farm.'

'Even if he *has*, what's to stop Thelma from jumping her?'

Connie smirked at me. 'You think Kimberly can't take Thelma?'

'Sure, in a fair fight. But maybe she gets jumped from behind. Thelma almost nailed *me*. She isn't that easy.'

'Well, she knew which buttons to push on you, didn't she?'

'There's no point arguing,' Billie broke in. 'We're going up to the lagoon, and that's final.'

'Is it?'

'Yeah, it is.'

'We'll see about that.'

Billie gave her an annoyed glance, but said nothing. For a while after that, none of us spoke.

We were nearly back to our camp when Connie said to her mother, 'It sure is nice to know you care more about Kimberly than you do about me.'

'Don't give me that,' Billie said.

'I've got a splitting headache – and my shoulder's killing me. I'm an absolute wreck, but you're gonna make me hike all the way up to the lagoon just to help Kimberly – who doesn't even *want* our help.'

'But maybe she needs it.'

'Shit, she ran *away* from us. Why should we wipe

ourselves out when she doesn't even . . . ?'

'You know why,' Billie told her.

'I do? Really? That's news to me.'

'She's your sister, for one thing.'

'My *half*-sister.'

'Oh, that's nice. Very nice. If your father could hear you say that . . .'

'Well, he can't. And I don't appreciate you throwing him in my face all the time.'

'He's your father *and* Kimberly's.'

'Big deal.'

'If you don't come with us,' Billie said, 'I can't go. I'm not about to leave you by yourself.'

'Fine.'

'You *have* to do this for her.'

'Yeah? Do I? And what'd she ever do for me?'

They glowered at each other.

'Practically *raised* you, maybe?' Billie said.

'Oh, for Godsake . . .'

'Stayed *home* instead of going away to college. Because of you.'

'She didn't have to do that.'

'No, she didn't *have* to. She wanted to.'

'Didn't wanta miss out on all those fine opportunities to boss me around.'

I couldn't help it. I asked, 'Why *didn't* Kimberly go away to college?'

'She wanted to stay with the family,' Billie explained. 'She never came straight out and said so, but that was the reason. We certainly could've *afforded* to send her anywhere, and she had the grades. I think it was almost entirely because of Connie.'

'My fault.' Connie raised her hand.

'Not your "fault." You were . . . ten or eleven at the time. When Kimberly was just about your age, a year or two older, maybe – that's when Thelma went off to college. Kimberly always . . . She loved Thelma so much. It hurt her so much when Thelma left home.' Billie's eyes filled with tears. She sniffed, wiped her eyes, and said to Connie, 'She just couldn't . . . put *you* through that. You two were so close. She knew how you would miss her.'

Now, tears began to glimmer in Connie's eyes. 'So it *was* my fault.'

'Don't be silly. She loved you, that's all. She didn't want to leave you without your big sister. And she would've missed *you* too much.' Billie looked at me and wiped her eyes. 'That's why,' she said.

I came out with a lame, 'Oh. Just wondering.'

Billie was done crying, but Connie kept it up for a few more minutes. When she finished, she sniffed and rubbed her eyes and said, 'I *still* don't think Kimberly needs any help from us, but I'll go along. I mean, what choice do I have, anyway? It's not like you're gonna let me stay here by myself while *you* two run off to save her bacon. As if her bacon *needs* any saving. I just hope we don't screw things up for her, that's all.'

The surprising thing is that, after all her complaints, Connie ended up taking the lead. She seemed to be in a hurry, too.

Billie's talk must've gotten through to her, somehow – reminded her that Kimberly was more than just a young woman put on this earth to annoy her, boss her around, and turn the heads of her boyfriends.

Leading us upstream through the jungle, it was as if Connie had magically forgotten to be self-absorbed – as if all that mattered was the bond between her and Kimberly.

She could be a wonderful human being for short periods of time.

I'd seen it before. It wouldn't last. But it was nice to see, on the rare occasions when it happened. I found myself actually *liking* Connie again.

Not that I'd ever stopped liking her body. From the neck down, she'd always been really fine. Her face wasn't bad, either. Behind her face is where the troubles lurked – inside her mouth, and in her brain. Her words and her thoughts. And, of course, the actions that came from the thoughts.

I liked *all* of Connie, though, as she led us up the middle of the stream that day.

And she actually did stay that way.

She never got a chance to revert.

The self-centered, whiny, pushy, obnoxious bitch had taken her last bow.

In a way, I almost wish she *hadn't* turned into a caring, decent person for her last hour or so. Might be easier. Maybe I wouldn't miss her so much, now. On the other hand, it's sort of nice – even wonderful – that she wasn't being a shit toward the end of things.

God, I miss her.

I miss her almost as much as I miss Billie and Kimberly.

No, not really. Who am I trying to kid?

I miss Connie a lot, but I miss Billie and Kimberly worse. It kills me to think that I'll never see them again.

And yet, here I sit.

Writing in my journal instead of going to find them.

Why is that?

Simple. If I go looking, I might get killed. God knows, I barely escaped with my life last time.

I'm fairly safe here.

Wesley and Thelma probably think I'm dead. At least for the time being.

Also, there's one other thing.

I really do not want to find any of my women dead.

Which is what might happen if I go looking.

I'd hate that.

It's better, not knowing. This way, I can at least hang on to the possibility that they might not be dead.

Or not *all* of them.

If even just one of them is still alive . . .

If I had to choose one, I wonder which would it be? Not Connie, I'm afraid; she was a bitch too much of the time. Not nearly as attractive as her mother or half-sister, either. She was better than plain, but both of them were beautiful.

So it's between Billie and Kimberly.

It would be sick for me to choose which of them should die. So let's say this: which would I rather have living with me till we get rescued from here?

(If we ever *do* get rescued, which is seeming less likely all the time. God, what if I have to live the rest of my life on this island without any of them? Just me. Never mind. I want to go on with my game of who to pick.)

Kimberly or Billie?

Not an easy choice.

Kimberly is a hothead, sometimes. She can be awfully tough and scary, and would definitely take charge of everything. She would run my life. Which might not be such a bad thing.

Billie is more easy-going and sensible. She's sweet, cheerful and compassionate. She wouldn't push me around. We'd be like great friends. We already are – were – awfully good friends, I think.

Obviously, the smart pick is Billie. We'd be great together. Making love with her would be incredible, too. She has a fabulous body, and knows it, and would probably relish the chance to share it.

I'd give anything, though, for just one time with Kimberly.

Who am I kidding? How about one time with *anyone*?

Losers can't be choosers.

Speaking of losers, I should stop playing games and go out and try to *find* Kimberly, Billie and Connie.

Not yet. I can't go and look for them until I've caught up on my journal. It might be the only way anyone will ever be able to learn what has happened here.

And it gives me an excuse to stay put.

Also, the writing of it helps me to remember them. I describe what they did, what they said, what they wore and how they looked, and it's almost as if they're with me again.

I have them with me whenever I write about them.

Hey, here's a thought. Maybe I'll *never* stop writing about them. When I catch up to the present, I'll just start making things up. Just to keep going.

My journal can turn into the literary equivalent of the Winchester House. I just keep going, building more rooms for my ghosts.

Not a bad idea, but I don't have a hell of a lot of paper left.

When I run out, I'll start writing in the sand.

Here lies one whose name was writ in sand.

That was somebody's epitaph, I think. Keats?

This is far off the track, and getting weird. I'm too tired and way too depressed to go on any more right now. Anyway, it's almost dark.

I'm going to quit now.

Tomorrow will be plenty soon enough to finish off what I can remember about how we got creamed. Then things will be up to date, and then I'll have to figure out what to do next.

Build a staircase to the ceiling, perhaps???

Oh, God.

I wonder if they *are* dead.

If not, what the hell is happening to them – being *done* to them – while I sit here lonesome on the beach fucking around with this stupid journal???

Night Journey

This is the next day.

Last night, I got brave. Or, more likely, just desperate.

So this chapter won't be about our 'last stand,' after all.

Fine with me. I'm not exactly looking forward to the task. I will get to it, but not right now.

Instead, this chapter will be about what happened last night.

After dark, I snuck upstream for a look at the scene of the crime.

It started out as a way to stop feeling like such a worthless loser. I was taking action. I would stalk the night, revisit the places that held such horrible memories, *face* what had happened to us, and search for answers.

Maybe I would find my women alive, and rescue them.

Maybe I would find their bodies.

Maybe I would come upon Wesley and Thelma, and slit their throats.

I had my razor.

I was Rambo.

I was Rambo until I left the beach behind. The moment I waded upstream into the shadows of the jungle – and out of the moonlight – I stopped being Rambo and became Chicken Little. I could see almost nothing, just a few pale speckles and scattered tatters of dim light that somehow made it down through the trees.

I was tempted to turn back. If I went on, I would probably fall in the dark and bust open my face.

I went on, anyway. Taking tiny steps. Hunkering down low so I wouldn't have so far to fall. Keeping both my arms forward to catch myself.

That way, I made slow progress up the stream.

I fell several times, banging up my hands and knees but not getting hurt in any serious way.

Frequently, I stopped to rest, stand up straight, and stretch to get the kinks out. Then I'd bend over again and continue on my way. In spite of the rest stops, all the bending tired me out and made me ache. I finally decided to take my chances and walk upright.

It felt good, walking tall.

I had farther to fall, and the falls hurt more, but I felt sort of proud of myself. I stayed high and even quickened my pace.

Sometimes, I felt as if Billie, Kimberly and Connie were walking with me through the night. I couldn't see them, but they were there. In front of me, behind me, wading by my side.

Other times, I felt alone.

Worse than alone. There can be comfort and peace in being truly alone. The bad kind of alone is not when you're all by yourself, but when your only company is an unseen stranger, imagined or real, creeping toward you in the dark. You have nobody to help you. There's no safe place to run. All you can do is keep going and hope for the best.

That sort of aloneness gives you goosebumps scurrying up your spine. It makes your scalp crawl. It makes you feel like someone has shoved an icy hand against your crotch.

That's the way I felt, off and on, while I was making my semi-blind way up the stream last night.

Off and on.

Coldly spooked when I felt the loneliness.

Warm and safe when the women seemed to be with me.

Off and on. I knew it was only my mind playing games, but I couldn't control it.

Sometimes, I nearly screamed with fright and ran like hell.

Other times, surrounded by my phantom ladies, I loved the darkness and warmth of the night.

I felt the good way as I approached the lagoon.

Raising my eyes, I saw the moonlit slab of rock where Kimberly had stretched herself flat, days ago, to scan the lagoon for signs of Thelma and Wesley. I climbed onto it. I lay down on it, in exactly the place where Kimberly had been. The warmth of the rock seeped through my shirt and shorts.

She was with me. Her heat was in me.

That's how I felt, anyhow. It was only in my mind, but maybe that's no great reason to discount it.

Lying there, I slowly scanned the lagoon.

In places, it sparkled with points of silver moonlight. Mostly, though, it looked black.

This was not a *forbidding* blackness.

The opposite. One look, and I wanted to be in it. Could hardly wait.

I told myself that I hadn't come up here for a dip in the lagoon; I'd come to look for the women.

To search for them beyond the far side of the lagoon, above the waterfall and farther upstream where we'd last been together. I wouldn't find them here. Maybe not there, either, but that was the place to start.

To get there, I needed to cross the lagoon.

On my feet, I looked all around. No glow of firelight was anywhere to be seen. Nor did I see a sign of anyone's presence. I listened. The only sounds were birds and bugs, plus some of the usual jungle shrieks and jibbers (God knows what they came from), and the quiet splashing sounds of the waterfall on the other side of the lagoon.

Bits of moonlight lit the falls. Otherwise, they were black except for a few dim, gray streamers of froth at the bottom.

I wanted to feel the waterfall spilling onto me. I wanted to feel the *lagoon* and the night air. I wanted to be gliding through the black water, naked.

I took off my shirt and shoes and socks.

Then I took off my shorts. Naked, I crouched and set them down. I pulled the straight razor out of the right front pocket.

Though I wanted complete freedom in the water – nothing to carry – I suddenly found myself reluctant to leave the razor behind. Someone might steal it. Or I might chance upon Wesley or Thelma. Without the razor, how would I defend myself?

After giving the matter some thought, I put on my right sock and slipped the razor down inside it against my ankle.

Which was exactly the same way I'd carried Andrew's Swiss Army knife up the tree to cut down Keith. I started to remember about that. It was more than a week ago, but seemed like it had just happened. I could *feel* the tree against my body, *see* Keith hanging . . .

'Don't think about it,' I said. Even though I spoke in a whisper, the sound of my voice unnerved me a little.

Who *else* might've heard it?

Standing up straight, I looked around. I stood motionless and listened. And started to feel very exposed and vulnerable.

I began imagining that someone was out there, hidden in the darkness, spying on me, creeping closer.

As fast as I could, I climbed down the rocky bank and eased myself into the water. My legs vanished. A moment later, everything below my waist was gone, as if I'd been sawed in half by a magician.

Right away, I felt safer.

It would be no trick, at all, to disappear entirely.

My chills began to fade. My goosebumps started to go away. My tight muscles relaxed. A pleasant warmth seemed to be spreading through my whole body.

I felt even better as I waded into deeper water. When it reached my neck, I looked down and there was none of me left to see.

I had become invisible.

Except for my head, of course. Even though I couldn't see it, I knew that it showed.

If anyone was watching.

So I ducked below the surface to make my head invisible.

Now, I was completely gone. Completely safe. I was all alone in the warm water, surrounded by a jungle where my enemies might be lurking . . . I felt wonderful. I was not only safe, but invincible.

Staying below, I swam. The water flowed along my body, warm and smooth. After a while, my lungs began to ache. I stayed below, anyway. Soon, I heard the shooshing and plottering of the waterfall.

Underneath the falls, I found footing on the rocky bottom. I turned around and came up slowly. The curtain of dropping water pattered on top of my head, ran down the sides of my face, splashed softly into the water still covering my shoulders.

My head was no longer invisible.

I didn't feel frightened, though – maybe because it would be so easy to disappear again.

I stood up straight.

And shivered as I did it. This was no shiver of fear, though. This was excitement. I felt daring and powerful as more and more of my body came out of the lagoon and into full view of anyone who might be watching.

How different this was from my last time here! Only a couple of days ago, I'd stood battered and aching and desolate beneath these very falls. I'll have to write about that in more detail. Soon. Not now, though. For now, I want to tell about last night.

And how I continued to rise up under the falls.

When I was bare down to my waist, I shut my eyes. The falling water splashed onto the top of my head, onto my shoulders and outstretched arms. It slid down my body like warm oil.

This was where Connie had stood, naked, rubbing herself with her wadded T-shirt. She'd stood with her back to me.

In my mind, I turned her around.

I became her.

I was Connie standing under the waterfall, arms out, trembling as the water spilled down my naked body, showing myself to an imaginary Rupert.

Which sounds a trifle odd, now that I try to write about it.

Let's just say I let my imagination run wild for a while, there at the falls last night. I had so many different emotions swarming through me, I'm lucky I didn't go nuts entirely and stay that way.

After a while, though, I remembered my reasons for coming up to the lagoon.

Namely, to search for Connie, Billie and Kimberly.

Not for their spirits, but for their bodies – alive or dead.

And to see if I could get some idea about where Wesley and Thelma might be.

To kill them, if I could.

So I waded over to the flat rock where we'd taken Connie after she'd been knocked out. I boosted myself up, got to my feet, and climbed to the top of the falls.

Even though I'd finally gotten back to business, I still felt strange. I was dripping wet and shivering – trembling from head to toe. My *jaw* even shook. The night probably hadn't turned any colder while I'd been in the lagoon, but it felt as if the temperature had dropped about twenty degrees. Also, I was gripped by a weird mixture of fear and excitement.

At the top of the falls, I stood in a patch of moonlight and gazed down at the lagoon.

My lagoon.

It seemed like a wonderful place just then, and all mine. It was my own private swimming hole, a place where I could be completely free and completely safe, where I could dwell in my memories of Kimberly, Connie and Billie – where they would come alive in my fantasies.

Better to have imaginary friends and lovers than none at all.

In some ways, they might even be an improvement over the real thing. If they only exist in your mind, they can't get killed.

Plus, they cooperate better than . . .

(That's me, going off the deep end again. Maybe I was having – *am* having? – a slight encounter with a touch of mental breakdown. Could that be? Tee hee hee. And I ain't even gotten to the BAD part yet. The bad part about last night, that is – as opposed to the bad part when we got attacked several days ago and all three of my women . . . Never mind. That's for later, too. I should get back to last night.)

I'll skip over some of the weird shit I was feeling and thinking, etc., while I roamed the jungle naked with the razor in my sock. I've got so much to write about, anyway, without dwelling on stuff like that. (Not to mention that I've already filled up more than three-quarters of my notebook. I have about a hundred empty pages left, and that's counting both sides of the paper.)

Here's how it went last night. From the top of the falls, I followed the stream uphill, climbing through the shadows and the moonlight toward the place among the rocks where we'd found Kimberly on the day I think of as 'the last stand.'

I wanted to see where it had happened.

That would be the best place to start my search.

The Calm Before The Storm

Before I go on with the rest of what happened last night, I'd better tell what happened to me and the women at the chasm. Last night will make more sense that way.

When I left off, we were wading upstream, Connie in the lead. Earlier, Kimberly had run away from us on the beach. She was afraid we might try to tone down her vengeance, so she wanted a crack at Wesley without us.

We were afraid that, going after him alone, she might get herself killed.

We hurried up the stream. Though we splashed quite a bit, we didn't speak.

Connie and I slapped mosquitoes, now and then. They weren't as bad as they'd been on the day we made our first trip to the lagoon, but plenty of them buzzed around us and settled on us and sucked our blood and tickled, so we both worked at smacking them flat. (The critters didn't bother Billie, of course. My theory is that they didn't want to spoil her fabulous body by marking it with little red bumps.)

Anyway, we waded up the stream at a good, quick pace, and didn't speak at all for quite a while. We were afraid of giving away our position. None of us, I think, looked forward to a premature encounter with the enemy. If it came to a fight, we wanted Kimberly to be with us.

About halfway to our destination, though, Billie broke into song.

'*Once a jol-ly swagman . . . !*'

Connie twisted around. 'Mom!'

'What?'

'Shhhh!!!!'

'Let's all sing,' Billie suggested.

Connie's attitude had improved so much that she didn't blurt out, 'Fuck you!' Instead, she asked, 'What on earth for?'

'It's a great day for singing.' Billie looked over her shoulder at me, and smiled. 'Don't you think so, Rupert?'

'They'll hear us,' I said, and whacked my neck to mash a mosquito.

'That's the idea,' she said. 'Let's get their attention, if we don't already have it.'

Connie lifted her eyebrows. 'So they'll worry about us instead of Kimberly?'

'Exactly,' Billie said. 'It might not even occur to them that Kimberly isn't with us.'

'As long as they don't *see* us,' I added.

Billie grinned. 'If they're busy watching us, they aren't watching Kimberly.'

'Okay,' I said. 'But we'd better be ready for them.'

'What the hell,' Connie said.

'Let's do it,' said Billie.

Off we went, marching up the stream, the three of us singing 'Waltzing Matilda' at the top of our lungs. Billie and Connie seemed to know the lyrics by heart – Andrew, the Navy lifer, had probably learned the song on shore leave in Australia, or something, and taught it to them. I knew most of the words, myself. (I've made it a point, since

I was a little kid, to memorize song lyrics, poems, all sorts of quotes that impress me.) We sounded damn good, bellowing it out.

Even though the song is mostly about death and ghosts, it's so jaunty that I felt great singing it.

We were flaunting ourselves, taunting Wesley and Thelma if they were near enough to hear our cheerfully defiant marching song.

After 'Waltzing Matilda,' we sang 'Hit the Road, Jack.' I didn't know the words at first, but caught on after listening to Billie and Connie. Then we sang, 'Hey, Jude,' which we all knew most of the words to.

For our next song, I suggested, 'We're off to See the Wizard.'

Billie laughed. 'Oh, that's rich.' Rich, mostly, because I was lugging an ax. 'You make a cute Tin Woodsman,' she said. 'I'll be the Cowardly Lion.'

Cute. She'd called me cute.

'Gimme a break,' Connie said. 'We're choosing *parts*? What does that leave me, the Scarecrow? Fat chance. What was he looking for, a brain? Thanks, but no thanks.'

'You can be Dorothy,' I told her, smiling.

'What if I don't *want* to be Dorothy? Dorothy's a woos.'

'That leaves Toto,' Billie said.

'A dog. Thanks a heap, Mother. If we're gonna sing the damn song, let's just get on with it, okay? You guys can pretend to be whoever you want, just include me out.'

'Party pooper,' Billie said.

'You and the horse you rode in on.'

'Cowardly Lions don't ride horses,' I pointed out.

Connie gave me a narrow look, then smiled. 'And doughnut holes don't fly,' she said, 'but maybe you can take a leap at one, anyway.'

'Let's sing,' Billie said.

Without any more discussion, we started in on 'The Wizard of Oz.'

Turned out, none of us knew the words very well. We made an energetic botch of the song, then quit when we reached the flat, slanting rock just below the lagoon.

This time, nobody went sneaking up the rock to take a look around. Connie leading the way, the three of us climbed its face. We stood at the top in full view of anyone who might be watching.

We saw nobody.

'Now what?' Connie whispered.

'Kimberly was planning to come in from the rear,' Billie said. 'She'll probably be over on the other side.'

'Somewhere upstream,' I added.

'So I guess we swim across,' Billie said.

'Not me,' I said. 'I can't swim anywhere with this ax.'

'Leave it here?' Billie asked.

'Somebody might swipe it. Besides, what if we need it?'

'Guess you're right,' she said. 'Maybe we'd better walk around to the other side.'

I expected Connie to say, 'Be my guest,' then dive in and swim across. I wouldn't have blamed her, either. *I* wanted to dive in. The water looked wonderful. Also, it would've been very soothing on our mosquito bites.

Connie surprised me, saying, 'I'll go first.' Then she turned to the left and began to make her way along the shoreline. Billie followed her, and I took up the rear.

It wasn't easy going. A lot of climbing. A lot of ducking under branches. A lot of squeezing through tight places. A lot of tricky footwork, crossing ledges and steep slopes and deadfalls. A lot of huffing and sweating.

I felt responsible. After a while, I said, 'Are you two sure you wouldn't rather go on and swim across? I can meet you on the other side.'

'This is the *last* place we oughta start splitting up,' Billie said.

'You got a death wish?' Connie asked me.

'I just feel bad about making you do this.'

'You're doing *us* the favor,' Billie said. 'Hell, you're hauling around our major piece of weaponry.'

She was right about that.

And very sweet to point it out.

They both seemed to accept this rough haul as an unavoidable part of our mission to hook up with Kimberly, and didn't blame me.

We stayed as close as possible to the water. That way, we had a good view of the lagoon and most of the opposite shore, including the waterfall. We kept our eyes open for Kimberly. And we watched for any signs of Wesley or Thelma.

Being at the rear, I watched our backs.

I couldn't help, from time to time, also watching the backs of Billie and Connie.

Billie's close-cropped hair, dripping with sweat, clung to her head in dark ringlets. Her back, richly dark from the sun (sunblock only goes so far), gleamed as if she'd been dipped in melted butter. Her back was crossed by the single rope of her tomahawk sling, and by the three coils of the long rope. The tomahawk bounced and swayed against her right hip as she walked. The seat of her black bikini pants was packed with her full, firm buttocks. I remember thinking, as I followed her, how I would've loved to see her wearing a thong like Connie's.

As for Connie, her short, blond hair looked almost exactly like her mother's. But that's where the resemblances stopped. She didn't have the broad shoulders, the wide back, or the impressive hips and rump. From behind, she looked like skin and bones while her mother looked like flesh and blood.

She wore the towel-vest, which covered most of her back. Below the rear of the vest, she was naked except for a waistband and a strip of orange fabric that descended (and very nearly vanished) between her buttocks. Her cheeks were brown and shiny, but had a few red bumps from the mosquitoes.

Both women were wonderful to watch.

For about an hour, I worked my way along behind them, struggling with the weight of the ax, keeping an eye out for trouble, and for Kimberly, and savoring my views of Billie and Connie.

I'm glad that I didn't try to be a perfect gentleman and avoid looking at them; pretty soon they would be gone and I might never have another chance to see them.

I didn't know that at the time.

I only knew that we were together on a mission, that I could admire them from behind to my heart's content, that I loved them both, and that this was one of those few, special times I would always look back on with fondness and sorrow.

The great times are often that way.

In the middle of everything, you suddenly realize that you're having a perfect, golden experience. And you realize how few they are. And how this one is bound to end too soon. You know that it will always be a wonderful memory, that the loss of it will give you a soft ache in the heart.

This was one of those times.

It had begun, I realize now, with 'Waltzing Matilda.'

It ended upstream, in the rocks beyond the lagoon, at the edge of the chasm.

By the time we reached the other side of the lagoon, we were drenched with sweat and gasping for breath. Instead of pausing to rest, however, we climbed the rocks alongside the waterfall.

We no sooner reached the top than Kimberly shouted, 'Over here!'

We spotted her standing on a boulder by the side of the stream, waving her arms back and forth. She was uphill from us, about a hundred feet away. Her spear leaned against the boulder, close enough for her to crouch and grab in case of an emergency. But if she fell on it . . .

The idea made me grimace.

While we approached her, she climbed down.

Didn't fall and get skewered.

Scooted on her rump down the face of the rock, then jumped to the ground.

'Was that you guys singing?' she asked.

'Who else *would* it be?' Connie said.

She smiled. 'I couldn't believe my ears. You're coming to my rescue belting out songs?'

'You obviously didn't require rescuing,' Billie said.

'It's the thought that counts.'

'We would've sung "The Gary Owen," ' I told her, 'but I don't know the words.'

'The Gary what?' Connie asked.

Kimberly wrinkled her nose. 'Is that the Seventh Cavalry song?' she asked.

'Right.' I hummed a few bars.

Billie grinned. She said, 'Ah, John Wayne.'

'George Armstrong Custer,' I said.

'That would've been choice,' Kimberly said.

'You being part Sioux, and all . . .'

'Anyway, I'm glad you came.'

'We thought you might be able to use some help,' Billie told her. 'Even if you *didn't* want us getting in your way.'

'Hey, I'm sorry about that. I got a little carried away down there. Anyway, as it turns out, you don't have to worry about me going nuts and torturing the hell out of Wesley. The bastard's dead.'

'Whoa!' Connie said. (I think she meant it to mean, 'Wow!')

'You found him?' I asked.

She nodded. 'Let's go. I'll show you.' She started leading us through the strange terrain to the right of the stream.

'What about Thelma?' Billie asked.

'No sign of her. But at least we don't have to worry about Wesley anymore.'

We followed Kimberly on a zigzag route through a maze of boulders, bushes, trees, and rock piles that jutted up like miniature mountains. Though we walked through patches of shadows, there was more sunlight than we'd seen since the beach. A gentle breeze blew. It cooled my sweat, and kept the mosquitoes away.

'He's through *here*?' Connie asked. 'How did you ever find him?'

'Took a while. This is upstream from the falls, like Thelma said.'

'But conveniently close to the falls and lagoon,' I pointed out.

'Yep. To me, it seemed like just exactly the right sort of area. You could hide an army through here. So I scouted around for a while. I climbed that.' She pointed at a tall cluster of rocks, not far ahead of us.

'You must've been here a while,' Billie said.

'I hurried. I was pretty sure you guys would come after me, sooner or later, and I wanted a chance to find Wesley before you got here. *Thought* I'd find him alive.'

'That's what we were afraid of,' Connie told her. 'That's how come we tried to hurry.'

'What took you so long?'

'We had to go around the lagoon,' I explained. 'We couldn't swim across because of the ax.'

'I'm glad you showed up when you did.' She smiled. 'Better late than never.' She seemed quite cheerful. 'Anyway, I was up there when I spotted something that looked like a pair of red panties on the ground. I figured they must be Thelma's. So what I did, I climbed down and went over to check them out. They were right by the edge of a chasm. I sort of peered over the edge, and there he was, down at the bottom. I could hardly believe my eyes. It was Wesley, all right.'

'And he's definitely dead?' I asked.

'I'd say so. You'll see.'

'So,' Connie said, 'now we only have to worry about Thelma.' She glanced nervously at several nearby places where the gal might be lurking.

Billie said, 'Don't worry. She isn't likely to jump all four of us.'

'I can't figure her out,' Kimberly said. 'Looks like she told us the truth, after all, about killing Wesley. His head's bashed in, just like she said. So how come she went for Rupert with the razor? I mean, we figured Wesley must've sent her. That idea doesn't quite work anymore.'

'She must've had some other reason,' Billie suggested.

'You try putting moves on her?' Connie asked me.

I blushed and blurted, 'No!'

Connie smirked. 'Not your type?'

'Not even close.'

'She must've had some kind of reason,' Billie said, frowning slightly as if puzzled.

Kimberly smiled. 'We'll just have to ask her when she shows up.'

'I'm hoping she *doesn't*,' I said. 'If I never see her again in my whole life, it won't be too soon.'

'She'll show up.'

'What makes you so sure?' I asked.

'You've got her favorite razor.' As Kimberly said that, she gave me a look and a smile that not only let me know she was kidding around, but somehow made me feel as if everything would turn out fine and dandy.

God, how I would love to see that look again, that smile. Nevermore.

I shouldn't say that. I shouldn't give up hope. Not till I've seen her dead body with my own eyes. And even *that* might not make anything certain.

Plenty around here is not what it seems to be.

I've started drifting again. Procrastinating. The problem is, I just don't want to tell about what's coming. I've got to, though.

The Last Stand

We arrived at the chasm.

Maybe 'chasm' isn't the best word to describe it – this wasn't the Grand Canyon. It was actually a long, narrow space between a couple of neighboring rock formations. I would guess it was thirty feet long, and about six or eight feet from edge to edge at the place where we were approaching it. At one end, the gap narrowed down to nothing. At the other end, it stopped at the open air of a drop-off.

Striding toward the gap, Kimberly tossed her spear to the ground and rid herself of the tomahawk. She didn't halt, though, until she reached the very edge. There, she bent over as if taking a bow, and planted her hands on her knees.

The rest of us held back.

'He's down there?' Connie asked.

'Yep. Come and take a look.'

'I'd just as soon not, if it's all the same.'

Kimberly straightened up. Swiveling at the hips, she looked back at us. 'Doesn't anyone want to see him?'

I raised my hand.

'Well, come on over here.'

'I'll hold the ax for you,' Billie told me, so I gave it to her.

Then I forced myself to step forward. The last thing I really wanted was to look at another dead guy. God knows, two were more than enough. But I needed to see for myself that Wesley was down there, and that he wasn't alive.

I couldn't force myself to walk all the way to the edge, as Kimberly had done. When I got close to it, I went down on all fours. I crawled the rest of the way.

The chasm wasn't nearly as deep as I'd feared.

Deep enough, though. Fifteen or twenty feet, probably, with very steep walls on both sides. The bottom looked like a flat but slightly tilted slab of rock. A few bushes sprouted here and there out of crevices in the walls and floor.

The whole time I was busy inspecting the dimensions and general appearance of the chasm, I was trying *not* to see the body.

It was just to the left down there.

I kept seeing it in my peripheral vision while I studied everything *except* the body.

I finally had to look, though.

He was sprawled face down. At first glance, he might've been a guy who'd drifted off to sleep while doing a bit of nude sunbathing. But his skin was a bad color. And he had a hole in his ass where there shouldn't be one – in the middle of his right buttock. And the back of his head was a ruin of mashed, black mush. Also, his left leg showed a lot of bone from the knee down; some sort of animal must've been working on it – an animal a lot larger than the ones I saw crawling on him and buzzing over him.

'You don't get much deader than that,' Kimberly said. She was by my side, bent over, her hair hanging down so I couldn't see her face. It's just as well that her face was out of sight. It must've worn a look of delight. Because that's what I heard in her voice. 'There's a fine example of what we call "dead meat,"' she said.

'Guess so,' I muttered, unable to work up much enthusiasm.

When she stepped back, I crawled away from the edge and stood up.

'Nobody else interested?' she asked, and took off Keith's shirt as she walked over to where she'd left her tomahawk and spear.

'I can live without seeing him,' Billie said.

'Let me have your rope,' Kimberly said.

Billie frowned. 'What for?'

'I'm going down.'

'You're kidding,' I muttered. 'You don't want to do that.'

'Sure I do.' Kimberly had *never* seemed so perky. It was scary. 'Have to make sure it's him.'

'Of course it's him. Who else could it be?'

'Gilligan?' she suggested. 'The professor? D.B. Cooper? Who knows? Could be almost anyone.'

'It's Wesley,' I said.

Connie scowled at her. 'You *told* us it's Wesley.'

'I'm sure it *is* him. I'm just not *sure* sure. That's why I need to go down and turn him over.'

Turn him over?

'Oh jeez,' I said. 'Don't. You don't want to *touch* him.'

She gave me a strange smile and said, 'Sure I do.'

'Be my guest,' Billie said. Nose wrinkled, she lifted the coils of rope off her shoulder and swung them over her head. She held them out to Kimberly, who took them.

'There's really no reason to go down there,' I protested. 'Really. I mean, you know and I know that it's Wesley, so . . .'

'Maybe *you* know, bucko.'

'*You* know, too.'

'I know no such thing.'

'It's not funny!'

'Am I being funny?'

'You're being *strange*.'

'He's right,' Connie said.

'How about we just call it quits and go back to the beach,' Billie suggested.

The quirky grin vanished from Kimberly's face. 'I'm gonna do what I'm gonna do. What I'm gonna do is go down and pay a visit to our dead friend because if he's *not* Wesley I wanta know it and if he *is* Wesley . . .' She shrugged.

'What?' Billie asked.

'Nothing. I just have to know for sure it's him. That's all. You know what? I'm not so sure, anymore. The more I think about it, the more this guy doesn't look *big* enough to be Wesley.'

'That's a crock,' I said.

Without another word, Billie walked to the edge and peered down. Then she made a sound. 'Uhhh.' After about a minute, she turned around and came back to us. She looked ill. 'It's gotta be Wesley,' she muttered. 'Who else *could* it be? Anyway, I think people are *supposed* to look smaller when they're dead.'

'*You* think he looks smaller?' Connie blurted.

'Well . . . sort of. Wesley was a pretty big guy . . .'

'The dead guy's big,' I pointed out.

'I'm not sure he's *as* big.'

Connie muttered, 'Jesus.'

'He's got Kimberly's spear hole in his ass,' I said. 'And his head's caved in, just the way Thelma . . .'

'Making him conveniently difficult to identify,' Kimberly

said. 'And anybody could've poked a hole in someone's butt.'

'In *whose* butt?' I blurted. 'Who else *is* there?'

Kimberly's smile returned. Not her spectacular smile -- her bizarre and gleeful one. 'Remains to be seen, Watson.'

With that, she twirled around and made her spritely way to the edge of the chasm. Holding one end of the rope, she let the rest of it fall over the edge. Then she faced us and shook her head. 'Not long enough. We'll have to add on the tomahawk ropes.'

By that time, we were all ready to cooperate. We hadn't had much faith in Kimberly's judgment, but Billie's doubts had turned the trick. *She* wasn't one hundred per cent sure the body belonged to Wesley, so we really needed to make an absolutely positive ID.

While I stood guard with the ax, the women took apart their tomahawk slings.

Billie tied the knots. The three shorter pieces added at least twelve feet to the length of the rope.

Kimberly held one end and tossed the rest of it over the edge. 'Reaches,' she announced.

I looked around for a good place to tie off the upper end. A tree trunk, for instance. Or a solid jut of rock. There was nothing of the sort near enough to the edge. 'I guess we'll have to lower you,' I said.

'Nope. I'll just climb down.'

Apparently, she'd already figured out what to do. She took the ax from me, carried it toward the edge, and turned the ax so its haft pointed away from the chasm. Then she squatted and shoved the blade into a crack in the rocks. Standing up, she stomped it deeper.

She tied a loop at her end of the rope and slipped it down the haft until it stopped against the steel head.

'That should do it,' she said. 'Rupe, how about hanging on to the ax handle? Just keep it pushed down, and try not to let the head pop out of the crack.'

I nodded. 'Okay, but . . .'

'Or stand on the ax. Whatever.'

'Okay.' Crouching, I clutched the wooden handle just below the loop of rope. 'Got it,' I said.

'Good guy,' she said. She gave my shoulder a gentle squeeze, then moved around in front of me. Briefly, we were forehead to forehead. Then she crawled backward, the rope on the ground between her knees.

'Be careful,' Billie said.

'For Godsake, don't fall,' Connie said.

They both moved in closer. Billie stood near my left side, while Connie sank down to one knee on my right. They were ready to help if anything should go wrong.

So far, Kimberly hadn't even taken hold of the rope. Hands pressed against the edge of the chasm, she lowered her legs. Then she stopped. She held herself there, braced up with stiff arms in front of me, the ledge pushing a long dent across both her thighs. Her shoulders and arms, usually so slender and smooth, bulged with curves of muscle. So did her breasts. They swelled, smooth and round, ballooning the pouches of her white bikini. Her dark skin dripped sweat and glistened.

'Rupe,' she said.

I met her eyes.

'I'm gonna lose my knife.'

I looked at it.

I'd been trying to avoid looking there.

As usual, the Swiss Army knife was tucked in between her bare skin and waistband at the very front of her bikini pants. Its top end stuck up more than usual – about half an inch. The thickness of the handle held the pants away from her body, and made a bulge all the way down.

I saw her problem right away; if she tried to lower herself any further, the rock ledge would push at the bottom end of the knife, thrusting it up and out.

'Take it,' she said.

'Uh . . .'

She sort of rolled her eyes upward. 'Just do it. Please.'

'*I'll* get it,' Connie said, sounding annoyed. Up on one knee, though, she was too far away. She started to put her other knee down.

'Never mind,' I said. Leaning over the ax, I planted my left hand on the ground to hold myself steady while I reached for the knife with my right hand.

I found myself gazing nearly straight down into wedges of open space on either side of the knife handle. Twin triangles formed by red plastic, white spandex, and bare skin. Smooth, flawless, private skin and curls of black hair.

The view sucked my breath out, made my heart start to slam, and sent a quick surge through my groin. I grew hard as I reached down to rescue the knife.

I tried to pinch the tip of the handle where it jutted out above her waistband.

Not enough there to get a firm grip on.

So I slipped my thumb and forefinger down inside. By accident, they brushed ever so softly against her skin. I felt the smoothness, and moaned. I murmured, 'Sorry,' in a shaky voice.

I was taking too long.

I squeezed the sides of the handle between my thumb and forefinger, and slowly lifted. The knife slid upward. I could feel the tightness of it, trapped like it was. But it came up smoothly. When it was nearly all the way out, I stole a glimpse down deep inside the gaping front of her pants.

Then the elastic snapped back. Her pants shut like a mouth.

'Got it,' I murmured.

'Thanks,' Kimberly said.

Thank you, I thought. Didn't say it, though.

I raised my head and forced a smile. The look she gave me, she knew what had happened. She'd *intended* it. Or maybe I just read that into her look, and all she'd really intended was to have me stop the knife from falling out. Who knows?

'If you need any help down there . . .' I said. The words were out before I realized they could be taken in a couple of different ways.

I expected Connie to pop out with a nasty crack. She didn't, though.

Kimberly said, 'I might want you to lower the knife to me. We'll see.'

'Sure. Just let me know.'

She bent her arms. The stone edge rubbed its way up her thighs, her groin and belly. Propped up on her elbows, she grabbed the rope with one hand.

I took my position beside the ax. Keeping the knife snug inside my right hand, I held the ax handle down with my left. By the time I looked at Kimberly again, only the top of her head showed. A moment later, it vanished below the rim.

With Kimberly out of view, I focused on the ax and the rope. They looked fine. The ax seemed to be solidly planted in the crack. The rope, taut and stiff, vibrated slightly.

Connie was still beside me on one knee.

Billie still stood near the edge, watching Kimberly's descent.

Someone yelled '*YAHHHHHH!*'

The noise of it almost stopped my heart. For an instant, I thought Kimberly'd fallen. The yell didn't sound like her voice, though.

Sounded like a man's voice.

I raised my head.

He came at us from the other side of the chasm, yelling as he charged. He didn't look like Wesley. He *was* Wesley, though. And he *was* bigger than the guy in the chasm.

Even though I only saw him for a few seconds, I remember every detail as if I'd snapped a photo of him. Or caught him on videotape, to be more accurate – they're *moving* pictures. Often, I see them in slow motion.

Somewhere, Wesley had gotten hold of a blue cap. He wore it backward, the plastic adjustable tabs across the middle of his forehead so he looked like some sort of fat, white gangsta rapper.

He also wore Thelma's large, red brassiere. He seemed to be using it as a harness to hold a bandage in place against his left boob; the red cup on that side was stuffed to bulging. The right cup had been cut away, so his hairy tit bulged out through the frame, bouncing and flopping as he dashed toward the chasm.

Since the night of the ambush – the last time I'd seen Wesley – he had also found a leather belt. If he'd come upon a pair of pants to go with it, though, he'd chosen to go without. He wore the belt around his waist, and hunting knives in leather sheaths at each hip.

On his feet, he wore a pair of high-topped sneakers.

He wore nothing else except his own sweat, hair, and hard-on.

He was pretty damn funny-looking, in a way.

But there wasn't much amusing about how he ran at us yelling like a madman and waving machetes overhead with both hands.

Even though I'm able to see him in slow motion, everything actually happened very fast. He had almost reached the far edge of the chasm by the time I raised my head and saw him coming.

Connie made a squeaky little noise.

Billie let out a loud gasp.

Wesley was in mid-leap before any of us started to move. Connie started trying to get off her knee. Billie began to turn and take a step backward. On my knees, I opened my hand and glanced down at the shiny red plastic handle of the Swiss Army knife, the silvery edges of the blades and tools that were safely folded away.

No chance of getting a blade out in time.

I started trying to get off my knees.

Billie, glancing over her shoulder, flinched and gaped. Her arms began to rise as she continued to twist around. Something about her expression and posture reminded me of a football player lunging for an interception.

In that instant, I knew Thelma must be attacking from the rear.

I heard Wesley's sneaker whap close by. Still in a crouch, I turned my head and glimpsed him on our side of the chasm – but not directly in front of me. Off a bit to my right. Charging straight at Connie.

I tried to stand up faster.

Connie had managed to get up. She was in the midst of turning her back to him, flinging her arms forward as if reaching for help.

That's where it stops.

That's all I remember about our 'last stand.'

Just at that point, I imagine, Thelma must've nailed me from behind.

Perchance To Dream

Here's my guess. While I was out cold from a blow to the head, someone 'disposed' of me.

That is, threw or shoved me over the edge of the chasm.

My guess is also that the fall didn't finish me off because I landed on the dead guy.

Lucky me.

My buddy, Matt.

Short for Mattress.

I slept on him for a long time, in a condition known as 'dead to the world.'

What's the difference, I wonder, between being in a coma and simply being knocked out cold? Just that one lasts longer? I don't know, and it doesn't much matter.

At some point, I 'came to' in the night.

I opened my eyes, saw a starry sky above me, wondered vaguely where I was, decided I must be on a camping trip, then faded out again.

I came to again with the sun baking me. I wished someone would make the sun go away; it felt way too hot, and made my head throb. Then the sun went away and stopped bothering me.

Bugs bothered me, off and on. Mostly, I ignored them.

Sometimes, I found myself enjoying how they tickled.

I must've had a hundred dreams. I could write to the last page of this notebook, and not be able to finish describing all the dreams that rambled through my sore head (many of which I'd like to forget, but can't) while I was sprawled there at the bottom of the chasm.

They were much more vivid and realistic than regular dreams.

Some of them were extremely erotic. Those mostly featured Kimberly, but I had some doozies with Billie and Connie, along with various combinations of the three.

Thelma found her way into some of my dreams. Those were usually sexy, but in a nightmarish way. Often her razor played a part. The Thelma dreams were really sick and perverted and repulsive.

The same goes for most of my other nightmares.

Horrible.

In one, for example, I was climbing the tree to cut down Keith's body after he'd been hanged. Which was lousy enough in real life. In my dream, though, it got worse. He suddenly swung toward me by his neck and embraced me – wrapped his arms and legs around me – and started to chew off my nose.

That one was nasty, but brief.

I had several nightmares that seemed endless.

Of those, one that I remember vividly involved a group of women who came walking up the beach toward me on a beautiful, sunny day. I didn't know who they were at first. For one thing, they were naked so I couldn't tell them apart by what they wore. For another, they didn't have their heads. Their necks ended at pulpy, bloodless stumps.

I was pretty turned on, but also spooked.

They said I could save them, if I wanted to badly enough. (This in spite of having no heads.) I was eager to save them, and asked how. They said, 'You have to match us up.'

That's when I realized that each woman was holding something out of sight behind her back.

They brought their arms around to the front.

Each woman was carrying a head.

Among the heads, I recognized the faces of Connie, Billie, Kimberly, Thelma, Wesley, Miss Curtis (my fifth-grade teacher whom I'd had a terrible crush on), Ardeth Swan (a girlfriend from high school – never got to first base with her), and a total stranger (I think) who looked sort of cute except for all the rings and bolts and pins sticking out all over her face and ears.

The last head belonged to my own mother. God knows what it was doing there, but it sure added to the creepy weirdness of the nightmare.

Right off the bat, it was clear to me that none of the ladies was holding on to her own head.

Wesley's head explained the rules of the game. 'If you wanta save us, you've gotta match up our heads correctly before sundown. Think you can do that, little buddy?'

'I wouldn't save you if I could,' I told him.

Besides, Wesley's body wasn't even there. Of the nine decapitated bodies standing in front of me on the beach, each and every one appeared to be a properly equipped female.

I took Wesley's noggin out of the hands of a heavy-set gal, and tossed it down the beach. Then I rushed over to Thelma's head, plucked it out of the hands of a slim gal I suspected of being Connie, and hurried with it over to the stocky gal who'd been holding Wesley's head. I plonked it down on her neck stub.

Thelma, now properly assembled, smiled and wiggled her fingers at me.

I won't go through the whole nightmare. I don't want to even *think* about some of what happened, much less write it down. So I'll skip the worst parts, and just tell about the stuff that isn't quite as disturbing.

Through the whole dream, whether I was laughing or feeling horny or confused or disgusted or terrified, I always had this terrible, heavy feeling of dread. Nobody'd explained what would happen if I failed to match the heads correctly with the bodies before sundown – aside from the obvious, that I wouldn't 'save' the women. But I had a feeling that my fate might be something too creepy for words.

Sundown was fast approaching.

So I raced back and forth, snatching heads out of hands, rushing this way and that, shoving them down onto neck stubs.

It wasn't as simple as it might sound.

I'd taken care of Wesley and Thelma right off the bat. Two down, seven to go. I'd seen enough of Connie and Kimberly to recognize their bodies, so they presented no problem (except when I dropped Connie's head and it rolled away and I had to chase it down the beach). Four down, five to go.

I tried to do Billie next, figuring she'd be a cinch. After all, she'd been running around forever in nothing but her bikini, and I'd seen her breasts completely naked the night she tried to tackle Thelma but ended up diving through the sand. (I remembered, even in my dream, about how they'd looked looming out loose over her bikini top.)

I grabbed Billie's head from the hands of a body I didn't recognize, then hurried it over to the broad, lush figure I knew to be her.

When I plonked it onto the neck, Billie's mouth said,

'Dumb move, Rupert. You don't know your own mother when you see her?'

Yuck!

Down the line, I spotted an identical body.

To me, they both looked like Billie.

Whoa, Nelly. Here comes Freud, Oedipus leering by his side.

The hell with it. This is no time to start worrying about what might be lurking in my subconscious. Screw id.

Anyway, I was shocked by that part of the dream, but the mistake had a silver lining. I quickly matched two heads to the proper bodies: Billie's and my mother's.

Next, I went for the head of the stranger.

Its ears, nostrils, lips, and even eyebrows bristled with all manner of metallic ornaments. I took her head out of Kimberly's hands and rushed it down the row of ladies to a pale, skinny gal who had rings dangling from her pierced nipples, clitoris, etc. Easy.

That done, only two heads remained.

My cute blonde fifth-grade teacher, Miss Curtis. And my high-school girlfriend, Ardeth Swan.

Unfortunately, *three* headless bodies remained.

That's because my first move of the game had been tossing away Wesley's head.

It wouldn't have matched any of the three remaining bodies, anyway.

Off on the horizon, the sun was sinking slowly into the sea.

Miss Curtis and Ardeth gave me no trouble.

Miss Curtis had a petite, slender body with a nice tan, cup-sized breasts with turgid dark nipples, and a shiny tuft of blond hair between her legs.

Ardeth Swan, a freckled and pimply tub, had lost her

head but not her modesty. She kept an arm across her huge breasts, a hand clamped to her crotch.

When I put Miss Curtis's head on her neck, she gave me a warm smile and said, 'You always were such a fine young man, Thomas.'

I didn't know who the hell Thomas might be, but I thanked her anyway.

After returning Ardeth's head, I simply smiled at her. She said, 'Fuck off, meatball.'

Even in my nightmares . . .

Only a small curve of orange sun remained above the horizon.

I faced the final headless body.

I had no head to give it.

Thinking I might spot a head I'd missed, I looked around.

Everyone had vanished.

Everyone was gone except me and the lone, headless woman. We stood close together on the empty beach, facing each other. (She wasn't 'facing' me, of course, as she didn't possess one.)

What she did possess was an absolutely fabulous, incredible body.

Her skin gleamed all over with a tawny, golden tan.

She was at least six feet tall, from neck to toe. She had long, slender arms and legs, broad shoulders, breasts that were high firm mounds with stiff jutting nipples. Her hips were wide and smooth, her belly flat. Lower, she had a glossy curve without so much as a trace of whiskers – as if she'd never grown any hair at all down there.

'I don't know what to do,' I told her. 'I'm out of heads.'

She shrugged her shoulders, which made her breasts lift and descend wonderfully.

'Do you know where your head is?' I asked her.

Again, that lovely shrug.

I checked the horizon and saw the last sliver of the sun easing out of sight.

Fast as I could, I snatched off my own head and shoved it onto her neck.

'There!' I yelled in triumph.

The yell didn't come from *my* mouth, though. I was looking at my mouth, my face, my head, on top of that gorgeous body.

Not a match!

In my haste to provide a head for her, I'd forgotten that the rules called for a match.

Not just any old head would do.

But *mine* did!

Figure that one out.

Anyway, I watched my own face give me a very nice, friendly smile.

Then my dream woman said, 'Thanks, Rupert.' (Not my voice, I'm glad to report. It sounded more like Lauren Bacall in *To Have and Have Not*, and a lot like Billie.) 'You won,' she told me. 'You saved us all, do you know that? You should be very proud of yourself.'

It made me feel really good.

'Of course,' she said, 'now *you* don't have a head.'

'Oh, that's okay.' I can be quite the gallant fellow, sometimes. 'I don't need it that much,' I told her. 'I'm just glad I was able to match everyone up.'

'Do you know what you get for winning?'

I shook my head. (Well, maybe not. I thought I did, though.)

'You get me,' she said.

'Oh boy!' I said.

She came forward. She took me in her arms, and I felt her body against me. Unfortunately, she had my face. When she tried to kiss me, I turned away.

'What's wrong?' she asked.

'I don't know about this. I don't think I wanta be kissing my own face.'

'Okay. That can be fixed. Whose do you want?'

'You can change your face?'

I watched myself give me a knowing smile. 'Sure. Just tell me who you want me to be.'

'Yourself,' I said.

'I *am* myself. I'm your dream lover. I'm whoever you want me to be.'

'I sure don't want you being me.'

'Who, then?' she asked.

'Can it be anyone?'

'Anyone you'd like.'

'How about Kimberly?'

'Excellent choice,' she said. Immediately, the face of my dream lover stopped being me and became Kimberly.

Then things really sizzled.

Somewhere along the way, my nightmare had gotten left behind, leaving me with a fantastic erotic dream. Probably the best dream I've ever had.

It stayed great, too. The worst thing about it, from the moment after I saved her with the donation of my head, was when I woke up very suddenly and the dream ended.

I remembered her (Oh, God, did I ever!), but she had fled, along with my sleep, and I couldn't bring her back.

I would gladly let myself get knocked out today, if I thought she would return.

Of all the dreams and nightmares that came to me at the

bottom of the chasm, though, she only put in the one appearance.

In my last dream down there, I found myself on the beach in a wheelchair, trying to get away from someone. I couldn't turn my head around to see who was chasing me, but I was plenty scared. I kept shoving at the wheel rims, trying to pick up speed, but the wheels were bogged down in the sand. They kept sinking deeper and deeper, until my chair wouldn't move at all.

Finally, screaming in terror, I hurled myself out of the chair and started to run away. My legs worked fine. What the hell had I been doing in the wheelchair? Elated, I sprinted for safety. But my feet started sinking in the sand.

With each step, I sank deeper. Pretty soon, the sand reached my waist. No matter how hard I tried, I couldn't wade any farther. I was trapped. It hugged me like tight, heavy trousers.

I was terrified.

Now, *he'd* catch me. He would come running up behind me with his ax or machete or . . . chainsaw.

It'll be a chainsaw, I suddenly realized.

I couldn't hear it, though. Not yet.

Had he given up the chase?

I listened. Ocean sounds, bird sounds, bug sounds, but no cough, sputter and roar of a chainsaw.

I smiled with relief.

All of a sudden, down deep in the sand, hands caressed my legs.

I woke up with a yell of fright and a splitting headache, and that was the end of my odyssey through a hundred dreams and nightmares at the bottom of the chasm.

Some of my worst nightmares, though, were more

pleasant than what I found on my return to reality.

I was sprawled on my back, my head pounding with pain. I felt as if every bone in my body had been hammered. In some places, I felt numb. In others, I itched. In still others, sharp pains stabbed me.

Above me, swarms of flies and other winged bugs zipped this way and that. Some landed on me, while others were happy to circle.

A vulture suddenly flapped up into my line of vision, startling me.

I saw the chasm walls towering above me on both sides.

The gray sky above the chasm held a promise of sunrise – or night.

Beneath me, I felt Matt.

Waking Up Is Hard To Do

Matt felt like lumpy, warm goo.

I shouldn't complain, though. Without him, *I* would probably be lumpy, warm goo.

Still, he disgusted me.

I had been napping for at least a couple of days, probably longer, on top of a naked, decomposing corpse.

I, at least, wasn't naked. Thank God I had my shorts on. Where my bare back pressed against him, we seemed to be stuck together. My skin, there, itched like crazy. Also, I felt squirming, crawling things; various critters that had apparently gotten sandwiched between us.

Let's not dwell on all that.

I won't even *mention* the smell.

The moment I realized where I was – and what was under me – I let out a cry and rolled off him.

It made quite a sound when we came unstuck. You might get a similar effect by dropping a large, hot pizza on the tile floor of your kitchen and letting it stay there for a couple of hours before you peel it off.

When you peel it off, that's when you get the sound.

Rolling off Matt, I took some of him with me. I could feel gop and stuff glued to my back.

I started to crawl away from him. Then I threw up.

Then I crawled farther. It's a wonder I could move at all. Aside from all my other complaints, I felt like a passenger on a twilt-a-whirl. I kept crawling, though, wanting to put miles between me and Matt.

I probably made ten feet before I collapsed.

I lay there groaning, sleepless and full of agony.

The next time I lifted my head, the chasm was dark. I sat up and leaned back against a curving surface of rock.

The full moon, directly overhead, shone pale light down between the steep walls. It lit most of the chasm's floor. Including Matt.

My silent partner.

He seemed almost like an old friend.

A long-lost buddy I might've shared some good times with once, but who had recently undergone some major changes for the worse – especially in the personal hygiene department.

I had no idea who he might be.

Gazing at his moonlit corpse over there, though, I found myself fancying him as an old prospector. He was Walter Huston. I was Bogart. We'd run into some tough luck – his a lot tougher than mine.

'Reckon we won't be buying no rabbit farm, Lenny,' I said to him.

Wrong movie. Wrong characters. But it's what I said, anyway.

'Shit happens,' I told him.

I thought about crawling over to him and taking a look at his face. For all I knew, I might recognize him.

Could he be Keith?

Maybe Wesley and Thelma had disinterred Keith, brought his body here to trick us . . .

No.

Matt was too large to be Keith.

He couldn't possibly be Andrew, either. Again, wrong size. Besides, they would've had to fish his body out of the sea.

So who the hell *was* he?

Or she? Matt might be a female. After all, I'd never seen the body's frontal areas. She couldn't be a woman from our group, though; all of ours had been up at the top while the body was down here.

Not that I'd actually seen Thelma up there. But I figure it must've been Thelma who attacked us from the rear.

Anyway, Matt seemed too large to be Thelma, and his shape was all wrong.

His shape seemed wrong, in fact, to be any woman at all.

Not that he *couldn't* have been one. Kimberly and Billie had looked at him, though, and they'd assumed he was a man: Wesley, in fact. Though we'd had doubts about his identity, none of us had doubted that the body was a *he*.

I wondered, though.

Matt was probably no Matilda, but I was curious.

Would I recognize him – or her?

Only one way to find out.

I didn't want to move, though.

I especially didn't want to take a good, close look at the stiff.

A. It stank.

B. His or her face was bound to be a wreck.

C. He or she was a critter magnet.

D. If I got any closer, I might start getting the creeps.

E. Or throw up again.

F. All of the above.

So I stayed put.

Then I squinted up at the top of the chasm and wondered what had happened.

Obviously, I'd been knocked out cold and dumped into the chasm. What about the women, though?

They hadn't won the battle, that was for sure.

If they'd won, I wouldn't have found myself waking up at the bottom of the chasm, days later, alone except for a corpse.

They would have taken care of me.

Not necessarily, I told myself. Suppose they won the fight, but only *after* I'd gone over the edge? Someone climbs down to check on me. Kimberly. She mistakes me for dead, so they go off and leave me here.

That didn't seem likely.

Not being an idiot, Kimberly would've noticed that I was alive.

Thinking about Kimberly, I recalled the last time I'd seen her. She had been climbing down a rope into the chasm. She'd just dropped out of sight below the edge moments before the attack came.

She wasn't down here, now. I had already looked around. Nobody was down here except for me and the corpse. I scanned the moonlit bottom again, anyway. No sign of Kimberly, or anyone else.

She'd most likely scurried back up the rope to join the fight.

A losing fight, almost for sure.

The last I saw, Wesley had been hot on Connie's tail. Seconds after I went down, he'd probably whacked her head off with one of those machetes. Then he and Thelma had probably made quick work of Billie.

So Kimberly, late in joining the fray, would've found herself standing alone against those two.

She was tough enough to win.

If she'd won, though, where was she? Why had she left me down here?

They're dead, I thought. *All of them. Kimberly, Billie and Connie. Dead.*

Then I almost went nuts, but I kept a grip on one thin thread of hope: that they had somehow won the battle. They'd thought I was dead, and left me. And they'd gone on back to our camp at the beach. If I could get out of the chasm, I would find them there, alive and well.

God, they'd be so glad to see me!

Not half as glad as I'd be, though, to see them.

We would have a great celebration.

I knew they were dead.

Sometimes, though, kidding yourself isn't the worst course of action. Instead of self-destructing, I got myself out of the chasm.

For starters, I struggled to my feet. Then I roamed back and forth, checking in the shadows and bushes to make absolutely sure that Kimberly wasn't down here.

I found no one.

I found no heads or other parts.

I found nothing worth finding.

Not even the rope. After the end of the battle, someone must've pulled it up. (Why leave behind a perfectly good rope?)

Not that it would've done me much good. I could barely hold myself upright, much less climb out of the chasm on a rope.

I did try to climb out without one.

I never got very high, fortunately, because I kept falling.

I fell three times.

Then I made my way to the open end of the chasm.

It overlooked a steep drop-off.

I studied the situation for a minute or two. The darkness hid most of what I wanted to see. But I did notice that the treetops beyond the cliff were *above* me. Very encouraging: I was somewhat lower than the treetops.

A fall might not kill me.

That was about all I really cared to know.

I lowered myself over the edge.

Braced up with stiff, shaking arms, I remembered when Kimberly had paused in almost the same position and asked me to rescue her Swiss Army knife.

What had happened to the knife?

Just before being taken out of the picture, I'd seen it in my hand.

Had I somehow slipped it into a pocket of my shorts?

Not in my seat pockets, that was for sure. I'd spent plenty of time on my back and would've felt it pushing against my butt. It didn't seem to be in my front pockets, either; they held the straight razor, Andrew's lighter, Billie's small plastic bottle of sunblock, and a pack of smoked fish. The way I was braced up against the face of the cliff, I could feel them all being pressed into my thighs.

No Swiss Army knife there. No big surprise.

Maybe the knife had ended up at the bottom of the chasm, though. If I'd still been holding on to it when I went over the edge . . .

I scrambled back up, got to my feet, and staggered over to the area where I had landed.

The area included Matt. Or Matilda.

Which goes to show how much I wanted the knife.

A good knife like that could make all the difference.

Also, it held memories.

I wanted it badly.

313

After sinking to my knees – perhaps a yard from the body – I dug Andrew's lighter out of my pocket. I gave it a flick. A small spear-head of flame leaped from its top.

By the shimmery yellow glow, I searched the ground. Staying on my knees, I circled the area, sweeping my gaze back and forth, trying not to look at the body.

Looking at it anyway, from time to time.

After a while, you get used to anything.

Desperate to find the knife, I finally considered the possibility that the corpse might be hiding it. The knife couldn't have fallen *underneath* the body, but it might've dropped out of sight in any of several places.

My lighter was little use on some of them.

I had to reach into the darkness under the chin and on both sides of the neck. I fingered the spaces under the armpits. I traced the entire body, crawling around it and running my fingertips along the crevice where its skin was pressed against the rock floor. I spread the legs apart and searched between them.

That's when I confirmed that the body was not a woman, after all.

But I didn't find the knife.

So then I turned the body over. (In for a penny, in for a pound.) As he rolled out of the way, I felt almost positive that the knife would show up, at last.

Kidding myself.

It wasn't there, of course.

And, of course, I couldn't stop myself from gazing at the front of the body.

The man had a pulpy ruin where his face should've been. Also, the left side of his chest was split open.

My guess is that Wesley and Thelma couldn't be sure whether he would land face up or face down when they gave him the old heave-ho into the chasm. They wanted to make sure he would pass for Wesley, either way, so they didn't spare any efforts in mutilating him.

Who was he, though? He certainly wasn't Keith or Andrew. Where in hell had they gotten their hands on a spare man to use for their trap?

Giving up my search for Kimberly's knife, I put away the lighter and returned to the open end of the chasm. I eased myself over the edge, and began to make my way down the sheer wall of rock.

I made it to the bottom in record time.

No bones got broken, though. Nor did I find myself unconscious. I was able to pick myself up again and get moving a few hours later, a while after the sun came up.

I found my way, without much trouble, back to the lagoon. I came upon its shoreline near the south end. After emptying my pants pockets on a rock, I took off my sneakers and socks. (How great it felt to have bare feet!)

I climbed down into the water and washed my hands the best I could, then cupped water to my mouth.

Delicious!

Cool, clear water, just like the song. (Not very cool, as a matter of fact, but it tasted wonderful anyhow.)

After gulping down quite a load of it, I waded out until most of the lagoon came into sight.

Nobody else seemed to be there.

I submerged myself. The water felt like a soothing ointment on my battered, bruised and bitten skin. Staying under, I rubbed my face. I rubbed my shoulders, arms, chest, sides and belly, using my hands to wipe away the layers of filth.

Then I took off my shorts and worked for a while at scrubbing them. They certainly didn't come clean, but I got rid of the worst of the mess. Done with them, I waded toward shore and tossed them onto the nearest rock. Waiting no longer, I bent over and rubbed all the itchy, sore, grimy places from my waist on down to my feet.

Later, I swam to the waterfall. I stood underneath it, the water splashing on my head and shoulders, running down me, spilling down me, flooding down me, washing off the last of the sweat and blood and whatever bits of Matt might still be clinging to my back.

I must've stood under it for half an hour.

Then I returned to the south end of the lagoon and climbed out. Nearby, I found a large slab of rock with a fairly flat surface. I crawled onto it and lay down.

I slept. If dreams came, I don't remember them.

Later that day, I walked out onto our section of the beach.

By then, I'd stopped kidding myself; I knew the women wouldn't be there.

The camp looked as if it hadn't been touched since our departure, some days earlier.

The fire was dead.

But I found my book bag, opened it up, and took out my journal and one of the pens.

My journal – my only companion, now.

I sat down in the sand, crossed my legs, placed the journal on my lap, and opened it. After riffling through the great thickness of it, I came to a blank page.

I wrote, 'DAY? ANYBODY'S GUESS.' I turned that page and wrote on the next, 'Musings On My Return To The Journal.'

When A Body Meets A Body

It took one hell of a long time to write all that. Yesterday morning, I started to write about my hike upstream the previous night. I was only about half done with that when I realized everything would make better sense if I went back in time and told the whole business about our 'last stand.'

I can't seem to be brief about this stuff. Next thing I know I'll spend all day writing – and still have plenty left to go.

I haven't been building fires since my return to the beach (trying to stay inconspicuous), so writing after dark is out of the question. I had to call it quits before I'd even gotten myself off the top of Matt.

This morning, I finished about the chasm, and brought myself back to the beach.

Now, I'm ready to tell the rest of what happened when I went upstream (two nights ago, now) to search for the women. I'd made my way about halfway through before breaking off to backtrack. But I need to get to the bad part, and get it over with, before I'm free to stop writing and do whatever comes next.

I was last seen above the waterfall, running naked through the jungle with the straight razor in my sock.

I found the place where Billie, Connie and I had joined up with Kimberly. Without her to lead the way, though, I had a difficult time finding the chasm from there. I became lost. More than once, I arrived at a boulder or tree that I recognized because I'd recently walked past it. I was roaming in circles.

It didn't bother me. I was in no hurry to reach the chasm. I didn't *want* to reach it, in fact. But the chasm (the area above it, actually) was the place where I needed to go, so I kept searching for it.

Eventually, I got there. Peering around a corner of rock, I scanned the scene of our battle.

No bodies littered the moonlit field.

I murmured, 'Thank God.'

Then I burst into tears. I couldn't help it.

I'd fully expected to find the remains of my three women on the ground near the top of the chasm. If not all of them, at least one or two.

Relief overpowered me.

The relief lasted about as long as my tears. I no sooner recovered from the crying than things came back into perspective; the absence of their bodies was an excellent sign. It didn't, however, guarantee they were still alive.

Wesley and Thelma might've killed my women and dragged them away: buried them, burned them, sunk them, tossed them off a ledge, hauled them off somewhere to play nasty games with – God only knows.

Or they might've taken my women away alive – as prisoners.

Stepping into the open, I wondered if I might be walking into another trap. After all, this was enemy territory and we'd been ambushed here before.

I crouched, drew the razor out of my sock, and flipped

318

open its blade. Then I made my way slowly toward the area where we'd been attacked. I crept along, turning, checking to my rear and sides, glancing in every direction.

Not far from the edge of the chasm, I found Connie's beach-towel vest. The last time I saw her, she'd been wearing it. Now it lay crumpled in shadow beside a block of stone. I clamped the razor handle between my teeth, then crouched and picked up the vest. I spread it open and studied it. The stripes looked like different shades of gray in the moonlight.

The vest appeared to be free of blood – another good sign.

I couldn't leave it behind. I wanted to keep my hands free, though. Wearing the vest seemed like the best solution, so I put it on.

And felt closer to Connie. As if the vest was a living part of her, keeping company with me. (This explained a lot about why Kimberly had gone around almost constantly in her dead husband's Hawaiian shirt.)

While still crouched in the place where I'd found the vest, I spotted a wadded rag and picked it up. Though it was dark with dry blood, I wasn't alarmed. It appeared to be the piece of old T-shirt that Connie'd been using as a bandage for her shoulder. She must've lost it along with the vest.

I dropped it, took the razor out of my teeth, stood up and continued my search.

I probably looked like a madman, roaming through the night with my wicked straight razor – and wearing not a stitch except for the vest and one sock. A demented Crusoe. A castaway Sweeney Todd.

Anyway, I continued my search of the battlefield.

The ax and rope were gone. I found none of our makeshift spears or tomahawks, either.

Nor could I find the Swiss Army knife.

I looked very carefully for that, not only walking a grid pattern over most of the area, but getting down on all fours to study the ground in the vicinity where I'd last been holding it.

The knife wasn't there. Except for Connie's vest and bandage, it appeared that nothing had been left behind. Someone must've carried away everything that had fallen (including the women?).

I didn't find blood on the ground, though. Which gave me more reason for hope. If Wesley had used his machete on anyone, vast quantities would've gotten spilled. Even though several days had gone by and I was doing my search by moonlight, a mess like that should've been easy to spot.

Unless someone had cleaned it up.

I pictured Thelma on her knees with a bucket and scrub brush. Ridiculous.

In some other setting, dirt and leaves might've been spread around to cover telltale blood. Not here, though. Most of this area was bare rock.

If blood had been spilled, much of it would've remained for me to find.

Nobody'd been chopped or slashed or stabbed to death, not on our field of battle.

Before leaving, I crawled to the edge of the chasm and peered down.

Nothing at the bottom except Matt.

He appeared to be on his back, the way I'd left him.

Staring up at me.

He was *not* staring up at me; he had no eyes. Down

there after turning him over, I'd gotten a good look at his face. It had been smashed apart: nose flat, cheekbones and mouth demolished, nasty little craters where his eyes should've been.

But I *felt* him staring up at me. My skin crawled.

What if he gets up and starts climbing out?

A dumb thought, but mine.

It creeped me out plenty.

The moment I was sure that nothing new had been tossed into the chasm, I backed away from the edge.

One more quick look around the scene of our 'last stand,' then I scrammed.

For a while, I couldn't get Matt out of my head. We'd been almost like buddies when I was down at the bottom with him. But now I felt as if he hated me. Maybe because I'd gone off and left him?

I pictured his mutilated, rotten corpse scurrying up the chasm wall, coming after me.

Stupid. But you know how it is. You get some sort of spooky crap into your mind, and it's hard to get rid of.

Trying to get away, I got lost and went in circles for a while. I half expected to rush around a boulder and bump into Matt. Didn't happen, though. Finally, I came to the stream.

By then, I figured I'd given him the slip. (I know, I know, I'm nuts. I was spooked. So sue me.)

Anyway, I felt better and better as I followed the stream downhill toward the lagoon. An irrational relief at leaving Matt behind. More than that, though, I felt a growing sense of elation about my women.

Sure, they might be dead.

I doubted it, though.

No bodies at the scene of the fight. And no blood.

It now seemed more likely than not that they'd been taken alive.

If you take people alive, you probably want to keep them that way. Otherwise, why not just go on and kill them in the first place? Save yourself the trouble of tying them, taking them somewhere, risking an uprising or an escape.

By the time I reached the top of the waterfall, I felt certain that I would be able to find my women alive, and rescue them.

I felt great!

So great that I had an urge to leap off the falls – in spite of knowing the water at the bottom was only waist-deep.

Already wrecked enough from various plummets, I fought off the urge and made my way down to the lagoon by foot. I stopped on the flat rock by the side of the falls and made sure the razor was secure in my sock. Then I took off Connie's towel-vest and rolled it into a bundle.

After lowering myself into the water, I raised the vest overhead with one hand. I kept it dry all the way to the other side of the lagoon. Not climbing out, I tossed it onto the same rock where I'd left my shorts, etc.

Then I spent about fifteen minutes having a very pleasant time: floating on my back, sometimes swimming, just relaxing in the smooth warmth of the water, relishing the way it slid over my body, always very aware that it was like a magic vanishing fluid: I could make parts of me, or all of me, disappear at will.

For a while, I felt as if I'd found a wonderful new home.

I would abandon our camp at the beach, and live at the lagoon.

Over near the north end, I saw a place where a slab of rock the size of a dining-room table slanted down into the water. I had probably seen it before, but paid no attention.

This time, though, it caught my eye. Though the rest of the shoreline was either dark or dappled with specks of moonlight, the special rock was brightly illuminated. It must've been aligned perfectly with the moon and a break in the treetops. It looked pale and smooth like a patch of snow.

I wanted to climb on.

I wanted to lounge on that glowing white slab and bathe in the moonlight.

I swam most of the way over to it, then waded.

When I first started wading, the water came as high as my shoulders. With each step, the level lowered a little. It was waist-deep when I stepped into something soft and squishy that wrapped around my foot and tripped me. I fell headlong with a splash, and my foot pulled free.

Whatever had grabbed my foot, it wasn't like anything that I'd ever stepped on before.

I didn't know *what* the hell it might be.

Standing again, I turned around. Nothing to see except black water and a few shiny coins of moonlight shimmering on the surface.

I had my ideas about what had tripped me.

I needed to find out for sure.

So I took a deep breath and bent down into the water, reaching toward the bottom with both hands. At first, nothing. I walked slowly, moving my arms.

Instead of finding the thing with my hands, I bumped it with my right foot. I kept my balance, though, and didn't fall. After coming up for air, I went down again, bending and crouching, and explored it.

A naked woman.

She was split wide open from sternum to crotch.

She had a load of stones where her guts should've been.

When I figured it out, I screamed or something. I'm not sure what I did, exactly, but I took in a mouthful of lagoon. I popped up choking. I *would've* screamed my head off then, except that I couldn't breathe. I could only cough and gasp for air and cough some more.

When I was breathing again, I just stood there and shook.

I wanted to be miles away.

But how could I leave without knowing who it was?

I'd touched her enough to know that she was a woman, that she'd been gutted and stuffed with rocks – probably to keep her down. I hadn't explored her well enough, however, to identify her.

So down I went again, quickly, before I had time to change my mind.

The first part I found was a shoulder. I held on to it with one hand, and explored with the other.

I started with her face, feeling it with my fingertips but trying to keep away from her eyes. I did *not* want to touch her eyes; they might be open – or gone.

Her mouth was open. I fingered her lips, touched the edges of her teeth, and tried to imagine the face that went with them. Which of the women had nice, straight teeth?

In my memory, all of them.

I ran my fingers through her hair. It felt limp and slippery and very short. Kimberly had much longer hair than this, so she was ruled out (unless someone had cut it). Thelma, Connie and Billie all wore their hair very short.

I had my hopes pinned on Thelma – though she seemed unlikely, being Wesley's ally.

After surfacing to take another breath, I went down again.

I wasn't exactly thrilled about touching the breasts of a

corpse, but I figured the size of them would tell me plenty. So I took them in my hands. (My first time ever to actually handle bare breasts, and it has to be like this.) They were too large for Kimberly or Connie. Though big, they didn't feel enormous like Thelma's. They seemed to be about Billie's size.

Billie.

God, I sure didn't want it being her. But it *had* to be Billie. Nobody else had breasts the right size.

In a frenzy of despair, I went at the body with both hands. I felt her wide shoulders, and how her sides tapered in, then flared out at the hips. I felt the solid thickness of her thighs.

Not just the breasts had Billie's shape and size.

She felt like Billie all the way up and down.

No!

I went a little nuts and straddled her and dug into her split torso with both hands and started snatching out the rocks that someone had packed in to keep her down.

Someone?

Wesley!

Wesley-fucking-Duncan Beaverton III.

How could he do it to her! How could he kill my Billie? How could he ruin her this way?

I suddenly thought, If Billie's like this, why not the others?

Why not Kimberly and Connie? Maybe they, too, were sprawled on the bottom of the lagoon, hollowed out and stuffed with stones.

I kept digging rocks out of the woman under me.

When I ran out of breath, I flung my head up out of the water and yelled at the top of my lungs, *'Wesley! You fucking cocksucking load of shit! I'm gonna kill you! I'm gonna cut you to pieces and make you EAT 'em, you motherfucking asshole!'*

I cried while I yelled.

And I kept on yelling.

I yelled a lot of things that don't even bear repeating.

With all the yelling and crying, I wore myself out. Finally, I quit. Then I just stood in the waist-deep water, panting for air.

It took me a long while to calm down enough to let me hold my breath and go under again.

She still held plenty of ballast.

Instead of unloading the rest of it by the handful, I crouched beside her, took her by the upper arm and the back of her thigh, and lifted.

Turned her over.

Dumped her out like a canoe.

Right away, she began to rise. I kept hold of her arm, and stood up. There were soft lapping sounds when she broke the surface. I could see, just barely, the dim, pale shape of her. In a few places, the moon put white marks on the skin of her back and rump. The patches of light scooted down her body as I floated her toward shore.

I climbed onto the tilted slab of rock.

Squatting at its edge, I lifted her by the arms. I staggered backward and dragged her up with me. She made sloshy sounds like someone rising out of a bathtub.

I let go of her arms, but stayed kneeling above her head.

The moon shone down like a spotlight onto us. A white spotlight, dimmed for gloomy atmosphere.

Bright enough, though, to let me see a few things.

She'd been beaten. Her back and buttocks were stained in places with gray blotches that appeared to be bruises. They were also criss-crossed with stripes as if she'd been whipped.

She'd also been stabbed in the back many times. Each wound was a narrow slot, more than an inch long, with puffy edges. (Probably made by a blade about the width of the knives that I'd seen on Wesley's belt when he leaped across the chasm.) I had a difficult time finding all of them – some were hidden among the lash marks. So I crawled alongside her body, searching them out, studying and counting them.

I found eighteen stab wounds in her back.

I found none in her buttocks.

But I made a startling discovery there – something I might've noticed right away if my attention hadn't been focused so completely on her injuries.

Bruises and lash-marks aside, her buttocks were the same pale shade of gray as her lower back and her thighs.

Where was her tan line?

Billie, I knew, had stark borders between her tanned skin and the parts covered by her bikini. Where she wasn't tawny, she was as pale as milk.

With her black bikini pants gone, she would certainly look as if she'd changed into a new, white pair.

She shouldn't be all one shade, like this.

For a few moments, I knew this wasn't Billie. Then doubts came.

Not enough time had passed, since I'd seen her last, for her tan to fade so completely. But several days had gone by. If she'd spent them naked in the sun, the white of her buttocks might've darkened enough to match the rest of her.

And what about being submerged in the lagoon? Over a period of time, the water might've done something to her skin color.

She hadn't been in it very long, though.

Not very long at all.

From the start, I'd been vaguely aware that she seemed to be in decent shape for a dead person. I hadn't given the matter much thought, though, except to be thankful that she wasn't as repulsive as she might be. That is, she didn't feel slimy or stiff or rotten.

(Compared to Matt, she was a regular Sleeping Beauty.)

Suddenly, it dawned on me that she was *extremely* fresh.

I picked up one of her hands. Holding it close to my face, I studied the fingertips. They were pruned, all right. But not that much.

I compared them to my own wrinkled fingertips.

I'm no damn forensic pathologist, but it was suddenly obvious that she hadn't been in the water for more than about an hour.

She had probably still been alive while I was above the falls trying to find our battleground.

If I hadn't gotten lost up there (twice) . . .

If I hadn't spent so much time looking around . . .

I might've returned to the lagoon in time to find her being murdered, gutted, stuffed, sunk.

Maybe I could have saved her.

Or maybe I would've gotten myself murdered, gutted . . .

Life and death, a matter of destinations and delays.

Only they don't tell you the right or wrong place to be, or when.

I couldn't bear the thought that I might've missed a chance, by such a slim margin, to save Billie's life.

I turned the woman over.

Glimpsed the terrible chasm down the middle of her torso. Looked a bit longer at her breasts: bruises, welts, scratches, but no stab wounds. Then made myself gaze at her face.

It was gray in the moonlight, etched and pocked with black shadows.

Enough of it showed, though.

This was not Billie's face.

This was the face of a woman I had never seen before, not even in my dreams.

I swam back to the place where I'd left my stuff, found Andrew's lighter, and returned to the body. Kneeling by her side, I studied her by the lighter's small, shaky flame.

She was definitely a stranger.

Physically, she bore a lot of resemblance to Billie. They seemed to be similar in age, size, build, and hair color. Even their faces had much in common. I could see that this wasn't Billie, but it would've been hard to describe the differences. This woman's face had obviously been attractive, even beautiful, before her death.

Her face, by the way, showed no signs of injury.

(Wesley hadn't wanted to spoil her looks, more than likely – just torture and murder her.)

Before leaving, I dragged her a small distance away from the lagoon. I hid her in among some rocks – so I'd be spared the sight of her, maybe, if I should return to the lagoon in the near future.

Speculations

I'm now nearly caught up to the present. A good thing, too, because I've only got a few pages left in my notebook.

I've had plenty of time to think about things.

I think the dead woman was probably linked, somehow, to Matt. I think they lived together, here on the island, before our arrival. My guess is that they were married to each other.

Wesley murdered Matt first – probably just before Thelma came into our camp and told us she'd bashed Wesley's brains in. He would've expected us to go looking for his body as soon as we heard the news, so it would've been in position at the bottom of the chasm on Day Six, waiting for us. That was two days before I got thrown down on top of Matt's remains.

Wesley kept the woman alive, abusing her, and didn't get around to killing her until shortly before I found her body in the lagoon two nights ago.

Obviously, Thelma had a hand in things, too. They're in it together. Partners, allies, accomplices.

Some of this is just speculation, of course.

But it makes sense to me.

I wonder about a lot of things, though.

If I'm right about Matt and the woman being inhabitants

of the island, did they live in a house? Is their house the place where Wesley got his hands on such things as the ax and rope?

Where *is* their house?

If I find it, will I also find Kimberly, Billie and Connie? I think so.

I think so, yes. If they are still alive, I'll probably find them at the house.

Last Words

Okay. I'm up to date with my journal, now. In fact, I'm done with it. I have no more reason to procrastinate. I can't build my Winchester House of words; there's no more room for words – or hardly enough to matter.

Tomorrow, I'll set out to search for my women. I don't expect I'll be returning to our beach. I plan to travel light; wearing Connie's towel-vest, Andrew's shorts, and my own socks and shoes. I'll carry the lighter in my pocket, of course. And I'll take along Billie's sun-block, mostly because it reminds me of her and it smells good. My only weapon will be Thelma's straight razor.

I'll take my journal with me in the book bag, along with a couple of pens that haven't yet run out of ink (in case I should stumble upon paper but no writing implement), my swimming trunks (though I haven't worn them since acquiring Andrew's shorts), the pink blouse that Billie gave me (though I now prefer to wear Connie's vest), and a few remaining items of food.

I'll leave just about everything else behind. Including Andrew's camera. I haven't used it yet, so I can't see a good reason to lug it around.

The less I have to carry, the better.

I do wish that I had something of Kimberly's, though.

Her Swiss Army knife (Andrew's before it came into her possession) would have been a great treasure. I haven't been able to find it anywhere, though.

I have nothing of Kimberly's to carry with me.

Only my memories of her.

With luck, though, I'll be with all three of my women soon.

If I can find the mystery house, they'll be nearby. I'd bet on it.

Whether or not I find them alive, I'll take care of Wesley and Thelma.

I'll make it hard for them, too.

Very hard.

Bet on it.

I'll make them pay for every hurt they've done to my women.

Which sounds like a mean-spirited, brutal way to end my journal. But so be it.

Obviously, I'll tell the rest of my story if I'm able. To do that, I'll need to find a new source of paper. And I'll have to still be alive.

Both good tricks.

So long.

The Rest Of The Story

My Quest For The Mystery House

I've gotten hold of a new notebook.

A lot has happened since my last entry.

I'll take my time, though, and tell about it in the proper sequence – starting with the morning when I went off to hunt for the house.

The island obviously had no shortage of vacant beachfront property, so nobody in their right mind would've built a house somewhere deep in the jungle. You'd want an ocean view. You'd want easy access to the water.

If I just followed the shoreline, I was almost certain to spot the home of Matt and the dead woman.

I started out early in the morning. After a light breakfast of smoked fish, I filled an empty booze bottle with water from the stream (just in case), put the bottle in my book bag, shouldered the bag and set off, heading north.

This had been our route on the morning of the 'last stand,' until Kimberly ran off without us.

Now, I was alone as I hiked the beach.

Though I started my journey with eagerness, sure of success, my optimism dwindled along the way. There might not *be* any house. Its existence was nothing more than a theory of mine.

For all I knew at the time (I've found out plenty since), Matt and the woman hadn't necessarily been residents of the island. They might've come to it for a brief visit – parked their boat and come ashore to do some exploring, have a picnic, who knows? Or they might've been castaways: survivors from a boat wreck or airplane crash. If so, I was searching for a home that didn't exist.

No, no, I told myself. There *has* to be a house. If not, where did Wesley get his hands on the ax, the rope, the machetes, the sheath knives he wore on his belt, the belt itself . . . ?

That argument comforted me for a while.

But then I remembered how, within a day or two after being marooned, Billie and I had come up with the theory that Wesley must've made a prior visit to the island.

He had obviously toured the region to search for a good island to use. Just as obviously, he would've taken steps to avoid becoming a victim of his own plot. That is, he planned to maroon the bunch of us, but he sure didn't want to find himself trapped on an island without the means to ensure his own survival.

So we had figured out, way back at the start of the whole mess, that he must've come ashore earlier and hidden a load of supplies.

Supplies that might've included the ax, rope, etc.

By the time I'd spent a few hours hiking along the shore, I had pretty much convinced myself that I wouldn't be finding any house. The house was a phantom, thrown together by bad logic and wishful thinking.

It would've been too convenient, too easy.

Find them all in a shack by the shore. Go sneaking in late at night, commando-style . . .

No, it wasn't going to be that simple.

I would probably need to hunt for them in the jungle. In the region above the lagoon and in the areas beyond where I'd never been before. Who knows? Maybe they had a cave.

The problem was, I didn't want to go looking for them in the jungle.

I wanted to stay on the beach, where I could feel the sun and the soft breezes, where I had a fine, open view in all directions and nobody could sneak up on me.

Besides, the house *might* exist.

Even if it didn't, there were plenty of good reasons to continue along the beach. No telling what I might find. We'd always intended to explore the boundaries of our island, but had never gotten around to it. Thanks to Wesley, there'd always been more urgent matters to deal with first.

I was finally getting around to it.

I decided to keep at it, too. Any journey into the jungle would have to wait for a day or two, or however long it might take me to circle the island.

I felt as if I'd been granted a reprieve.

Then I found the house.

Some time earlier, I had rounded the north end of the island and started back along the eastern shore. I'd been hiking southward for quite a while when I came to a cove.

From a distance, the cove had been out of sight. I'd seen nothing ahead except more beach – ocean on one side, jungle on the other. Though my view had been obstructed, here and there, by rocky areas, I assumed that I was approaching a continuous shore-line.

I was climbing over a low spine of rocks when I first

noticed a break in the beach ahead.

Seeing my forward progress blocked by water, I felt frustrated and annoyed; it was an inconvenience that would force me to walk a lot farther than I'd expected. Within a few seconds, though, my curiosity took over.

I could see across the water to where the beach started again, but very little of what lay to the right. The trees at the edge of the jungle got in the way. What seemed to be ahead, however, was a small bay, or cove, that looked at least five times as large as our little inlet on the other side of the island.

Hurrying down from the rocks, I ran through the sand. With each stride, more of the cove's opposite shore came into sight. More and more.

Nothing but sand and rocks; jungle further back.

When the boat loomed into view, it scared the shit out of me. I dived for the sand.

Stretched out on the beach with my head up, I gazed at the vessel.

There'd been no need to panic; it wasn't under way, as I'd thought.

I saw anchor lines stretching down into the water.

I saw nobody aboard.

It was a big white cabin cruiser – about a forty-footer.

Matt's boat, I figured.

And our ticket out of here.

Now all I've gotta do is find my women . . .

That's what ran through my mind, for a few seconds. I was elated. Then scared, realizing I might've already been seen. Just because the boat *looked* deserted . . .

I stared hard at it, and wondered if Wesley or Thelma might be staring back at me through a window or port.

No sign of anyone.

I scurried on my belly for the edge of the jungle. In the shelter of the bushes and trees, I got to my feet. Then I snuck through the thick foliage until the cove came into view again.

From my new position, I had a full, wide view.

Off to the right, perhaps a hundred yards beyond the anchored cabin cruiser, a dock jutted out from the shore. Floating at the end of the dock were two dinghies. One of them had probably been used to transport people (Matt and the woman?) ashore from the anchored cruiser. The other looked a lot like *our* dinghy.

I'd last seen it heading north, Wesley aboard, when he was making his getaway after splitting open Andrew's head.

He must've brought our dinghy here, and docked it.

I hardly got a chance to think about the dinghies, though, because the house suddenly caught my attention.

For my high-school graduation present, just last summer, my parents took me on a special trip.

It started with spending a week in Memphis, Tennessee.

There, I almost got trampled to death by a mob of spectators in the lobby of the Peabody Hotel when I tried to catch a glimpse of the damn ducks that march through twice a day. I almost got *scared* to death when we visited the Civil Rights Museum at the old Lorraine Motel where Martin Luther King got shot. My white parents and I were pretty much the only people of that shade roaming through the museum, which seems to be a monument to the evils of the white man.

Memphis wasn't all bad, though. It had delicious barbeque and fabulous music. Every night, we walked from our hotel to Beale Street, where the blues were born. Beale Street was great.

While staying in Memphis, we also visited Elvis's home, Graceland.

The house on the cove didn't remind me of Graceland.

No, this house was what I'd *imagined* Graceland would be like: a huge plantation-style mansion.

Graceland had turned out to be smaller, more modern than I'd expected. But I had a chance to see plenty of actual plantation houses after leaving Memphis.

My *real* graduation present wasn't the visit to Memphis, but a trip down Old Man River on an authentic paddlewheel steamboat, the *Mississippi Queen*. (For one thing, I'm a big fan of Mark Twain.) We spent six days and nights on the river, and ended up in New Orleans.

Along the way, we stopped at places like Vicksburg and Natchez. And visited God-only-knows how many antebellum homes. These were plantation houses built in the period before the War Between the States. Big old hunchers, usually three storys high, full of narrow stairways and tiny rooms, their outsides loaded with columns, balconies and verandas.

They were very interesting until you'd been through about two of them. After that, they mostly looked alike. (Mom is big on antiques and Dad is a Civil War buff, so they were happy as pigs in slop. My fondness for Mark Twain didn't extend far enough, though, to cover endless, dreary tours of mansions.)

The deal is, the white mansion beyond the cove looked as if it had been plucked off the grounds of an old cotton or tobacco plantation on the Mississippi, and plonked down here.

I gaped at it, stunned.

What the hell was an ante-bellum mansion doing on a little lost island like this one?

My imagination told me that a Southern Gentleman had settled here, long ago. Maybe he'd lost his original plantation house during the War Between the States (most of them went up in smoke, though you wouldn't think so if you ever got pushed into touring them), so he'd sailed to this island to start over again – far from the Yankees – and built this home in the image of the one he'd lost.

Sort of a romantic notion, and probably wrong.

Maybe it was built in the 1980s by a rich guy with a weird fondness for Scarlett O'Hara (or Rhett).

I kept staring at it from my hiding place at the edge of the jungle.

I would've been pretty thrilled to find any house at all. But *this*!

I felt as if I'd taken one small step into *The Twilight Zone*. All I needed was Connie to give me the 'doo-*de*-do-do' music and her Serling intro – *One Rupert Conway, eighteen, took a little walk along the beach one day in search of his missing ladies. Instead of finding the ladies, he found himself venturing into a strange land ruled by the limits of the imagination* . . .

I stared at the mansion for a long time.

It had probably been the home of Matt and the woman I'd found in the lagoon. Just as the cabin cruiser and one of the dinghies must've been theirs.

Theirs until Wesley came along.

He had taken everything from them: their home, their boats, their lives.

And then he'd taken over.

All his, now.

Maybe he'd brought us to this island – killed our men and captured our women – because he wanted belles for his cotillions.

Or servants for his mansion.

Or slaves.

Recon

After watching for a long time and seeing nobody, I made my way through the jungle. I moved cautiously, stopping often to check around and listen. Usually, I stayed away from the cove. Every so often, though, I snuck closer to it for another look.

I saw nobody: not on the cabin cruiser, not on the dinghies or dock, not in the water or along the shore, not in or around the mansion. Nowhere.

Nor did I hear any voices or other sounds, such as pounding, that would tell of people nearby. Of course, it would've taken some major noise to reach me through all the squawks and squeals and shrieks from the birds and other animals. (Some of the shrieks sounded almost human, but I figured they probably came from birds.)

Finally, when I took a left and snuck toward the cove, I came to a lawn instead of the shoreline – a broad field of grass that led to the rear of the mansion. The lawn looked as if it had been well-kept until recently. It needed a mowing.

At the far side of the lawn was a red tractor mower. It didn't seem to belong there. The way things looked, someone might've started to cut the grass, but quit before getting very far and never got a chance to put the tractor away.

Off beyond it, past the side of the house, were a couple of brick outbuildings. One had an open door large enough for the mower to fit through.

I couldn't see what was inside. Just a small, empty space near the front – probably where the mower should go.

In places where you keep your lawn mower, you usually store other equipment and tools. Things like shovels, picks, pruning shears, hammers, saws . . .

Axes.

My heart pounded a little faster.

This could be the place where Wesley had gotten hold of the ax.

Maybe the rope, too. The rope he'd used for hanging Keith.

He'd strung Keith up during our first night on the island. So he must've come here immediately after blowing up the yacht. Is that when he killed Matt and the woman?

No. Impossible. Neither of them had been dead that long. Matt had probably been alive for most of the first week – killed only when they needed a body to double for Wesley. And the woman must've been killed the very same night I found her body in the lagoon.

Wesley had probably held both of them captive from Day One until their deaths.

Where had he kept them?

In one of the outbuildings?

Aboard the yacht?

Inside the mansion itself? Maybe in a bedroom or attic or cellar?

Somewhere else?

The place where Matt and the woman had been kept was, almost for sure, the prison where Wesley now held Kimberly, Billie and Connie.

If they're still alive.

He took them alive. Otherwise, I would've found their bodies at the battlefield.

He took them alive, and he's *keeping* them alive.

I had to believe that.

I had to hang on to that belief, no matter what. It was like a rope over the edge of a chasm – only not a shallow chasm like the one beyond the falls.

One so deep I would fall for a mile. If I lost my hold, down I'd go, screaming all the way to the bottom.

They're alive, I told myself. I just need to find where Wesley's keeping them, set them free, and take Wesley and Thelma out of the picture.

Not necessarily in that order.

What should I do first? I wondered.

Find someone. If not my women, at least find Wesley or Thelma.

Get up and go, I told myself.

But I stayed put.

I just couldn't force myself to break cover.

That's because Thelma and Wesley were almost sure to be nearby. If one of them should spot me sneaking around, I'd lose any chance of taking them by surprise.

Then I'd probably lose my life.

If that happened, I'd not only be dead (which I hoped to avoid for as long as possible), but I would pretty much cease having a chance to rescue my women. If *I* couldn't save them, who would?

More than likely, I was their only hope.

Barring some sort of miraculous rescue by outside forces, they would remain at Wesley's mercy for weeks, months . . . maybe even for years.

Maybe for the rest of their lives.

For their sakes (not just for my own), I needed to be extremely careful, take no chances; under no circumstances allow myself to be captured or killed.

What I oughta do, I thought, is get the hell off the island and bring back help.

It sounded like a chicken way out.

But it also seemed like the smartest move – by a long shot.

Take the cabin cruiser to the nearest inhabited island, get in touch with the authorities, and come back with a rescue team.

For a while there, it seemed like the perfect solution to my problem.

I could wait for dark, then swim out to the cabin cruiser, cut the anchor lines, start the engine . . .

Start it with what key?

Even if Matt and the woman had been trusting or stupid enough to leave the boat's key in the ignition, Wesley wasn't. He would've gone out there, at some point. Checked the vessel from stem to stern. Taken whatever he felt an urge to take.

Not much chance he would've left the starter key behind.

Not a crafty bastard like Wesley.

And I'm not exactly the kind of guy who knows the first thing about how to hotwire an Evinrude or Johnson, or whatever. Without the key, I had no chance in the world of starting the engine.

Where would I find the ignition key?

Probably in Wesley's pocket.

Great. If I could hunt down Wesley and take the key off him, I wouldn't *need* to run off on the boat and go for help.

So much for fleeing on the cabin cruiser.

Just as well. It would've been the 'smart' thing to do, but I sort of hated the idea.

I don't really think I *could've* done it – left the island without knowing what had happened to my women, whether they were even still alive. And if I *had* found them alive, I couldn't have gone off without rescuing them.

Sometimes, you just can't do the 'smart' thing because it leaves out the heart.

That sounds sort of sappy.

The deal is, those three women had gotten to mean a lot to me. (Not just that they made me horny, either.) I couldn't abandon them, not even if that would've been the best way to save them.

I *could* make them wait, though.

They'd been captured (if captured) at least five or six days ago, maybe longer. A few more hours shouldn't matter very much to them. The hours might make plenty of difference to me, though.

I needed to wait until dark.

Darkness would hide me, so I'd be able to move about without so much risk of being spotted. Also, somebody might put on a light.

I *really* hoped for a light; it would give me a location.

It might even light my way to Wesley and Thelma.

Night, however, was a long time off.

I crept away from the edge of the lawn. When I was surrounded by jungle so thick I could see no trace of the lawn or mansion, I lay down on my back to rest. I used my book bag for a pillow.

There seemed to be little hope of falling asleep. I was too nervous and excited. Also, I ached nearly everywhere from my injuries. The plan was simply to rest and wait for night to come.

Shutting my eyes, I thought about my plans. Soon, I began daydreaming about the women. The next thing I knew, I found myself waking up in the dark.

Not knowing where the night might take me, I decided against leaving my book bag behind. I sure didn't want to lose it – not with the journal inside. The only way to make sure it stayed safe was to keep it with me.

I made my way back to the edge of the lawn. The windows of the mansion – those within sight – all looked dark. There was no light anywhere except for what came from the moon and stars.

Staying hidden, I kept watch for a long time. Nobody appeared. No lights came on.

Maybe I had the wrong house.

Maybe this house had nothing to do with Wesley, and was simply deserted.

No, no. Our dinghy was at the dock.

This had to be the right house.

But maybe Wesley wasn't using it. He might've simply raided the place, taken what he wanted (including the man and woman who lived here), and returned to some secret base camp in the jungle.

If he wasn't here, I'd already wasted hours upon hours.

I suddenly couldn't stand the thought of waiting any longer, so I broke cover and dashed across the lawn. Nobody yelled. Nobody shot at me. Nothing happened. I stopped at the side of the house, near its rear corner. Leaning against the wall, I tried to catch my breath and calm down.

So far, so good.

I'll just walk around the whole building, I thought. Check to see if there are any lights on.

If the place is dark, I'll try to get in.

The Game

I was about to push myself away from the wall when a fluttery, dim glow seemed to drift out the window just to my left and hover in the darkness. The murky light was so faint, at first, that I wondered if it might be a trick of the moonlight – or my imagination.

It grew brighter.

I gazed at it, stunned. For a while, I couldn't move. Then I forced myself to sneak toward the window.

I was afraid of what I might find, but I *had* to look. My heart slammed. My stomach trembled. My legs felt weak and unstable.

The fact is, I was shaking all over by the time I reached the window and peered in.

The room on the other side was lit by candles and several kerosine lamps with glass chimneys. Thelma, walking about with a candle in her hand, ignited more candles while I watched.

She wore a glossy, royal blue robe that looked like satin. It was too short for her. She had to reach high, now and then, to light wall sconces. Each time she did that, the lower half of her ass showed. Not a pretty sight. Her big buttocks, ruddy from a sunburn, looked dimpled and lumpy. They were bruised, too, and striped with red marks from being lashed.

Her legs also looked banged up – a lot more so than they'd been the last time I'd seen her.

When she turned in my direction, I saw that her robe wasn't shut all the way. She was bare down her middle – except for the loosely tied sash that crossed her belly. The opening was too narrow to let me see much. Only that she'd gotten a sunburn all the way down.

I realized she was coming straight toward me, so I dropped to a crouch.

Directly above my head, the window scooted upward. Thelma sighed.

What if she leans out!

She can't, I told myself. A screen's in the way.

I wondered if she could see me, anyway. Screen or no screen, she might be able to spot the top of my head if she looked downward.

Or she might hear my slamming heart.

No sounds of alarm came from her, though. Just that one sigh. A few seconds later, I heard her bare feet thumping away.

Up again, I put my face to the window screen.

Thelma seemed to be gone. The room she'd left behind was bright with tiny flames. She had lit perhaps twenty of them with her candle, but those twenty were caught and doubled by a mirror that stretched the length of one entire wall – the wall way over to the left, not the one straight across the room from me, so I'd probably not been reflected in it.

Attached to that mirror wall, at about waist-height, was a wooden rail. It looked like the sort of rail that ballet dancers use during practice.

Dance practice would also explain the long, full-length mirror.

In one corner of the room stood a baby grand piano.

In another corner was a sound system. It appeared to have a turntable, radio, twin speakers, the works.

I saw light fixtures on the ceiling.

Lamps with cords snaking across the floor to wall outlets.

So the mansion came with electricity, after all.

I wondered if there might be a generator, somewhere, that had broken down on Wesley and Thelma. Or maybe they just didn't know how to work it.

Possibly, they'd made a choice not to use any electricity. Maybe they feared it would give them away, somehow. Or perhaps they simply preferred candlelight.

Most of the floor was empty. To give the dancers plenty of prancing space, I suppose.

The room was more than a dance studio, though. Apparently, it doubled as a reading room, or library. It had a few small tables, lamps, and some thickly padded chairs over near the wall to my right. A wall of floor-to-ceiling bookshelves.

Movement in the mirror suddenly caught my eyes.

It reflected the doorway near the middle of the bookshelf wall.

I saw Wesley before he even came in.

If I can see him in the mirror, he can probably see me.

I ducked and waited, my heart hammering.

A few quiet sounds came: bare feet, wood creaking, a noise like a chair being scooted, the *snick* of a striking match. Then Wesley said, 'What would you like if you win tonight, my dear?'

A voice murmured, 'Nothing.'

'Oh, you must want something.' Wesley sounded very cheerful. 'What'll it be?'

'As if she's gonna win, anyhow,' Thelma said. 'Hasn't got a chance.'

'Of *course* she has a chance. There's always a chance.'

'Yeah, sure,' Thelma said. 'There's a *chance* I'll get struck by lightning.'

'Name your prize, my dear.'

I eased myself higher until I could see in.

The girl stood with her back to me, facing Wesley. She was slender and several inches shorter than Thelma. She had blond hair in a ponytail. She wore a short-sleeved white blouse, a tartan kilt that seemed mostly green and blue, forest green knee socks, and no shoes. The mirror, off to her left, gave me a side view of her face.

I had never seen her before.

My guess was that she might be thirteen or fourteen years old.

Matt's daughter? Daughter of the lagoon woman with the rocks in her belly?

I wanted her to be Kimberly, Billie, or Connie. I'd come here to find them, not some stranger. Where were *my* women?

My mission wasn't a complete failure, though; at least I'd found my two enemies.

Thelma, off to the girl's right, was facing Wesley.

Wesley sat in a padded armchair, grinning at the girl. He wore a square white bandage on his chest. It reminded me of a pirate's eye patch, the way it covered only one side while his other boob bulged out, bare.

Because of how he sat deep in the chair, with one leg crossed, he looked naked. I'd had that glimpse of him in the mirror, though, while he'd been coming in from the hallway. He'd been wearing a belt, two sheathed knives, and some sort of blue bikini-style shorts – briefs or a swimming suit, I couldn't tell which. The way he was seated, I couldn't see any of that.

Except for his bandage, he looked like an acre of bare, hairy skin. (He even had hair on the tops of his shoulders.) He had a dark tan.

Other than his chest wound, he didn't have any signs of injury. Nobody'd been whipping him, slapping him, punching him, kicking him, biting him. (I'm aware, of course, that he was sitting on a good wound. I couldn't see it, though.)

Pinched between Wesley's thumb and forefinger was the long, silver tube of a cigarette holder – but not the one I'd seen him using on the yacht. (That had been ivory.) A cigarette was plugged into the end of it. A thin, pale stream of smoke climbed the air in front of his face.

'Your prize, Erin?' he asked again.

The girl's shoulders shrugged slightly. A moment later, she muttered, 'Doesn't matter.'

Wesley seemed amused. 'Of course it matters! Certainly! You must have an incentive. We can't have you giving up too easily, can we?'

The way Erin looked from behind, she had already given up.

'What would you like more than anything else in the whole world?' Wesley asked. 'But no fair asking for your mother and father.'

After a few moments, Erin said in a soft voice I almost couldn't hear, 'Let us go?'

Thelma gave a snort.

Wesley said, 'Let who go?'

'My sister and I.'

'Good try! I'm afraid that's out of the question, though. Name something realistic.'

'Like what?'

'How about a Pepsi?'

Thelma snorted again.

'Okay,' the girl said. 'But one for Alice, too.'

'Alice can win her own.'

'If she can't have one, I don't want one, either.'

Wesley blew smoke at her. 'Have it your way. I'm trying to be nice, offer you a prize. Where's your gratitude?'

Erin said nothing.

Wesley took a puff, then gave a nod to Thelma.

She stepped up behind Erin, reached around her, and ripped open the front of her blouse. She peeled the blouse off the girl's shoulders and down her back. Then she stepped aside and tossed it to the floor.

Erin was bare down to her kilt. She had narrow, fragile shoulders. Her back was smooth and tanned, and looked as if it might've had a few days to heal since her last beating. It had seen a lot of abuse, though. Along with livid blotches, there were several old, fading yellowish bruises. Along with numerous crusty brown scabs that criss-crossed her back, she had pale, shiny pink stripes where older scabs had come off.

She just stood in front of Wesley, arms hanging by her sides, not even trying to cover herself.

The mirror gave me a side view of her breasts. They came to points and looked like small, soft cones. They were almost as tanned as her back.

'Lovely,' Wesley said. 'You're a very lovely girl, Erin.'

She didn't respond.

'When someone gives you a compliment, you're supposed to say thank you.'

'Thank you,' she mumbled.

'I'd like you to put up a good fight, tonight,' he told her. 'No slacking, like last time.'

She just stood there, limp, her head and arms hanging.

'Let's start the fun,' he said.

Thelma's blue satin robe fell to the floor. She looked as if she'd watched a lot of television wrestling, the way she stomped toward Erin.

But this was no 'gorgeous lady of wrestling.'

This was a monster, battle-scarred, growling, hunched over, arms open, fingers hooked like claws. She attacked from behind, hugged Erin, hoisted her up, swung her around and hurled her.

Flung her in my direction.

The girl came toward me, feet first. Under her kilt, she was bare all the way to her waist.

In midair, she made a frightened noise as if she suddenly realized she had a long way to fall.

She hit the hardwood floor, thudding and bumping as she tumbled, letting out whimpers and grunts, her skin squeaking as she skidded. When she came to a stop, she just lay there on her back and sobbed. Her kilt was up around her hips. I had a hell of a view. I felt guilty, looking. I couldn't *help* looking, though.

I mean, the way she was sprawled out on the floor with her feet no more than about two yards in front of my window.

It ran through my mind that I ought to help her.

But what could I do? I'm not a big guy. I didn't have a gun. My only weapon was the straight razor in the pocket of my shorts. If I just tried to Rambo my way in and save the day, Thelma would wipe me out. She probably wouldn't even need Wesley's help.

I watched her storm across the floor, her huge breasts swinging and flopping. Her eyes were fixed on Erin.

Who didn't even try to get up or defend herself.

'Fight, ya little twat,' Thelma gasped. She clamped the girl's head between her ankles and hopped. Erin's trapped head was jerked up off the floor, then slammed down.

Then Thelma dropped on top of her.

A lot happened, after that – nasty stuff I don't want to write about.

I'm ashamed of myself for watching. Looking back on it now, I know that I should've done whatever I could to stop it. But I was enthralled. Horrified and disgusted, but entranced. I'd never seen anything like this before. As much as I felt sorry for Erin and wanted to help her, I couldn't force myself to stop watching the spectacle.

I told myself there was nothing I could do, anyway.

Which was pure shit. I could've stopped it. One way or another.

Didn't want to, that was the thing.

The girl never did put up any struggle.

Thelma didn't let that stop her. She stripped off Erin's knee socks, wrestled her, squeezed her, tugged the kilt down Erin's legs, kissed her and sucked her and bit her, pinched her, twisted her, slapped and probed her.

They were a rolling tangle of bare flesh. Both of them gasping for air. Both of them groaning and whimpering. Both shiny with sweat and spittle and God-knows-what.

I watched from my window.

Wesley watched from his chair across the room, puffing cigarettes, leaning forward, eyes fixed on the action. He squirmed around a lot. Sometimes, he licked his lips.

I only glanced at him from time to time. Mostly, I watched Thelma and Erin.

By the time I noticed that Wesley had gotten out of his chair, he no longer had his shorts on. His belt was gone, too. He wore nothing but his bandages. His cigarette holder jutted upward from between his teeth, and smoke drifted into his right eye as he strolled toward the women.

His penis led the way, big and solid, pointing at the ceiling.

From his right hand dangled a length of electric cord. (I don't know where it came from – hadn't noticed it before.) Its end trailed along on the floor beside him.

When he got to where Thelma was working on Erin, he began to use the cord on them. He didn't seem to care whether he hit Thelma or the girl. Either of them seemed fine with him.

He started off by casually flicking them with the cord. Toying with them. Slowly, though, he worked himself into a frenzy. He became like a madman. Wild-eyed, huffing for breath, slobbering down his chin, he pranced around them, swinging the cord so hard it whistled. It cracked against their skin. Made them jerk rigid with pain. They writhed and shrieked and bled on the floor.

Through all of this, Thelma never stopped holding on to Erin. Never stopped offering the girl's body to Wesley's lash. And never stopped hurting Erin with her own hands and mouth.

Again, I don't want to dwell on all the nasty details.

I'll skip to the finish.

This is how it ended – with Thelma on her back on the floor, Erin on top of her.

Thelma used her arms and legs to pin the girl to her – face up and spread-eagled. They were both very bloody from the whipping and other things that had been done to them. But now, with Thelma holding Erin helpless,

Wesley dropped on top of them both.

He raped Erin.

While he did it, Thelma went nuts on the bottom as if *she* was the one getting screwed.

Then it was over.

They unpiled. Thelma and Wesley took Erin by her arms, helped her up, and walked her out of the room.

I sank down against the wall under the window, shaky and exhausted. Dazed by what I'd seen.

I wished I hadn't watched.

Also, though, I wished I could get to see it all again.

I know, sick.

The thing is, you don't get a chance to see something like that every day.

Like a car accident.

Only better.

Never mind. I know I shouldn't have watched. I should've risked my life to stop it. But I didn't. How come?

A. I'm a miserable, horny pervert.

B. I didn't even know the girl.

C. Thelma and/or Wesley would've killed me.

D. I owe my allegiance to Kimberly, Billie and Connie, not to some stranger.

E. All of the above.

After The Game

After they left the room, I didn't know where they might be. I figured they would probably return pretty soon, though, if only to gather their clothes and put out the candles and lamps. You don't leave flames untended, not for long. Not unless you want to burn down your house.

I could burn the place down!

Standing up, I peered through the window.

Nobody'd come back into the room, yet.

All I needed to do was remove the window screen (or slit it with my razor), climb in and spread around some kerosine, toss a candle . . .

And maybe burn up Kimberly, Billie and Connie – not to mention Erin and her sister, Alice.

As far as I knew, they might all be locked inside the house, somewhere.

Maybe others, too.

I couldn't take any sort of action until I knew where they were being kept.

I'd missed a great opportunity to find them, I realized. While Wesley and Thelma were busy brutalizing Erin in the dance room, I should have gone exploring. I probably could've searched the whole house – with no danger of being caught. Instead, I'd just planted myself at the window and gotten my kicks watching the show.

I'd blown it.

Maybe I'd blown my single, best chance to find and save my women.

All because I'm a low-life, horny pervert.

On the other hand . . . I didn't know in advance that they'd be spending an hour or more messing with that girl. If I *hadn't* stayed and watched, maybe I would've been in the house when they got done. I might've bumped smack into them and gotten myself nailed.

Being a low-life, horny pervert might've saved my life.

Might've saved my women, too, since there was nobody to rescue them except me.

You just never know.

Maybe it was a good thing that I stayed and watched.

While I stood outside the window, peering in and thinking about all that stuff, Thelma came back into the room. She was still naked, but no longer bloody. Apparently, she'd gone off somewhere to wash up.

She hurried about, crouching to pick up what they'd left behind: her robe, Wesley's pants and belt, Erin's kilt and blouse and knee socks. Clutching them to her bosom, she circled the room and blew out the candles and lamp flames.

When she finished, the room was dark except for faint light from the doorway – and its reflection in the mirror. The mirror showed her backside as she hurried down the hall. Then she disappeared.

I decided to climb in through the window and try to catch up with her.

The only safe way to play: keep my eyes on Thelma and Wesley. So long as I never let them out of my sight, they wouldn't be able to take me by surprise.

Also, they were sure to lead me to my women. (Unless my women were dead, which I couldn't allow myself to believe.)

The window screen was attached to the sill by small hook-and-eye catches. A simple flip of two hooks, and the screen should swing out for me.

But the hooks were on the inside.

At the bottom of the screen, just above one of the hooks, I sliced a small flap with my razor, I pushed against it with the tip of my forefinger. The flap lifted inward. I inserted my finger to the second knuckle and shoved the hook sideways. It was tight in the steel eye. But it suddenly popped out.

I started to work on the screen above the other catch. When the flap was made, I put away my razor. Then I poked my finger in. I shoved at the hook. It slipped free.

The screen went loose at the bottom.

I stuck my index fingers into both the flaps.

I started easing the screen toward me. It came easily.

But all of a sudden, a door banged shut somewhere to my right – in the direction of the front of the house. The sound, though not very loud, startled the hell out of me. I jumped. I felt as if I'd gotten zapped by lightning – a hot current sizzling through my heart and every vein and artery.

I damn near fell down.

Somehow, though, I kept my hold on the screen. I eased it gently back into place, in spite of my quaking hands. Then I let myself collapse.

I lay on the ground, head up, eyes on the grounds by the front of the mansion. I no longer sizzled from the sudden fright, but my heart wouldn't slow down. It whammed like a madman. I had a hard time catching my breath, too. I was a wreck.

Nobody walked into view.

I heard voices, though. Probably Wesley and Thelma, but the sounds were soft and masked by a thousand jungle noises. I didn't have a clue about what was being said.

After a few seconds, the voices faded out completely.

I pushed myself off the ground and ran alongside the house. Glancing around the corner of the veranda, I found my quarry; Wesley and Thelma, walking Erin toward the jungle.

They had their backs to me.

Thelma's right hand clutched Erin by the arm. She carried a flaming torch in her left hand. It lit the three of them with an aura of shimmering gold.

Thelma wore shoes, and nothing else. Erin wore nothing at all. Wesley, holding her by the right arm, wore his knife belt, a bandage on his right buttock, and high-top sneakers.

Erin limped along between her two captors. She'd been cleaned so that she no longer looked as if she'd been rolling in blood. But I could see a mad pattern of stripes on her back and buttocks.

Her head hung. She looked hugely weary.

They led her away from the mansion, following a dirt pathway that curved to the left and vanished into the jungle.

I watched until *they* vanished into the jungle. When all I could see was the haze of Thelma's torchlight, I broke cover. I dashed past the side of the veranda and across the front lawn (book bag whapping against my back), and didn't slow down until I came to the dirt path.

Crouching low, I crept forward. With bushes in the way, I could no longer see the glow of Thelma's torch. But she and the others couldn't have gone far. They had to be just a short distance ahead.

I snuck around a curve in the path.

And found them.

Found them on the path, no more than fifty feet in front of me.

Loading Erin into a cage.

A cage the size of a small room, bars on all sides, bars across the top, a door of bars in front.

At the fading edges of the torchlight, I could just barely see a second cage. A space the width of a sidewalk separated it, from Erin's cage – enough distance to stop the prisoners from reaching each other, touching.

A girl stood in the second cage, her face pressed between two of the bars. She was poorly lit. She looked too small, though, to be any of my women.

I guessed she might be Alice, Erin's sister.

Wesley shoved Erin through the door of the first cage, then swung it shut and locked it with a key.

He had a whole bunch of keys. They hung on a ring the size of a bracelet. After locking Erin in her cage, he slipped the key-ring over his right wrist.

I figured he and Thelma might turn around soon, to start back, so I scurried off the path and crawled in among the bushes and tree trunks. I'd just gotten myself turned around when they came down the path.

I couldn't see them, so they couldn't see me, either.

I saw the glow of the torch, though. It drifted slowly by, no more than six feet in front of me but high off the ground.

Wesley and Thelma weren't talking. I couldn't hear their footsteps, either. All I heard was the soft jangle of the keys.

The light moved on and vanished. The jangle faded away.

I didn't move.

What if it was a trick? Maybe Wesley stayed behind to spring a trap on me. He could've given the key-ring to Thelma.

Don't be ridiculous, I told myself. They almost certainly think I'm dead, and they *sure* don't know I've tracked them down.

Unless they do.

Unless they spotted me somehow. Somewhere. When I followed them over here to the cages. When I spied on them through the window. Or earlier. Maybe they'd even spotted me before dark.

No.

They don't know I'm here. They think I'm dead. Wesley didn't stay behind to jump me. He and Thelma are on their way back to the mansion.

Probably.

I sure hoped so.

I couldn't see myself staying put all night, hiding there in the bushes on the off-chance that Wesley might be waiting to jump me at the cages.

So I crawled out.

On hands and knees, I looked both ways – up and down the path.

No sign of anybody.

I couldn't see the light of Thelma's torch, either.

Nor could I see the cages. They'd been eaten by the darkness.

Getting to my feet but staying low, I hurried down the path to where it opened with a view of the front lawn and mansion. Thelma and Wesley had almost reached the veranda.

As I watched, Thelma stepped over to a bucket by the side of the veranda stairs. She swept her torch down and plunged its blazing end into the bucket.

No more light.

At least it seemed that way for a few seconds. But then I saw – or thought I saw – Wesley and Thelma climb the veranda stairs. Vague, moving blurs, not quite as dark as the darkness that gave them shape.

One small, pale bit was slightly more distinct than the rest. I figured it must be the bandage on Wesley's ass.

All traces vanished at the top of the stairs, killed by the shadows from the veranda's roof.

Then a door bammed.

They'd gone inside the mansion.

I hoped.

Waiting no longer, I turned around and rushed up the path toward the cages.

Caged Birds

In the absence of Thelma's torchlight, I couldn't see the path. I couldn't see anything at all except for a few different shades of darkness that were flecked, here and there, with dabs of white from the moon.

I remembered Andrew's cigarette lighter. I could feel it in the right front pocket of my shorts, along with the straight razor and Billie's sunblock. They bumped and brushed against my thigh as I walked.

I dug the lighter out. Got my thumb ready to flick it. Then changed my mind.

In the darkness, I was almost invisible.

I *like* being invisible.

You're so safe and powerful when nobody can see you.

I slipped the lighter down inside my pocket, then made my way slowly forward, watching and listening.

Soon, I heard voices. Girl voices, softly spoken, coming from ahead and over to my right. I crept toward them. When I was near enough to understand the words, I crouched down and listened.

'Don't be dumb,' one girl said. 'We aren't old enough.'

'You're the dumb one.' This sounded like Erin's voice, though it seemed more lively than the other times I'd heard it. 'It isn't how old you are, it's whether you're having periods yet.'

'Who says so?'

'Dad.'

'How come he didn't tell me?'

'Maybe you never asked.'

'Mom never said so.'

'Mom never said anything about *anything*. Not that sort of stuff. That's how come I asked Dad.'

'You asked him when you can start having babies?'

'Sure.'

'How come?'

'Just wondered.'

'So if you already know, how come you're asking *me*?'

Erin didn't answer at first. When she spoke again, she sounded more like the timid kid I'd heard in the room with Thelma and Wesley. 'It's just . . . do you think he's gonna make us have babies?'

'Jeez, don't ask me.'

'That's what's gonna happen, I think. You know?'

'I honestly don't think you can have a baby till you're eighteen.'

'Eighteen? You're nuts. You don't have to be any eighteen.'

'Do, too.'

'Ask Connie.'

Connie!

My heart gave a quick lurch.

'No way. Are you kidding? I'm not gonna wake her up just to ask her some dumb question. She'd kill me.'

'Would not.'

'I'm not gonna.'

'Well anyway, I happen to know for a fact you don't

have to be any eighteen. You only gotta be old enough to be having your periods, because that means you've got eggs going. Once that's happening, you can have all the babies you want.'

'No. Huh-uh. You've gotta be eighteen.'

'You're out of your mind.'

'Am not. I read it someplace.'

'Eighteen must've meant something else.'

'Like what?'

'How should I know? I didn't read it. I just think we're all gonna end up having babies if we keep letting Wesley screw us.'

'Who's *letting* him?'

'He's doing it anyway, isn't he? I mean, how many times have *you* ever stopped him?'

Alice didn't answer.

For a little while, neither of them spoke. Then Erin said, 'I wonder how many times it takes.'

'For what?'

'You know. To make you pregnant.'

'You tell me. You know everything.'

'I don't know that,' Erin admitted. 'I wonder if you have to do it, like, twenty times or something.'

'I wouldn't know. You should've asked Dad.'

'Very funny. But don't you think we'd maybe be pregnant by now if it only took once or twice or something?'

Alice sighed. 'I guess so.'

'But we aren't, right? He did us both the day he showed up for the first time. Then he got me twice more before he went away. So that makes a total of three, all the way back then.'

'Twice for me,' Alice said.

'But we had our periods since then, so obviously it

wasn't enough. So how many *does* it take?'

'Who knows?'

'At least it's not *us* all the time, now that he's got everyone else.'

Everyone else!

I couldn't keep silent any longer. 'Excuse me,' I said.

They both gasped.

'It's okay,' I told them. 'Don't be scared. I'm a friend. I'm here to rescue you.'

Erin said, 'Rupert?'

I couldn't believe my ears.

'Yes,' I said. 'You know who I am?'

'Just a guess. They told us all about you. Where are you? I can't see you.'

I crept closer. No moonlight, at all, made it down to where the cages were. I could see nothing. Not the cages, not the girls, not even my own hands. It was like being shut up at night in a closet.

Reaching out with one hand, I touched bars. 'I'm at your cage.'

'I can't see you,' Erin said.

'I can't see you, either,' I said.

'Are you sure?' Alice asked. 'You can't see either one of us?'

'If we can't see each other *or* him,' Erin said, 'how is he supposed to be able to see us?'

'It's possible. It all depends.'

'Alice is just worried 'cause we don't have much on.'

'That's okay. I can't see a thing.'

'She's Alice, by the way. I'm Erin. We're Alice and Erin Sherman. We're fourteen, and we're twins.'

'Identical twins?' I asked.

'No,' Alice said.

'Yes,' said Erin.

'We are not.'

'In the technical sense, we are. Only we just don't look exactly alike, that's all. Alice thinks she's prettier than me.'

'Liar.'

'But *I'm* actually the pretty one,' Erin said. I imagined her smiling as she said that.

'You're so full of crap,' Alice said, 'it's not even funny.'

I started moving sideways, following the bars. They felt warm in my hands. They were at least an inch thick. The gaps between them seemed to be about four inches across.

'What're you doing?' Erin asked. 'Rupert?'

'I'll get between your cages so we won't have to talk so loud.'

'Have you been here long?' she asked.

I blushed, but nobody could see it. 'No,' I lied. 'Just got here.'

'Everyone thinks you're dead.'

'The reports of my death are greatly exaggerated,' I explained – Mark Twain had said it first.

'Boy, this is great,' Erin said. 'You being alive.'

'And not in a cage,' added Alice.

I found the corner of Erin's cage, and crawled around it. To make sure I was between the cages, I stretched out my arms. I touched bars to my right and left. So I sat down and crossed my legs. 'Okay,' I said.

From both sides came quiet sounds – rustling, sliding, breathing, a couple of small moans – as the girls moved in closer. The moans had come from my right, from Erin. After the beating she'd taken in the room, it probably hurt her a lot to move.

'Are you there?' she asked.

As quietly as I could, I slid myself toward Erin's cage. I

stopped when my upper arm touched a bar.

'Can you get us out of here?' Alice asked.

'I sure hope so. One way or another. Is there any way to open these things without a key?'

'Nope,' Erin said. Her voice was much closer to me than Alice's. I thought I could feel her breath on my arm. Though I couldn't see even a hint of her, I pictured her sitting cross-legged, leaning forward, elbows on her thighs, the tips of her breasts almost touching her forearms, her face only inches from the bars.

I wished I could see her.

I thought about the lighter in my pocket.

I didn't go for it, though. Better for us all to stay invisible, at least for the time being.

'You can't get in or out,' Erin said, 'unless you've got keys. These're really strong cages.'

'They were made to hold gorillas,' Alice explained.

Monkey Business

'*Gorillas?*' I asked.

'This used to be a gorilla zoo,' Erin said.

'Before we moved here,' her sister added.

'Yeah, a *long* time before we moved here. We've only been on the island a couple of years.'

'It'll be two years in June,' Alice said.

'The gorillas were all dead before we ever got here. *Long* dead. Like before we were even born. This guy massacred them all. How do you like that? The same guy that brought them here.'

'To save them,' Alice added.

'Yeah,' Erin said. 'There was some sort of revolution going on some place in Africa. Like back in the sixties? And this guy was afraid all the gorillas might get killed off.'

'He was a naturalist,' Alice explained.

'You know, like that *Gorillas in the Mist* woman. Sigourney Weaver?'

'Dian Fossey,' Alice said.

'Yeah,' Erin said, 'like that.'

'He lived right here in the big house when he wasn't running around places like Africa.'

'So anyway,' Erin said, 'he captured like a dozen of these gorillas and shipped them over here to this island. He had the cages built especially for them. Made himself a nice little private zoo.'

'It wasn't really a zoo,' Alice pointed out.

'Not if you wanta get *technical*,' Erin said. 'It wasn't like a *public* zoo. He kept the apes for himself, like pets. Then one day he slaughtered them all.'

'Killed them?' I asked. 'Why'd he do that?'

'Maybe he got tired of them,' Alice suggested.

'Or they done him wrong,' Erin said. Again, I pictured her smiling.

'Nobody knows why,' Alice said.

Then Erin went on. 'He must've gone nuts, or something. He chopped them all up in their cages with a machete, and then he shot himself in the head. Anyway, that's how come the cages are here.'

'We weren't permitted to play in them,' Alice said.

'Now we gotta *live* in them,' Erin said.

'Who else is here?' I asked.

'In the cages, you mean?'

'Yeah.'

'Connie and her mother, and Kimberly.'

All of them!

I started to cry. I tried to be quiet about it, but couldn't help letting out a few little noises. Erin and Alice didn't say anything. It was like they were both sitting in their cages, listening to me.

Then something rubbed the top of my head.

I flinched.

'It's just me,' Erin whispered.

Her hand gently stroked my hair, then eased down along my cheek. Petting me.

I'd started crying out of relief at the news my women were here and alive. With Erin caressing my face, though,

I started crying for her, for what had been done to her.

And for myself because I'd allowed it to happen.

I'd enjoyed watching.

'It's okay,' she said softly. 'They're fine.'

'Are not,' Alice said.

'They're as fine as *we* are.'

'You call that "fine"?'

In a softer voice, Erin said to me, 'They're really gonna be shocked. They thought you were dead, for sure. You fell off a cliff or something?'

I nodded. I tried to stop crying.

'That was *after* Thelma got him in the head,' Alice reminded her.

'Yeah,' Erin said. 'Anyway, they were awfully upset about you getting killed. They thought you were the greatest.'

'Me?'

'Yeah. They're gonna go nuts when they see you.'

'They're in . . . some of the . . . other cages?' Even though I was getting better, I could only talk between sobs.

'Connie's in the one next to mine,' Alice said. 'Then's Kimberly. Billie's cage is on the other side of Kimberly's. And then the rest of 'em are empty.'

I said, 'Maybe I'd better . . . go over now, and . . .'

'No.' Erin's hand dropped to my shoulder and squeezed it. 'Don't go yet. Please? They're probably all asleep, anyway. Can't you just stay here and talk to us for a little while more? Please?'

I didn't much want to go over and see my women, anyway, until I'd completely finished the crying. Besides, I wanted to find out a lot more about what had been going on. I said, 'Okay. I won't go yet.'

'Thanks,' Erin said.

'How long . . . when did they get here?'

'Connie and the others? About a week ago.'

'This is their seventh night,' Alice said.

'What about you two?' I asked.

'It's night twenty-four,' Alice said.

I gasped, 'What!'

'Yeah,' Erin said. 'Twenty-four.'

'My God!'

'Wesley put us in the day he got here.'

'The *first* time he came,' Alice pointed out.

'He knew about the cages,' Erin said.

'He'd read about them.'

'Yeah. An article in some old *National Geographic* magazine, or something, and he wondered if they were still here, and could he see them.'

'He said maybe he'd buy them if they were in good enough shape.'

Erin's hand glided down my arm. She found my hand, and took hold of it. Then she continued with the story. 'Anyhow, Alice and I were off swimming, so we weren't around when he came along. Mom and Dad had to fill us in. I guess they were showing him the cages, and all of a sudden he grabbed Mom and put a razor to her throat. So then Dad was afraid to do anything, 'cause he didn't want Mom to get her throat slashed. Wesley made them both get in cages, and locked them in. Then Alice and I got back home and he put us in cages, too.'

'We could've gotten away,' Alice said.

'Yeah. It would've been a cinch. There was only Wesley. He didn't have a gun or anything, either. But he said he'd kill Mom and Dad if we didn't do everything he told us.'

'And he told us to get in the cages.'

'So then he ended up killing them, anyhow – only not right away.'

'Maybe not Mom.' Alice sounded a little offended.

'If he didn't kill her, where is she?'

I figured I knew where she was, but I kept my mouth shut.

'I don't know,' Alice muttered.

For my benefit, Erin explained, 'He kept Mom in one of the cages just like the rest of us. Dad, too, but they took him away a long time ago. With Mom, she was here the whole time till she got away.'

'When was that?' I asked.

'A few nights ago.'

'Four,' Alice said. 'Counting tonight.'

Four. That would've been the night I hiked upstream, searched our battlefield, and found the woman at the bottom of the lagoon.

'Yeah,' Erin said. 'They were bringing Mom back to her cage after . . . it was her night for going to the house. She hadn't ever tried anything before. Because of us, you know? What Wesley said he'd do to us if she ever tried to escape. But she figured we didn't stand any chance *unless* she made a getaway. Then she could sneak back, you know? And save us. So she waited till they were trying to put her back inside her cage, and then she shoved free and made a run for it. They both went chasing after her, though. And they got her.'

'Maybe they did, and maybe they didn't,' Alice said.

'They got her.'

'Just because they said so . . .'

'Come on, Alice. You think they would've been acting like that if they *hadn't* caught Mom? You know darn well.'

Alice went silent.

I thought about asking more questions. What time had their mother made her break? Were they familiar with the lagoon? How far was the lagoon from here?

But I didn't have to ask.

The dead woman I'd found in the water *had* to be their mother. Who else could it be?

And Matt, I'd already figured out, was their father.

Wesley had made orphans out of these kids.

One of his many crimes, and one of his worst.

'Anyhow,' Erin said, 'back to what I was saying. The day Wesley got here? We all ended up in cages. Then he hung around for a couple of days. He never did anything to Dad, but he like . . . took turns . . . fooled around with the rest of us.'

'He likes to hurt people,' Alice muttered.

'He'd take us out of our cages. Just one at a time. And make us do stuff.'

'Awful stuff,' Alice added.

'And if we didn't do everything just right, he'd make someone else pay for it. Like he wanted me to . . . do something to him. I wouldn't. So then he put me back in my cage and took Mom out. He whipped her right in front of us, then made *her* do it to him. 'Cause I'd said I wouldn't.'

Erin's hand felt hot and sweaty, holding mine. I gave it a gentle squeeze.

'Anyhow,' she said, 'he did that sort of stuff to us right from the start, when he was here the first time. He didn't stay very long, that time. When he went away, he left us in our cages with some food and water, and said he'd come back.'

'But not when,' Alice added.

'Yeah. After a while, we started to think he wasn't

gonna come back at all. We got really low on the food and water. Before it was totally gone, though, we heard this huge explosion.'

'Our yacht going up in smoke?' I asked.

'Yeah. And next thing we knew, he was back. He came in from the jungle, all smiling and happy.'

'And not wearing a stitch,' Alice added.

'He hardly ever does,' Erin said. 'Like he thinks everybody wants to be looking at his *thing* all the time.'

'Which they don't.'

'Not me.'

'Did he say how he blew up the yacht?' I asked.

'Sure,' Erin said. 'He bragged all about how easy it was. He used that razor of his to cut open a fuel line. Down in the engine compartment? Then he made a fuse out of a bedsheet. After he lit it, he snuck overboard and swam away underwater.'

'He was laughing about it,' Alice said. 'He thought he was so smart.'

'He outsmarted us, all right,' I told them. 'We all thought he blew it up by accident and got himself killed.'

'That's what he wanted you to think,' Erin explained. 'Billie says you figured it out pretty quick, though.'

'Well, we guessed. After people started getting murdered. I mean, who else *could've* been doing it? As far as we knew, the island was uninhabited. We didn't know there was a whole family . . . Are there any others?'

'Other what?' Erin asked.

'People. Families. Houses. Do you have neighbors?'

'We're it.'

'Nobody here but us,' Alice said.

'We had the island all to ourselves. It was great. Until Wesley came along.'

'Mom and Dad brought us here so we'd be safe,' Alice said. 'That's a good one, huh?'

'We lived in Los Angeles,' Erin said. 'We moved when the riot happened. That was the last straw, you know? They were afraid we'd all get killed, or something. They wanted to take us someplace where we wouldn't need to worry about stuff like crime and drugs.'

'And look what happened,' Alice said.

'We *know* what happened,' Erin told her. 'But it was great while it lasted.' To me, she said, 'We did home study. No school. Mom and Dad taught us. She used to be a schoolteacher, and Dad was a writer. It was great, not going to some awful school full of nasty kids. And we went swimming and fishing almost every day. It was the greatest, till Wesley came along and ruined everything.'

'I wish we'd stayed in Los Angeles,' Alice said.

'No, you don't.'

'Mom and Dad'd still be alive.'

'Maybe. But you never know. Maybe the quake would've killed us all.'

'Would've been better than this.'

'No, it wouldn't have been.'

'I'd *rather* be dead,' Alice blurted. 'I'd rather be dead any day of the week than get . . . Rupert, you don't know what he does to us.'

'Huh-uh,' I said.

I wasn't about to let on that I'd watched him and Thelma with Erin. It would've been too embarrassing. And it would've made the twins wonder what was wrong with me – how come I watched them mess with Erin, but didn't try to help her?

'They *play* with us,' Alice said. 'It's bad enough we've gotta stay in these *cages*, but it's a lot worse when they take

381

us out. They take us out to *play* with us. They play *dress-up* with us. They play *house* with us. They make us eat with them and dance for them and fight with them. Anything they can think of, they make us do. And it always ends up the same way, with getting beaten to a pulp and getting fucked.'

'Hey,' Erin said. 'You don't have to get crude about it.'

'It *is* crude. Everything *about* it is crude! I *wish* I was dead!'

'No, you . . .'

'Hey! Knock it off! Jesus H. Christ, it's the middle of the night. Some of us are trying to *sleep* around here, thank you very much.'

'Connie?' I said.

Silence.

Then she asked, 'Who said that?'

'Me.'

More silence.

Then, 'Rupert?'

'That's my name, don't wear it out.'

'Holy fucking shit! Rupert!'

Reunion

'Rupert?' Now Billie had joined in, obviously awakened by Connie's excited voice. 'Is that you?'

'Yeah. How are you?'

Instead of answering, she sort of gasped, 'Oh, my God' in a shaky voice.

'Haul it over here so we don't have to yell,' Kimberly greeted me.

'Hi, Kimberly,' I said.

'You're a little late for arriving in the nick of time,' she said, 'but better late than never. Come on over here.'

I whispered, 'I'd better go. But don't worry, I'll take care of everything.' I eased my hand out of Erin's.

'You'll get us out of here, won't you?' Alice asked.

'Yeah. Somehow.'

'Just be careful,' Erin told me. 'And come back to our side of things when you get a chance, okay?'

'Sure. Thanks.'

'We don't even know what you look like,' she said.

I thought about the lighter in my pocket. She'd pretty much invited me to strike it up. I wanted to do it. The flame would give me a close-up look at her, sitting there in her cage. I'd get a chance to see her twin sister, too.

Both of them probably naked.

A good way to find out whether they were really identical.

But they'd already been badly treated – to put it mildly. I didn't want myself adding to their troubles by lighting them up and embarrassing them.

So I kept the cigarette lighter in my pocket.

I said, 'You want to know what I look like? I'm so gorgeous I make Tom Cruise look like he got hit by an ugly-stick.'

Soft laughter came from Erin.

'Really?' Alice asked.

From farther away, Connie said, 'What kind of shit are you handing those girls, Rupe? Tell 'em the truth! You look like a fucking chimp! An albino chimp that lost all its hair!'

She was sure in fine form.

'I don't, either,' I said to Erin. 'Chimps have tails.'

'You'd better go,' Erin said, 'or she'll start saying *really* bad stuff about you.'

'Okay. See you later. You, too, Alice.'

I made my way out of the space between their cages. I got to my feet in front of Alice's cage. Running a hand along its bars to keep myself oriented, I hurried toward the cages where Connie and my other women were waiting for me.

'What've you got, nine lives?' Connie asked when I was in front of her cage.

'Just lucky.' I kept moving slowly, following its bars. 'Something broke my fall.'

'You must've been hurt,' Kimberly said. Her voice came from a distance ahead of me. 'It was a long way down.'

'Got banged up pretty good. That's why it took me so long to get here. I was out cold for a couple of days or so, then I was too messed up to do much.'

'We're lucky you're alive at all,' Billie said from her cage on the far side of Kimberly's.'

'And lucky that you finally *found* us,' Kimberly added.

'Yeah.' Connie sounded a little annoyed. 'Better late than never.'

Reaching out, I felt no more bars. I'd apparently arrived at the corner of Connie's cage. Leaving it behind, I crossed an open space. My searching hand bumped against steel.

And got grabbed around the wrist.

'Stay.' Kimberly's voice. Her hand clutching me.

It felt strong and warm. Heat from it seemed to flow up my arm and spread through my whole body.

'You've gotta get us out of here,' she said.

'I will. Are you all okay?'

'Yeah, right,' Connie said. 'They've had us for a *week*. All they wanta do is figure out new ways to fuck us over.'

In a low voice, Kimberly said, 'They've raped all of us.'

'Even you?'

'Yeah, even me.'

'How?'

'What do you mean, how?'

'You're so . . . tough.'

'They make you go along,' she muttered.

'It's my fault,' Connie said. She sounded different, suddenly. Quiet and upset. 'They use me. If Mom or Kimberly don't go along, *I'm* the one who gets it. They don't want me getting wrecked, so they . . . keep cooperating. No matter what Wesley wants.'

'You've gotta get the keys away from him,' Kimberly said. Her hand tightened around my wrist.

'I will,' I said. 'Are you all okay, though? I mean, I know you're not *okay*, but . . .'

'We're fucked,' Connie said.

'We're fine,' Billie said.

'We *are not*.'

'Our injuries aren't too serious,' Kimberly explained. 'Superficial stuff. We probably don't need a hospital, nothing that bad.'

'I had you all figured for dead,' I told them.

'Hate to disappoint you,' Connie muttered.

'I couldn't find your bodies, though. I went back to where we had the fight. I thought . . . you'd all still be there. But when I couldn't find your bodies . . .'

'We gave up,' Kimberly said.

'Thanks to me,' Connie said. 'My fault. I plead guilty.'

'Wesley got her down,' Billie explained from her distant cage. 'You were already out of it, by then. Thelma'd clobbered you in the head with a rock. You never even saw it coming. Next thing I knew, Connie was flat on her face.'

'I was still on the rope,' Kimberly said. 'By the time I got to the top, Wesley had a foot planted on her back. He was all set to kill her with a machete. We *had* to give up.'

'Glad you did.'

'You wouldn't be so glad,' Connie said, 'if *you* had to go through this shit.'

'Rupert?' Billie asked. 'Do you remember all our talk, those first few days, about Wesley's motive? How we figured he wanted to kill everyone?'

'Yeah, for the money.'

'We were wrong. It didn't have anything to do with money. He wanted *us*. The three of us. He had this fantasy about trapping everyone in a remote place, killing the men, and keeping us as his prisoners.'

'He admitted it?'

'Yeah. Told me all about it. He had me alone – Thelma'd

wandered off somewhere – so I started asking questions. He happened to be in a talkative mood. Real pleased with himself. He'd just finished . . . having a fine old time with me. So I found out a lot. For starters, we were all together the first time he met Thelma. So right from the beginning, he knew what we looked like. Me, Connie, and Kimberly.'

'Three hot babes,' Connie muttered.

Billie said, 'He told me that he'd never in his life scored with anything but bow-wows. Women like us would never even *think* about going out with him.'

''Cause he's a fucking loser,' Connie threw in.

'From then on,' Billie said, 'everything was a set-up. He started by going after Thelma. She was easy.'

'Being also a fucking loser,' Connie added.

I half expected Kimberly to speak up in her sister's defense, but she kept silent.

Billie said, 'What Thelma didn't know is that he only wanted her as a way of getting at the rest of us. He figured he would have plenty of access to us if he married her. Then – surprise, surprise – it turned out she was as kinky as he was.'

'A match made in Bedlam,' Kimberly muttered.

'Both of 'em a couple of fucking sadists,' Connie said.

'Was Thelma in on everything?' I asked.

Billie answered. 'She sure didn't know her loving husband had the hots for every other woman in her family. He kept that to himself. Along with his big plan to blow up the boat and maroon us.'

'He knew the cages were here,' Kimberly said.

'He did *research*,' Billie explained. 'My God, he hadn't even gone on an actual *date* with Thelma before he started studying up – trying to find just the right place for his little caper. He thought about cabins in the mountains, ghost towns, abandoned factories, warehouses, barns — every sort of place he could imagine where nobody'd be likely to get in his way. Where he could keep us for as long as he wanted, and do anything to us that suited his fancy.'

'Fucking degenerate,' Connie said.

Billie ignored her. 'It wasn't long before he realized that an uninhabited island would be perfect. You're cut off from everyone. You've got the run of the place, so you don't have to keep your prisoners hidden away. Nobody around to hear them scream. And it's tough for them to escape.'

'Tough, all right,' Kimberly said, her voice low. 'Look what happened to Dorothy.'

'Who?' I asked.

'Their mother. Dorothy. She made a break for it — Christ, just a few nights ago — but they ran her down and nailed her.'

'I heard about it,' I muttered.

'Those poor children,' Billie said, keeping her voice quiet, not wanting Alice and Erin to hear her. 'They've been through worse than any of us. They've been in the cages for almost a month. They've lost their mother *and* father. And . . . Wesley and Thelma do such *awful* things to them. My God, they're only kids.'

'Kids with tits and . . .'

'Knock it off, Connie,' Kimberly snapped. In a softer voice, she said, 'Billie, go ahead and finish what you were saying about Wesley looking for an island. Rupert oughta hear this.'

'Yeah,' Connie said. 'So he can put it in his fucking journal.'

'You still keeping it?' Kimberly asked me.

'I ran out of paper.'

'Aw, ain't that a shame,' Connie said.

'Finish it after you save us,' Kimberly told me. 'And put in how Wesley planned it all, how he picked which island, and everything. It'll help show he had premeditation.'

'Like he's ever gonna stand trial,' Connie said.

'However it all turns out,' Kimberly said, 'it'll be a good thing if Rupert has a detailed record of the whole situation. It might be the only way anyone ever finds out what happened here.'

'If I'm dead anyhow,' Connie said, 'I'm not exactly gonna *give* a rat's ass.'

'Billie, go ahead and tell him the rest.'

'Okay. Let me see.' She was silent for a few seconds, then said, 'Wesley decided an island would be the perfect sort of place, so he started doing research. At first, he thought mostly in terms of islands in places like Wisconsin and Michigan. You know, on lakes and rivers. He concentrated on the Midwest. Probably because he was raised in that area. Grew up near Chicago. The minute he broadened his horizons, though, he realized that the Bahamas would be ideal. Beautiful, tropical islands with great weather. Conveniently located off the coast of Florida. Handy airline service. The best part was, he found out that there're hundreds of uninhabited islands in the area.'

'He didn't pick an uninhabited one,' I pointed out.

'That's because he read about the cages. He ran across an old magazine article . . .'

'Erin and Alice told me about that.'

'When he saw the bit about gorilla cages . . .'

'Thought he'd died and gone to Heaven,' Kimberly said.

'In case you haven't noticed,' Connie said, 'we're in Wesley Heaven.'

'Everything seemed to be falling into place for him,' Billie explained. 'It was almost uncanny. First, he finds the absolutely perfect place for fulfilling his nasty little daydreams about us. On paper, anyway. Then, it turns out that Andrew and I are about to have our twentieth wedding anniversary.' With mock eagerness and an edge of bitterness unusual for her, Billie proclaimed, 'Why not celebrate it with the whole family aboard a rented yacht in the Bahamas?'

'It did sound great,' Kimberly admitted.

'It *was* great . . . until . . .' Billie stopped speaking. I heard her start to cry.

For Andrew, her husband. That's what I figured. Or maybe she was crying because of everything. Not only had she been made a widow during her twentieth anniversary celebration, but she and her daughter were locked in cages, kept like slaves for the amusement of a couple of demented perverts. She might've been crying for the others, too. Kimberly's husband had also been murdered, and Kimberly'd ended up in a cage. The twins, too – Erin and Alice.

All five of them had lost people they loved. All five had been toyed with by Wesley and Thelma – beaten, whipped, raped, and God-only-knows what else.

It's a wonder that they weren't *all* bawling their heads off.

You can't cry all the time, though. This was Billie's time for it.

Kimberly still held my wrist.

'Let go,' I whispered.

Her fingers opened. I slipped my hand free, then felt my way along the front of her cage. I crossed the open area and came to Billie's cage. She was still crying.

'Billie?' I asked.

'Rupert?'

I pressed my body against her cage and reached through the bars with both arms. 'Over here.'

She found my arms and moved in between them. We hugged each other, bars sandwiched between our bodies. She sobbed quietly. The sobbing and gasping made her shake. I started to caress her back, but the smoothness there was broken by ridges – welts and scabs from the beatings she'd taken. She twitched slightly when I touched one.

'I'm sorry,' I whispered.

'It's okay, honey.'

Then I was crying, too.

I stopped caressing her back, afraid of hurting her. As I lowered my arms, she said, 'No, hold me. Don't stop.'

So I put them around her again, but very gently.

Jealous Dogs

'What the hell are you two doing over there?' Connie called out.

'Shut up,' Kimberly told her.

'We aren't doing anything,' I said. Which was true. We were only embracing each other while Billie continued to cry.

'Thank God you're all right,' Billie whispered. Her breath tickled my lips. Then she had her mouth there, wet and open, pushing against my mouth. It was a kiss, but not like any kiss I'd ever had before. She was still sort of crying while we kissed. It was strange, but awfully nice.

I'd been trying to ignore the fact that her bare breasts were pressed against me. You don't want to notice that sort of thing when a woman is crying in your arms. But now that she'd begun kissing me, it seemed okay to think about them.

They were pushed out between the bars, soft and springy against my chest.

While we kissed, I squirmed so I could feel them slide on me. We were both sweaty. Our skin was slippery as if we'd been oiled. Her nipples were stiff, and rubbed against my chest like little tongues.

I tried to pull away so Billie wouldn't feel how hard I

was getting. But she held me tightly, so I couldn't.

Her kiss was astonishing and wet.

By the time it ended, Billie didn't seem to be crying anymore. We were both gasping for air, though. And she didn't let me go. She kept her arms around me, just like before the kiss. We stayed pressed together.

'Thank you, honey,' she whispered.

'My pleasure.'

She made a quiet 'Hmmm' sound, but didn't say anything.

'Are you okay?' Kimberly asked.

'A lot better, now,' Billie said.

'I'll bet,' Connie called.

'Why do you always have to be such a snot?' That one came from Erin – the first I'd heard from either of the twins since I'd left their cages. I grinned.

'Up yours,' Connie yelled at her.

'Same to you and many more.'

Alice got into the act. 'Erin! Shhh!'

'She's such a bitch.'

'*You're* a shit-eating little twat!' Connie shouted.

'Cut it out, children,' Kimberly said. 'Let's not fight among ourselves.'

'Blow it out your ass,' Connie told her.

Kimberly laughed.

Billie, still in my arms, called out, 'Connie. Stop it. What the hell is the matter with you!'

'Oh, nothing. What could possibly be wrong? My mother's over there in the dark, bare-ass naked and messing around with my guy . . .'

'We're not messing around,' Billie said.

'My *former* guy. My *ex*-guy. My worthless fucking loser of a wimp . . .'

Very quietly, Billie whispered to me, 'You should go over to her. Give her a hug.'

'You've gotta be kidding.'

'I mean it. Go.'

'I don't think she'd like that at all.'

'Sure she would. Go on over to her, let her know you care about her.'

'I want to stay with you.'

'I know.'

'Don't you want me here?'

'Sure. But Connie . . . she's really hurting. Go over and be nice to her.'

'She hates me.'

'No, she doesn't. When she thought you were dead . . . she was devastated.'

That was fairly hard to believe. 'Really?'

'Yes, really. I've never seen her so upset. Now, go over to her. Please.' She kissed me again. This was a quick one, a thanks-and-get-going sort of kiss. Then her arms went away from me.

'Okay,' I said. I felt almost sick with disappointment, but I had to do what Billie asked. Whispering, 'Is it okay if I come back later?' I slid my hands all the way down her back. I was gentle about her wounds.

'Sure,' she told me. 'Later. But help Connie first.'

She wore nothing around her waist. My hands curved down over her buttocks. She didn't try to stop me.

But she kissed me once more, and whispered, 'Go on, now.'

I stopped caressing her and brought my hands back through the bars. As I stepped away from the front of her cage, I said fairly loudly, so everyone could hear and stop wondering what was up, 'So, what about Thelma? She didn't know anything about Wesley's plans?'

'Not a thing,' Billie said, sounding a little surprised about the return to that subject. 'She actually believed he'd blown himself up.'

'Why didn't he tell her?'

Billie was probably wondering why I was still standing near the front of her cage, instead of heading for Connie's. The truth is, I wanted to please Billie, but wasn't very eager about confronting her daughter.

Connie was not in one of her finer moods.

'He planned all along to kill her,' Billie explained.

'What?'

'Wesley intended from the start to murder Andrew, Keith, you and Thelma. That's what he told me.'

'Why Thelma?'

'You ever take a good look at her?' Connie called out. 'Oh, yes. Forgot. Sure you have. But apparently *you* found her so attractive you wanted to wrestle naked with her. You got this thing for older women, don't you? Thelma, my mom, Kimberly. Bet you'd like to wrestle naked with . . .'

'Knock it off,' Kimberly told her.

'Wesley hated Thelma,' Billie said, speaking loudly and firmly. 'He hated everything about her, but most of all that she was so much like him.'

'Bet he didn't tell you *that*,' I said.

'You're right. That was a personal observation. But he did say he hated her. Called her ugly and disgusting. He fully intended to kill her as soon as he'd finished off the men. He'd had enough of her. He didn't want her getting in the way. He only wanted *us*.' She lowered her voice. 'And the twins, too. He didn't know about them. He picked this island because it had the cages; the twins were a special bonus for him.' Lowering her voice even more, she whispered, 'Go and see Connie. Go on.'

'I will,' I whispered back. Then I asked in my normal voice, 'Why *didn't* he kill Thelma?'

'Because she saved his ass,' Kimberly said.

'When we tried to ambush him at the beach?' I asked.

'Right,' Billie said. 'It went sort of like we thought: he was wounded so badly that he needed her help. After they got away, he put on a big show of breaking down and confessing. He basically admitted everything.'

'Not that he hated her, though,' Kimberly added.

'No, not that. He kept that to himself. Claimed he loved her. Said he'd done all this for *her*, because he knew how much she despised us.'

'How could she possibly despise you?' I asked.

'For one thing, we tried to kill her husband.'

'She didn't take kindly to that,' Kimberly added. 'Also, she just hates our guts on general principle.'

''Cause she's a jealous fucking dog,' Connie called out.

I heard a bit of grim humor in Kimberly's voice as she said, 'Apparently, we make Thelma feel ugly.'

'Make her feel like the worthless loser she is,' Connie said.

'And she's been making us pay for it,' Kimberly explained. 'She's been having a great time with us.'

Billie said, 'She's worse than Wesley.'

Connie let out a harsh laugh. 'At least Thelma hasn't got a dick.'

'She makes up for it,' Billie said.

'They're a hell of a team,' Kimberly said.

I knew that. But I didn't say anything. Nobody was supposed to know I'd watched them in action with Erin.

'Does that about cover it?' Billie asked.

I didn't know who she was asking.

'That's the important stuff,' Kimberly said. 'He doesn't have to know everything.'

'I bet he'd *enjoy* hearing all the juicy details,' Connie said. 'He can write all about 'em in his diary. Isn't that right, Rupe?'

'I ran out of . . .'

'Oh, yeah, right. But you wanta hear it all anyway, don't you? Wouldn't you just love for us to tell you how they raped us? Which orifices Wesley preferred, and how Thelma . . .'

'Shut up!' Kimberly snapped.

'Connie?' Billie sounded worried. 'What's the matter with you? Stop that.'

'Come on over *here*, Rupert,' Connie said. 'I'll tell you the *good* stuff. I'll give you an earful.'

'Thanks, anyway,' I said. 'I don't . . .'

'You wanta know what Thelma did to Kimberly with a stick yesterday?'

'You'd better shut your mouth,' Kimberly said.

'Come on over, and I'll tell you all about how Mom sucked Wesley's cock.'

'Rupert,' Billie said. She sounded upset, but still fairly calm. And she wasn't whispering. Apparently, it was all right now for Connie to hear what she had to say. 'Go on over to her,' she told me. 'Quick, okay? She's sounding . . . I don't know, I'm afraid she's about to lose it.'

'*Lose it?*' Connie blurted. 'You're afraid I'm gonna *lose* it? Ho ho ho! Surprise, surprise! It's lost!'

I started to hurry in the direction of her cage.

'Connie?' I asked.

'Over here, Rupert. Right over here.' The mocking, coaxing tone of her voice gave me the creeps. 'I'm *waiting* for you.'

'Hey,' I said. 'Take it easy.'

'You miss me?'

'Sure.'

'Bet you missed my mother more.'

Right on the money, I thought. I said, 'No, I didn't.'

'Liar, liar, pants on fire.'

From the direction of her voice, she seemed to be straight in front of me. I stopped walking, and faced her cage. Reaching out, I moved my hand from side to side.

The cage was too far away to touch.

Just the way I wanted it.

'How about Kimmmmm-berly?' she asked. 'Bet you missed herrrr.'

'I missed all of you.'

'Bullll. Bull, bull, bull! You missed her more than me. You missed 'em both more than me. Admit it. You wanta fuck 'em, don't you! Or maybe you've already done it. Have you? Huh? Have you fucked my mom yet, Rupie? Or the fabulous Kimmmm-berly? Have you? How were they? Were they good and . . . ?'

'And you called *Thelma* a jealous dog?' I said.

Which was not the best thing to say, just then.

Connie screamed.

Not a fright-scream like you hear in the movies. This was a rage-scream, a shrieking snarl. '*RAHHHHHHHHHHHHHHHHHHHH!!!*'

She sounded nuts.

My skin crawled.

I dug the lighter out of my pocket, raised it in front of me and thumbed it. A yellow flame spurted up.

'Kill that light!' Kimberly gasped.

I didn't.

I kept it going, and stared at Connie.

Still shrieking, she clung to the bars of her cage about halfway up the front. Her feet were planted wide apart, her knees bent, her back hunched. She jerked her body back and forth, up and down, as if she were trying to shake apart the cage.

Which didn't budge.

I'd expected her to be filthy, for some reason. She looked clean, though. Clean, but shiny and dripping with sweat.

'Rupert!' Kimberly snapped. 'Put that light out! They might see it from the house!'

My thumb stayed, holding down on the gas lever. The flame stayed up.

Connie stopped all her jerking and shaking. She stopped the shrieking, too. But she didn't climb down. She clung to the bars, panting for air, and grinned at me.

She was too high on the bars for me to see her old shoulder injury from the time Thelma had thrown the rock over the falls. Her short blond hair was wet and clinging to her scalp, but there wasn't any blood on it that I could see.

Her face looked okay.

If you forget about the wide, mad eyes and peeled-back lips. If you ignore the fact that she grinned at me like a maniac.

Which is to say, they'd been careful not to wreck her face.

From the neck down, her bare skin was a map of bruises, raw abrasions, scabs, welts, scratches and cuts.

The usual handiwork of Wesley and Thelma.

I groaned at the sight of her.

I muttered, 'My God, Connie.'

'Pretty as a picture,' she said. She tilted her head to one side, and licked her lips. 'Gimme a little kiss?'

Kimberly said, 'You'd better get out of here, Rupe. They might've heard the screams. If they looked out and saw your light . . .'

'Come here,' Connie said. 'Come, come, come.' Leering, she thrust her pelvis toward the bars. Somebody had shaved her. Instead of pubic hair, she had smooth, glistening skin. 'Come and gimme a little kiss. Gimme a little kiss on the lips.'

As if to punish me for looking, for seeing what I shouldn't, my lighter suddenly died.

Blackness clamped down on us all.

I let up on the gas lever and got ready to strike the lighter again.

'Go!' Kimberly said. 'Get going!'

'No, no no,' Connie said. 'Come. Come right over here, Rupie. I got something for you.'

'Rupert,' Billie called from her distant cage. 'Leave. Right now. Run. If *they* get their hands on you, we're all finished. We won't have a hope.'

Turning away from Connie's cage, I scanned the darkness. In the jungle and down the trail, I saw a bit of moonlight – and nothing else but black and vague shapes of gray. No sign of the house. No sign of anyone.

I heard plenty.

Jungle noises.

Nothing that sounded like anyone approaching us.

If Wesley and Thelma realized I was out here, though, they wouldn't come dashing after me, yelling and waving a torch. They would come in darkness and silence.

It might already be too late for me.

'I got something for you, Rupie. Come a little closer. Or are you scared? You aren't scared of me, are you? I won't hurt you. Promise. I'll make you feel *real* good.'

'Bye, everyone,' I said.

'Oh, no you don't!' Connie cried out.

I hurried away from her cage. Behind me, she shrieked and raged and called me horrible names.

Into The Lair

I stumbled through the jungle, feeling my way in the darkness, until I came to the edge of the mansion's grounds. Staying in the bushes, I crouched low and peered out.

After the nearly complete blackness near the cages, the moonlit lawn and house seemed amazingly bright.

No sign of Wesley or Thelma.

I'd last seen them entering the house. Were they still inside?

Off behind me, Connie continued yelling things like, 'You bastard, come back here!' Billie and Kimberly were talking to her, trying to calm her down. Their voices, and Connie's wild shouts, got mixed in with the usual squeals and squawks of jungle creatures.

I doubted that they could be heard inside the house. Even Connie's first and loudest raging shriek had probably gone unnoticed by Wesley and Thelma. They might've caught the noise if they'd been standing, quiet and listening, near an open window in one of the front rooms. But the chances were against it. In a huge house like that, they were more likely *not* at a front window.

They probably weren't standing quiet, either, straining to hear sounds from outside. More likely, they were *doing* something in there. Moving around, talking, sleeping, whatever.

It was unlikely that they'd heard Connie.

There seemed to be a better chance that they'd noticed the glow from my cigarette lighter. For one little dab of flame, it had really knocked a hole in the darkness. A fairly narrow strip of jungle separated the cages from the mansion's lawn. If the foliage wasn't really thick, the light might've been visible from the mansion.

It would've gone unnoticed, though, unless Wesley or Thelma happened to be watching from a front window.

After a while, I reached the conclusion that we'd overreacted. I could have stayed with the gals.

Better safe than sorry, though.

I *am* their only chance.

Besides, it's just as well that I got away when I did. Things had gone a little haywire with Connie. No telling what might've happened.

My departure improved the situation with her. After a while, she quietened down. Within about fifteen minutes, no more voices were reaching me.

By then, too, it was obvious that nobody had shown up to check on the prisoners.

I tried to figure out what to do.

There seemed to be three choices:

1. Do nothing.
2. Sneak back to Billie's cage.
3. Sneak into the mansion.

Doing nothing sounded pretty good. It held the least risk of unpleasantness – or death. As long as I remained hidden in the jungle, I stood a good chance of staying alive. It might also be the smartest course of action, since I didn't know exactly where Wesley and Thelma might be.

I was very tempted, though, to sneak back to Billie's cage. If I could do it with complete stealth and somehow get her attention without any of the others catching on . . . My God, no telling what might happen. I got excited, just thinking about it.

But why restrict myself to Billie? I could sneak over to *any* of the cages.

Wouldn't want to get near Connie, of course.

How about Kimberly? Man!

No. Kimberly'd be all business. She might grab my hand, but she wouldn't want to mess around.

What about paying Erin a visit?

I liked Erin.

She seemed to like me, too.

She's too young, I told myself. You can't *do* anything with her.

Who says so? She's only four years younger than me. That isn't so much. When I'm thirty, she'll be twenty-six.

But she's only fourteen now.

So what? In some cultures, people get married *when they're fourteen.*

I imagined myself over at Erin's cage. Touching her in the dark. Both of us exploring each other through the bars. In my mind, I could almost feel the smoothness and warmth of her small, pointy breasts.

The more excited I got, the more guilty I felt.

I couldn't let myself sneak back to the cages.

If I went to Billie, I might end up going to Erin.

Which would be a very wrong thing to do, in spite of the arguments I could give myself in its favor. How could I even *think* about trying to mess around with Erin? I'd be no better than Wesley.

I was angry at myself.

Maybe I wanted to punish myself for being so tempted over Erin. Or maybe the awful urge to take advantage of her – the wrongness of it – sort of shone a spotlight on the *right* thing that needed to be done.

I'll go back to the cages, all right. I'll go back when I've got Wesley's key-ring in my hand.

And not before.

There weren't three choices anymore.

Only one.

Number three: sneak into the mansion.

Staying in the jungle's darkness, I made my way along the perimeter of the lawn until I came to the area that faced the side of the house.

Then I gazed out.

Directly ahead of me, a short sprint away, was the window where I'd watched their vicious abuse of Erin.

The window was dark.

No light showed anywhere.

I saw no sign of Wesley or Thelma. Most likely, though, they were someplace inside the house. I'd seen them go in. There was no reason to believe they'd left.

But they might've left.

They might be almost anywhere.

Just waiting to nail me.

I broke from cover and dashed through the long grass. I was so scared that I did that thing where you separate into two people: one of them doing this crazy and dangerous thing while the other watches, astonished, from a distance – sort of cheering on the fool.

I thought, *Oh, man, you're asking for it.*

But I kept running, and didn't stop until I reached the side of the house. I leaned my shoulder against the wall. I gasped for air. It didn't take long to get my breath back, but my heart wouldn't slow down. It pounded like mad. Because it knew what was coming.

The dash across the lawn had been the safe part.

I stepped over to the window. Pressing my face against the screen, I peered in.

Saw nothing.

Actually, I could see a lot. This wasn't the sort of blackness I'd found at the cages. The room seemed to be filled with a dim mist – moonlight that had spilled in from the window and spread itself around.

Enough to show me that the room was cluttered with darkness.

Plenty of darkness to hide two people – or twenty.

Exploring the bottom of the screen, I found the pair of flaps that I'd made earlier with my razor.

What if Thelma found them?

I wished I hadn't thought of that. If she or Wesley had spotted my handiwork with the screen, they'd *know* a prowler had paid them a visit. They'd be ready and waiting.

But they probably hadn't spotted it.

They probably hadn't so much as entered the room after Thelma's return visit to pick up the clothes, blow out the candles, and so forth.

I poked my index fingers through the flaps, bent my fingertips downward and swung the screen toward me.

A few seconds later, I had my head inside. Without the screen in the way, the view was much better.

I could see the darkness a lot more clearly.

I stood there, the screen pressing against the back of my head while I scanned the room.

Black blotches all over the place.

Nothing appeared to be moving, though.

There was a lingering, somewhat foul odor of cigarette

smoke. I smelled candles and blood, too. Or thought I did; those might've only existed in my imagination.

I pictured Wesley and Thelma sitting cross-legged in the middle of the floor, smiling as they patiently waited for me to enter their lair.

With the moonlit outdoors behind me, I would be easy to see. Like a black bust of Pallas perched upon the windowsill.

I went ahead and started to climb in, anyway.

The 'other' me seemed to stand back and shake his head and warn me, *It's gonna be your ass.*

The book bag on my back caused some trouble. I had to elbow the screen up out of its way. Finally, though, I got myself over the sill and into the room.

Sidestepping away from the window, I put a wall to my back.

Then I just stood still and listened to the house. The only human sounds came from me: my own breathing and heartbeat – and my stomach gurgling now and then.

Too long since my last meal.

I had food with me, but this was no time to pause for a snack.

I dug into the right front pocket of my shorts. First, I took out the lighter. I switched it to my left hand, then reached down again and brought out the straight razor.

I kept its blade shut.

Wanted it ready, but not *that* ready.

Then I tried to make myself flick the lighter.

The Bic was slippery in my hand. My thumb didn't want to move.

Go on and do it, I thought. What've you got to lose? If they aren't in the room, they won't see it, anyway. If they *are* here, you're already a dead duck and just don't know it yet.

I struck the lighter.

So did a guy standing off to my left in the corner of the room.

I jumped. I gasped, 'Yah!'

Then I realized the guy over there was a mirror-made duplicate of yours truly.

(I know, I know, I'm an idiot.)

I killed the light and stood in the darkness for a long time, waiting for someone to come and investigate my odd little yell.

Nobody came.

I ignited the lighter again. This time, the guy in the mirror didn't scare me. In fact, I appreciated him; he doubled the brightness.

We both stood motionless and scanned the room.

It seemed to be deserted, except for us.

I started walking slowly. He and his flame followed me.

When the floor suddenly went slick under my foot, I skidded but didn't fall.

I turned around and bent over to see what I'd stepped in. On the floor was a wet, reddish smear. This was where Thelma and Wesley had finished their fun with Erin. Thelma had come back into the room for their clothes and to blow out the lights, but she hadn't bothered to wipe up the blood, sweat, and so on.

Now, I'd made skid marks in it.

After taking a step backward, I found a clear imprint of my sneaker's tread pattern.

I killed the flame. I dropped the razor into my pocket. Holding the lighter in my teeth, I slipped the book bag off my back and brought it around in front of me.

Inside, I found the towel-vest that Connie had made. I held it between my knees while I put the pack on again.

Standing in the dark, I lifted one foot, wiped the bottom of its sneaker, stepped backward, wiped the other, and repeated the process. Then I got down on my knees and lit the lighter. My mirror-double and I crawled forward, mopping away our tracks. We stopped at the edge of the wet, blood-smeared area. The skids could stay; since they didn't show tread marks, they might've been made by someone barefoot.

We stood up and walked backward slowly. No new tracks were being made.

In darkness again, I rolled the towel-vest and returned it to my book bag. This took a while. Also, the towel made my hands wet and sticky. I had to wipe them on my shorts.

When I lit the lighter, my double reappeared. He didn't last long – only until we got close to the doorway and I killed the flame again.

Keeping the lighter in my left hand, I took out my razor and stepped through the doorway into the corridor.

Sleeping Dogs

Room by room, corridor by corridor, stairway by stairway, I searched the enormous house. Last summer's long, boring tours of ante-bellum mansions along the Mississippi paid off: the general layout of this mansion was similar to many of those I'd seen. I felt as if I'd been here before. Much of the time, I sensed what was coming.

Though I held on to the lighter, I didn't use it.

I searched in darkness, creeping along, often stopping to listen.

After a while, I put the razor back into my pocket; I needed a free hand for feeling my way.

The house seemed terribly silent.

Except for the thousand times its floors moaned and squawked under my footsteps.

I made very little sound, myself. My breathing and heartbeat *seemed* noisy, as did the frequent growling of my hungry stomach — but they were quiet compared to the outcries of the wood under my feet.

The flooring of the house seemed to be in cahoots with Wesley and Thelma. Sure it is, I thought. It *likes* those naked bodies tumbling around on it, enjoys the feel of all that bare skin, loves having its planks oiled with blood and sweat and semen. I was here to put a stop to such things.

So, of course, it wanted to cry out warnings.

(You think odd thoughts at times like that. It gets you, being alone in the darkness, never knowing if you're about to stumble and fall down, or crash into a wall, or knock over a lamp, or bump into someone who wants to slit your throat.)

It would take me hours to write about every stumble and collision, fright and false alarm I had while searching the mansion – the nightmarish scenarios that fumbled through my mind – the terror I felt each time I crept around a corner or entered a new room.

The searching seemed to take hours.

I expected the sun to come up.

To be realistic about it, though, I probably spent no more than an hour sneaking through the place before I found Wesley and Thelma.

I was beginning to think that they weren't in the house, after all. Maybe they spent their nights on the cabin cruiser. But then, as I climbed the stairs to the third and final story, I detected a quiet, grumbly sound. I stopped moving, and listened. The sound went away, but soon came again. Again, there was silence. Then came a harsh snort.

Some sort of animal snuffling around?

After listening a while longer, I realized that the sounds were probably being made by someone asleep.

Asleep and snoring.

Ever so slowly, I started climbing again. I set my feet down gently and eased my weight onto each tread. Most of them squeaked, anyway. Every time that happened, I cringed, stood still and listened until I heard the snoring again.

At last, I reached the top of the stairs.

I found myself in the middle of a hall, surrounded by walls with open doors. From where I stood, I could see into four moonlit rooms – one near each corner.

The snoring sounds, more distinct than ever, seemed to be coming from the doorway in front of me and over to the right. I stopped beside the newel post, and faced the sounds.

The doorway looked vaguely pale in the darkness.

I snuck carefully toward it.

This had to be Wesley and Thelma's quarters.

With the entire house at their disposal, why had they chosen to sleep in such an out-of-the-way room? It seemed very strange, especially considering Wesley's wounds. Why climb three flights of stairs when there were plenty of fine, comfortable rooms on the ground floor?

I stopped at the doorway. I peered in.

The two windows at the other side of the room were bright with moonlight.

Of course!

This is the room with the view.

From this height, they could probably look down through gaps in the foliage and see the cages.

Watch the women.

From here, they probably could've seen the glow of my cigarette lighter.

But only if they'd been looking.

The way things sounded, they *hadn't* been looking. If they'd seen my light, they sure wouldn't have gone ahead and turned in for the night.

Along with the snoring, a sound of deep, slow breathing came from inside the room.

Both of them were in there, both asleep.

Apparently.

In a way, I was glad I'd finally found them. The mystery of their whereabouts, at least, was solved.

But part of me wished I hadn't found them.

What the hell was I supposed to do, now?

I could think of only two possible courses of action.

1. Get the hell out of the house.

2. Enter their room.

To be honest, I *ached* to get out of there. If I stayed, bad stuff was bound to happen.

I thought about getting out and setting fire to the house. It would be a fairly safe, effective way to kill Wesley and Thelma.

Not a half-bad idea.

Trapped this high up, their chances of escape would amount to zilch.

There was only one drawback.

(Seems like there's *always* a drawback.)

Wesley had probably taken the cage keys into the room with him. If I burnt down the house, what would happen to the keys? For starters, I might not be able to find them in the rubble. For enders, what if they melted in the heat? I'm no expert on the melting temperature of gorilla cage keys. After going down with the blazing house, they might be reduced to puddles – or at least distorted enough to be useless.

In which case, how would I get the cages open?

If that's the only drawback, I thought, then what you've gotta do is sneak into the room and find the keys. Take the keys, *then* get the hell out of the house and set it on fire.

It seemed like a very good idea.

It had only one drawback: to get my hands on the keys, I would have to enter the room and look around.

And how could I hope to find them in the dark?

Into my head came a voice that sounded like Kimberly. It said, 'Quit thinking about all this shit. Just do it.'

She was right.

Or *I* was right, since the voice wasn't really Kimberly's, but mine.

I didn't want to do it.

But I'd found Wesley and Thelma. They were sleeping. Asleep, they were helpless. They were in my power. This might be the best chance I would ever get. If I chickened out, I would hate myself forever.

If I blew it, the women would be the ones to pay.

Before entering the room, I slipped the razor out of my pocket. I thumbed open its blade.

By then, I was doing that schizo thing again: standing outside of myself, a critical and worried observer.

You must be outa your ever-lovin' mind, I thought.

I stepped over the threshold.

The floor squawked.

One of the sleepers snorted. (Wesley, I think.) The other continued to take those long, easy breaths.

They're dead to the world, I told myself.

Unless they're faking it.

And then I thought, *What you oughta do is slit their throats right now.*

I knew I couldn't do that, though. You'd have to be damn cold-blooded to murder people in their sleep. And even if I could bring myself to nail Wesley that way, Thelma was a whole different story.

Being a woman.

How could I slit the throat of a woman?

I couldn't, that's how.

(But I could burn her by setting fire to the house? Apparently. Even while deploring the notion of slitting throats, I fully intended to burn the house down around those two monsters. Go figure.)

Stopping just inside the room, I saw Wesley and Thelma sharing a bed. At least, I supposed it must be them.

I couldn't see them very well at all.

On each side of the double bed was a lamp table. The lamp tables and the bed stood against the wall between the windows, so they were bypassed by most of the moonlight.

Wesley and Thelma (at that time, I could only assume it was them) lay side by side – vague, dark shapes on the white sheet.

The body on the left side of the double bed appeared to be larger than the one on the right. The snores came from there. Also, the body had a patch of white that I took to be Wesley's chest bandage.

Which put him on the left, Thelma on the right.

I made my way toward Wesley's side of the bed. He was the keeper of the keys. If I were him, I would've placed them on the lamp table, where they'd be within easy reach.

I needed a free hand. I wanted to hang on to my razor, though, so the lighter went into my pocket.

Both the sleepers continued to make their usual noises while I crept closer and closer to Wesley's lamp table.

When I got there, I turned sideways so I could keep my eyes on them.

If you stare at people, though, they seem to feel it.

One or the other of them would wake up, for sure.

So I looked toward the doorway, instead, while I gently patted the top of the lamp table.

Not gently enough.

Searching blindly, I nudged the key-ring with my fingertips. It moved, scraping against the wood. A few of the keys must've bumped into each other. They made two or three clinking sounds.

Wesley snored on.

Thelma popped up off her back.

I froze.

She sat there on the mattress on the other side of Wesley, not moving, not saying a word.

I couldn't tell which way her head was turned.

She *had* to be staring at me, though.

Could she see me?

I didn't move. I tried not to breathe.

Maybe I can wait her out.

If she couldn't see me, and if I made no sounds, she might relax after a while, lie down and go back to sleep.

Pretty soon, I had to breathe. I did it slowly. She probably couldn't hear me over Wesley's loud snores.

She still sat there.

I was turning into a wreck. I felt as if I couldn't get enough air. My heart raced. My whole body trembled – including my hands.

The key-ring was pressed against the tabletop by the fingertips of my left hand. If my trembling got much worse, I might not be able to stop myself from giving the keys another jangle.

I thought about lifting my hand.

But taking it away might cause a jangle.

Maybe I oughta just snatch them up and run like hell.

No no no no no!

Wait her out, I told myself. Any second now, she'll lie down. Before long, she'll be sound asleep.

'Come here, Rupert,' she whispered.

I flinched and gasped and clutched the keys. They clanked together for a moment before my hand squeezed them silent. Wesley made a choky-sounding snort. Moaning, he rolled onto his side. Which put his back toward me, his face toward Thelma. She stayed silent. After a few seconds that felt like an hour, Wesley resumed snoring.

I stood by the bed, the keys in one hand, the razor in the other.

I stared at Thelma.

Though I couldn't see her eyes – or even which way her head was turned – I knew she was watching me.

Slowly, I began sidestepping toward the foot of the bed.

She'll think I'm coming, I told myself. Right up to the instant I bolt for the door.

At the foot of the bed, however, I didn't bolt.

One step in the wrong direction, and Thelma would let out a shout. I knew it. I didn't have the slightest doubt. Her outcry would wake up Wesley, and they'd both come after me.

Deal with her alone, or deal with them both.

Also, I was curious. It seemed very strange that she'd whispered, *Come here, Rupert.* Why had she done that instead of yell?

She continued to sit upright while I crept past the foot of the bed. Wesley continued to snore.

When I rounded the corner, she eased herself sideways and lowered her legs. She sat on the edge of the mattress and waited for me.

A pace or two away from her, I stopped.

She grabbed the front of my belt. Not resisting, I let her pull me until I was standing in front of her. She pulled me closer to her. I stepped in between her knees. Her legs rubbed against mine.

Still gripping me by the belt, she whispered, 'Give me the keys.'

This time, her whisper didn't seem to disturb her husband. He kept snoring, and he didn't move. The way I towered over Thelma's head, I had a fine view of him. I just couldn't tell whether or not his eyes were open.

'I don't have 'em,' I whispered.

'Wesley?' Not a whisper. Not terribly loud, either, but enough to make him sputter and give out a moaning noise that sounded like a question.

I had the keys in one hand, the razor in the other.

One quick slash with the razor . . .

Even if she deserved such a fate – and she did – I couldn't do it to her. Not this way, surprising her in the dark. For one thing, she was a woman. For another, it would've been cold-blooded to kill her except as a last resort, to save myself.

Wesley's snoring had stopped.

Instead of slitting Thelma's throat, I pushed my left fist against her body. It met warm, yielding skin. Her hand fumbled with my fingers. I opened them and she took the keys. They jingled a few times, then went silent.

'Mmmmm?' Wesley asked.

'Nothing, honey.'

'Mmm.'

A few seconds later, he was snoring again.

I heard a couple of quiet clinks – Thelma setting the keys down somewhere, I suppose. Maybe on the mattress behind her.

Still clutching my belt with one hand, she used her other hand to rub the front of my shorts. Then she slowly slid my zipper down. She reached in.

Something like that should've gotten me hard really quick. But I was damn scared, and Thelma wasn't quite in the same class as the other gals. In fact, I might've been

just as horny if she'd been Wesley. I was shrunk up so small
I'm surprised she could find what she was hunting for.

She found it, though.

And started working on it.

I remembered the time by the campfire, and how she'd
tried to split me with a razor.

The same razor I was holding in my right hand while she
squeezed and stroked and pulled on me.

I knew she didn't have a weapon, this time. Not in her
hands.

One hand held me by the belt, the other by the dong.

Reaching out with my left hand, I found the top of her
head. I caressed her short, damp hair. I slid my fingers in
and held on. Then I felt along the side of her head with the
wrist of my right hand.

I located her ear.

I put the razor against it – in the valley between the top
of her ear and the side of her head.

The hand inside my pants quit trying to arouse me.

It took hold.

'Let go or I'll cut you,' I whispered.

'I'll rip your cock off.'

'Just give me the keys, and I'll get out of here.'

'In your dreams, dickhead.'

Wesley was still snoring.

'I won't hurt you,' I whispered. 'I'll just go.'

'Fuck me,' she whispered. 'Fuck me, and maybe I'll let
you have 'em.'

You've gotta be kidding, I thought.

'Right now.' She gave me a gentle tug.

'I can't. Not with *him* there.'

'Want me to wake him up?'

'He'll wake up anyway if I . . . do what you want.'

'Who knows? Let's find out.'

'How about somewhere else?' I suggested. 'If we go to a different room . . .'

'Here. Right here beside him.'

'Just let go of me and give me the keys. Please?'

'That my razor?' she asked.

'Yeah.'

'Wanta shave me?'

'No.'

'You sure? I haven't had a nice, close shave since I lost it.'

'Since you tried to kill me with it.'

'If you aren't gonna give me a shave, how about putting it away?'

'I'm going to cut off your ear if you don't give me the keys.'

She made a quiet, laughing sound. 'Go on ahead, then.'

As I started to think about doing it, she said, 'If you had the guts to go around cutting people, me and Wesley'd be dead right now with our throats slit open. You're just too nice a fella for that sort of shit.'

'Think so, do you?'

'I know so. And anyhow . . .' She gave me a squeeze. Not hard, but hard enough. It made me flinch, gave me a sick feeling. 'I got you by the nuts, boy. You're gonna do what *I* say. Now, take that razor away from my ear, or I'll scramble your eggs for you.'

I hesitated.

She squeezed harder.

Maybe I should've gone ahead and sliced off her ear when she did that. Instead, I groaned and bent over a little, trying to ease the pain.

'Okay,' I whispered.

I lifted the blade away from her ear.

The hand holding my belt let go. It brushed against my belly. 'Give,' Thelma said.

'What?'

'The razor.'

'How do I know you won't cut off my whang?'

She laughed softly. 'You won't be much good to me without it.'

'Okay,' I whispered.

I could hardly believe that Wesley was sleeping through all this. My luck wasn't likely to continue forever, though.

I tried to concentrate on what I needed to do.

'The razor,' Thelma said.

'Let go of me, and I'll give it to you.'

'Think I'm an idiot?'

'It'll be a fair trade,' I whispered.

'Long as I've got hold, you're gonna do whatever I say.'

'You'd better let go,' I said.

'The razor.'

I let go. I'd been holding a lot more than the razor. It seemed like about a gallon. I opened up on her.

She still clutched me for a second or two. Probably not sure what was going on – what was that hot liquid squirting all over her hand and up her arm? Then she must've figured it out. She went, *'Yuuuuuh!'* Her hand leaped away. *'You bastard!'* she shouted.

I was probably catching her in the chest, so I reached down and gave myself some elevation.

'Wesley!'

She got his name out. A moment later, she began to sputter and spit as I hosed her face.

I backed off fast.

Wesley sat up in bed. 'What . . . ?'

421

'Get him!' Thelma squealed. She sounded as if she'd lost her mind. *'Kill the little shit!'*

I couldn't wait around to finish what I'd started. I couldn't manage to quit, either. So I whirled around and ran for the door, still squirting.

The Chase Is On

From behind me, I heard thuds and voices.

'Who?' Wesley asked. He sounded mighty damn scared. 'Who was it?'

'Rupert!'

'He's dead!'

'My ass!'

Just outside their door, the wet floor sent my feet sliding. I gasped and flapped my arms. My legs flew out from under me. My butt whammed the floor.

Behind me, Thelma was still talking. 'He snuck right in here. Had my razor. Gonna slit our throats!'

'You sure?'

'*Yes!* He *peed* on me, the little cocksucker!'

I was *still* peeing. My shorts were drenched.

My feet stuck out into space. I pushed myself forward. My legs lowered. My feet found a plank of flat, slippery wood, which I figured to be the second stair down from the top.

'The keys!' Wesley blurted. 'He got the keys!'

'I got 'em,' Thelma said.

'You sure?'

I switched the razor to my left hand, reached up with my right, grabbed the banister, and pulled.

'Right in my hand,' Thelma said. 'He *had* 'em, but I got 'em away from him.'

On my feet, I looked back toward the doorway. Thank God Wesley and Thelma had decided to have a discussion instead of a hot pursuit.

'Good going,' Wesley said. 'Here, give them to me.'

The way they were thumping around in the room as they talked, I figured they must be grabbing stuff. Not just the keys, either. Weapons, more than likely.

What if they've got flashlights?

I took a step down. My feet skidded on the wet stair. I might've fallen again, but I kept a good grip on the banister. In the meantime, I was still going. You can't just shut things down at the drop of a hat, not if you've been holding it a while, and especially if you're scared. Anyway, I'd probably only been at it for half a minute or less even though it seemed like ages.

Somewhere along the way, my tool had gotten out of alignment with my open fly. Which meant I'd been splattering the insides of my own shorts. A lot came back at me, the rebound drenching my groin and spilling down my legs and soaking my socks.

'Come on, come on,' Wesley said.

'You ready?'

'Yeah. Here, take these.'

I hobbled down the slippery stairs, my sneakers squelching.

From above and behind me came the thuds of quick footfalls.

I tried to move faster.

I wished I could see where I was going.

Suddenly, I could.

They'd turned on the lights!

The mansion had its power on, after all.

I suddenly missed the darkness. The darkness seemed like an old friend that used to hide me in its closet.

Now I was out in plain sight.

But at least I could see, and move faster.

I was about three steps up from the bottom of the stairway. I leaped. The book bag sort of lifted off my back. A second after I landed on the floor, the pack swung down and gave me an extra shove. As I stumbled, a spear shot by. (Connie's special fishing spear with the carved barbs.) It missed me by inches. It clattered and skidded on the hardwood, and went scooting down the hallway.

I thought about chasing after it.

Which would mean leaving the stairs behind.

Which would mean a fight, not an escape.

Two against one.

The spear wasn't worth it.

From the sound of things, Wesley and Thelma were already rushing down the stairs.

Not daring to look up at them, I made my turn-around and lunged for the next stairway. About to start my race down, I heard someone cry, *'Yeeee!'* Then came some quick thuds.

I looked.

Wesley seemed to be poised on top of his head, about halfway from the bottom of the stairs. He was barefoot, bare-ass, bare everything. Except for the soiled white squares patching his boob and butt, all he wore was a belt around his waist.

I glimpsed an empty leather sheath at one hip as his legs and rump slammed down. The hunting knife was in his hand. He held on to it all the way as he somersaulted and crashed down the rest of the stairs.

He came to a stop on his back.

He was all sprawled out.

He looked unconscious or dead.

Up near the top of the stairway, he must've slipped on my pee.

And now he was out of the picture.

Now there was only Thelma . . .

Maybe she'll fall, too.

She came sliding down the banister like a demented swashbuckler – legs wide apart, rail squeaking between her buttocks, a strange and terrible grin on her face, both arms raised, a machete in each hand.

She didn't seem worried about the wooden knob atop the newel post at the bottom of her banister.

I was tempted to stick around and watch, but didn't dare.

I turned away and started leaping down the stairs toward the mansion's ground floor.

Somehow, Thelma dealt with the newel post. I heard thumps, but no outcry. Seconds later, I looked over my shoulder just in time to see her start down my stairway. This time, not sliding on the banister.

Pounding her way down the middle of the stairs, machetes waving above her, sweat (and maybe some of my urine) flying off her hair and skin, jowls and arms and thighs shaking, her enormous breasts hopping up and down, swinging every which way.

Each heavy step sounded like a battering ram trying to demolish the stairway. I felt the tremors through my own feet as I raced for the bottom. I also felt air coming in through my fly, and realized I'd finally run out of piss.

About four steps from the bottom, I jumped.

I landed on both feet. The book bag whapped my back.

I plunged across the foyer, staggering more than running toward the front door. The razor would do me no good – not against Thelma's machetes. Afraid of hurting myself with it, I whipped its blade shut on my way to the door.

I put on the brakes. Skidded. Not able to stop in time, I twisted sideways and slammed against the door. As I reached for the handle, I glanced back.

Thelma, chugging her way down, had about three steps to go.

I lurched backward, jerking the door open.

The veranda was brightly lit by a couple of spotlights on the front lawn. It surprised me. I wished they'd been off. Wesley or Thelma must've activated them, somehow, the better to chase me down.

It worked both ways, though. *I* could see better, too.

On my way out the door, something struck me in the back. It felt like a fist slugging my book bag. A punch, but no real pain.

The moment I got outside, I dodged to the right. As I raced for the end of the veranda, I took a quick look over my shoulder.

Thelma didn't slow down enough. After charging onto the veranda, her momentum swung her out wide. Yelling *'Wahhh!'*, she crashed a shoulder against a front column. The blow knocked her to a quick halt. The way her tits swung, I half thought they might fly off and land in the front yard. But they stayed attached and rebounded as she bounced off the column. She couldn't stay on her feet after that.

I watched her crash onto the floor of the veranda.

She hit it hard with her right side.

I quit running as she skidded and rolled onto her back. By then, however, I had almost reached the railing at the end of the veranda. A fine distance for my escape. But a bad distance for any hope of rushing back and jumping Thelma; she would have plenty of time to recover and get up.

Even as I watched, she rolled off her back and raised her head and met my eyes.

She had a machete in her left hand. Her right hand was empty.

She started to push herself up.

I suddenly spotted her other machete. It lay on the veranda floor about midway between us.

How had it gotten there?

I remembered the blow to my back.

But that had happened while I was still in the doorway.

My guess (later confirmed by gashes in my book bag and journal) is that Thelma had thrown the machete at me. It must've penetrated my book bag and had probably been sticking out for a few seconds while I dashed along the veranda. Then, shaking loose, it had fallen to the floor.

Thelma saw me looking at it.

She glanced at it.

We looked at each other.

I suddenly felt as if I'd become the star of a Sergio Leone film. We're just waiting for the music to stop. That'll be the signal. With the final note, we both break into mad dashes for the machete – in slow motion.

But there was no music.

This was no film.

Neither of us waited.

There was no slow motion, either, but I can play it that way in my mind. When it happened, though, it happened fast.

As I sprinted for the weapon, Thelma scurried forward and onto her feet. She already *had* a machete. And she raised it high, ready to chop me.

I had the greater speed, though. My chances looked good for reaching the other machete first.

By maybe half a second.

Then I'd have to swoop down and snatch it off the floor and swing it up in time to stop Thelma from whacking my head off.

The distance between us closed fast.

She wasn't even *paying attention* to the damn machete.

Her eyes were on *me*.

She knew she had me. *I* knew she had me.

This was just me. Rupert Conway, not Clint Eastwood or Bruce Willis, Arnold Schwarzenegger or Mel Gibson. This was real life, not a scene in an action movie. These were real machetes.

I was about to get myself killed.

Thelma, threatening the veranda floor with each thundering stride, yelled *'Yahhhh!'*

I yelled, *'No!'* and swerved away from our collision course and dived over the white-painted railing. I smashed through some bushes. They scratched me, but broke my fall.

Thelma didn't leap the railing. She must've gone ahead to the second machete, picked it up, then run back to the veranda stairs.

Which gave me a little time.

I used the time to pocket the razor, shuck off my book bag, stuff the bag under the bushes for safe keeping, scramble to my feet and get a start on my dash for the corner of the house.

When I looked back, Thelma was charging down the

veranda stairs. She turned toward me and broke into a run, pumping her two machetes.

Now that we were out in the open, I figured she didn't stand a chance of catching me.

Not unless I fell down and broke my leg, or something.

I'd never broken a leg in my life, so it didn't seem likely to happen tonight.

After turning the corner of the house, I slowed down a little. No point in wearing myself out. Anyway, I needed to think.

For a while there, my survival had looked iffy.

Now that I'd gotten out of the mansion alive, I had to make up my mind about what to do next.

I wanted the keys to the gorilla cages.

They were probably still inside the house.

I could hardly go after them with Thelma on my tail.

Wesley might not remain out of action for long. It had looked like a very nasty fall, though. It could've put him out of commission for hours, or days, or for ever.

So Thelma seemed to be my main problem. Sure, I could outrun her. I could hide, or run circles around her. But I didn't want to fight her. Not while she had those machetes.

They were my real problem.

She had to be disarmed.

Bet she can't swim with them, I thought.

The lagoon crossed my mind, but I rejected it. For one thing, how do you get there from here? For another, the ocean was dead ahead.

Swim out to the boat, I thought.

I remembered the two dinghies tied at the dock.

Can't leave either of them behind.

Dealing with them would take a while.

Suddenly, I wished I hadn't slowed down. I poured it on and sprinted at top speed for the shore.

How The Chase Ends

If I'd had another ten seconds, maybe I would've had time to slice through the mooring line of the second dinghy. As it was, I only cut through one.

My plan, formed as I dashed for the cove, had been to cut both the dinghies loose, hop into one, and tow the second away from the dock. Which would force Thelma to swim after me, leaving her machetes behind.

Probably not such a terrific plan, anyway.

But I didn't get a chance to find out, because Thelma came pounding onto the dock before I even had a chance to *start* cutting the second rope.

I dropped the line of the first dinghy, sprang up and ran like hell for the end of the dock.

My sneakers clumped on the planks. Thelma, barefoot, slapped and thudded after me, wheezing for breath.

Again, she didn't stand a chance of catching up.

On my way to the end of the dock, I flipped the razor shut and dropped it into my pocket.

I raced to the very edge, then dived.

My dive carried me way out over the water. I hit the surface flat out with a whop that hurt. Then the water shut down on top of me. I stayed under and kicked hard, trying to pick up speed.

No big splashing sound came from behind me. I kept waiting for it. My headstart hadn't been much; Thelma should've already reached the end of the dock.

Obviously, she'd decided not to jump in.

Needing air anyway, I kicked to the surface. As I filled my lungs, I looked back.

I was closer to the dock than I'd expected or hoped. The shoes had probably slowed me down – as had my big, baggy shorts. Even though I wanted more distance between myself and Thelma, I began treading water.

The shoes made it tough, but I wasn't about to kick them off and lose them. Pumping my feet as if I were racing a bicycle, I managed to keep my head above the surface.

Thelma, pale in the moonlight, was stepping down into the first dinghy. She held her arms out for balance. Beyond her hands, the blades of her machetes gleamed like silver.

She set the weapons down inside the boat. Then she bent over the outboard motor.

For a few seconds, I could only see her rump and the backs of her thighs. Then the drifting dinghy gave me a side view. Thelma had already planted one hand against the motor's cowl. With the other, she jerked its starter cord. Her breasts swung like crazy. The motor coughed but didn't start. She gave the cord another pull. The motor sputtered and caught.

Next thing I knew, she was sitting down and steering the boat in my direction.

I started swimming like mad for the cabin cruiser.

In this race, Thelma had the advantage. The dinghy was no speed-demon, but it moved faster than I could swim.

I had a fair headstart.

Not good enough, though. At the rate Thelma was coming, she'd overtake me long before I'd reach the cruiser.

I swam as fast as I could, and didn't look back. The growing noise of the motor told me all I needed to know.

From the sound of things, Thelma was straight behind me, coming on, probably planning to run me over and chop me with her propeller blades.

I caught a deep breath and plunged for the bottom.

The motor sounded like a tinny, grumbling buzz as the dinghy passed over me. Abruptly, the pitch lowered. My guess, Thelma'd throttled down.

The noise faded, then swelled.

Thelma had turned around.

She's going to stay up there, I realized. Circle and wait me out. Knows I can't stay down forever. When I come up for air, she'll try to nail me.

Rolling onto my back, I looked up and saw the moonlight shining on the water. I also saw the dark underbelly of the dinghy. It glided over the surface like a shadow.

I had a shark's-eye view of the dinghy.

Inside my head, I started hearing the theme music from *Jaws*.

If I were a Great White, I could shoot straight up and ram the dinghy hard enough to capsize it. In the water, Thelma'd be at my mercy.

Ramming the dinghy wasn't likely to work, though, me being a little guy and having nothing to push off against. If I shot up like that, playing shark, I might rock the dinghy a little bit. Mostly, though, I'd simply end up shoving myself downward off its hull.

While I considered these things, the boat slowly circled above me. And my lungs began to burn from holding air too long.

Getting some fresh air shouldn't be terribly difficult. I could probably surface a safe distance from the dinghy, grab a breath, and have enough time to submerge before Thelma could reach me. Just a matter of picking the right moment to pop up. And being quick about it.

A fresh breath would give me extra time, but it wouldn't solve my main problem.

If I could keep going up and snatching breaths . . .

Doing that, I might swim all the way to the cruiser. Or back to the dock.

What would that accomplish? She'd be right there, ready to chop me.

Sooner or later, she'll run out of gas.

At first, the idea thrilled me.

No gas, no motor. The dinghy would be useless to her. She'd end up drifting around aimlessly. She'd either have to sit there and hope for the best, or start swimming.

Perfect!

But I had no idea how empty her tank might be. For all I knew, the gas might last for an hour.

An hour of me bursting to the surface, every minute or two? No way. I might be able to pull off a stunt like that three or four times, but then she'd catch on. I wouldn't last ten minutes.

Unless the dinghy was already running on fumes . . .

Not much chance of that.

But maybe I could think of a way to kill her motor. Something that didn't involve an endless wait.

By the time I'd gotten that far with my thoughts, my lungs ached so much that I could no longer think straight. I looked for the dinghy.

Damn!

It had just reached the far curve of its circle – as far away as it was likely to get. With each passing moment, now, it would be moving closer to me.

I rushed for the surface, jabbing my arms up, kicking hard. I went up so fast that I almost lost my shorts. I felt them slipping, but didn't dare make a grab for them.

When they were down around my thighs, I remembered the razor in my pocket.

If I lost the shorts, I'd lose the razor.

So I reached down, grabbed the waist with one hand and held on. An instant later, I burst up out of the water. I gasped for air. With both hands, I pulled up my shorts.

Thelma's head suddenly jerked sideways. She'd spotted me. She shoved the steering arm. The bow swung sharply and pointed at me. The motor noise swelled to a roar.

I dived.

A near miss. I felt the shivering water of the prop-wash against my back.

That'd be one way to stop the motor, I thought. Let it hit me.

Which probably *would* stop it. But the price seemed a bit steep.

During family vacation as a kid, I'd spent enough time in outboard motor boats to have them quit on me any number of times. Not always because of a fuel problem. If the prop hit a large rock . . . got tangled with weeds.

Yes!

Staying as deep as possible, I shoved a hand into my pocket and dug out the razor. I slid the razor under the top of my right sock. Then I tugged the shorts down and off.

After missing its chance at me, the boat had slowed down and resumed its casual circling.

I wadded the shorts.

Holding them in both hands, I started toward the surface.

Probably lose a few fingers, I thought.

Might be worth it, if it works.

I watched the gliding black belly of the boat. Slowed my climb. Watched. Waited. Felt the push of water as the bow passed over my head.

And suddenly shot both arms up, ramming my shorts into the propeller. In an instant, they were ripped from my grip. I jerked my arms down.

Fingers and hands intact.

Above me, the motor groaned, coughed and quit.

Yes, yes, yes!

Motor dead, the dinghy glided on by. I started swimming underwater to stay with it.

In a few seconds, I managed to get underneath it again.

A few seconds after that, the dinghy wobbled. Then the entire submerged portion of the motor swung up and broke the surface – taking along the remains of my shorts.

You can swing these outboard motors up on their hinges to get at the props. I'd done it myself a few times. So I knew that Thelma had to be standing at the stern, bent over the motor, both her hands busy.

A good, precarious position.

I lunged for the surface.

Reached high.

As my face cleared the water, I grabbed the gunnel with both hands and jerked down on it like a guy desperate to climb aboard.

My side of the dinghy lurched downward.

The other side jumped up.

Thelma, looming above me, was bent over the raised motor just as I'd hoped. Both her hands were on it. By the time I saw her, she had already turned her head to see what had gone wrong.

Already lost any chance of staying on her feet.

Crying out with alarm, she flung up her arms. She swayed sideways, shoulder first. For a moment, she stood on her right leg while her left leg lifted like a boy dog about to wet a tree. But her left leg kept rising higher. Then she was plunging down over the side of the dinghy. The gunnel jerked out of my grip and the dinghy scooted off. I kicked to keep my head up.

Thelma's right shoulder struck the water.

The rest of her followed.

Then came a concussion that buffeted me, shoved at me, and slapped a load of water into my face.

Blind from the drenching, I began to swim after the dinghy.

My goal was to reach it, climb aboard, and take control of the machetes. Once I had them, Thelma wouldn't dare give me any more trouble.

I'd have nothing more to fear from her *or* Wesley.

As I swam, I blinked the water out of my eyes. The dinghy was about twenty feet away.

No sweat.

I glanced back. No sign of Thelma. She still hadn't come up. Though glad she wasn't hot on my tail, I felt a twist of worry.

Maybe she'd drowned.

I actually thought about going back to see if she needed help. Which sounds nuts. But I had this idea that she might be grateful, might even change her tune and decide to stop fighting me. Maybe we would join forces, be a team . . .

She grabbed my left ankle.

Stopped me cold and jerked me down.

When her other hand clutched the back of my right leg, it gripped me *above* the top of my sock – missing the razor, thank God.

I felt myself being dragged backward.

A hand released me, grabbed me higher on the leg.

Knowing Thelma, she'd be going for my nuts. So I squeezed my legs together to stop her from reaching between them. Just in the nick of time, too.

She shoved a hand between my thighs. As she drove it in, prying her way deeper into the crevice, I suddenly tried to fling myself over. Her one hand stayed trapped between my thighs. Her other let go of my calf. I twisted, flung myself about, and kicked with both legs. In seconds, Thelma no longer had me.

I clawed to the surface. Gasping to fill my lungs, I whirled around as her head popped out of the water. She sucked in a single big breath. Then I clutched her shoulders with both my hands and drove her down.

She didn't go *straight* down – she went over backward, me on top.

She fought me. When I lost hold of her slippery shoulders, she wrapped her arms around my back. She gave me a hug as if trying to crush my ribcage. My arms were free, so I grabbed her by the hair and one ear, and twisted her head.

Both of us kicked and squirmed.

I quickly lost track of who was on top – or where the top might be. We both stayed underwater, though. Neither of us could breathe.

And neither of us let go.

We stayed in our clinch as if each of us figured we had the upper hand.

It seemed like hours that we struggled under the water in that fierce embrace. It might've been as long as a minute.

Finally, Thelma seemed to tire out. Her thrashing and writhing and kicking slowed down. Her arms no longer squeezed my ribcage so hard. Soon after that, she ceased all her struggles. Her arms loosened their hold, then slid away from my back.

I let go of her ear. With the hand that clutched her hair, I eased her away from me.

She seemed limp.

Unconscious, maybe dead.

Maybe faking.

Keeping my grip on her hair, I rose to the surface. I breathed, but held her head under – at arm's length, just in case she was playing 'possum.

I had to tread water furiously to keep my own head up. With so much motion on my part, I might not be able to detect movements by Thelma. Until it was too late.

Unnerving.

I felt like a murderer *and* a sitting duck.

It became very difficult to keep on holding her down. I thought she might already be dead. But I also half expected to feel her suddenly slide the razor out of my sock. Scared of both things, I gave her head a shove backward and let go.

A few seconds later, her head popped up. I glimpsed her face in the moonlight – eyes abulge, lips tight. I felt sure she must be alive, after all. But she didn't start gasping and huffing for air. In silence except for the slurping sounds of the water, her head tilted back and the rest of her body came sliding to the surface.

The next thing I knew, she was floating on her back. Sprawled out loose and open, arms spread, legs wide. She looked as if she'd maybe zonked out while relaxing in her back-yard swimming pool.

She sure didn't look dead.

It was uncanny.

It gave me the willies.

Treading water, I watched her for signs of life.

She just drifted lazily, being lifted and turned a little, now and then, by the motions of the water under her back. After gazing at her for a while, I noticed she was farther off than before.

I didn't want her to get away.

Not yet.

I wasn't about to *swim* after her, though. So I twisted myself around and swam to the dinghy.

I made a stop at its stern. Reaching up, I spent a minute or two untangling my shorts from the propeller. They'd gotten torn up pretty good. I tossed them into the boat, anyway. Then I managed to throw myself aboard without capsizing the thing.

While I put on the shredded remains of my shorts, I checked on Thelma. She was pretty far off, but still spread out on her back, the same as before.

It didn't seem right.

If I'd drowned her, she should've sunk. If I *hadn't* drowned her, she ought to be either swimming somewhere or floundering in the water, gasping and coughing.

Just didn't make any sense for her to be floating like that, as if asleep.

I lowered the outboard back into the water and got it started. Keeping it throttled down, I turned the dinghy toward Thelma. I puttered toward her very slowly.

The prow was aimed between her legs.

I steered to the side a little earlier than I needed to, just to avoid temptation.

I tried to miss her completely.

But the port side of the dinghy gave her left foot a gentle nudge. She didn't so much as flinch. She simply remained sprawled on her back, and began to swivel counter-clockwise.

She reminded me of the knife thrower's assistant in a circus act. The beautiful gal in a skimpy outfit who gets strapped to a wheel, gets twirled, gets the fun of being the knife target.

Except Thelma wasn't beautiful and she didn't have a skimpy outfit on. She was naked. Her huge breasts, shiny and pale in the moonlight, sort of drooped off the sides of her chest like a couple of seasick voyagers getting ready to woops.

The bump by the dinghy made her spin half a turn.

She appeared to resume spinning when I started to circle around her with the boat.

The waves of my wake made her tilt and bob.

She seemed oblivious of it all.

Reaching down between my knees, I grabbed one of the machetes. I picked it up and waved it overhead. 'Hey!' I shouted. 'Thelma! Look what I've got?'

She just lay there in the middle of my wave-circles.

I threw the machete at her.

It was supposed to be more of a toss, really. A gentle, underhand toss – the way you might throw a ball to a little kid.

Intended to startle her, make her flinch or try to dodge out of the way.

It wasn't even meant, actually, to hit her.

For some reason, the toss went haywire. For some reason, I swung my arm up with more force than I'd planned on. Instead of making a shallow arc through the air so it would fall fairly harmlessly on or near Thelma, the machete went high.

Maybe all 'Freudian slips' aren't verbal.

Maybe this was a slip-of-the-arm.

Who knows? Maybe there was no subconscious intent, and it just happened because my coordination was loused up from all the running and swimming and stuff.

Anyway, I was surprised and shocked to see that I hadn't given the machete such a gentle toss, after all.

It flew almost straight up, tumbling end over end.

I said, 'Oh, shit.'

As it flipped higher and higher, I had no idea where it might come down. For all I knew, it might land on me.

We're talking a very large knife, built for whacking its way through sugar cane or jungle or something. The blade didn't have much of a point, but it must've been two feet long – broad and heavy.

It tumbled blade over handle on the way up.

To a height of at least thirty feet.

At the very top, it made a tight U-turn. Then it started down, still tumbling.

Right away, I saw that I was no longer in danger of being Ground Zero.

Thelma was.

'Thelma!' I shouted. 'Watch out!'

She didn't react – just floated spread-eagled on her back like a naked and unlovely knife thrower's assistant.

She's dead, I told myself. Don't worry about it.

But I yelled 'Thelma!' again, anyway.

And watched the machete fall, whipping end over end.

Maybe it would miss her, after all. Or maybe she would be struck by its handle, not its blade.

It struck blade first. It caught her just below the navel. It sank in almost to the handle.

Thelma screamed.

She was punched underwater by the blow. Her scream went gurgly, then silent.

She vanished, swallowed by the black.

My own scream ended when I ran out of breath. Gasping and whimpering, I gave the motor full throttle and sped away at top speed – which seemed way too slow.

I glanced back.

No sign of Thelma.

After that, I didn't look back any more. I was scared of what I might see.

I sort of thought she might be swimming after me.

One To Go

I took the other machete with me, climbed onto the dock, and tied up the dinghy. Still feeling creeped out, I wouldn't look behind me at the cove as I hurried to the foot of the dock. Nor when I walked through the thick grass at the rear of the mansion.

The whole thing had been too damn weird.

Also, I'd never killed anyone before.

I felt pretty strange about killing Thelma.

It was bad enough that I'd ended the life of a human being. But she was a woman, too. You're not supposed to hurt women, much less kill them. Also, she was Kimberly's sister; I didn't feel good at all about that.

On the other hand, it wasn't as if Thelma hadn't deserved what she got. She'd thrown in with Wesley, who'd murdered her own father and her own sister's husband. Along with Wesley, she'd done some vicious, sick things to Billie, Connie and Kimberly. To those kids, too – Erin and Alice – not to mention helping Wesley murder their parents.

If that weren't enough, she'd tried to kill *me* a few times – including the attempt at the lagoon that had nearly wiped out Connie. I was damn lucky to still be alive.

Also, it wasn't as if I'd murdered her in cold blood. Our struggle in the cove had been self-defense, on my

445

part. I'd only been trying to stay alive.

And the final deal with the machete had been sort of an accident. Which wouldn't have happened if she hadn't been playing dead, or whatever the hell she'd been up to.

She had nobody to blame but herself.

In a way, I felt sort of angry at Thelma for making me kill her.

In another way, though . . .

Maybe I'd better not write it.

Oh, why the hell not? Who am I trying to impress? The whole idea is to tell what happened – accurately, without any phoney stuff . . .

It's not that I didn't feel sort of rotten in some ways about killing Thelma. Especially because she was Kimberly's sister, and I hated the idea of causing Kimberly any more grief.

But here's the deal.

There was part of me that felt absolutely *great* about killing Thelma.

We'd gone one-on-one, her or me, a fight to the finish, and I'd wasted her ass.

Sure, I felt sort of horrified and disgusted and guilty and spooked and *very* tired – but holy Jesus I was so excited by it that I felt all trembly inside. As I walked through the grass of the back lawn, I clenched my teeth and pumped my machete at the sky and hissed, 'Yes! Yes! Yes!'

One down, one to go.

And with any luck, the 'one to go' might already be out of the picture. Wesley'd taken a major fall down those stairs. At the very least, he'd been injured so badly that Thelma'd gone after me without him. Maybe he'd broken a leg. Maybe his neck.

In a way, I hoped the fall hadn't killed him.

Just busted him up enough to make him easy for me.

Even from the back yard, I could see light in a few of the mansion's windows. Wesley or Thelma had turned on some lights to help them chase me down. From the look of things, nobody'd gotten around, yet, to turning them off.

A good sign.

It might mean that Wesley was at least disabled.

I planned to enter by the front door, so I walked through the yard alongside the house, past the window where I'd watched Wesley and Thelma brutalize Erin, and on past the corner of the veranda. The front area was still brightly illuminated by the spotlights.

On my way to the veranda stairs, I spotted my book bag under the bush where I'd left it. It could stay there until I'd finished with Wesley.

I also happened to catch a look at myself. My shorts had been so demolished by the outboard motor that they no longer had pockets. I'd lost Andrew's lighter, Billie's sunblock, and the snacks of smoked fish that I'd never gotten around to eating. A good thing I'd transferred the straight razor to my sock. The razor was still in place.

So little remained of my shorts after their run-in with the prop that they'd hardly been worth putting back on. Andrew's belt was scarred but intact. Most of the area below the belt, however, was either shredded or completely missing. A few flaps hung here and there. Otherwise, there was nothing much save fringe and gaps and me.

Which I sort of liked.

I wouldn't want to walk down Broadway wearing them, but hell, this was a tropical island. A wilderness. Nobody here but me and my women.

And Wesley.

Can't forget Wesley.

Not quite yet.

Machete in one hand, razor still in my sock, I trotted up the veranda stairs. The front door stood wide open. Was that how Thelma had left it? Of course. She sure hadn't slowed down to shut it after her mad dash onto the veranda.

I stepped through the doorway.

Looked all around, fast, to make sure nobody was coming.

Then turned my attention to the stairway. I could see to the top of it. But not to the place where Wesley had landed after tumbling down from the top story.

I sure hoped he was still there.

Very slowly, I made my way to the foot of the stairs.

There, I stopped and listened. My heart was thumping awfully loud and fast. That was about all I heard other than the outside sounds – the usual jungle noises – squeals and screeches and twitters and stuff.

Nothing inside the house.

Nothing that might come from Wesley.

I switched the machete to my left hand so I could use my right to hold the banister. Then I started to climb. I set each foot down with great care. Silently. Once in a while, a stair creaked under my weight. Each time that happened, I halted, waited and listened.

Nothing from Wesley.

Maybe he *is* dead, I thought.

Or just sleeping.

No, not sleeping. Not where I'd last seen him. I should've been able to hear his snores.

Which left three possibilities:

1. He was dead where he'd fallen.
2. He was too hurt to move, lying very still and silent, aware of my approach.
3. He was gone.

Number one would've been okay with me, but I was pulling for number two. Still pumped from my encounter with Thelma, I looked forward to dealing with him.

I did *not* want possibility number three.

But that's what I got.

After all that slow sneaking up the stairs, I finally climbed high enough to see the next floor. I wanted – expected – really thought for sure that I would find Wesley's naked body sprawled out there on the hardwood floor.

Crippled, but alive.

Or dead would've been just fine and dandy.

But not this.

I groaned and clutched the banister. Shivers scurried up my back.

He might be anywhere.

I twisted sideways and glanced down the stairs.

Thank God, he wasn't sneaking up behind me.

Thinking that perhaps he'd managed to crawl a short distance from where he'd originally landed, I climbed the final six or seven stairs.

No sign of him.

He might've gone into one of the rooms off the hallway, or back upstairs, or downstairs . . . or anywhere.

Now what? I wondered.

Easy. I'll find him, or he'll find me.

I thought about doing a room-by-room search. But quickly gave up the idea. A search like that would be scary, dangerous and time-consuming. Possibly a *waste* of time, too.

He might not even be in the house.

He might've gone over to the cages.

What if he's with the gals, right now? Doing things to them?

Whatever he might be doing, he wasn't attacking me at

the moment. He wasn't available for me to deal with. I needed to figure out my next move.

Go to the cages?

No, no, no! Find the keys, and *then* go to the cages.

Wesley hadn't seemed to be carrying the keys when he fell down the stairs. Which meant they were probably still in the upstairs room, unless he'd returned for them.

I dashed up the stairs. Most of them were pretty wet, so I kept a hand on the banister, ready to catch me if I should slip. But I reached the top without any trouble.

Though the hallway was lit, the bedroom was dark. I rushed in and searched the wall near the doorway until my hand hit the switch. An overhead light came on.

No keys on the rumpled white sheets of the bed. I snatched up both the pillows. Still no keys. Nor could I find them on the floor or nightstand or dresser. After scurrying around the room, I even dropped to my knees and looked under the bed.

Not a completely thorough search.

No luck. By then, however, I wasn't *expecting* to find them. Wesley had returned to the room, all right. He'd either hidden the key-ring, or taken it with him.

Taken the keys to the cages?

I rushed to one of the windows.

Seeing little more than my own reflection in the upper pane, I crouched and peered out through the screen.

Out beyond the moonpale front lawn, a small area of the jungle shimmered with an orange-yellow glow of firelight.

It gave me a nasty sinking in my stomach.

I muttered, 'Oh, jeez.'

And ran from the room.

Return To The Cages

On my way down, I took a fast detour and grabbed up Connie's fishing spear.

Spear in one hand, machete in the other, razor in my sock, I trotted the rest of the way downstairs and raced out of the mansion. I leaped down the veranda steps. I sprinted across the front lawn, leaving the lights behind.

From ground level, I couldn't see the fireglow. Too much jungle in the way. I was certain the glow had come from the area of the cages, though.

And wondered if I might be running into a trap.

Wesley seemed good at traps.

Maybe he wanted to play it safe just in case I should win against Thelma. Maybe he'd even watched us, and knew I'd taken her out.

And figured I'd be coming after him next.

Just his style, he might light a fire to draw me into position. But he wouldn't be *at* the fire. He'd be nearby, instead, waiting to ambush me.

With that in mind, I changed course. Instead of heading straight for the cages, I veered to the left and ran to a far corner of the lawn before entering the jungle. I went in fairly deep, then turned to the right and started making my way back.

I was quick about it. If Wesley had gone to the cages for some reason other than to ambush me, he needed to be stopped fast. There wasn't much need for quiet, either. With all the regular jungle noises, he wasn't likely to hear me crashing through the bushes. Not, at least, until I was very close to him.

When I spied the glow in the distance and off to my right, I slowed down. It seemed to come from a strange height, shining on leaves and limbs about ten or fifteen feet above ground level.

I couldn't recall any hills near the cages. Had Wesley climbed a tree and planted a fiery torch among its branches?

Reminding myself that he was probably *not* at the torch, I hunkered down and crept closer to the area. I listened for voices, but heard none.

I figured Wesley would probably jump me at any moment.

The last time I'd seen him, he had been holding one knife and wearing a belt with one empty sheath. There'd probably been a second sheath on his other hip, holding his other knife.

So I could expect him to be armed with two hunting knives.

At least. No telling what else he might've grabbed before coming over to the cages.

Not the ax, I hoped.

I hadn't seen the ax since our 'last stand,' when we'd used it as an anchor for the rope. Hadn't seen the Swiss Army knife since then, either.

Wesley or Thelma must've taken both those weapons.

The Swiss Army knife didn't worry me much. Though wickedly sharp, my razor was sharper. And the little pocket knife was outclassed, big-time, by my machete.

The ax was a different story, though.

If Wesley snuck up on me with the ax . . . or some major weapon I didn't even know about, such as a chainsaw . . . or even a gun . . .

No gun, I told myself. If he'd found a usable firearm, he would've started using it a long time ago.

Probably.

But God only knew what other sorts of weapons he might've found. If he'd looked in those storage buildings behind the house . . . A family that keeps a tractor mower might own a vast assortment of nasty tools: a chainsaw, a scythe, hedge-trimmers, a pickax, a sledge hammer.

Most of those, I figured, wouldn't be much worse than the ax. The ax had to be somewhere. Not in his hands, I hoped.

I'd seen, close up, the damage it had done to Andrew's head.

The ax really scared me.

Scared the living hell out of me until the moment I found out what Wesley *did* have.

Then I *wished* he'd had the ax instead.

Wait, wait. Time out. That was jumping ahead. The last thing I want to do is jump ahead – bring myself closer to when I need to write about what's coming, anyway, much too soon for my taste.

I wish I could just skip the whole business.

I've come this far, though. I've already written about all sorts of nasty shit that hurt to write about because it was so disgusting or horrible or personally embarrassing. What's coming is worse than anything else, so far. I'd love to stop writing, right now, and avoid the rest.

That'd be chicken, though.

It's not as if I haven't known what's coming. For days, ever since I first started to write 'The Rest of the Story,' I've known how things turned out at the cages that night. I've known how painful it would be to write about. Now that the time is just about here, I can't just call it off. Even though that's exactly what I'd *like* to do.

I mean, it's the end of the story. I've gone through several ballpoint pens, my entire spiral notebook and most of a smaller notebook that I found in Erin's bedroom (everything is on Erin's paper since 'Last Words' at the end of my journal) all to keep track of what has happened from the time Wesley stranded us on this island. I've probably spent some seventy to eighty hours writing. I didn't go to all that trouble just to go yellow and quit before telling how things came to an end.

So, here goes.

Sneaking toward the fireglow, I found myself in the bushes behind one of the seven gorilla cages. From where I crouched, the cage was only a dim, black shape. It appeared to be empty, but I couldn't be sure. The fire was still a good distance off.

Keeping the spear and machete in my hands, I crawled between the bushes and scurried across a strip of open ground toward the back of the cage. Before I got close enough for the bars to interfere with my spear, I turned to the right and hurried to the cage's far corner. I slipped around that corner. As I crept along the side of the cage, I looked through its bars.

The fire came from that direction. It was high and far away, as if Wesley had flung a blazing torch on top of one of the cages. The back-light let me see that the cage beside me was empty. So was the next cage down. The torch seemed to be directly above the third cage.

Much farther away than it might sound.

Each cage was shaped like a rectangle, about twelve feet high, fifteen feet wide and maybe twenty-five feet long. There was an open space of about five feet between cages. So the torch must've been some seventy or eighty feet away from me.

Because of the distance, my angle of vision and all the bars in the way, I couldn't see if anyone was up on top of the cage with the torch.

But I could see a woman inside the cage. Her face was anybody's guess. I recognized her figure, though, in spite of the distance, bars, and murky light. She stood near the middle of her cage, almost directly under the torch, her naked body half-concealed by shadows but unmistakably Billie.

She didn't walk anywhere, but turned around slowly as if looking for someone.

Maybe looking for me.

Facing my way, she seemed to stare at me. She probably couldn't see me, though, in the heavy darkness at my end of the cages.

So where's Wesley? I wondered. Up on Billie's cage with the torch, or waiting to jump out of the jungle and take me from behind?

I needed a clear look at the top of her cage.

If I could climb *this* cage . . .

No. I might've been strong enough to shinny up the bars, but I sure couldn't do it without setting down my spear and machete.

Which weren't going to leave my hands. Not, at least, unless I knew for sure that Wesley wouldn't be jumping me.

Keeping hold of the weapons, I retraced my way into the jungle. In among the bushes and trees, I watched the glow of the torch and took a route parallel to the row of gorilla cages. I stayed far enough back to keep the cages and the blaze of the torch out of sight.

For a while, I planned to sneak in near Billie's cage and try to see if Wesley was on top.

But if I could spot him, he could spot me.

I hit upon a better idea.

Don't look for him – ask.

Sticking to my route, I continued through the jungle. Past the torchlight. And on, and on, leaving the glow farther and farther behind me.

When I judged that I'd covered enough distance, I started sneaking to the right.

I thought I had probably overshot Erin's cage, and would need to backtrack and search for it. Luck was with me, though. I came out of the jungle behind the middle of her cage.

After a quick look from side to side, I started crawling across the strip of open ground.

Erin didn't seem to be aware of my approach. She stood at the door of her cage. Though she was merely a dim shape in the darkness, she appeared to have her back toward me. Her hands were raised to about the height of her head, and seemed to be gripping the bars of her door.

Pausing, I looked to my right and saw Alice's cage. The girl was hunkered down – as if cowering or trying to hide – at the back corner nearest to Erin's cage.

I couldn't see anyone inside Connie's cage. Which was closer to the torchlight, but a fair distance away from me. I figured she must be in it – just out of sight. Maybe lying down.

The next cage was Kimberly's. The light was better, way over there. Not so much darkness as a shivery glow. What with the distance and my angle, though, I couldn't exactly tell where Connie's cage left off, Kimberly's began or ended, or Billie's began.

Someone seemed to be roaming around down there, in among the confusion of bars. I supposed it must be Kimberly, but I couldn't be sure.

I tried to spot the torch.

Couldn't, though. Not the torch, just its glow.

At the other end of the cages, I'd been a lot closer to it. From my new position, the bright aura of torchlight might've been coming from on top of Kimberly's cage. I figured the torch was probably still above Billie's, though.

Anyway, I stopped inspecting the place and finished crawling across to Erin's cage. When I was almost there, I turned myself sideways. I lay down flat, mashing the tall grass on the ground alongside the bars. The grass was maybe six inches high, so it would help to conceal me. It felt cool and wet. I put the spear and machete by my sides, and propped myself up on my elbows.

Erin still stood at the door of her cage.

I called out to her. It was a whisper, really. She didn't respond, so I whispered her name more loudly. The pale blot of her head jerked. Her hands fell away from the bars. The width of her body narrowed, then widened, as she turned around.

'Erin,' I whispered again.

She started walking toward me. She had a slight hitch to her gait – a limp.

Which gave me a sudden, harsh reminder of what I'd watched them do to her. Wesley and Thelma. In the downstairs room. How they'd brought Erin in wearing a white blouse, a cute tartan kilt, and knee socks. How they'd stripped her, brutalized her, done such horrible, sick things to her . . . All while I watched, guilty and aroused. It made me feel strange, just thinking about it. I had to squirm a little in the dewy grass.

'Rupert?' she whispered.

'Yeah.'

She stopped at the bars and lay down on her side of them, matching my position, her head turned, her face close to mine.

'How are you?' she asked.

'Okay. What's going on here?'

'Wesley came.'

'Where is he?'

'Up on top of the cages. I think so, anyhow. It's kinda hard to keep track of him all the time.'

'Is everybody okay?'

'Rupert?' Alice's voice, her whisper loud.

I turned my head and found her. She was still at the corner of her cage, but no longer in a hunched position. She was poised there on all fours like a dog, her face to the bars. 'Don't leave me out of everything,' she said.

'You were asleep, anyway,' Erin told her.

'Was not.'

'We'd better keep our voices down,' I said. 'Come on,' I told Erin. I picked up my two weapons. Then she and I crawled, side by side, the bars between us.

I wished there was more light. I wanted to be able to see her and Alice. But this was better than last time, when the darkness had been almost total. This time, at least I could make out their shapes – sort of. Basically, they weren't much more than pale blurs without any distinct features.

At the corner of her cage, Erin halted. I crawled around

it, turned myself so I faced the rear, put down my spear and machete, and sat in the grass between the two cages.

Alice on my left, Erin on my right.

Like old times, except this time we were gathered at the back of the passageway, not the front.

'I thought you were asleep,' I told Alice. 'That's why I didn't . . .'

'It's okay,' she said. 'I'm sure glad you're back.'

'Is everybody okay?' I asked.

'All depends,' Alice said. 'What do you . . . ?'

'We're fine,' Erin said. 'I mean, you know. Not exactly fine and *dandy*, but we're the same as before.'

'He hasn't been *at* us,' Alice explained.

'Where'd you go?'

'Over to the house, for starters. I went looking for the keys, so I could come back and let everybody out.'

'Did you find them?' Erin asked.

'Wesley doesn't have them?'

'I don't think so.'

'I *know* he hasn't got them,' Alice said.

'Well, he didn't unlock any cages.'

'He walked *by*. You could *see* what he had and didn't. And he didn't have any keys. Not if they weren't, like, stuck up his kazoo.'

'He couldn't *fit* them up his kazoo,' Erin pointed out, sounding a trifle annoyed. 'That big brass ring? No way.'

'It was a figure of speech, stupid.'

'Anyway, I guess she's right. We would've seen the keys if he'd had them.'

'What did he have?' I asked.

'A boner,' Alice said.

'Very nice,' Erin said.

'Well, he did.'

'I'm sure Rupert wants to hear all about it.'

I was blushing, but the darkness kept it hidden. 'What sort of weapons did he have?' I asked.

Erin said, 'Two knives. Does the torch count?'

'I guess.'

'Okay, then the torch. And a can of gas.'

'*A what?*'

'A can of gasoline.'

'We keep *tons* of it around for the generator,' Alice explained.

'For a lot of things,' Erin added.

'Mostly for the generator, though. We've got *tons*.'

'Wesley has about two gallons,' Erin said. 'He took the can up with him.'

'He says he's gonna incinerate us,' Alice said.

Me And The Twins

'He won't do it,' Erin said. 'It's just a threat. If he burns us up, he won't be able to mess around with us any more. It'd wreck everything for him.'

'Yeah? Well just suppose he only burns *some* of us?'

Erin didn't have a quick answer for that.

'He's already doused Billie,' Alice added.

I felt my stomach sink and shrivel. 'Are you sure?'

'It was the first thing he did,' Erin explained. 'He showed up, I don't know, like maybe an hour or so after you took off? With the torch and gas.'

'And no pants on, as per usual,' Alice added, sounding disgusted.

'So he parades by our cages, and says how we're all going to help him set up a surprise for you.'

'He called you a chickenshit motherfucking asswipe,' Alice explained.

'Real nice,' Erin said. 'You don't have to tell him *everything*.'

'*I'd* want to know it, if somebody called me . . .'

'Doesn't matter,' I said. 'What about the surprise?'

'He said you paid him a visit at the house, and that you ran away, but Thelma'd gone after you. He said Thelma would probably kill you . . .'

'Nail your puny little butt,' Alice elaborated.

'But just in case she *didn't* get you, he wanted to have a surprise ready. He said you'd probably come over here to the cages, first thing. So we should be expecting you, and we'd better not yell and try to warn you off.'

'He said he'd toast our twats.'

'Alice! Stop it!'

'I'm just telling what he said.'

'Well, don't. For Godsake. You don't have to be so *crass*.'

'You talk just as bad. Only not around *Rupert*.'

'Hey, girls. Come on.'

'She's got the hots for you, Rupert.'

'I do not.'

'Like you'd ever admit it to *him*. But she does, Rupert. Trust me. She told me so.'

'Liar.'

'You're the liar.'

'I never said I had the *hots* for him.'

'Maybe not in those exact words, but . . .'

'Can't we talk about it some other time?' I suggested. 'I mean, if I don't take care of Wesley . . . Does he ever come over to this end of things?'

'Hasn't yet,' Erin said. 'The closest he's come is Kimberly's cage. He hasn't gotten on top of Connie's or ours.'

'Not that he couldn't,' Alice said.

'Yeah, he could if he wanted to. If he didn't want to move the ladder, he could always just go ahead and jump. It isn't that far between . . .'

'What ladder?' I asked.

'*Our* ladder,' Alice said.

'He got it at our house,' Erin explained. 'Like everything

else, just about. He's been keeping it handy ever since he put us in the cages. It's one of his things. He climbs up on top of the cages and sort of . . . messes around. You know, looks down at us. Teases us. He keeps a box of stuff up there. Things he can drop on us whenever he feels like playing "bombardier."'

'Mostly books,' Alice said.

'He drops *books* on you?'

'Yeah,' Alice said, 'and they can hurt. Even a paperback hurts if it catches you with its spine.'

'Especially a *corner* of the spine,' Erin added. 'The deal is, Wesley doesn't want to bomb us with anything we might use against him. He figures we can't do much damage with a book.'

'Sometimes, he bombs us with pages,' Alice said. 'He'll rip one out and wad it up, then set it on fire and drop it through the bars.'

'You can usually dodge them,' Erin said. 'He just likes to hear us scream.'

'And watch us try to get out of the way. He *loves* to make us jump around. You know, because we aren't wearing a stitch of clothes, or anything.'

'He dumps buckets of water on us from up there, too.'

'All kinds of stuff,' Alice added.

'It'd take all night,' Erin said, 'to tell you *every*thing he drops on us. I mean, he's had a lot of time on his hands with nothing to do but mess with us.'

'His favorite thing, he lies down and dangles his dong through the bars. Then he'll . . .'

'God, Alice. That's not . . .'

'I'm just trying to tell what he does.'

'Rupert doesn't need to hear it. You know? Jeez!'

I decided to bring us back to the subject. 'So Wesley got

this ladder, tonight, and used it to climb up to the top of Billie's cage?'

'Right,' Erin said.

'Then what?'

'Then he pulled it up after him. And he put it across the gap between Billie's cage and Kimberly's to make it easy for him to cross back and forth. He can just use the ladder like a bridge, you know? Instead of having to jump.'

'That's why he hasn't come over here,' Alice said.

'I don't think he's real eager to jump. It'd be pretty tricky. There's nothing up there but bars.'

'And the ladder,' Alice added.

'He can get around pretty well, walking on the bars. He's had a lot of practice.'

'He's part ape,' Alice said.

'Thinks he's King Kong,' Erin said.

'*Thinks* he's King Dong.'

'You'll have to excuse my sister,' Erin said. 'She isn't usually like this.'

'It's all right,' I said.

'See?' Alice asked. 'I *told* you it was okay with Rupert.'

'He's just being polite.'

I stayed quiet at that, not wanting to get involved in their little squabbles. The thing is, I didn't really mind Alice's language. It's hard to be offended by stuff like that when you've got a guy like Wesley nearby. It's hard to be anything except scared. But I did find myself a little bit amused, now and then. And sometimes embarrassed.

And turned on. I mean, there I was, sitting on the ground between Erin and Alice. They were stark-naked. I might as well have been naked, too, considering the condition of my shorts.

Even though I couldn't see the girls, I sort of knew what

they looked like. After all, I'd had time to study every inch of Erin when she'd been in the room with Wesley and Thelma. And Alice was her twin sister. What I couldn't actually see because of the darkness, I had no trouble imagining.

On top of all that, Alice's talk about things like twats and dongs and boners only made things worse – or better, depending on how you look at things.

Plus, I couldn't quite stop thinking about Erin having the 'hots' for me. Apparently, she hadn't used that exact word. Whatever words she might've used, though, she'd made it clear to Alice that she liked me.

Interesting news. Incredible news. Wonderful news.

Too bad it had to come at a time when everyone was in so much danger that I figured we probably wouldn't all make it through the night.

Anyway, that sums up what was going on with me, and why I said that I didn't have any problem with Alice's language. I wasn't being polite, I was being truthful.

Trying to get things on track again, I said, 'So you think Wesley won't try to jump from cage to cage?'

'I haven't even seen him try *that* in broad daylight,' Erin answered.

'Doesn't mean he *can't*,' Alice pointed out.

'If he wants to come this way,' Erin said, 'I bet he'll bring the ladder with him. Put it down across each gap. We'd hear that, if he tried it.'

'The ladder's aluminum,' Alice explained.

'So we don't need to worry about him sneaking over,' Erin said.

'Unless he *does* jump the gaps. We'd hear him when he lands on *this* cage, but . . .'

'He's too smart to try it.'

'Or unless he gets down off the cages,' I suggested. 'Then he could sneak over here on the ground . . .'

'Kimberly's gonna warn us if he climbs down.'

'She's *supposed* to,' Alice corrected.

'Yeah. We sort of set up a few tricks of our own. If Wesley does anything we need to know about, Kimberly's gonna pass the word to Connie, and Connie'll tell Alice.'

'Except Connie's asleep,' Alice said.

'Maybe she is and maybe she isn't,' Erin said. 'Anyway, he won't climb down. He's right where he wants to be, up above everything where nobody can get at him.'

'I have a spear.'

The girls were silent for a second or two. Then Erin asked, 'Can you hit him with it?'

'I don't know.'

'You'd better not even try,' Alice said. 'Even if you get him, he'll probably still be able to set Billie on fire. All he has to do is drop the torch.'

'What if I wait till the torch goes out?' I asked.

For a couple of seconds, nobody answered. Then Alice spoke up. 'I don't know.'

'It might be a really long wait,' Erin said. 'And when it does burn out, he'll just dip it in the gas and light it back up.'

'With what?' I asked.

'Huh?'

'How would he relight it?'

'Oh, he's got a couple of Dad's cigarette lighters. Keeps them in the box up there for lighting his paper wads.'

'And cigarettes,' Alice said. 'The creep smokes like a chimney. That's something *else* he uses on us. His butts. He gets a big charge out of flicking them at us.'

'He doesn't have to be on top of the cages for that,' Erin

explained. 'He mostly does it from the sides. Yells "incoming" and fires the things through the bars. They aren't as easy to dodge as the paper balls.'

'They can really sting, too,' Alice said.

'That's horrible,' I muttered.

'It isn't half as horrible as *some* of what he does to us.'

'Rupert doesn't want to hear about it.'

'And Thelma's even worse than Wesley,' Alice went on. 'She comes right into the cages with us, sometimes and ...'

'Knock it off,' Erin said. 'I mean it.'

'I think she must be part lesbo ...'

'They're both a couple of sicko freaks,' Erin said. 'Let's just let it go at that, okay? You haven't gotta go and blab about every little perverted thing they've *done* to us.'

'Rupert doesn't mind. Do you, Rupert?'

'Well ...'

'*I* mind,' Erin said. 'Jeez. So just cut it out. It's embarrassing. Rupert doesn't need to hear every disgusting detail.'

'Let him speak for himself. Do you want to hear what Thelma likes to do?'

I looked for a way out, and found it.

'She's dead, by the way.'

'What?' Erin blurted.

'I killed her. Over in the cove.'

'Wow.'

'Fan*tas*tic,' Alice said.

'Good going,' Erin told me. Something suddenly touched my thigh, so I flinched. Then I realized it was Erin's hand. It gave my leg a gentle squeeze. 'How'd you get her?' she asked.

'With one of those machetes.'

'Holy cow.'

'Fan*tas*tic,' Alice repeated.

Erin's hand slipped under the tatters of my shorts.

'So Wesley,' I said, 'is the only sicko freak we have to worry about.'

Her warm, small hand glided a ways up my thigh. It came close to my groin before reversing direction. I had to squirm.

'What about the bucket?' I asked. 'You said Wesley liked to take it up on top of the cages and dump water on you?'

'What about it?' Alice asked.

'If I can get my hands on a bucket of water, maybe I can take care of things if Wesley tries to set Billie on fire.'

Erin squeezed my leg. 'Yeah!' she whispered. 'That's a great idea.'

'Where do I find it?'

'I don't know.'

Alice said, 'I hate to embarrass you again, Erin.'

'Then don't.'

'The thing is, Rupert, we've each got a bucket in our cage. For you know what.'

I was surprised. It certainly made sense for them to have buckets in their cages, but I hadn't given the matter any thought. I hadn't seen any buckets, either.

Looking over my shoulder, I tried to spot one in Erin's cage. Too much darkness.

'Real nice,' she was saying to her sister. Even as she complained, her hand crept higher up my thigh.

'You think Rupert doesn't go to the bathroom?' Alice asked her. '*Everyone* goes to the bathroom. We just happen to do it in buckets.'

'Which won't do Rupert any good at all, because we can't exactly *hand* them to him.' In a more pleasant tone of voice, she said, 'My dumb sister seems to have forgotten that the buckets won't fit through the bars. Thelma has to . . . *used* to come in and take care of them.'

'Maybe we can *make* one fit through the bars,' Alice suggested.

'They're metal or steel or . . .'

'Doesn't mean they can't be bent.'

Erin's hand stopped moving. 'We'd have to fold one in *half* to get it through the bars. We'd have to, like, jump on it or something. And we're barefoot. Besides which, even if we *could* smash one small enough, the thing would make so much noise that Wesley'd probably hear us.'

'What about Wesley's bucket?' I asked. 'Where's the one he uses?'

'Who knows?' Alice said.

Erin's hand resumed caressing my thigh. 'It might be anywhere,' she said. 'Maybe back at the house, even. If you wanted to go back to the house, you'd be sure to find *some*thing. Cooking pots you could fill with water. Pitchers, waste baskets . . .'

'What about a fire extinguisher?' I asked.

'We keep one on the boat,' Erin said.

'Not in the house, though?'

'We've been in these cages for almost a month,' Alice pointed out. 'Who knows where anything is?'

'But I bet you could find something and fill it with water back at the house.'

'You'd *better* do it, too,' Alice said. 'I mean, Billie's gonna get burnt to a crisp if you don't have a way to put her out. She's all fueled up and ready to go.'

'Maybe I'd better do that,' I admitted.

Suddenly, I knew where to find a bucket. Back at the mansion, over near the veranda stairs. Earlier, I'd seen

Thelma put out her torch in it.

I was awfully reluctant to leave, though. I felt sort of safe, hidden between the cages, the girls on both sides of me.

And Erin's hand kept roaming my leg.

Her hand was our secret. She was letting it stray pretty far up my thigh.

It was driving me a little crazy.

Anyway, I couldn't just stand up and walk away.

'What else should I get?' I asked, just to delay things.

'What do you mean?' Alice asked.

What if I reach between the bars and touch Erin?

'Back at the house,' I said. 'Is there anything else? Something I should get while I'm there?'

'Like what?' Erin asked.

If I try anything funny, she might quit. Just leave her alone. Let her do what she wants.

Where was I?

'Are there any guns in the house?' I asked.

'No way,' Erin said.

'That's one reason we left Los Angeles,' Alice said. 'To get *away* from things like guns.'

'I could sure use one now,' I said. 'What about bows and arrows?'

'No.'

'Just get the water,' Alice said. 'You'd better hurry, too. I mean, there's no telling. He might go ahead and light her up, just for the fun of it.'

Erin's hand eased up higher than ever. I flinched and caught my breath. Her hand flew off like a startled bird. And crashed against a bar of her cage with a low, ringing thud. She yelped.

'Jeez, I'm sorry,' I whispered. 'Are you okay?'

'My hand.'

'I'm really sorry.'

'What happened?' Alice asked.

'Nothing,' Erin told her. 'I bumped the bars.'

'What were you doing?'

'Nothing.'

'We were holding hands,' I explained. Which sounded better, I thought, than the truth.

'You shouldn't go holding her hand,' Alice said. 'You don't know where it's been.'

'Very funny,' Erin said.

'I'd better get going,' I said.

'Not so fast. Rupie? Come here.'

The Fire Storm

'Rupie? Come herrrrre.'

The voice made me cringe. For one thing, it was too loud. For another, it belonged to Connie, and she didn't sound much less crazy than last time.

'My God,' I muttered.

Alice was already scurrying across her cage, apparently hoping to shush her.

On my knees, I grabbed my spear and machete.

'What're you gonna do?' Erin whispered.

'I don't know. Make her be quiet.'

'I know you're there, Rupie! Now come on, pull your cock outa that bitch and come on over. I been waiting for you!'

I scrambled out from between the cages. On my feet but hunched low, I dashed through the grass behind Alice's cage.

'What is it with you, boy?'

'Be quiet!' Alice gasped.

'When you aren't fucking the old ladies, you're fucking the babies.'

'Shut up!' Alice pleaded. Her voice came from my left, and not far ahead. I slowed down.

'Why not me? You some kinda fucking geek?'

'Be quiet, Connie!' I snapped.

'RUPERT! GREETINGS!'

Wesley's shout slammed through me, knocking my breath out, stopping me cold.

It had come from far away.

From where he apparently still stood on top of Billie's cage.

Sounding cheerful, Connie sang out, 'Look who's fucked now.'

'Before you make any rash decisions,' Wesley called, 'let me advise you that the lives of the ladies are in your hands. I'm fully prepared to annihilate them all, Rupert, unless you give me your full cooperation.'

I felt sick and weak. I seemed to be trembling all over. My heart pounded hard and terribly fast.

'Do you hear me?' Wesley called.

I didn't answer.

'In that case, do you have any last words for Billie? I took the trouble of dousing her with gasoline. She'll make one hell of a torch. You'll be needing sunglasses, little buddy. Better put 'em on!'

I shouted, 'What do you want?'

'Go to the front of the cages,' he commanded.

'Okay.'

I found the bars at the back of Alice's cage. Keeping track of them with my left arm, I rounded the corner. I rushed between the cages. On one side, Alice said, 'Be careful.'

On the other, Connie hurried along with me. This much closer to Wesley's torch, the light was somewhat better. Connie's shape was fairly visible. Her eyes, mouth, nipples and what I took to be several injuries looked like holes or rips in the pale canvas of her skin. She seemed to be leaping sideways to stay with me.

As she leaped along, she ranted. 'See what you get? Huh? This is what happens, Rupie. This is what you get. You were mine. Mine! You blew it. Blew it big-time, boy. Now you're gonna pay. You're fucked. Big-time. Wesley's gonna ream . . .'

She ran out of cage. One moment she was springing along beside me, the next she wasn't. I heard the bars ring from the impact. She let out a grunt, sounding surprised and hurt.

I looked back and saw her prancing away from the bars as if she'd been hurled back by a giant, invisible spring. Then she slammed down on the floor of her cage.

She sounded like a slab of steak tossed onto a counter top.

Which made me realize the floor of her cage must be concrete. Until that moment, I hadn't given any real thought to the subject. I'd just assumed the gals must have earth and bars under their feet.

Not that it seemed to matter, either way.

Concrete was probably better when the cages needed cleaning. It would hurt you more, however, if you fell on it.

Connie appeared to be sprawled on her back. She wasn't trying to get up.

Had she knocked herself out?

I really didn't care, except to be glad that she, at least, might not be causing me any more trouble for a while.

God knows, she'd already caused enough.

After her crash, I slowed down but kept moving. For a couple of moments, I forgot about Wesley.

Then he called, 'There you are!'

I turned toward the sound of his voice.

And there he was. Standing on top of Billie's cage – legs spread, a blazing torch raised in his right hand, his left hand propped on his hip. In the firelight, his body gleamed like gold. A golden statue. Hercules gone to flab.

He'd lost the chest bandage; maybe in his fall down the stairs. The fall must've opened his wound, too. The split across the front of his left boob looked like a grim mouth, puffy-lipped and dribbling blood as if it had recently caught a fist. It made thin, dark streamers down his chest and belly, down to his leather belt. A few strands of blood had worked their way down his left thigh.

The wound obviously didn't bother him much. Neither did I. He was getting a charge out of the whole situation. Two things gave it away: his grin and his hard-on.

'Step right this way, little buddy,' he called to me.

As I walked toward him, I saw that Connie still lay sprawled on the bottom of her cage.

Knocked out or faking? I wondered.

Hope she split her head open, I thought.

The next cage over, Kimberly stood at her bars, watching me. Her raised hands clutched the bars to either side of her head. She didn't try to cover herself. Maybe she thought I couldn't really see her. I could, though. She was much closer to the torch than Connie. The air in which she stood seemed to be tinted with its dim, hazy glow. She looked almost distinct, but veiled. As if draped with a shroud of wispy black fabric that revealed her, but cloaked her with darkness.

I could actually recognize her face. I could see the entire front of her body – ribcage and breasts, the dark coins of her nipples, all the long slender way down past the dot of her navel, the hollows slanting down and inward from her hips to the smooth mound between the tops of her legs, and then her legs, parted and slim and sturdy. All visible, but darkly veiled.

All wounded. In spite of the murky light, I saw dark places where her skin should've been unblemished. I saw smudges, stains, patterns of narrow marks and stripes.

My throat turned thick and tight because of how she'd been hurt. I felt my eyes sting. At the same time, heat surged through me. It made me feel ashamed, but I couldn't help it.

'Don't let him get you,' Kimberly said as I walked by, staring at her. 'If he gets you . . .'

'Shut up, down there!' Wesley called.

'. . . he gets you, we're all sunk.'

'Hey!'

'Kill him, Rupert.'

'I'll try.'

'One more word and momma-bear's going up in flames!'

Kimberly's right hand slipped sideways between the bars. She raised two fingers.

I don't think she meant it to be the peace sign from the bygone days of the hippies.

I think she meant it to be Winston Churchill's V.

Hell, I *know* that's what it was. A Navy brat like her, Andrew's daughter, descended from a Sioux warrior, tough and proud.

V for Victory.

'Keep coming,' Wesley told me.

I gave Kimberly a nod, and walked on past the end of her cage. Up top, a ladder crossed the open space between her cage and Billie's. Just as the twins had said.

The ladder was extended to a length of about fifteen feet. Five or six feet at its middle bridged the gap. The rest of it overlapped the tops of the cages, maybe five feet on each side.

Wesley was standing away from the ladder, more toward

the middle of Billie's cage. Near his feet, I saw the gasoline can and a cardboard box.

The box that held his 'bombardier' goodies.

'Okay,' he said. 'Stop right there.'

I stopped.

Billie stood almost directly beneath him, well-lit by his torch. The light wavered and shimmied on her body as if she was underwater. Her skin, copper in the shifting glow, gleamed with wetness.

The gasoline.

Her short hair was drenched, matted to her skull in tight golden coils.

Again, the gasoline.

And gasoline darkened the concrete under her bare feet. It had spread out around her, forming a shallow and lopsided puddle in the middle of her cage.

When I looked up from the puddle, she gave me a shrug.

Like a little girl who'd peed on the floor, couldn't help it, and was left embarrassed and resigned.

Why was she standing in the middle of the gas?

Wesley's orders, I supposed.

He must've commanded her to stand still while he poured the gasoline onto her head, while it ran down her body and made the puddle. Then he'd ordered her to remain standing in the same place.

Move a muscle, and I'll torch you.

And I had no bucket of water for her. Because I'd stayed too long with Erin and Alice, because of Erin's hand on my leg.

And because of Connie's roaring jealousy.

I should've had the water for Billie.

Her toilet bucket was off in a rear corner of her cage,

upside-down. Apparently, she'd been using it as a seat. Obviously, it had nothing in it.

She's gonna burn!

I could think of only one way to save her: stop Wesley from setting the gas on fire.

'Look at you, look at you,' he said. 'You've gone quite native.'

'What do you want?'

'My first order of business is to neutralize *you*, don't you think?'

'I'll do anything you say,' I told him.

'Excellent. Drop your weapons.'

'Don't,' Billie said, her voice firm and clear. 'You're the only chance we've got.'

'Shut up, Billie darling.'

'He'll burn you,' I said.

'Let him.'

'No, I can't.'

Above her, Wesley bent over. He reached into the cardboard box with his left hand, and came up with a paperback book. He lifted it by a corner of its front cover, so that the book hung open. Then he lowered the torch and held its flame beneath the pages.

'No!' I shouted.

Fire crawled up the book.

'Don't do it!'

I threw down my spear and machete.

Wesley tossed the book underhand. It tumbled through the night, blazing. And dropped onto the grass near my feet.

'That was sure a close call,' he announced.

'Fucking bastard,' I said, stomping out the flames.

'Oooo, such language! You've been listening to Connie.

A very bad influence, that girl.'

'What do you want?' I asked.

'Let me see. What do I want? I want you to step into your new accommodation, over there.' Swinging his torch, he pointed out the empty cage beside Billie's cage. 'Step right in and shut the door.'

With my first step in that direction, Billie gasped, 'No! Rupert, you can't honey. If he locks you up . . .'

'I'm not gonna let him burn you.'

'Very wise, little buddy.'

'You have to take him down,' she said.

'Shut up with that kind of talk, bitch! I'll cook your cunt right now!'

Ignoring him, staring me in the eyes, Billie said, 'Kill Wesley. At least maybe you'll be able to save the others. Let him burn me, but kill him.'

'You asked for it!' Wesley yelled. He bent down and reached into the cardboard box.

'Wait!' I blurted. 'Wait a minute!'

He looked at me.

'If you burn her up, you won't have her to mess with anymore.'

He grinned. 'Oh, I don't know about that.'

'You get turned on by her pain, don't you? If she's dead, she won't even feel what you do to her. She won't flinch or cry out or bleed or anything. It won't matter how hard you whip her, or . . .'

'Who needs her?' Wesley asked. Even as he said it, though, he took his arm out of the box, no book in his hand, and stood up. 'I've got all the rest of them. And there'll be plenty more, once they start having babies for me.' Grinning, he shook his head. 'Good old Thelma, she always wanted babies. God save us all. Can you picture it?

What if they came out looking like her? Who'd want 'em? Wouldn't be good for shit, girls ugly as that.'

'Billie'll have beautiful babies,' I said. 'Just look at Connie. That's *proof* of how her babies will look. And you want to burn her up? Are you nuts?'

'You've got a point there, little buddy. I tell you what, go on and step into that cage, and maybe we can give her a stay of execution.'

'Okay.'

'Wait,' Kimberly said. 'What happened to Thelma? Where is she?'

Wesley let out a harsh laugh. 'Gosh! I forgot to ask! How's my Thelma? I sure hope you didn't *hurt* my dear, sweet little wife.'

I looked over at Kimberly's cage. She stood at its nearest corner, facing me. 'I'm really sorry,' I told her. 'She was trying to kill me, and I . . . I'm pretty sure she's dead. She went down in the cove.'

Kimberly was silent for a moment. Then she murmured, 'It's all right. I mean . . .'

'All right?' Wesley blurted. 'It's fucking *perfect*! Thank you very much for ridding me of the ugly cow! She did have her uses, but . . . I do believe that we're all much better off without her. My God, what a pig! Three cheers for Rupert! Hip hip hooray!' On hooray, he thrust his torch high. 'Hip hip . . . hooray!' Up went the torch. 'Hip hip . . . hooray!' He rammed the torch at the sky.

Then, laughing, he performed a weird little dance on top of Billie's cage: stomping his feet on the bars, waving the torch, twisting and shaking, swinging his hips, thrusting with his pelvis. He probably would've jumped and twirled, but was afraid of stepping between the bars.

I *hoped* for him to slip and fall. I even thought about

snatching up the spear and making a try for him while he danced. But Billie would burn if anything happened to make him drop the torch.

His wild gyrations sent sweat pouring down his body, flying off his hair and skin.

'So long, Thelma!' he yelled. 'Nice knowing you! Nice, my ass! Ha hah!'

Billie, looking straight up at him, suddenly blinked and ducked her head and rubbed her face.

Then *she* began to dance.

In silence, she swayed and turned, swung her shoulders, jumped from one foot to another.

Wesley noticed. He quit dancing himself, and bent over. Huffing for breath, he looked down at Billie through the bars. 'What the hell do you think you're doing?'

'Dancing.'

'Knock it off.'

She didn't stop. Though she remained in the center of her cage as if shackled there by Wesley's threats, she hopped from foot to foot, waved her arms, bowed, twirled, shook and leaped.

'You've got nothing to dance about,' Wesley said.

'Do, too,' she called out.

'Knock it off.'

'It's my rain dance!' she shouted. 'I'm calling up a storm!'

And her dance suddenly broke into a savage frenzy. It wasn't like anything I'd ever seen before. The way she leaped and writhed, she must've had manic drumbeats in her head.

Instead of ordering her to halt, Wesley stared down at her, captivated by the view.

I was captivated by the view.

It wasn't something you could look away from. Not if you were a guy.

My God, it was like watching some sort of pagan ritual, the way she cavorted naked in the firelight, bowing and rising, spinning, whimpering and grunting with the effort, her feet splashing in the puddle of gas, her shiny buttocks flexing, her glossy breasts jumping and bouncing and swinging, her face agleam and streaming as if dipped in oil, sweat leaping like melted gold off her hair and nose and chin and nipples and fingertips, sweat spilling down her neck and chest and breasts, down her back and belly, her buttocks, her pubis, her legs, sliding down like golden run-off from a torrent of rain.

A downpour.

A squawl.

It's my rain dance! I'm calling up a storm!

Spoken to Wesley.

Meant for me.

Dropping to a crouch, I grabbed the spear out of the grass. Wesley still stood atop the cage, bent over and watching Billie.

He didn't look at me as I straightened up, raised the spear above my shoulder and hurled it at him.

Wesley's Last Stand

He still had his head down when the spear struck him. It caught him near the top of his left shoulder, punched him there but didn't stick, bounced off the bone and leaped out of the thin covering of flesh, its other end whipping upward as if a pole-vaulter was taking off from his shoulder.

He roared.

The whole spear leaped off into the dark behind him.

He raised his sweat-slick, dripping face. His eyes bulged. He bared his teeth at me.

Straight below him, Billie had stopped dancing. She stood in the puddle of gas in the middle of her cage, her head tipped back. Her body gleamed and dripped as if she had just climbed out of a swimming pool. She whined with her struggle to breathe.

'You dirty little fuck!' Wesley shouted at me.

And jammed the torch down between the bars at his feet and let it go.

'No!' I yelled.

The torch fell.

A moment later, it touched off the gasoline. The gas erupted with a heavy *WHOP!* like a mainsail snapped by the wind. The sudden brilliance hurt my eyes. As I squinted, a hot wind rolled against my body.

Wesley had been right about needing sunglasses.

The cage looked as if a bonfire had erupted in the middle of its concrete floor.

I saw Billie in there. All firelit and bright and shiny, her back to me.

Running. Leaping onto her upside-down bucket. Using it like a step for leaping again. High up at the far back corner of her cage, she caught hold and latched herself to the bars, curled tight with her knees up.

Depending for her life on the sweat of her mad dance, sweat meant to sluice the gasoline off her skin and bathe her with saving moisture.

I didn't know if it would work.

Afraid to see her burn, I turned my gaze to the top of the cage.

Where flames leaped for Wesley.

They wrapped the cardboard of his 'bombardier' box, licked the sides of his gasoline tin.

With a squeal of alarm, he kicked the gas container and knocked it flying. The punt sent it well past the far side of Billie's cage, sprinkling gas from its spout. It clamored against the empty cage that he'd intended as my cell.

I looked back at Wesley to find him prancing across the bars like a ballerina as the flames tried to climb his legs. Just as he got away from them, he lost his footing. He crashed down belly-first on the ladder. It jumped and shuddered under him, raising a terrible racket.

Before the ladder had a chance to settle down, he shoved himself to his hands and knees and started crawling across it.

Away from the fire of his own making.

A fire that had already fallen to half its size.

But he didn't know that. He wasn't looking back. If he'd

seen how the fire had diminished so abruptly, he probably wouldn't have been so quick to flee.

Billie still clung to the bars at the distant corner of her cage.

She still had her hair.

From shoulders to buttocks, her skin looked ruddy, shiny wet, uncharred.

She'd made it!

Now the job was to kill Wesley.

I snatched up the machete and raced for him.

Halfway across the gap, he saw me coming. He let out a yelp and crawled faster, the ladder shaking and clattering beneath him.

I ran full-speed between the cages. With the ladder looming over me, Wesley almost to the other side, I leaped and reached high, slashing with my machete.

Missed him, the ladder, everything.

I'm not a tall guy. I must've missed the ladder by a foot.

Gave him a good scare, though. He'd squealed when I swung at him. As I put on the brakes, the clamor of the ladder let me know he was scurrying like mad.

The ladder noise suddenly stopped.

I turned around in time to see Wesley look for me over his shoulder and try to stand up.

He should've been watching his feet.

The right one stepped down between two of the bars. He cried, *'Yaaah!'* as his leg shot down. He flapped his arms. His other leg bent at the knee and scooted out from under him. His bare ass struck the bars.

And there he sat, his right leg hanging down into Kimberly's cage.

He made whimpery, frightened sounds.

Before he could even start to free himself, Kimberly jumped.

My God what a jump!

'Yes!' someone yelled.

Billie.

She stood at the side of her cage, the fire behind her fluttering low, Wesley's blazing torch in her upraised hand.

Kimberly dangled beneath Wesley.

She hung with both hands from his right ankle.

Golden in the torchlight, arms stretched so high that her breasts were nearly flat – long, low slopes topped by hard and jutting nipples – her entire body taut and thin as if she were being stretched from both ends.

Wesley tried to kick free of her.

His leg hardly moved at all. Just enough to sway Kimberly back and forth with an easy, gentle motion.

'Let go of me!' he shouted.

Kimberly didn't answer. She just held on.

Wesley pulled a knife out of its sheath on his belt. He wouldn't be able to reach her with it. He could throw it, though.

'Look out!' I yelled, and ran between the cages.

Billie shouted, 'He's got a knife! Watch out!'

With an underhand toss, I flung my machete toward Billie's cage. It hit bars, but fell near enough for her to reach it. I faced Kimberly's cage just as Wesley let out a cry of pain.

Kimberly had started to swing.

Still hanging from his ankle, she flung her legs forward and up.

A kid on a swing, pumping for the sky.

'Stop!' Wesley wailed. 'Stop it! Fuck!'

I jumped, reached high, grabbed two bars, squeezed

bars between my knees, and began my struggle for the top of Kimberly's cage. Slow going, awkward. I made progress, though.

As I pulled and scurried my way higher, Wesley's voice raged in my ears. 'My leg! Let go! Shit! You're gonna rip it off! Fuck! Let go! *Ahhhhh!*'

Kimberly no longer acted like a kid on a swing. The smooth, graceful pumping action was gone. She'd turned wild, bucking beneath him, twisting, kicking her legs toward the barred ceiling.

She had a knife protruding from her left thigh.

I hadn't even seen it hit her. Wesley must've hurled it down through the bars while I'd been looking somewhere else.

No wonder she'd gone wild.

She swung like a rabid Tarzan, a mad and naked Jane trying to ride her vine to the moon.

Through Wesley's shouts and shrieks, I heard a gristly, popping noise.

His thigh bone bursting out of its hip joint.

His scream gave me goosebumps.

'Don't kill him!' someone yelled.

A girl's voice from far off.

Erin.

'Don't kill Wesley!' she shouted. 'He's gotta tell where the keys are!'

And then my left hand caught hold of the crossbar at the top of the cage. I reached up with my right, grabbed hold and pulled myself up.

Wesley kept his eyes on me as I clambered over the edge. Suddenly, I found myself perched atop Kimberly's cage, my hands and knees on the roof bars, Wesley a distance to my right and just beyond the end of the ladder.

Though one leg lay across the top of the bars, he squirmed and swayed like a human torso – or like one of those inflatable punching toys that swings back and forth when you hit it, and keeps coming up.

'Help!' he blurted at me. His face was streaked with sweat and tears, tremulous with torchglow and shadows, twisted ugly with pain. 'Please!' he cried out. 'Make her stop! Please!'

Though he pleaded, he held his second knife high, its blade pinched between his thumb and forefinger.

'Put down the knife!' I shouted.

He couldn't seem to make up his mind whether to throw it at me or Kimberly.

Looking down, I saw her rising toward me on his leg. She seemed to be looking at me. In another moment, she was sprawled out beneath me like a lover. She lingered there, just below the bars, all shadowy and open.

Screaming, Wesley jerked the knife back toward his ear.

He'd made up his mind.

Kimberly.

His tormenter, and such an easy target inches below the bars, motionless, trapped in the moment before starting her downward course.

Yelling, I sprang.

Hurled myself – not so much *at* Wesley as *between* him and Kimberly.

I heard a thunk.

A grunt.

I landed flat and hard on the bars. They pounded me. They rang out. I slid on them.

Below my face was Kimberly's face.

Eyes squeezed nearly shut, mouth open, teeth bared.

Her face huge and beautiful but torn with pain.

Then shrinking.

At first, I didn't know why.

But as her face became smaller, more and more of Kimberly came into view.

Her neck, shoulders.

Her arms reaching overhead like a surrendering prisoner.

Her chest.

The knife handle jutting up between her breasts.

Her belly, her groin, thighs.

The knife handle jutting up from her left thigh.

Her long, spread legs.

All becoming smaller.

Then the shrinking stopped. She shook as if she'd suddenly been hit by a monstrous gust of wind. It shoved at the front of her whole body – spread her face, mashed her breasts, distorted her everywhere for a moment – then moved on.

I was vaguely aware of yelling.

Billie was yelling.

I was yelling.

Somehow, I missed the noise of Kimberly's body smacking the concrete. It must've been drowned out by our cries of shock and despair.

I don't know how long I lay sprawled on the bars, gazing down at her.

I couldn't believe this had happened.

I wanted it to be a dream.

Or a trial run. I wanted another chance, a way to try things differently.

A way to save her.

'The bitch was gonna rip my leg off,' Wesley said. 'I couldn't just let her rip my leg off, could I?'

I raised my head.

'Hey,' he said. 'Hey, look. Just settle down. It was an accident, okay? Accidents happen.'

In The Land Of Pain

When the sun came up, Kimberly still lay sprawled on the bottom of her cage. A pool of blood had spread out around her, much like the gasoline that had puddled the floor of Billie's cage, but dark.

Billie and Connie stood at the front corners of their cages, facing me.

I faced Wesley.

Alice and Erin watched from their distant cages.

Four spectators, four witnesses.

One executioner.

One motherfucking son of a bitch about to die hard.

During the night, I had lowered him to the ground. Billie and I had belted him around the neck to a bar of her cage. Neither of us spoke to him. He cried and begged and made excuses and carried on about a lot of stuff. We didn't listen, though.

When we asked him about the cage keys, he said, 'I'm not telling. If I tell, you got no reason not to kill me. They're real bastards, these cages. Nobody's getting out, ever. Not without the keys.'

Billie stood guard over him with the machete while I went away.

I spoke briefly to Connie, who was conscious but confused. She'd been out cold during the action, and had no idea that Kimberly'd been killed. When I told her, she seemed to shrivel. She sank down in a corner of her cage and covered her face.

I went on to Alice and Erin, and explained what had happened. Then I returned to the mansion.

I searched all over the place, looking for the keys. While trying to find them, I came across a few sections of rope which appeared to be our old ropes, taken from the scene of the big battle at the chasm.

Also, I found Kimberly's Swiss Army knife.

I quickly hid the knife away for later. I didn't want to use it on Wesley, foul it with him. I wanted it as a keepsake, a reminder of Kimberly to be savored in times to come.

Downstairs, I gathered some food and water for my women.

I returned to the cages. After handing out the provisions, I took over with Wesley. He hadn't given Billie any trouble. She gave the belt to me, and I dragged him by the neck. He tried to crawl, but it wasn't easy because of his dislocated leg. He screamed and choked a lot.

It took plenty of effort, but I finally managed to stand him up and tie him to the front door of Kimberly's cage. He could only stand on one leg, the other being useless. I kept him upright by tossing two ropes over the crossbar at the top of the door and tying them under his armpits. Then I stretched his arms out to the sides and lashed them to upright bars. I took the belt off him, got rid of its two empty knife sheaths, and used it to strap his good leg to the bars.

By then, Billie's torch had burned itself out.

I wanted light to work by.

So I took a few steps backward from Wesley, and lay

down on the ground. Billie called to me a couple of times. I didn't answer, though. I didn't want to go to her. She would hold me. We would weep. It would be comforting and nice. I would probably even end up with a hard-on.

I wanted no part of that.

I wanted no part of gentleness or sex or love.

It would ruin me for what I needed to do.

So I lay there on my back, in a position almost the same as Kimberly's. I pictured how it might look from the air: Kimberly and I stretched out like wings. Airplane wings. Angel wings. Eagle wings.

Wesley between us like the body between our wings. And what did that make us? What did that make him?

I'm starting to ramble.

No more of that.

I stayed on my back, not sleeping, until dawn arrived. Then I got up and went to Wesley.

Billie, Connie, Alice and Erin were already standing in their cages to watch. As if they'd all risen early, afraid they might oversleep and miss out.

Wesley watched my approach.

He was a wreck before I even got started. Aside from his dislocated, swollen leg, he had three spear wounds – the old ones in the boob and buttock, plus the one in the shoulder that I'd given him last night. He was also battered from falling down the stairs last night.

By the look on his face, he must've guessed that even worse was on its way.

Then he saw me pull the razor out of my sock.

When I flicked open its blade, he started to sob.

'Hey,' he said. 'Look. Don't. Don't hurt me.'

Billie called from her corner, 'Just tell us where the keys are, Wesley.'

His eyes were latched on the razor. He licked his cracked lips. 'I'll tell. Okay? Put that away. Put it away and I'll tell.'

I stepped up very close to him. Reaching down with my left hand, I grabbed him. His eyes bulged. I said, 'Where's your fucking boner now, tough guy?'

'Please,' he blubbered.

'Cut his cock off!' Connie shouted. 'Make him eat it!'

'Good thing *she's* locked up,' I said.

He nodded vigorously. His face dripped sweat and tears. 'Don't . . . do it,' he said. 'Please. I'm begging you. I'll tell where the keys are. Please.'

'Okay.' I let go.

'Thank you.' He sniffled. 'Thank you.'

'You're welcome,' I said, and sliced off the underside of his left forearm from wrist to elbow.

While he screamed, I stuffed it into his mouth.

'Eat *that*,' I said. 'You'll need snacks. This is gonna take a while.'

He wouldn't eat it, though. He gasped and choked and managed to spit it out.

'*The keys!*' he squealed.

Off to my right, Connie vomited. She was hunched over, face between bars, trying to get most of her mess to land outside the cage.

I looked at Billie. She stood with her arms up, hands gripping the bars. I saw where Wesley or Thelma or both of them had left marks on her, and I saw a fierce look in her eyes.

'It's not just for Kimberly,' I told her.

'I know that, honey.'

I faced Wesley.

'Tell me where the keys are,' I said.

'Bedroom,' he gasped. 'Upstairs.'

'Where in the bedroom?'

'Under mattress.'

'Liar,' I said, and sliced him across the left eye. My razor cut in through the closed lid, slit his eyeball and nicked the bridge of his nose.

It took him a long time to stop screaming.

I stood back and waited. Most of my audience had had enough. Making no complaints, they'd simply turned away and gone to far corners of their cages. Only Billie still watched.

When our eyes met, she nodded.

'I *told* you where the keys are!' Wesley blurted when he was finally capable of speech again.

'Not enough,' I said.

'What do you want? I'll do anything!'

'Apologize to Billie.'

'I'm sorry!' he cried out. 'Billie, I'm sorry! Forgive me!'

I took off one of his ears.

When he could speak again, he gasped, 'I did what you wanted!'

'Not enough,' I said.

'*What?*'

'You didn't apologize to Connie.'

'But . . . but . . . !'

I shoved my razor into the rip across his left boob, made so long ago by Kimberly's spear but reopened last night. I ran the blade through it, slow and deep.

When Wesley could talk again, he cried out, 'I'm sorry, Connie! I'm sorry, Alice! I'm sorry, Erin. Okay? Okay?'

'You forgot a few people,' I explained, and cut off his right nipple.

Had to wait.

Then, 'Who? Who?'

'Try to remember.'

I made him scream again.

Had to wait.

Then he shouted, 'I'm sorry, Andrew! I'm sorry, Keith! I'm sorry, Dorothy! I'm sorry, James!'

'Finished?'

'No?' he wondered.

'Who, then?' I asked.

'I don't know! You? I'm sorry, Rupert!'

I hurt him again.

Had to wait.

Then, 'Who? Please! Who?'

'Apologize to your wife. Don't you think Thelma deserves an apology?'

'Yes! I'm sorry, Thelma!' he cried out.

I sliced off a pretty good section down the front of his left thigh, and slapped him across the face with it a couple of times.

Had to wait.

Then, *'What? What? Who?'*

'You forgot Kimberly.'

'Kimberly? No, I . . . Yes! I'm sorry, Kimberly! I'm sorry, Kimberly! I'm sorry, *everybody! Everybody!'*

'Very good,' I said.

He hung there against the bars of the cage door, sobbing wildly, blood all over, and blubbered, 'Thank you. Thank you.'

Fool thought I was done.

'One more thing,' I said.

He shuddered. *'Yes! Yes! Anything! Please! Whatever you say! Anything!'*

'Make Kimberly be alive.'

'*What? No! I can't! I would, but I can't! Please! I can't do that! She's dead! I can't bring her back to life.*'

'Didn't think so,' I told him.

That's when I did what Connie had suggested in the first place. When his mouth was full, I clapped a hand across his lips and kept it there until he was dead.

Then I went over to Billie's cage.

Without being asked, she handed the machete to me.

I returned to Wesley.

'This is for Kimberly, too,' I said.

With one blow, I chopped off his head. It fell and thudded against the ground, and rolled. It came to a stop, face up, the tip of Wesley's penis peering out from between his lips like a curious passenger.

Then I chopped off his arms and legs.

I found a wheelbarrow in one of the storage buildings behind the mansion, brought it over, piled it with Wesley, then rolled him off into the jungle and dumped him in some bushes.

Far enough away so we wouldn't have to smell him rot.

King Of The Island

Almost three weeks have gone by since that morning.

My women are still in their cages.

Including Kimberly. After disposing of Wesley's body, I did what was necessary. I tried for a while to break into the cage. I couldn't get in, though. So she would have to stay.

There were sacks of concrete in the storage building where I'd found the wheelbarrow.

I mixed the concrete in the wheelbarrow with a shovel. I carried it in a bucket up the ladder, and dumped it through the bars. The heavy gray glop fell on Kimberly, bombed her, splatted her body and spread out, rolling like lava, some spilling down her sides to join the concrete of the floor.

I don't want to get into how I felt. Or which parts of Kimberly I covered first. Or last.

After many trips up the ladder with the paint bucket, none of her showed anymore.

Wesley's two knives, one in her thigh and one in her chest, stuck up out of the gray mass like miniature Excaliburs. But no hero arrived with the strength or magic to draw them out.

I gave the concrete a while to set, then mixed more batches in the wheelbarrow and hauled them up to the top and poured. I couldn't pull out the knives, but I could bury them.

When I finally quit, Kimberly's resting place was a long, low hill of concrete at the bottom of her cage.

Billie had watched all this from her cage. She'd given me useful advice, from time to time. She'd spoken softly, sadly. It was good having her there. To Connie, Alice and Erin, I'd apparently turned into a leper. It didn't bother me, though. Mostly, I felt numb.

We didn't say anything over Kimberly.

Maybe we each did, privately. At least those of us who loved her.

Which probably included only me and Billie, when you come right down to it.

I thought about singing 'Danny Boy' for her. I couldn't do it, though. Maybe someday.

After cleaning up the tools, I returned to the mansion and took a long, hot shower. Then I stayed in. I went to where I'd hidden the Swiss Army knife. With the knife in my hand, I searched for a good bedroom. I picked Erin's, on the second floor. I flopped on her bed.

I stroked my cheek with the knife's smooth plastic handle, and remembered Kimberly. Next thing you know, I started bawling. I cried like crazy, like I'd never cried before. And then eventually I fell asleep.

I dreamed of Kimberly running on the beach. It was *our* beach on the inlet. She ran toward me, smiling. She wore her white bikini, and her husband's gaudy Hawaiian shirt. As usual, the shirt wasn't buttoned. It flowed behind her as she ran. And so did her long black hair. She was tanned, sleek, gorgeous. I couldn't believe my eyes. It must've been a mistake about her being dead. Maybe I'd only dreamed that she'd been killed.

She came into my arms, held me gently, kissed me on the mouth.

After the kiss, I murmured, 'I thought you were dead.'

'You think too much, Rupert.'

'You're not, then?'

Her smile. Her fabulous smile. 'Of course not. Do I look dead? Do I *feel* dead?'

No, she didn't. She looked and felt alive and very wonderful. Shaking my head, I began to weep in my dream. She kissed my tears away. 'Do you love me?' she whispered.

'Yes.'

'Would you like to marry me, Rupert?'

'Yes!' I blurted. 'Yes!' But suddenly I realized that I couldn't marry her, no matter how much I wanted to.

She saw the change in me. 'What's the matter?' she asked.

'I can't. I love Billie. I love both of you.'

Kimberly's smile beamed. 'Then marry us both,' she suggested. 'Why not? You're the king of the island, you can do whatever you want.'

'Okay, then. That's what we'll do.'

'Don't you think you'd better ask Billie, first?'

'Oh, yeah. Good idea.'

'I'll be back,' Kimberly said. She kissed me, whirled around and started running away down the beach.

'Wait!' I yelled. 'Don't go! Come back!'

I must've called out in my sleep, and I think that it was the sound of my own voice that woke me.

The room was dark.

I crept through the house and went outside. I walked across the front lawn, sad that the dream had lied about Kimberly being alive, but feeling less desolate than earlier.

Wherever else her soul might've gone, it had found a home inside of me.

I would hold her in my heart forever.

Along with Billie.

Though I approached silently and invisibly in the full darkness, Billie touched me when I tried to find the bars of her cage. She took my hands and guided me forward. We hugged each other. Hard bars pressed against us, but couldn't keep us apart. We filled the spaces between them with our warm, bare flesh.

It was as if Billie had been waiting for me, needing me.

We didn't talk. We hugged and kissed fiercely. It started with the solemn urgency of two survivors finding each other after long and lonely wanderings. There was joy and relief, and a terrible sadness for all that had been lost.

Then that changed, shifted into an urgency of lovers. Hearts pounding, we explored each other with hands and mouths. Caressing, squeezing, delving deep, stroking. We licked each other, sucked and tasted. Gasping for breath. Moaning and sighing. Whispering no words except, 'Yes,' and 'Oh, there,' and 'God.'

I won't even try to describe all we did.

We were together for hours. Sometimes, we simply embraced and quietly talked. Then we would get started again.

Eventually, Billie managed a contortion that allowed us to make love between the bars. It was a hell of a trick, and took a lot of strength on her part. She couldn't hold the position for very long.

It drove me crazy to be inside her that way. I'd never felt anything like it. So soft and warm and tight and slidy. And how it made me feel as if we were almost the same person for a while.

We've done it plenty of times since. I've learned to help by reaching through the bars and clutching her. That way, she doesn't need to work so hard at holding herself up.

It has been wonderful.

Kimberly's concrete tomb gives us sorrow, but also reminds us that life is a gift and we need to savor every moment that we're given.

Though they've been imprisoned in the cages for three weeks now since the deaths of Wesley, Thelma and Kimberly, all four of my women are doing well. I have provided them with clothing, blankets and pillows, plenty to eat and drink. I clean them regularly by pouring water onto them from the tops of their cages. They have soap, washcloths, drinking cups, toothbrushes. They have hung blankets to make cubicles for privacy.

Their toilet buckets cannot be removed from the cages, so we came up with a system of lining the buckets with plastic bags. The used bags are passed between the bars for disposal.

I give my women whatever they ask for: combs, brushes, mirrors, sanitary napkins, books, magazines – even a Gameboy and a portable radio, both of which run off rechargeable batteries. I have become a fairly good cook. The mansion has provisions enough to last us for a few months, so there is no need to worry about starving. I don't even ration the food.

My women want for very little, except their freedom.

It became obvious, after many tries during the first few days, that their cages were impregnable. I couldn't pick the locks. I couldn't force the doors or hinges. I had no saw or file capable of cutting through the bars. With a pickax, Billie tried to break out through her floor – only to find iron bars imbedded in the concrete.

Nobody treats me like a leper, anymore. Connie and the twins quickly got over their shock at what I'd done to Wesley. I couldn't be all that terrible, they must've supposed, since I was being so good to them. Besides, they knew that Wesley deserved everything he got.

The twins are great. They quarrel a lot between themselves, but they have become my great friends. Erin seems to be madly in love with me, which Alice thinks is ridiculous. They have been healing nicely (as have Connie and Billie). They are both incredibly beautiful, and continue to go around in their cages most of the time wearing few or no clothes.

Which certainly catches my attention. We don't fool around in any sexual ways, though. They are too young for such things. Also, I love Billie so much that I never seem to work up very much excitement over Alice or Erin.

As for Connie, she remained sullen and surly for about a week. She knew that she was to blame, at least partly, for Kimberly's death. She also found out, soon enough, that her mother and I were lovers. She gave us quite a hard time with that mouth of hers.

She seems to be over it, though. I think she has accepted the fact that it's stupid to be jealous over someone you never really liked that much in the first place. I was her boyfriend of convenience who'd stumbled into her life by an accident of the alphabet. I was not, and never had been, any great catch. So let her mother have me.

That's how I *think* she looks at it. We haven't actually discussed the matter.

It's hard to know what she feels. Lately, though, she has been a lot less snotty than usual. Eventually, we might even become friends. Who knows?

I could go on and on about Connie, Alice and Erin. And especially about Billie and me. I could write in lavish detail about all we've done, what we've said and how they've looked. The real story, though, pretty much ended with the death of Wesley.

Also, I've been spending too much time away from my women, writing in the privacy of Erin's room for hours each day.

Now that I'm caught up to the present, I'll be able to spend more time with them.

Eventually, I'll set them free.

The keys to their cages are bound to turn up, somewhere.

Maybe under the mattress where Wesley said they'd be.

So long for now.

The Horror Writers Association presents:
THE MUSEUM OF HORRORS
edited by Dennis Etchison

A special hardcover edition featuring all new stories by:

PETER STRAUB
JOYCE CAROL OATES
RICHARD LAYMON
BENTLEY LITTLE
RAMSEY CAMPBELL

*And: Peter Atkins, Melanie Tem, Tom Piccirilli,
Darren O. Godfrey, Joel Lane, Gordon Linzer, Conrad Williams,
Th. Metzger, Susan Fry, Charles L. Grant, Lisa Morton,
William F. Nolan, Robert Devereaux, and S. P. Somtow.*

"The connoisseur of the macabre will find a feast on this table."
—Tapestry Magazine

Dorchester Publishing Co., Inc.
P.O. Box 6640   0-8439-4928-7
Wayne, PA 19087-8640 $24.00 US/ $34.95 CAN

Please add $4.00 for shipping and handling NY residents, please add appropriate sales tax. No cash, stamps, or C.O.D.s. All orders take 7-10 days to be fulfilled after they are received by our order department. Canadian orders require $5.00 for shipping and must be paid in U.S. dollars. Prices and availability subject to change. Payment must accompany all orders.

Name _____
Address _____
City _____ State_____ Zip _____
E-mail_____
I have enclosed $ _____ in payment for the checked book(s). **Payment must accompany all orders.**

__Check here for a FREE catalog
Check out our website at www.dorchesterpub.com
for even more information on your favorite books and authors.

AMONG THE MISSING RICHARD LAYMON

At 2:32 in the morning a Jaguar roars along a lonely road high in the California mountains. Behind the wheel sits a beautiful woman wearing only a skimpy nightgown. She's left her husband behind. She's after a different kind of man—someone as wild. daring, and passionate as herself. The man she wants is waiting patiently for her . . . with wild plans of his own. When the woman stops to pick him up, he suggests they go to the Bend, where the river widens and there's a soft, sandy beach. With the stars overhead and moonlight on the water, it's an ideal place for love. But there will be no love tonight. In the morning a naked body will be found at the Bend—a body missing more than its clothes. And the man will be waiting for someone else.

___4788-8 $5.99 US/$6.99 CAN

THE TRAVELING VAMPIRE SHOW
RICHARD LAYMON

It's a hot August morning in 1963. All over the rural town of Grandville, tacked to the power poles and trees, taped to store windows, flyers have appeared announcing the one-night-only performance of The Traveling Vampire Show. The promised highlight of the show is the gorgeous Valeria, the only living vampire in captivity.

For three local teenagers, two boys and a girl, this is a show they can't miss. Even though the flyers say no one under eighteen will be admitted, they're determined to find a way. What follows is a story of friendship and courage, temptation and terror, when three friends go where they shouldn't go, and find much more than they ever expected.

__4850-7 $5.99 US/$6.99 CAN

IN THE DARK

RICHARD LAYMON

Nothing much happens to Jane Kerry, a young librarian. Then one day Jane finds an envelope containing a fifty-dollar bill and a note instructing her to "Look homeward, angel." Jane pulls a copy of the Thomas Wolfe novel of that title off the shelf and finds a second envelope. This one contains a hundred-dollar bill and another clue. Both are signed, "MOG (Master of Games)." But this is no ordinary game. As it goes on, it requires more and more of Jane's ingenuity, and pushes her into actions that she knows are crazy, immoral or criminal—and it becomes continually more dangerous. More than once, Jane must fight for her life, and she soon learns that MOG won't let her quit this game. She'll have to play to the bitter end.

___4916-3 $5.99 US/$6.99 CAN

ONE RAINY NIGHT
RICHARD LAYMON

"If you've missed Laymon, you've missed a treat."
—Stephen King

The strange black rain falls like a shroud on the small town of Bixby. It comes down in torrents, warm and unnatural. And as it falls, the town changes. One by one, the inhabitants fall prey to its horrifying effect. One by one, they become filled with hate and rage . . . and the need to kill. Formerly friendly neighbors turn to crazed maniacs. A stranger at a gas station shoves a nozzle down a customer's throat and pulls the trigger. A soaking-wet line of movie-goers smashes its way into a theater to slaughter the people inside. A loving wife attacks her husband, still beating his head against the floor long after he's dead. As the rain falls, blood flows in the gutters—and terror runs through the streets.

"No one writes like Laymon, and you're going to have a good time with anything he writes."
—Dean Koontz